Brag Dog
and Other Stories

The Best of Vereen Bell

Vereen Bell

Brag Dog
and Other Stories

The Best of Vereen Bell

Introduction by Vereen M. Bell, Jr.
Artwork by Marguerite Kirmse

Belgrade, Montana

The publisher has reprinted the text to reflect to the letter the original work, nothing added or expunged, to give the reader an authentic view of another age. This entails retaining several distasteful racial terms commonly printed in the era in which the author lived in order to present the text honestly. While we do not support the use of these terms, we feel a responsibility to accurately present the text.

© 2000 Mrs. Florence Long
Introduction © 2000 Vereen M. Bell, Jr.

Book and cover design © 2000 Wilderness Adventures Press

Published by Wilderness Adventures Press
45 Buckskin Road
Belgrade, MT 59714
800-925-3339
Website: www.wildadv.com
email: books@wildadv.com

All rights reserved, including the right to reproduce this book or portions thereof in any form or by any means, electronic or mechanical, including photocopying, recording, or by any information storage and retrieval system, without permission in writing from the publisher. All inquiries should be addressed to: Wilderness Adventures Press™, Division of Wilderness Adventures, Inc.™, 45 Buckskin Road, Belgrade, MT 59714.

Printed in the United States of America

Library of Congress Cataloging-in-Publication Data

Bell, Vereen, 1911–1944.
    Brag dog and other stories : the best of Vereen Bell / with an introduction by Vereen Bell, Jr.
    p. cm.
    ISBN 1-885106-84-X (alk. paper)
    1. Southern States—Social life and customs—Fiction. 2. Hunting stories, American. 3. Outdoor life—Fiction. 4. Dogs—Fiction. I. Title

PS3503.E4389 A6 2000
813'.54—dc21
00-043405

Table of Contents

Publisher's Preface ❧ vii
Introduction ❧ ix
Brag Dog ❧ 1
The Gopher Dog ❧ 15
Come Back Tuesday ❧ 25
Mortgage on a Dog ❧ 33
The Sometimes Dog ❧ 41
The Hunting Fool ❧ 49
A Dog for a Man ❧ 63
Sis ❧ 75
Field Trial ❧ 83
Trouble's Child ❧ 93
The Sounds of Geese ❧ 105
Jumping Horse Man ❧ 115
Trial by Marriage ❧ 127
Prairie Dogs ❧ 229
One Man's Dogs ❧ 237
About the Artist ❧ 243

Publisher's Preface

Several years ago one of our customers asked me if I had read any books written by Vereen Bell. I had to admit that I was not familiar with the author or his writings. My customer raved about his books and claimed he was the best writer of bird dog stories that he had read. I asked him how he compared with Horace Lytle, Archibald Rutledge, and Havilah Babcock. "He's better," replied my customer.

His comments piqued my interest. After a long search, I found a dealer who had three of Bell's books, *Two of a Kind, Swamp Water,* and *Brag Dog and Other Stories.* All of these were printed in the early 1940s as cheap paperbacks. When the books arrived, I took them home and spent the evening reading *Two of a Kind.* It was 2:00 AM when I finished the book. Here was a great storyteller—Bell not only had a magical way with words, it was obvious that he was a bird dog man and knew field trials and bird hunting. In three days I devoured his books. My customer was right: He was the best writer of bird dog stories.

I decided to bring back all of Vereen Bell's dog stories in a beautiful slipcased edition similar to our other special editions, *Meditations on Hunting, Big Woods,* and *Wildfowling Tales.* Darren Brown, our editoral manager, spent a year searching for more of Bell's writings. He located a number of great stories that were written for *Collier's* magazine and *The Saturday Evening Post* in the late 1930s that had never appeared in book form.

We have included here all of the sporting stories from his collection, *Brag Dog,* the entire novella, *Trial by Marriage,* and five other stories that appeared only in magazine form. This includes two nonfiction essays, *Prairie Dogs* and *One Man's Dogs,* that are every bit as interesting and entertaining as the rest of the stories. *Brag Dog* was originally printed by the U.S. Government for distribution to our soldiers during WWII in an Armed Services edition. *Trial by Marriage* was first published as a serial in *Collier's* magazine. It was then published in book form with the title *Two of a Kind* and again soon after under its new title, *Trial by Marriage.*

For years I have collected the etchings and drypoints of Marguerite Kirmse. In my opinion, she was the finest bird dog artist of the 20th century. Seven of her hunting dog scenes are reproduced in the book. I am proud to publish Vereen Bell's classic bird dog stories and hope you enjoy them as much as I have.

Chuck Johnson, Publisher

INTRODUCTION

My father, Vereen Bell, was born in Cairo, a placidly agricultural town in south Georgia, in 1911, the scion on his mother's side of a wealthy and by then distinguished family of Vereens who more or less presided over the fortunes of the more prosperous nearby community of Moultrie, Georgia, forty miles to the west. His grandfather, W.C. Vereen, the patriarch not only of his large family but of Moultrie and Colquitt County as well, had been an entrepreneur and, as I imagined him then and now, a benevolent nineteenth-century robber baron, opportunistically moving from South Carolina to Atlanta and finally to Moultrie, buying and losing banks, buying up timberlands, building sawmills and cotton mills, and in general consolidating enough hard-earned wealth to ensure his heirs financial security and businesses to be operated and developed for generations to come. By the time I was of an age to become sensible of all this, W.C. Vereen's restless opportunism and industry had stabilized into a patrician gentility.

Vereen Bell's father, R.C. Bell, had come into his own version of gentility by a different route. He had come from a family of farmers and merchants in west Georgia, slightly farther north (Jimmy Carter country), and had put himself through college and law school by teaching Latin in small rural schools even though, in order to do that, he had had to stay a chapter ahead in the textbook on his own learning curve. He was a respected and honorable attorney for many years and eventually became Chief Justice of the Georgia Supreme Court. He and my grandmother were broken irreparably when my father was killed in 1944, a long, long way from Cairo, Georgia, in the Battle of Leyte Gulf.

By the time he died, Vereen Bell had become a famous novelist and cut a glamorous figure in Georgia, and particularly in the part of it we had by then moved to, Thomasville, which was sophisticated and Yankeefied because of the plantations that encompassed and dominated Thomas County and its culture and also contributed to its status as legendary hunting territory. He had had a real job briefly as an editor at *American Boy* magazine (based in Detroit) and had honed his own writing skills under the tutelage of *American Boy's* chief editor, Harold Ober. He was regularly publishing hunting and fishing pieces in *Outdoor Life* and *Field and Stream* and fiction in *Saturday Evening Post, Collier's,* and *Liberty* magazine. His first novel, *Swamp Water*, was a highly successful bestseller and was made quickly into a movie produced by Darryl Zanuck, who hired Jean Renoir for his American debut as a director. Dana Andrews, Anne Baxter, Walter Brennan, and Walter Huston starred.

His second novel, *Two of a Kind* (also *Trial by Marriage* as reprinted here) was not so successful—partly because its main setting, bird dog field trials, must have seemed esoteric to the wider reading public; but it sold well, again made bestseller lists, and Vereen Bell's family continued to prosper.

I am probably romanticizing, but I have always believed that the Okefenokee Swamp, where *Swamp Water* was set, was my father's natural milieu. It was, and still is, wildly beautiful and remote, a thriving habitat for exotic and menacing wildlife, and stubbornly resistant over centuries to human management or exploitation. My father loved wilderness and wild things and had a hard time staying within the lines himself. He married suddenly and secretly, outside his class, so to speak—or so it must have seemed to his family—a year after he graduated from Davidson College (at the time a kind of finishing school for young Presbyterian men from respectable families). Luckily for him and everyone else, my mother (and her six luminous and hilarious siblings) turned out to be classier in all the best senses than the Vereens and Bells could have hoped for in their wildest dreams. Vereen Bell's father had wanted him to be an attorney and to follow an ordained path through law school into small town respectability—and into what must have seemed to him tedium. (There was some sort of quarrel on that account that is interestingly replayed in *Swamp Water* in the coded subplot dealing with Ben Ragan's relationship to his father, Thursday.)

When the war came, he had a wife and two young children and a thriving career and did not have to go into the service. In retrospect, though, it seems natural that he would have—not just out of the now anachronistic-seeming sense of duty that serious men of his generation took for granted, but also because of the sense of adventure. Because he had been a hunter, the navy, with its improvisational wartime logic, offered him the opportunity to stay stateside as a gunnery instructor, but he went to sea, anyway, as an air intelligence officer on the escort carrier, Gambier Bay. Presciently, the central symbolic character in *Swamp Water*, Tom Keefer, a renegade who has fled the law to live in the swamp, tells his young friend as he dies, choosing to die rather than come out into the normal world, that dying is not so bad, that it's one of the interesting things to do that, as he puts it, he ain't done yet.

Tom Keefer also believed that animals had souls, or at any rate ought to have, compared to human beings, and should be able to go to heaven as

Introduction

readily as any man or woman. My father loved wild things, as I say, as deeply as that, and his love of hunting dogs must have been for that strange wildness that possesses the best of them. Anyone who hunts with bird dogs knows what this means. They can be bred and trained into obedience, but at their most generic they are basically keen and indefatigable predators. Hunting is what they live for.

I once sent a pointer off to be trained and got him back from the trainer six weeks later with a tactful letter saying that Doc was going to be an excellent hunting companion, and we knew right away what that meant—that he was going to be more of a companion than a hunter, and we were right.

The dogs I have watched working at field trials, almost always rawboned pointers, especially at the Grand National, are so hardwired and obsessed that they seem demented, even supernatural.

The dogs in this collection of Vereen Bell's stories are not quite like that; they have been humanized to one degree or another by the requirements of narrative fiction. But I am sure that what got my father absorbed in the lore of bird dogs in the first place was ironically that aspect of their strange and scary natures that is beyond describing and about which nothing much can be said or written, really, because they are essentially nothing but hide, bone, muscle, a nose, and a tiny fixated brain. Set a pair of them loose in a stretch of south Georgia pine woods on a cold winter morning and watch them work, and it's hard not to feel for the duration of the moment that you have stepped over into another world, and that the dogs have taken you there. I am glad to know what that feels like, because it helps me to know how much rare, uncomplicated joy my father was able to pack into his short life. In his stories he shared it with others.

Vereen M. Bell, Jr.
July 2000

Brag Dog

Eph was outside when it happened. He was sitting under the chinaberry tree, writing in the dirt with a nail, trying, as usual, to study out some way to buy the wheel chair for Addie May. Of course she knew nothing at all about any wheel chair, but Eph guessed that Addie May'd be mighty happy if she could just glide out on the porch to talk to a passer-by, and then glide back in when the flies got too bad, without anybody's having to leave their work to tote her.

It was just then that Cleotha came in the house, and there the puppy was, chewing up her only half fit'n pair of go-to-meetin' shoes. She let go a stick of cordwood at him, and her daughter, little Valentine, screamed like she was stabbed. The puppy was knocked clean under the bed. Eph expected to drag him out cold dead, but before he could kneel down, the puppy came wobbling out, bleeding at the mouth, and one ear torn half off. The puppy sat down, his head tilted to favor his injured ear, and, licking his mouth, he regarded them in puzzlement, blinking that blind, white eye. He wagged his tail uncertainly.

Eph never had felt quite so roused up about anything. "You ever do dat again, Cleotha, and you gwine git hurt. Fun now on, you bees on prohibition, so you better be keerful, you hear me?"

Little naked Valentine had dropped the shriveled ear of raw corn she had been eating and went to the puppy. Eph knelt beside them, and the puppy began gnawing at his hand as if nothing had happened.

"Ol hardhead," Eph said tenderly. " 'E got a skull just like a rock in de river."

After that the puppy's name was Hardhead. Mr. Floyd Jessup had given the puppy to Eph. They had been fishing on the lake, and not catching anything. Mr. Floyd didn't mind, though; he kept whipping the fly rod, and popping the bass bug among the lily bonnets.

"How're you making out these days, Eph?" he asked afterwhile.

Eph hesitated a moment. His crop was no good, because it had been so almighty dry. He hardly had food enough for his family, much less his stock—you could hang your hat on the mule's hip bones. The lake was down low, too, so that the fish weren't biting and hardly anybody wanted a boatman any more. At home, Cleotha was a file-tongue she-cat, and Addie May, his wife, was crippled these eight years, and not long ago the good Lord had taken their boy, Luck, away from them. Luck had been a first-class

1

hand at tractors and such, and Eph concluded that some of the heavenly machinery had got itself out of fix and They'd just naturally had to call Luck in on the case.

But Eph couldn't bother Mr. Floyd with all that, so he answered, "Tol'able, Mr. Floyd, just tol'able."

"Haven't you a little granddaughter?"

"Yes, suh; Valentine."

"I've got a pointer puppy you can have, Eph. The kid will enjoy him, I guess. A cat scratched his eyes nearly out. One of them's gone, and he'll be blind in the other one within a month or so. But she can have the fun of him for that length of time."

Eph thought it would be fine for Valentine to have a puppy to play with, even a half-blind puppy. So the next time Mr. Floyd came fishing, he brought the puppy with him. That night on the way home the puppy chewed contentedly on Eph's ragged coat, not seeming to mind having one eye milky like a white marble and the other with webby stuff over it.

It was dark when Eph got home, and Addie May and Cleotha and Little Valentine were all in bed, but Eph roused them with a shout.

"Guess what I brung home!" he said into the darkness.

"I bet it ain't nothin' to eat," Cleotha said pessimistically.

"I know what it is," Valentine said suddenly, " 'cause it's already in the bed with me. It's a little old dog."

Cleotha came out of the bed with an angry bound, and lit a lamp. "A dog?" she shouted. Sure enough, it was a dog, in the bed with Valentine, giving her happy face a lathering.

"Father reserve us!" Cleotha said. "We ain't got a dust a' meal ner a drop a' grease in de house, and de old fool done brung home another mouth to feed."

Addie May turned painfully, so she could get a look at the puppy. "He's purty, ain't he?"

"Purty? I'll purty 'im," Cleotha said in a tight-lipped rage.

The puppy was lucky to be alive next morning. Three or four times during the night Cleotha had tried to slip out and put an end to that extra hungry mouth. But every time Addie May heard her, and called Eph. Sometimes Eph wondered if Addie May ever really went to sleep any more.

Eph lay awake and thought about the wheel chair. "If'n I was makin' any money," he thought, "I could bury a dime er fi'teen cents a week and in two years er maybe three er four, I'd dig up enough to pay for hit, cash. But I ain't makin' no money."

His brain began to ache from a confusion of thought. It wasn't possible for an old nigger like him to buy a wheel chair for his crippled wife. Yet he wanted it so bad he was tempted to call on the good Lord to pass a miracle. He was even tempted to point out to Him how wrong things had been going, with Luck dying, and Addie May getting crippled, and little Valentine being half hungry all the time; but he was afraid the Lord might think he was criticizing, so he kept his mouth shut.

With morning, rain came. Not a gulley-washer, the kind they needed to bring the lake up, but enough of one to help the corn some. By late summer they had bread

Brag Dog

to eat with their greens, and occasionally Eph would get his old Long Tom single-barreled full-choke shotgun and kill a rabbit or a crow for dinner.

Eph and little Valentine saw to it that the puppy got a little something to eat all the time. He seemed to prosper on corn bread and greens; in fact, his bones grew faster than his flesh, it looked like, giving him a gawky, thick-legged appearance.

The dog's good eye got better instead of worse, and gradually the spidery film over it was gone and the puppy could see almost as good as anybody.

"Well, now, let me see," Eph said, puzzled. "I guess I got to take de Hardhead back to Mr. Floyd."

"How come?" Cleotha asked.

"Well, he ain't went complete blind like Mr. Floyd thought. He goan make a bird dog now."

"You old fool, didn't Mr. Floyd gi'm to you? We gwine sell dat dog and git some money for him, maybe two dollars er two and a quarter. He's sho your dog."

But Eph thought he ought to take him back, so he rose before Valentine woke next morning, and he and the puppy started sadly to Tallahassee. When he finally got there, they went straight to Mr. Floyd's enormous country house on the other side of town.

"You walked twenty miles from the lake with this dog?" Mr. Floyd asked. "You lunatic, I gave you that dog. Now, you keep him."

"Yes, suh, but I feel kinda gilted 'bout him regittin' back his sights. He ought to be your little dog, Mr. Floyd."

"I gave him to you, understand? And listen, I don't want to hear of you selling that dog for two or three dollars. He's worth thirty right now, if that eye's all right. Take him to the kennels and let my dog man give him a distemper shot and some worm medicine and a square meal." He drew out a dollar bill and gave it to Eph. "That's bus money back, understand? I don't want you walking down here again, keeping a bird-dog puppy out in the hot sun all day."

Afterward, on the way to the department store, Eph had a curious mixture of feelings. Now that he was about to get the wheel chair, his fingers trembled violently in glad excitement. At the same time, the thought of parting with Hardhead put a sickness in his heart. He hurried into the store before he could change his mind.

"How much your w'eel chairs costes, suh?"

"We got one for twenty-five dollars," the clerk told him.

It was beautiful, with rubber tires and shiny bright wood and black spokes.

Eph didn't hesitate. "Well, dis yere's a thutty-dollar puppy, and I wants to turn him in on dat w'eel chair."

The clerk looked at Hardhead's gaunt frame and unsightly imperfections, and he had to put his hand over his mouth. "I'm afraid we couldn't do that, old man," he said. "Tell you what, though; you train that puppy and he'll be easier to sell. Won't make much difference what he looks like then."

Eph went out with the curious mixture of feelings, only this time they were backward. His hand on Hardhead's scrawny neck was glad. At the same time his whole insides seemed touched by his disappointment. He hadn't got the wheel chair.

Eph told Cleotha what Mr. Floyd had said about harming the puppy.

" 'E says if'n you boddered dis puppy, he gwine have you put in de callyboots, in de blackest corner of hit."

Addie May had them put her out on the porch, so she could tell passersby about Eph's trip from town. They sat her down carefully. Addie May looked at her yard and said, "If'n I had me a nickel, I'd buy me some flar seed, and I'd plant 'em right around this ere poach. Zeenies. Blue uns and yaller uns and pank uns." It wasn't often that Addie May let on about wanting anything. The next nickel Eph got his hand on, he was sure going to buy her some zinnia seed.

All afternoon Addie May sat there, speaking to the people who occasionally went by with fish poles and sacks on their way to the lake.

"Mawnin', Miz Davis," they would say to her, "how you?"

"Just tol'able," Addie May would answer. "It's sho Lawd hot, ain't it?"

"Ain't it?"

"Eph went to Ta'hassee, yestiddy, right in de b'ilin' sun."

"Did? W'en 'e comin' back, Miz Davis?"

" 'E come back yestiddy," Addie May would say casually. "On de bust."

MR. FLOYD HAD GIVEN Eph about a dozen cans of dog food to feed the Hardhead. "Feed him a can every three or four days, to sort of balance his diet. A dog needs more than corn bread, you know."

But when Eph came in from pulling fodder one afternoon, Cleotha had found the dog food. She cooked two cans of it in the frying pan. It looked like beef hash.

"Dat ain't people's sump'm-to-eat," Eph said. "Dat's dog rations."

"It eats good," Cleotha said complacently.

Eph dubiously took a spoonful of the stuff and sampled it, and it wasn't bad, sure enough. They had dog food for supper, but Eph couldn't eat any of it, knowing he wasn't supposed to. After supper, he went out and fed Hardhead corn bread and pot licker and tried to explain as best he could.

"It doan seem eggsactly fair," Eph admitted, "but at the same time we been sharin' wid you, so I guess you don't objeck to sharin' up wid us, specially since you don't know nothin' 'bout it nohow."

The lake got into such a shape that nobody fished it any more, and Eph had lots of time to spend trying to make his eroded clay farm land grow something. Hardhead always went with him plowing. While Eph plodded up and down the dry furrows, Hardhead would crouch under the sassafras bushes along the rail and wait for the birds. Presently they would come fluttering in, one or two at a time—larks and bluebirds and grassbirds, prospecting in Eph's plowed earth. Suddenly Hardhead, now a half-grown, long-legged dog, would come bounding out and circle the field with whippet-like speed, raising a considerable dust, and chase every bird out of the field. Then he went back to the sassafras bushes, panting, and waited for them to come back into the field again.

Eph watched his antics with pride. "Yes, suh, you got de bird-dog instank. W'en de fust frost comes, you and me is gwine a bird huntin', and I gwine learn you your bird-dog manners." A trained dog would bring a fine price, he thought with a sudden unhappiness.

Along about the first week in December, Eph got his old Long Tom down from the rafters, and the five shells he had saved.

Eph said, as they walked out of the yard, "All right, now git out and go. And recollect 'bout dis, Hardhead. Fun now on, I ain't your sugar tit to chaw on. I de Boss Man, and w'en I holler, you got to hear my voice."

Hardhead ran about excitedly, going faster and faster. Every now and then a field lark would jump up in front of him, and Hardhead would chase it, springing up in the air after the bird. Suddenly the dog cut short one of his absurdly long casts with a flash point, then moved in boldly and held.

Eph grinned in pleasure. "I hope dee's sup'm dere. I kin tolerate a bird-eatin' dog er a flushin' dog, but I can't abide no false pointer."

Hardhead's ears moved, listening to the man's voice. The muscles in his big-boned hind legs quivered. Eph came up until he stood beside the dog. Slowly he stroked the dog from his head to the tip of his shaking tail, and talked to him soothingly.

"Yes, suh, dat's de way a brag dog behaves hisself, and you's de brag dog fo' sho'." He saddened momentarily. "Doggone, I do wish ol' Luck was here now, a-lookin'. Me and you and Luck could had us some ideal hunts together, couldn't us, now?"

Hardhead's tremors gradually passed. Eph stopped stroking him and stepped in front of him. A rabbit came out in great frightened bounds. Hardhead went after him with a happy yelp. Eph chuckled.

"Chase him plumb out de county, and see do I keer," he said. "You in grammy school now, and you ain't sposed to be reading de high-school books." He walked on in the direction the dog had gone. "Anyhow, dat ol' rabbit did smell like a pa'tridge. He even fooled me."

That night, he told his family, "We gwine have us a ideal bird dog."

"How much he goan be wuth w'en you get 'em trained up?" Cleotha asked interestedly. "Ten or twelve dollars, you reckon?"

"Sheh, gal. Time I work on him three-four months, I 'spect he be wuth forty dollars."

"Y'ain't plannin' to sell him off?" Addie May asked. Little Valentine began to pucker up around the mouth like she had eaten a green persimmon.

"I ain't sure," Eph said unhappily.

"Yes, you is," Cleotha said ominously. "I ain't goin' round raggedy w'en dey's a forty-dollar dog in de yard!"

"Maybe he turn out bad," Addie May said hopefully. "If'n he ain't a bird dog, he ain't wuth nothin', is he, Eph?"

"Ain't wuth a nickel," Eph agreed.

"In dat case, Cleotha said, "be better to knock 'im in de haid, and den dey'll be one lesser hongrey mouth to feed."

For a while, Hardhead improved. But approaching maturity, he became a wild dog. Soon as they left the yard, Hardhead lit out, fast as he could run. For maybe ten minutes he was in sight, then he'd disappear in the distance, going hell-a-lickety. Eph's shouting never seemed to mean a thing to him. And that would be the last Eph saw of him that day usually. Sometimes Eph would see him find birds way off. He flushed them immediately, without hesitation, and chased them out of sight.

Finally Eph thought of putting a drag chain on Hardhead. The dog stood patiently while it was being attached, blinking that white-marble eye and twitching his mutilated ear and grinning in excitement. He ran somewhat one-sided, but he still ran wild, and presently he would be out of sight.

"Dang your fool time," Eph finally said when the dog came in one night, brier-scratched and happy, "how come you don't listen at me? I hope you run dem legs off up to de yelbows." The dog got up and came to Eph, and began biting imaginary fleas on the Negro's leg. "Git away fun here," Eph said. He was thinking about the lost wheel chair, and Hardhead's worthlessness made him sicklike. His hands fell upon the dog's big head, and he softened. "If de truth be told, you jist ain't no bird dog. You jist ain't got it into you. You jist a high-class yard dog, and fun now on dat's all you claims to be."

Cleotha, standing behind him, said, "I heered you say he wasn't no bird dog."

From then on, Cleotha was out to get rid of that hungry mouth, and several times, when Eph was in the field, she almost did it. Hardhead knew well enough how Cleotha felt about him, and he never let her get close to him. When he saw her coming, he got up and moved elsewhere. Being one-eyed didn't seem to make him any less alert. Sometimes Cleotha would come out with a plate of corn bread and pot licker in her outstretched hand, and a stick of cordwood behind her back, but hungry as he was, Hardhead wasn't fooled. He wagged his tail politely and went under the sagging old barn.

WHEN MR. FLOYD CAME back from Europe, the first thing he did was to drive to the lake to fish with Eph. In the past year the rains had done fine, and the bass were roiling the water.

"I guess you didn't know I was going to be your neighbor, Eph," Mr. Floyd said. "I'm buying the old Humphrey plantation that joins your little farm. Ten thousand acres of it. Plenty of birds on that place."

"Oh, Lawd, de birds on dat Humphrey place!" Eph said.

"By the way, what ever happened to that bird-dog puppy I gave you about three years ago?"

"We still got him, and proud of 'im. 'Course Cleotha, she don't keer 'bout him mightily. But Ol' Hardhead, 'e de best yard dog in Floridy."

"Is that so?" Mr. Floyd asked. "How is he on birds?"

Eph sighed. " 'E ain't no 'count as a bird dog, Mr. Floyd. We jist got him for a pet dog, sort of."

"Gun shy?"

"Oh, no, suh; 'e like to hear de guns."

"What's wrong with him?"

" 'E's a pure wild dog in de woods, Mr. Floyd. Sometimes I wish you could see de way 'e lickety-splits, like a fitified dog. Den, too, 'e hardheaded as a light'rd knot."

Brag Dog

"Does he find birds?"

"Well, I can't rightly say what-all he do do. I don't see him but jist a very few minutes, once I let 'im go. Ev'y now and den I see him find a covey. Den—blip!—he done fleshed 'em."

"Did you ever try hunting him from horseback?" Mr. Floyd asked.

"No, suh. Ner muleback either, 'cause ol' Kate's backbone would split me right in two."

"I want to see that dog hunt, Eph. Bring him over to the place Monday morning. We'll have a horse saddled for you."

Monday, Mr. Floyd told Mr. Mac, his dog man, to get out Bob, one of his best pointers. The horses were saddled when Hardhead arrived, followed at the end of a taut plowline by Eph.

Eph wiped his face with the back of his hand. "Dis lunytic done drug me two miles," he said. "W'en I gits back, I gwine hitch 'im up to de plow, and let ol' Kate loafer a w'ile."

Mr. Floyd looked at Hardhead. He saw a seventy-pound liver-and-white pointer with a great chest, long, big-boned legs, and a lithe waist hardly bigger than your two fists together. His ribs flared out under his tough hide like keg staves, and you could tell that fat would no more stay on him than it would on a white-hot stove. Eph tied him to a tree, and when the dog finally decided that the tree was too sturdy to be moved, he half-crouched at the end of his rope, panting excitedly and blinking at them with that milky eye.

They took the two dogs down to Blue Pasture on leash, and Mr. Floyd said, "All right, let's see what they'll do. Leave that check cord on Hardhead."

The dogs were released. "Better watch de big fool close right now, suh," Eph said, " 'cause you ain't gwine see him for long, dog bite his bullheaded time."

Mr. Floyd's dog, Bob, made a long swinging cast toward the branch at the left of Blue Pasture. But Hardhead split the middle, going wide open like a racing greyhound, the fifty-foot check cord they'd tied to him dancing and leaping wildly into the air. The horses spurred after him, and they did well to keep him in sight for fifteen minutes. Once they saw him swing with startling abruptness from a dead run to a cold point, never having slowed or put his nose to the ground. For that one instant, his work was perfect. There he stood, with his tail pointing at the pine tops and his head up as if he were looking over a stump, and that crooked ear twisted lopsided on top of his head. It lasted only a second. Hardhead ducked his head and bolted, busting the covey into twenty frightened pieces, slashing at them with his teeth. He came in with such a lightning rush he even caught one of the birds. He gave it a quick crunch, flung it aside, and then went helling after the others, chasing them out of sight.

"See dere how 'e do?" Eph said. "Ain't no 'count as a bird dog. But round de house he minds good, and he keeps de possums out de chicken house and de pigs out de yard, and he's a ideal play-pretty for Valentine."

That night when they came in, Mr. Floyd asked, "Well, Mac, what do you think?"

"It'll be a hell of a job to break him, Mr. Floyd," the dog man answered, "but if we can do it, he'll be one everlastin' pistol ball."

"That's what I think, too," Mr. Floyd said. "Eph, you've got a dog we figure can run in field trials. He's your dog, but I want to see a winner that was bred in my kennels; and I'm going to let you and Mac try to break him. I need another man around the kennels anyway, and from now you're working for me—and you better keep your lazy bones in a hustle."

That night as Hardhead dragged Eph home at a trot, the Negro said, "Now, ain't you sump'm! Mr. Floyd done made up his mind dat you a field-trial dog, and 'e want us to train you up. But 'e gwine find out just how hardheaded you is, 'fo' he gits through, and he gwine be plumb disagusted. But I ain't. It ain't gwine make de fust bit of diffence. You gwine still be de ol' nigger's brag dog, even if it ain't nothin' but de brag yard dog."

They went to work trying to break Hardhead, but he seemed to get wilder. In the woods they could never get near him. He ran wild as a buck deer and he never held a point for more than twenty seconds. They couldn't train him when they couldn't touch him. Sometimes Hardhead would come back that night, and then again he might be gone three days. After a day of fruitless search in the woods, they would wake up to find the dog lying wearily by the house, muddy and brier-slashed, and twitching in his sleep as he chased dream quail. One time he showed up with blood spots here and there on him. They dug the shot out, and found them to be No. 4's. Whoever let go at him had meant to kill him. They investigated and found out Hardhead had run down a yearling calf and killed it, just for the fun of it. The calf belonged to Mr. Donnelson, a farmer friend of Mr. Floyd's who lived fifteen miles away. Mr. Floyd paid for the calf and got everything straightened out.

"Damn his wild soul," he said afterward, "my ten thousand acres just cramped his style. He wanted room to stretch out and hunt."

Eph thought of the trick that they used finally to break Hardhead. Down in the Blue Pasture there were two coveys that Hardhead knew, and he inevitably went straight to them, first off, and sent them a-scattering. One day they took another bird dog out and located the two coveys precisely, without flushing them. Then Mr. Mac hid in the brush near the first covey, and Eph hid near the second covey, nearly a quarter mile down the pasture. Presently, far up the woods, they heard Mr. Floyd's shout, and they know Hardhead was loose. Then Mr. Mac could see him coming, his big feet drumming on the ground like a wild mustang's hoofs. Hardhead got wind of this first covey and swerved in and flash-pointed.

Mr. Mac made a dive for the trailing check cord. He got it just as Hardhead lunged forward to pop the birds. "Whoa!" he yelled and braced himself, but when the dog hit the end of the cord the man was jerked to his knees.

Hardhead turned a complete end-over-end flip, and hopped to his feet with an expression of mixed incredulity and frustration, his tongue hanging out sideways. He got another whiff of the quail, and stiffened. Then he tried to bust into 'em again, and Mr. Mac turned him tail over head again. Every time Hardhead moved he got snatched back on his tail. Mr. Mac made him stand there twenty minutes, with the birds not ten yards from him. Then he walked in and flushed the birds, shooting one of them down. He made Hardhead stand another minute, then let him go retrieve the bird the way he'd learned to do it in the yard. He retrieved with tender mouth, too, because the last bird he bit had had nails in it.

When Mr. Mac sent him on, he headed straight as a bullet for that second covey. He held his point a good bit longer this time, and when he did charge, Eph was on the other end of the cord, and Hardhead hit the ground again.

Later, when they were talking about it, they laughed about the look on Hardhead's face after he'd been stopped by the cord.

Mr. Mac observed. "He come up with a surprised expression, and he said to me: 'Well, Judas Priest, is that what you been wanting me to do all this time?'"

Eph shook his head, "Dat ain't what he said to me. After nearbout snatching my arms out dee sockeys, de ol' scoun'l looked at me, a-spittin' de dirt out'n his mouth, and he said, plain as day, 'Well, you finely cotched me, but I sho' give you a time of it!'"

When they had worked on him a few more months, they ran him at Quitman, at the Continentals—"Mr. Gerald Livin'ston's trials," Eph called them afterward—but Hardhead was too wild. Mr. Mac handled him, and Eph scouted. Hardhead found two coveys and held them staunchly. Then he got lost. The time was up when Eph finally found Hardhead three miles off the course, on point.

At Shuqualak, Mississippi, Hardhead won second. A big lemon pointer named Kentucky Buckaroo beat him, a hard-going young dog that had been burning up the field-trial circuit.

"Buck's the next champion, absolutely," they said.

After Shuqualak, Mr. Floyd came to Eph and handed him two hundred-dollar bills.

Eph's eyes widened. "W'at's dis yere for, Mr. Floyd?"

"That's what you get for having the next-best dog in the trials."

"Father, do!" Eph whispered. "I didn't know dey gave you no money for jist bird huntin'. Dese Sugar Log people is sho fine folks."

Mr. Floyd started to go, then turned back. "When we get back, I've got a brood bitch I'm going to send over to your place. We want to be getting some Hardheaded puppies."

Grand Junction, Tennessee, on field-trial week is dog-men's paradise. Any talk but bird-dog talk is beside the point. The great old dogs live again; dogs like Mary Montrose, who first won the National when she was a derby, and Becky Broomhill and Feagin's Mohawk Pal, both of whom also won it three times; John Proctor, champion and famous sire, whose blood has run hot as ever in his descendants, like Comanche Rap, and Ferris Jake, who won the 1921 championship, and Muscle Shoals Jake, who missed the championship, but took everything else, and his son, Air Pilot, who was headed for the top until automobile fumes in a garage ruined his nose, and his son, Air Pilot's Sam, who won in 1937, twenty-one years after his great-great-great-grandfather, John Proctor.

The wealthy dog owners are there, Johnsons and Teagles and Fleischmanns and Sages, and such, and field-trial judges like Hobart Ames, who owns the course, and Dr. Benton King, a little man on a big horse; and then the professional handlers, the real dog men—the Farriors, father and son, and Ches Harris, who has won more championships than any other living handler, and Dewey English and Clyde Morton and the Bevan Brothers and all the rest of them.

Eph had never seen so many handsome saddle horses in his life. He held Hardhead's collar and said, "Yes, suh, Hardhead, if'n you win next-best ag'in, we goan buy Addie May that sump'm-another!"

The first day was perfect, clear and brittle-cold and breathless. Hardhead was paired with a dog from Oklahoma who hunted well the first half of the long heat, then tired and slowed. Hardhead got off to a bad start, ambling too wide and getting lost, but Eph found him; from then on he hunted the course at a ground-eating pace.

"I'll bet he's in the second series," Mr. Mac said after the heat, as he put the leash on Hardhead's collar.

"He sure hustled," Mr. Floyd grinned. "Take him to the dog truck, Eph."

But it was Hardhead who took Eph to the dog truck. After three hours of the hardest bird hunting, most dogs would have been content to trot wearily at heel. Hardhead hunched his gaunt shoulders, stretched the leash taut as a fiddle string, and pulled.

Two or three men were watching. One of them asked Eph, "Hey, George, ain't that the one they call Hardhead? The one they just took up?"

Jogging along, Eph grinned and said, "Dis de ol' fool hisse'f, gen'lmen."

"I'll bet a hundred to two on that dog against the field," the man said to his friends, "provided they call him back for the second series."

"You think I didn't see the way he drug that nigger by here?" one of the others said. "You trying to catch a fish?"

"I throwed out my net."

But when night of the second day came, there was a new favorite. He was a yellow pointer from Oklahoma, and his name was Ambling Sam. When he ran he outhunted everything that had been put down, finding five coveys and nailing them tight. He traveled wide and fast, with a happy lighthearted style, and he handled like a show dog.

Eight dogs were called back for the second series, but everybody was pretty sure that the real race was between Hardhead, Ambling Sam and Kentucky Buckaroo. Hardhead and Buck were paired in the last brace. In the brace preceding them, Ambling Sam threw his chances away. After hunting nicely for two hours—though not so spectacularly as he had in his previous run—he jumped a doe deer, forgot his training, and chased her clean out of the country.

The judges called the last brace. Mr. Mac and Mr. Floyd and Eph took Hardhead out of the dog truck and gave him a tiny bit of water. The dog yawned nervously and looked things over, his leathery muscles quivering and his one good eye glinting fiercely.

Mr. Floyd pulled at his cigarette and whispered, "Look at him. He's right today."

Mr. Mac gave Eph a hard glance. "Don't lose him, Eph. He's sure hot. He can be the best dog in the world today—or he can be the wildest."

They brought him out front, Mr. Mac leaning back as the dog strained mulelike against the rope. Eph held the rope until Mr. Mac found the leash snap. "All right, I got him," he said, unsnapping the rope. He muttered, "He's hot as a pistol, Eph. Don't lose him now."

Buck stood waiting, eager, too, but well-mannered. A smooth-turned bird dog, Buck made an odd contrast with the gaunt, big-boned Hardhead, with his wild impatience and his bad eye and ear.

"Let 'im go!" the starting judge said.

Both dogs broke fast, but Hardhead jumped with the suppressed power of a spring out of a clock. He ran furiously, straining almost agonizingly for a longer stride. Easily losing Buckaroo, he was still going like this when he hit game, five minutes later. He was right in the middle of the covey in one bound, and they exploded around him. For one split second he seemed about to lunge forward after them. But he stood, on point, until the judges came.

"It's a stop to flush," one of them said. "I saw the birds."

Mr. Mac sent Hardhead on. The dog resumed his wicked wind-scorching stride. He swung out to the right, skirting a cornfield and leaving a vapor of dust behind him.

"Go hard, dog," Eph muttered, "but don't come up on no birds till you run off some o' dat hot."

Then Hardhead found two coveys within five minutes. The first he almost flushed again. Running wild, he suddenly stopped his front feet dead. His rear end kept going, swinging him around, and when he had stopped he was on birds.

Eph rode to the edge of the woods and shouted to the judges, waving his battered hat.

The brown body of the gallery shifted and broke, and the riders galloped to the point. Mr. Mac dismounted, his little twenty-eight-gauge gun in his left hand, and his quirt in the other. Hardhead stood frozen, his tail good and his front quarters still in the slight crouch in which he had stopped. Mr. Mac walked rapidly out front, kicking the bushes and flinging his quirt against the grass. When the birds got up, he fired the gun with one hand, watching to see that Hardhead didn't break.

The next find was a bit on the spectacular side. Slicing rapidly across a thinly covered grass field, Hardhead picked up a vagrant scent and wheeled at right angles. He didn't slow down, but his head was higher as he read the wind. The birds were feeding quietly two hundred yards away. He drew on them boldly, cockily, and abruptly pointed with high head and tail and all feet planted solid. Two birds were not eight feet from him, their frightened little black eyes shining as they squatted motionlessly in a barren furrow in plain view of everybody. Mr. Mac flushed the covey.

Kentucky Buckaroo had come to be known as one of the biggest going dogs on the field-trial circuit. Hardhead was bigger. Buck made several good finds, and handled them nicely, but it was Hardhead that everybody watched. In the distance they saw the Negro ride out to the edge of the woods and wave his hand, and again his shout of point drifted clearly down.

"That big dog's got 'em again," a brown man called. When the judge rode up, Mr. Mac dismounted and walked toward the motionless dog. Before he got close to him, Hardhead left the point and ran fifty yards out into the sedge and pointed again.

"Dey runnin' fun 'im," Eph thought nervously. This time the birds held, and Mr. Mac's boots exploded them out. Hardhead stood to wing and shot, and was sent on.

Eph grinned his relief. "De reason dat ol' head's so hard is 'cause she's packed plumb tight with brains!"

Hardhead swung out into the woods again, going like a ball of light through the cold shadows. An ice-water brook wandered down the woods; Eph hoped the dog would stop and drink, and get a few seconds rest. Hardhead drank, but he did it galloping up the shallow stream, splashing the chilled waters on the damp leaves of the banks. Then he jumped out and headed for the cornfield.

In ten minutes he was out of Eph's sight. Twenty minutes later Hardhead was lost and Mr. Mac had joined the search. They quirted their horses, riding high in the saddle and intently studying every distant whitish object that might be a pointer on birds.

"Dog take my sorry time," Eph thought fearfully. "I done gone and let 'im lost hisse'f!"

Another ten minutes they searched, without success. If they didn't find him before taking-up time, Hardhead was out of it. "Lemme me find 'im, Lord, lemme find 'im," Eph kept muttering. Then he thought of Luck, and he said. "If'n you kin look any better fun where you is, Luck, glance round and see do you see 'im."

A man shouted. "Hey, Mac, yon's your dog!"

Eph saw him, a mile away, beyond the gallery, slashing his way down a rise, moving with incredible swiftness, as always. At the bottom of the rise, Kentucky Buckaroo stood on point; even that far away, Eph could tell the judges were watching to see what Hardhead would do.

When Hardhead was two hundred yards away, he saw the point and stopped on the hillside, stylishly honoring; he held until the birds were flushed and Buck sent on.

"For a dog with one eye," a man was saying as Eph approached the gallery again, "he can see a damn long way."

"That's the most dog you'll ever look at, bud," another answered. "I've watched 'em all from Eugene M right on down, and that hardheaded son of a gun right yonder's my pick."

"Comanche Frank would've showed him a thing or two."

"Comanche Frank, hell."

"You wait a while. This race isn't over. See if your Hardhead is still balling the jack like that after three hours of it."

That's what the judges were watching too. Buckaroo was running a good race, and finding birds; and ordinarily his performance would have won. But Hardhead was too much dog. He had covered more ground, found more birds, and handled as well as Buck.

The gallery rode in quiet excitement. Hardhead was far out to the left, almost, it seemed, on the horizon. Buck was on the right and closer in. Buck cut across in front of the gallery. Ahead of him was a ravine, ten feet or so across. Buck slid down one side and galloped up the other, hardly slowing.

"Buck can't be very tired," somebody said, "the way he come out of that hole like a bat out of hell."

Brag Dog

While the riders looked for a place to cross the ravine, Hardhead came back in, his big feet thrumming on the red earth. Before he even reached the place, it was apparent that he was going to cross the ravine at exactly the same place Buck had crossed. Everybody stopped—the judges and reporters and spectators and dog men—to see if Hardhead would reveal any weariness in crossing that deep ravine.

The dog came on, that torn ear lying inside out on his head the way it did sometimes. For a split second it seemed that Hardhead didn't even see the ravine. Then he was there. He left the ground. In mid-air his tail gave a convulsive flirt that seemed to send him over. That unbelievable leap carried him across with two feet to spare. Within a few minutes he had overtaken Buckaroo and was headed for the horizon again.

The judges looked at their watches. Doctor King said, "You can take your dogs up."

ADDIE MAY DIDN'T KNOW exactly what to make of the wheel chair. A lot of the neighbors heard that Eph had bought it, and they were there when it came.

"How you do it, Eph?" Addie May said uncertainly.

"You jist gits in it and rolls right around," Eph said happily.

Addie May hesitated. "Ise scared of hit."

Eph laughed. "Hit's plumb harmless, honey."

They sat her in it, and she rolled carefully across the room, and, with growing confidence, turned it around and came back.

"Doggone," said Joe Ben Brown, "I gwine borry dat to ride to de store in!"

Cleotha looked at Eph angrily. "I see you aims to just th'ow dat best-dog money away."

Eph paid no attention to her. "How you likes it, Addie May?"

"Hit's sho Lord purty," she said, almost ready to cry in her happiness. "We'll put us a sheet over hit to keep it nice, and just let comp'ny set in it."

"Honey, dat ain't no comp'ny chair. Dat's your ev'yday chair, and you kin roll right where you pleases," Eph said. Hardhead came up and hasseled the chair with his flaring nostrils, and his tail gave a perfunctory wag. "Look at de ol' scoun'l," Eph said, "he know he done bought you dat fancy sump'm."

13

THE GOPHER DOG

Jud Lee stopped his wagon in front of The Golden Rule Grocery. The bird dog Fred, having trotted in under the shade of the wagon, lay down on the pavement and immediately went to sleep. Golden Rule Linkins, leaning against the doorway, called,

"Howdy do, Jud?"

"Just tolable, Rule. How you gitting along?"

"Poorly. It looks like my business is going to drindle right on down to nothing. Seems like I better hatch me up one of them premotion schemes," Linkins said unhappily. "You been fishing lately?"

"I've just about give it up, to tell the truth. Ain't been since day before yestiddy," Jud said. "Course I stopped off a minute at the creek coming in, to catch a mess for my old woman, on account of she's ailing." He held up a willow fork on which hung three bass, still flapping.

"You caught them at the creek this morning?" Rule asked in astonishment. "Why I fished the creek this morning myself and I never hung the first one. What'd you catch 'em with?"

"Same old thing." He leaned over in the wagon and picked up an object shaped roughly like a lizard, made of buckskin and studded with fish-hooks.

"Jud Lee's Dabbler," Rule breathed reverently, for the fame of this lure was wide. It was said that fish would follow Jud to the hard road to get at his dabbler. Many men had tried to imitate it, and even Jud had not been able to make another one as deadly. The imitations caught some fish, but not the way the original did. It had the magic motion. Once a big bass broke Jud's line and stole the lure; Jud went to town and got three sticks of dynamite and blasted here and there until he killed the right fish and recovered the dabbler.

"Jud," Rule said, "I don't guess you'd sell that dabbler, would you? It must be right old now, and it's gitting pretty chewed-up-like."

"I reckon I'll hang onto it a while longer," Jud said.

"I'd give you two dollars, if you was mind to sell."

Jud said he reckoned not, and they went into the store. Rule was right—business was bad. Things were very quiet. Jud bought a sack of flour and two bladders of snuff and some coal oil; as he started to pay, Rule said, "You just take them groceries and this here five-dollar bill and leave that dabbler with me, and we'll call it square, Jud."

"I couldn't hardly do—" He stopped short, for from behind the counter had strolled a big pointer with well-sprung ribs and a handsome head. "Never knew you had no bird-dog like that, Rule," Jud said." Where you git him at?"

"I come by him," Rule said complacently.

"Is he worth a damn?"

"He ain't bad," Rule said. "Ain't bad. I reckon I ought to keep my mouth shut but the fellow I got him from said your dog Fred was the daddy of him. Said he had his bitch locked up and old Fred come around one night and when he seen what dog it was he let him in."

At this information Jud put down his groceries and looked intently at the dog. "He walks lazylike, the way Fred does," Jud admitted. "But eyes is set a mite too close together."

"Come here, Bertie," Rule said. He fondled the dog's ears. "That fellow shore did hate to git shet of Bertie. I sort of know how he feels now."

"How come?" Jud asked quickly.

"Well, looks like I'm gonna have to let him go myself. My business is bad and I got to try to build it up. Ain't got time for hunting and fishing both. So I'm quitting hunting. Tears me all to pieces to do it, but I got to find Bertie a new home."

"Town ain't no fit place for a bird dog noway," Jud said. "Guess I oughtn't to be thinking about feeding another dog, but if you're set on letting him go I'll take him off your hands."

"He's a valuable dog, Jud, and with my business the way it is I just couldn't afford to outright give him away."

"Tell you what. I got a Genuwine Simulated Diamont I ordered out of a magazine I'll give you for him."

Rule shook his head, and after a long time he said, "I couldn't do that but tell you what I will do. I'll swap Bertie for that old chewed up dabbler of yours. And them three fish."

Jud's first impulse was to say no; but then he looked at the dog again. He liked fishing, but fishing was not hunting, and anyway this dog might really be Fred's own child. Finally he said, "Never thought I'd be studying about giving up my dabbler, but...let's go see your dog hunt."

"You can take my word for it that he's a good dog," Rule said.

"Ain't taking nobody's word about no bird dog," Jud said.

Rule hesitated. "Well, there's a patch of woods down back of my house. Don't guess it'd hurt to lock up a little while."

They locked the store and went to the woods and released Fred and Bertie. Bertie was fast, and he looked good hunting. Before fifteen minutes had passed, Bertie found a covey of birds and pointed them staunchly.

"Be durn if he didn't beat Fred to them birds," Jud said in amazement.

"You satisfied?" Rule asked.

The Gopher Dog

"Nearly bout," Jud admitted. "Let 'em hunt about another hour and I'll be plumb sure."

"I cain't do that!" Rule protested. "I've closed up my place of business. I got to go on back. You seen him hunt. Don't aim to rush you, Jud, but you'll have to decide right now. You want him or not?"

"If you put it that way," Jud said, "I guess I'll have to take him."

THAT FIRST COVEY was one of the few that Jud ever saw Bertie point. The next morning he postponed sharpening his wife's axe and he and Fred and Bertie hit for the dewey woods in the wagon.

"Now, you Bertie, let's see if you can hang it on your daddy again today," Jud said. The dogs swung away and disappeared. After a while, when Bertie didn't return, Jud went looking for him. When he found him, only Bertie's posterior showed. The rest of him was down in the hole of one of the land tortoises locally called gophers, and he was digging and whining excitedly.

"You git away from there," Jud shouted, outraged. Bertie gave no sign that he had heard. Jud picked up a lightwood knot and sent it whistling at Bertie, and this bouncing off his rump got Bertie's attention. He yipped and backed out, wagged his tail, and started hunting again.

"Any young dog would be liable to do that," Jud told himself but without conviction.

Before long Bertie pointed, to Jud's relief. Fred came up and backed dutifully. But it was not a covey of quail, it was a big tortoise—gopher—squatting in the grass with his head half pulled into his shell. Fred gave Bertie a look of disgust and went on hunting. Jud gave Bertie a licking.

The licking didn't do any good at all. Bertie found another tortoise hole and started digging.

Finally Jud was convinced. "I just be durned if I ain't let that Golden Rule Linkin git my prize dabbler in swap for a pea-headed gopher dog!" he thought, and jumped up and down in rage. Bertie would point a covey of birds if they got in his way, but they were secondary game to him. Once he got so far down into a gopher hole he couldn't get out, and Jud had to go to the nearest Negro shack and borrow a shovel and dig him out. "Should a-left the scoun'l in there, only it would a-been too mean a trick to play on the gophers."

He realized now what Rule had done. He had gone to a patch of woods he knew thoroughly, steered Bertie to a covey of birds, and immediately afterward ended the hunt. There had been no gophers in that patch of woods because Bertie had cleared them out long ago.

Bertie would bring in the smaller gophers by mouth; the larger ones he lay down and barked at.

For the next day or two Jud was not fit company for even the gophers Bertie brought in. His face stayed purple in anger, and his children hid from him under the bed and his wife kept a stick of stove wood handy and watched him closely.

Jud would have shot Bertie the first day, only that would have made the deal a total loss. "Anybody would pull a trick like that is crooked as a blacksnake," Jud shouted. "On top of that, he's probably been snickering around about swapping me a gopher dog and everybody knows about it and now I won't be able to sell him to nobody else!"

Jud sat on his front step with his chin in his hands for two days, thinking, rising only to eat some corn bread and syrup and sowbelly, or to go to bed. On the third day he sent the two small children down to hitch up the mule and wagon, and he got ready to go to town.

When he walked into the Golden Rule Grocery, Linkins smiled amiably and spoke friendly-like, but watched Jud carefully, at the same time whittling a stick with what seemed to be a very sharp knife. Out in the back a small Negro boy, Jud noted with irritation, was cleaning five or six fresh and beautiful bass.

Jud smiled pleasantly and said, "Hope everything's going to suit you, Rule. Yep, I shore do. I want to buy a sack o' tobacco and a can of coffee."

Rule regarded him suspiciously. He did not turn his back to Jud but reached up over his head and felt for the goods, and then tossed them on the counter, staying out of Jud's reach.

"Rule," Jud said finally, "I've sure had me a good time the last few days. That Bertie, he's some dog. A gopher dog."

"Gopher dog? He never fooled with gophers when I had him," Rule said.

"Oh, I know he just took it up. I know you wouldn't a-swapped me no gopher dog on purpose. I ain't mad about it. That old dabbler was really chewed to pieces anyway."

"I been doing all right with it," Rule said complacently.

"I really got the best of the deal, in some ways," Jud chuckled. "I swear, that Bertie dog just tickles me to death. When he gits to fooling with an old gopher, sometimes I laugh until I'm fit to bust."

Rule looked relieved. He folded his knife and quit whittling. "I shore am glad you feel that way about it."

Jud looked reminiscent and chuckled again. "When he gits to digging and barking, I just nearly die. He's been a whole heap of pleasure to me, old Bertie has."

"I never knowed you had no such-all sense of humor as that."

Jud said suddenly, "Oh, I was about to fergit. The other day Bertie found a tremenjous gopher, and I got to thinking back to recollect a bigger gopher, and then it came to me suddenlike: you know what would shore-enough build up your business? *A gopher contest!* You could offer out a twenty-five dollar prize for the biggest gopher brung in."

"Twenty-five dollars for a gopher?"

"I got it all thought out. Build a big pen outa chicken wire out there in the back, and everybody comes right through the store to chunk in their gopher. Why they'll be coming in and out all day long, to look er to turn in. You can make them that's passing through go down the right handed aisle and them coming out tother aisle, so as not be bumping into each other and interfering with folks buying things at the counters."

The Gopher Dog

For a moment Rule's eyes grew bright as he visualized the crowds streaming in and out. "But twenty-five dollars for the biggest gopher!" he said.

"Well, tell you what," Jud said hesitantly, "Me and Bertie's going to take a stab at it ourselves, and if I can quit laughing long enough to pick up the gophers he gits aholt of, me and him's bound to find the biggest 'un. Then, since you was the one let me in on Bertie, we'll split the prize money and it'll only cost you twelve and a half."

"Well, now you talking!" Rule said. He thought for a while. "Yes, sir, Jud, that sounds like just the kind of premotion scheme my business needs. Everybody and his brother will be out gopher-hunting, and they's plenty to be found. They'll come piling in here with they gophers and then they'll buy a bunch of stuff just to git on the good side of me so I'll give 'em the prize. And them as ain't gopher hunters will come to look at what's been brung in, and argue about seeing one bigger when they was a boy, and then they set there on the counter and talk and before long *they'll* remember something they need in the grocery line. Jud, be durned if you ain't turnt out to be a real friend."

"Here's the kind of fellow I am, Rule," Jud said solemnly, "when somebody does something for me, I aim to try to do just as much fer him. Er more, if possible."

"Well, to tell the gospel truth, I didn't expect you to be so crazy as all that about Bertie."

"Rule, I never before had no feeling in my heart like the one I got for old Bertie, and may the good Lord strike me dead if that ain't so."

Within twenty-four hours after the announcement of the big contest, the gophers began coming in. And every day they increased in number and size. Negroes brought them in croker sacks. Little boys brought them in toy wagons. Farmers brought them in the backs of wagons, carefully bedded down in fruit crates half filled with straw. Two men in the woods spied a big gopher at the same time and had a fight over him and while they were fighting the gopher got away.

Jud had been right about the popularity of the contest. The Golden Rule Grocery was now a busy place, and while of course most of the traffic was toward the gopher pen, many people did buy things. Meantime the population of the pen grew, until it was crawling two-deep in rusty old land tortoises who stared with beady eyes but did not seem overly nervous about their new environment. With three days still to go before the end of the contest, the pen had to be enlarged.

Jud looked the candidates over and thought: "Some pretty nice ones there. Me and Bertie had better git started."

The man next to him said, "Yon's the biggest 'un, that'n with the twinkle in his eye."

Another said, "Naw. That mottled 'un will outweigh him a pound."

"Wait until me and that damn gopher dog git to work," Jud muttered, "and then they'll see the biggest 'un."

Bertie was more than willing to do his part toward winning the contest. Fred went along too, simply because Jud had never found any way to keep him at home when he went to the woods. Fred pointed soon after they got into the woods, but to his surprise Jud walked right on past him to where Bertie was digging. Fred kept holding the point, watching out of the corner of his eye for Jud to come back. But now even Jud was digging, and a shower of dirt pattered on the leaves all around. Fred lay down. Finally when Jud didn't come he sprang into the birds and flushed them, then prepared to spring away from the lightwood knot that was sure to fly. But Jud had not noticed, even though the birds had flown right over him. Jud let out a whoop and dragged something out of the hole.

Fred approached curiously and saw that the thing causing Jud such satisfaction and Bertie such excitement was the grandfather of all gophers. Fred sat down in disgust.

Golden Rule Linkins had begun to get a little worried, because some of the gopher candidates looked as if they might be hard to beat, so he was pleased when Jud came in and allowed his entry to crawl majestically from the croker sack. Rule whistled.

"That," Rule said in admiration, "is the nicest 'un I've seen in forty years of woods rambling!"

The word of Jud Lee's gopher got around fast, and people shoved their way through the store to see. There were many ejaculations of amazement. Archibaldus Foord, a turpentine man who has worked many a crop of boxes and who was an authority on gophers, studied Jud's gopher from one side and then another, and they all waited for him to have his say. Finally he spat and said slowly, "Jud, he's shore a fine 'un!"

On Tuesday there was a little ceremony, and Jud was given the twenty-five dollars first prize. They all congratulated him, and even the losers admitted that he deserved to win. It was quite a triumph for Jud, and one or two of his friends felt that it was a proper answer to some who had often said that Jud never would amount to anything.

Afterward, when things had quieted down a little, Rule said, "Jud, I just don't believe there was no premotion scheme like this in the history of the county! I believe I got folks coming back to trade regular. To tell the truth it's remade my business. I'm shore in your debt."

"Wasn't nothing much," Jud said.

"By the way," Rule said suddenly, "what we gonna do with all them gophers?"

Jud held up a finger and smiled wisely. "I been saving the best for last. We ain't through premoting. What we gonna do now is paint every one them gophers on the back with "Golden Rule Grocery.'"

"And then what?"

"Then we gonna turn 'em a-loose right here in town. Everywhere they go they'll be reminding people to trade at your store."

Rule caught his breath. "Crawling billboards!"

"Reckon that's about it."

"Listen, you run git that sign painter, and start sobering him up enough to go to work."

Jud started out the door, and then stopped. "While I'm gone you could start washing them gophers up some."

"Washing them up?"

The Gopher Dog

"You ought to know they got to be clean to paint on 'em."

"That's the grocery business for you," Rule said cheerfully. "Cain't never tell what you'll have to do next. Washing gophers!"

When the painter was sober enough to walk he came down and surveyed the task. After looking at the sea of gophers he said, "It would take three days to paint them gophers free-hand. We better cut us a stencil and go work."

By midnight the job was done. On the back of every gopher was plainly painted *Golden Rule Grocery*.

"Jud," Rule said wearily, "we've done a day's work we won't never fergit."

"I expect that's about right," Jud agreed.

They pulled up the stakes of the pen and the gophers skidded and tumbled to the ground. They began to crawl around and disappear off into the darkness.

"Well, I better be gitting home," Jud said. "I'll come in tomorrow and see how you making out."

THE NEXT AFTERNOON when he sent Little Sister down to hitch up the mule and wagon, Fred saw the wagon being hitched and sneaked off into the woods so Jud couldn't catch him and shut him up. A mile or so down the road he would suddenly appear behind the wagon. "You needn't sneak off—I see you," Jud said. "Come to think of it, I'll take my old streak o' rust and kill a mess of birds on the way home."

He went into the house and got his gun, and then he called Bertie from under the house. "You're going too," he spat. He put him into the body of the wagon and tied him with haywire, and then wiped his hands on his overalls distastefully.

When Jud arrived in town, he found Golden Rule Linkins in a state of wild nervous excitement.

"Jud, our advertising scheme has done backfired on us!"

"It has?"

"Certain people has been seeing them gophers around town and has had a lot to say about it. They—" The phone rang. When Rule picked up the receiver, Jud could hear a woman's voice:

"Mr. Linkins, your turtle is in my living room under the *sofa*!"

"Ain't no turtle, ma'am. Just a harmless gopher. And he ain't mine."

"Well, he's got your name on him, and if you don't come get him *right now* I'll never buy another thing from you and I may not do it anyhow."

Rule hung up, and turned to Jud, wild-eyed. "You see? That's how it's been going all day. Them gophers has taken over the town, and people's looking at it the wrong way. I went out and tried to round them up, but couldn't find none. Then just time I git back, the phone goes to ringing to beat all hell," he cried. "Watch the store for me a minute. I got to run down to Mrs. Maud's house. If anybody calls up, tell 'em I'll be there tireckly."

He rushed out. Jud opened a can of sardines and sat on the counter and began eating them. A large gopher on the sidewalk, head up inquiringly, moved leisurely past the store front. The phone rang, and when Jud finally decided to answer it an angry voice shouted:

"Rule Linkins, this is Rob McVey, and in case you've forgot it I'm your best customer, and I thought I'd tell you I don't see the joke in having two of your gophers on my front terrace and you better come get 'em right now."

"I ain't interested," Jud said, and hung up.

The phone rang again. This time a nearly hysterical woman.

"I ain't interested," Jud said, and hung up.

That kept up until Rule came back in, panting feverishly. Jud was on his fourth can of sardines.

"Anybody call?" Rule demanded.

"Not a soul," Jud said. "Mighty quiet little place you got here."

The phone rang. Rule sprang to it, said he would be there at once, and headed for the door. Here he collided with a man in approximately the same high emotional state he himself was in.

Mel Wottle, the policeman, could hardly speak. "You—you—Linkins! I got the mayor and the city clerk and everybody else in the city hall trying to find an ordinance to arrest you under. Your dang gophers are all over town, falling in the reservoir, scaring women, gitting squushed by cars in the street! I never seen such goings-on!" Tears of anger rolled down his cheek. "You listen to me. Git busy and round up them gophers, or I'll—I'll—" His voice failed.

"But they's hundreds of 'em! How'm I gonna find 'em?"

"That's your worry!"

Jud coughed gently. "Rule, I don't want to butt in, but I got a little idea might be of some help. *I* know how you could find them gophers.

"How, for the Lord's sake?"

Jud nodded toward his wagon outside, where Bertie tugged impatiently at his wire. "Him."

Rule gasped in relief. "Jud, you've saved my life! Just loan me Bertie for a couple of hours!"

"Don't believe I could exactly *loan* him to you, Rule. He's a fine gopher dog, and for all I know you might slip off to the woods and git him hunting birds and ruin him for gopher hunting. It'll just about kill me to let old Bertie go, but seeing the tight fix you're in, I'll swap him back to you."

Rule turned slowly and faced him, and for the first time a glimmer of suspicion came into his eyes. As he thought about it more, the glimmer increased in intensity until it became a glare. "*Now* I begin to see! *Now*—" He started for his pocketknife, then noticed that Jud had started whittling. "Jud Lee, I'll—"

The phone rang. Rule leaped to it and talked briefly. Then he turned to Jud, wiped his forehead, and said, "How much?"

"Well, I guess that other twelve dollars and a half prize money ought to be about right," Jud said reasonably, and then as Rule stepped to the cash register he added, "and of course that old chewed-up dabbler I let you use."

With the dabbler hooked on the side of the wagon, and Fred out ranging for birds, Jud felt a lot better as they started through the woods that led home. He whistled

The Gopher Dog

pleasantly. Not far over to the left, Fred suddenly whirled and pointed. Jud stopped the mule and got down with his gun.

"Steady, now," he cautioned Fred, "and watch where the birds fall at."

He walked in front of the dog. No birds got up. Instead, a large gopher crawled unhurriedly out of the bush. On its back was painted *Golden Rule Grocery.* Jud swore and turned toward the dog.

But Fred had left, and now had begun to hunt the field nearby, moving with a curious air of satisfaction.

Come Back Tuesday

The car stopped at the front gate, and the bird dog under the sagging porch of the house lifted his head and barked once and lay back down. Jud Lee, lying barefooted on the porch, turned over and spat. The young man from the Planter's Bank got out of the car.

"I'm lucky to catch you at home this time, Mr. Lee," said the young man, whose name was Davis.

"Yep, you shore caught me," Jud said resentfully. "You must a' cut off your engine and coasted to the house. That ain't no way to do."

"It's pretty important, or I wouldn't have done it," said Davis apologetically. "You're going to have to move off the place."

"Where'll I move at? Ain't no other empty farms. How'll I feed my dog and young 'uns? The bank don't aim fer us to starve to death, I hope."

"But you're three years behind in your rent! 1938, 1939, and now 1940. It's only sixty dollars a year but you don't pay anything, and there's another tenant anxious to get this place."

"Tell you what. You come back in a week and I'll have enough to pay this year's rent. You cain't chunk me out if I pay for this year."

The young man sighed. "For two years you've been telling me you'd have the money next time I came."

"I hope God strikes me dead if I ain't got sixty dollars by next Tuesday!"

Davis hesitated a moment. "All right. I'll give you until Tuesday. But this is absolutely your last chance!"

Jud went back to sleep and forgot all about it, and he didn't think of it until the following Tuesday dawned and he remembered what he had said he hoped God would do. But then God knew everything, including the fact that he was lying when he had hoped to be struck dead, so of course God would not strike him dead.

At that moment Jud heard a car coming down the little woods road, and he was away to the thicket in a run, thinking exultantly, *Never slipped up on me this time.* He lay down and chewed a sweet-gum stem. Presently his small son came and said, "Ain't him, Pa. It's another old fool."

Jud went cautiously back to the house and found in the car at his gate a city man in khaki hunting clothes, and on the back seat two fine-looking pointers.

"Good morning!" said the man.

"Howdy," Jud said.

"Any quail around here?"

"They's some. Git down and come in."

The man got out of the car and lifted the buggy-sprocket latch on the gate and came in. "I'm Doctor Ingram. I wonder if I could get you to go with me and show me where the birds are."

"I'm right busy," Jud said dubiously.

"I'll pay you five dollars."

Jud turned to the two small children who peeked through the window. "Son, you and little sister go hitch up the mule and wagon. This here gentleman wants me to go out and kill him a mess of birds."

The doctor said quickly, "I'll do my own shooting. You're just to come along as guide."

"Well, I'll carry my old streak o' rust along just in case I have to sting my old dog's tail."

"We won't need your dog. I've two good dogs."

"Ain't no way to dispute old Fred from going, now that he done heard us mention about it. We could shut him up in the crib, only he'd climb outa the top."

"I could shut him up in my car."

"He'd chew up the inside er git sick on the seats, just fer spite. Better let him go. He ain't no trouble."

The doctor shrugged and let his dogs out. They romped around the yard. Fred rose lazily and came from under the porch, his hide sticky with turpentine where he had rubbed against a boxed pine to discourage the fleas. He yawned and watched the dogs until they approached him challengingly. When they seemed to want to fight, he yawned again and lay down.

The doctor got a red-wrapped package of meat from the car. "Like to give my dogs just a little nourishment before they go out," he explained.

He threw each of his pointers a piece of meat, which they swallowed in one gulp. Then he dropped a piece of it in front of Fred. Fred smelled the meat, and backed way from it.

"He don't know what it is," Jud explained.

They rode in the wagon until they reached an open pine woods, and here was an old wire fence and on the nearest rotting post a sign said, "No Hunting. A.L. Sidler."

"Here's where we start at," Jud said cheerfully, and he gave the mule a sound lick with the hickory switch and drove right on over the fence, breaking off the posts and pressing the wire to the ground.

"Mr. Sidler must be a good friend of yours," said the doctor.

"Friend of mine?" echoed Jud. "Why, he's the meanest old crank in this here country. I'd ruther go down to the callyboose to pick out a friend."

"You reckon you ought to leave his fence like that?" the doctor asked nervously.

Come Back Tuesday

"Oh, we'll prop it up when we come back," Jud said, "if we chance to come out this-a-way."

They released the dogs, and Jud drove on without a glance at them. Doctor Ingram sat up and interestedly watched the work of his dogs. They hunted nicely, swinging back and forth in front. He noticed that Jud's dog, Fred, quickly went out of sight. Several minutes passed and Fred did not show up again.

"That dog of yours ranges wide," he said, "but looks like he would report back."

"Liable to have birds somewhere."

"Aren't you going to look for him?"

"Naw, he'll come git us."

Presently, far ahead, Fred appeared. For a moment he stood there until sure they had seen him, and then he went away in the direction he had come, and when they followed they found him standing point in nice style.

"You mean he had pointed those birds and then came and got us when we didn't show up?"

"Why, shore. He ain't no fool. Git your gun and let 'er roar," Jud said. He peered at the grass. "Yon squats the birds, in that clump. You ruther shoot 'em on the ground er a-flying?"

"Flying, of course," Doctor Ingram answered in indignation, and walked in front of the rigid Fred.

When the quail covey came up with a thundering whir, he fired twice and, in his nervousness, missed.

Fred looked around in surprise when no birds fell, and Jud said, "Gimme that old streak o' rust. I see I got to do the bird-gitting, if there's any of it done."

"I'll do my own shooting," insisted the doctor.

He called his dogs in to hunt closely for the scattered single birds, but Fred had watched them down like a blue-darter, and quickly went to a pine top, caught scent, and again pointed. The other dogs backed dutifully. Doctor Ingram kicked the dead tree, and a hen quail came out like a hand grenade. Before he could shoot, there was a detonation by his ear and the bird dropped stone dead.

"I couldn't help it," Jud apologized. "Knowed you was going to miss, and I just had to let go."

"Wait until I miss, next time," the doctor said, with heat, rubbing his ear.

They hunted on, and after a while the doctor saw, far ahead, his dog standing motionless, and he said with quick pride," I see Lad has stopped."

"Backs sort of pretty, don't he?"

"What do you mean, 'backs'? He has birds!"

"Nope. Yonder stands Fred in that broom sage ahead of your dog. Yourn's just backing mine."

The doctor saw that it was true, and he swallowed hard. And as the afternoon wore on, his amazement grew, for Fred was plainly outhunting his own very good dogs and finding all the birds that were found.

"Where did you get that dog, anyway?" he asked, finally.

"Got him as a puppy from Lem Johnson—swapped him for a pig that got into my back field. Lem says he stole the puppy. But you cain't go by that—Lem'd just soon lie as tell the truth."

At that moment a figure in overalls jumped out from behind a bush and shouted furiously, "What you doing hunting on my land, Jud Lee?"

"Did we chance to wander onto your land, Mr. Sidler?" Jud asked in innocent surprise. "Well, I do declare!"

"I'll learn you!" said the angry landowner, and threw up his shotgun at them.

"Git, mule!" Jud said, and away they rocketed just as Sidler fired. Two of the bird shot struck the doctor's back and he howled.

When they were out of immediate danger, the doctor shouted above the banging wagon, "The dogs!"

"Shuh, old Fred done led them home by now. He knows what a cranky old fool that Sidler is."

When they got back to the house, they found not only Fred and the other two dogs—asleep under the house—but also the young man named Davis from the bank.

"Oh, my!" Jud said. "Durn' if I didn't forget and walk straight up on him."

"Well, Mr. Lee," said Davis. "I hope you've got some money."

Jud turned to the disheveled doctor. "Doc, you owe me five dollars, don't you?"

"I suppose so," he answered bitterly.

"Well, how about loaning me a little extra to go with it, until Saturday? I need fifty-five dollars more. This here's the rent man."

"Loan you fifty-five dollars?" The doctor laughed for the first time.

Davis said firmly, "It's no use, Mr. Lee. Better move out tomorrow or we'll have the sheriff come move you."

Jud said, "Doc, it looks like you *would* let me have the loan of fifty-five dollars."

A sudden thought seemed to come to the doctor. "If you really want sixty dollars, I know how you can get it."

"How?" Jud demanded.

"I'll give you sixty dollars for the dog."

"Fred?" Jud's face fell. "I guess I better hang on to the old fool."

Davis ejaculated, "You'd rather keep this dog than your farm, Jud?"

"I cain't sell my old dog," Jud said. "I just couldn't git shed of him. Anyway, he wouldn't hunt for nobody but me. Fellow stole him oncet and had to let go."

Davis sighed. "Okay. Tomorrow, Mr. Lee."

"Wait a minute," Jud said, suddenly. He ran into the house calling, "Ceely! Ceely! Where's our diamont at?" And presently he came back with a ring mounted with a glistening stone.

"Look here, Doc, I'll sell you our diamont ring."

"Where'd you get that?" Doctor Ingram asked, taking it.

"Ordered it out of a book. You can have it for fifty-five dollars."

Davis examined the ring. "That's nothing but glass with a quicksilver backing."

Come Back Tuesday

"You're plumb crazy. It's a Genuwine Simulated Diamont, just like it said in the magazine."

"I can't use a simulated diamond," the doctor said regretfully.

"Don't forget, Mr. Lee," said Davis, turning away.

"Wait, young man," said Doctor Ingram. "I believe I know how Lee can raise the money. There's a field trial in Laridian that starts Saturday, and there's a first stake of six hundred dollars and a second of about two hundred or so. The dog named Fred could come mighty close to winning one of those stakes, if Jud cared to enter him. I'd be willing to risk the entrance fee on it."

"You mean they'll pay Fred fer out-hunting them other dogs?" Jud asked.

"Is Jud's dog that good?" Davis asked.

"Unless today was an unusual hunt for him, he'll be hard to beat," the doctor said.

"Okay, Jud," Davis said. "I'm going to take this gentleman's word for it, and give you one more week. But this is absolutely your last chance."

THE SUN WAS JUST COMING up when Doctor Ingram and Jud Lee arrived at the starting point, with Fred asleep on the back seat. Several small cornstalk-and-lightwood fires were surrounded by men, while other men saddled the horses. Jud spotted a wagon with planks laid across for seats, and he said, "Yonder's where I aim to sit at. I ain't no horseback rider."

"You'll have to ride horseback while you're running your dog. Better pick out a mount now."

Jud looked over the horses that were for rent, and his eyes lit up when he saw, tied to the fence, a sleepy-looking mule. On its back was an ancient saddle, held together by tobacco twine and haywire.

"Now that yonder is a critter I got as much sense as," Jud said, and went over to speak for the services of the mule. As he approached, the mule opened one eye and let fly with a hind hoof that grazed Jud's thigh. To the animal's astonishment, Jud immediately kicked him back. After that, they seemed to understand each other.

The first brace of dogs was put down and they raced away. Jud and the doctor rode up toward the front of the gallery, and the doctor instructed Jud in field-trial procedure as they went along. Presently one of the dogs pointed, and when the handler dismounted and fired, Jud observed that no birds fell.

"Shuh, that fellow's nigh sorry a shot as you, Doc," he said.

"No birds are killed in a field trial," Doctor Ingram explained.

"Ain't?" Jud asked. "It's goodby farm for me, then."

"What do you mean?"

"You wait and see," Jud said slowly.

It so happened that the dog drawn to run against Fred was the champion of last year, a hard-going orange-and-white pointer named Bold Springs Rap. At the breakaway, Rap raced away in true field-trial style, while Fred went away leisurely. But gradually Fred widened and in a little while was out of sight.

With the other handler, Jud rode up front, his long frame forked over the plodding mule. The other handler, Olivant, periodically called, "Ha-a-ay, Rap," and blew his whistle, until Jud rubbed his ear and complained. "Durned if you don't keep up a racket." Rap found the first covey of birds, and pointed them in a picture-book style, and he was steady to wing and shot.

When the dog had been sent on again, Jud said, "That's a right nice little dog you got. He's shore to take second."

Olivant smiled. His smile faded as he saw Fred, far out to the right, pointing near a plum thicket.

They galloped over to the thicket and Jud dismounted. He whispered to Doctor Ingram, "You shore I ain't allowed to kill a bird?"

"That's right."

Jud shook his head, and walked in and flushed the birds. Jud raised his gun, and Fred lifted his head interestedly to see how many birds fell. When none at all fell, he looked at Jud in amazement, and was visibly stunned as he went on off in search of more game.

Meantime, Rap again had found a covey and his manners were exemplary. Jud said, "You wouldn't want to swap that dog for a Genuwine Simulated Diamond, would you?"

"I guess not."

"He's a right nice little dog," Jud admitted.

Fred seemed to have recovered from his shock, and he found the next covey.

Jud walked in. The birds got up. Jud fired and again no birds fell. Fred gave him a look of profound disgust, and lay down on the spot.

"Git up from there," Jud commanded. "I cain't help it if they won't let me kill none."

Fred reluctantly rose and trotted off, obviously seeing little reason for finding birds if Jud couldn't hit them. The judges looked at one another significantly, for anything less than constant energy and application on the part of a dog is disapproved. At this point, however, Fred luckily struck quail scent, and unenthusiastically pointed a covey that had been feeding in the field.

"Well," Jud muttered to Doctor Ingram as he dismounted, "this'll put a finish to it. The durn' fool has took all the missing he'll put up with."

As Jud walked past the dog, Fred rolled is eye upward, obviously telling him that this was his last chance. Jud kicked the thin grass, and a bird whirred up, then another, and then the rest of the covey, scatteringly—perfect targets. He fired, and all the birds kept going. Fred watched their flight momentarily, then without another glance at Jud he turned toward the gallery, threaded his way through the horses, jumped into the nearest wagon and lay down.

"Is your dog sick, Mr. Lee?" asked one of the judges, puzzled.

"No, he's just plumb disagusted," answered Jud.

He went to the wagon and got Fred by the scruff of the neck and put him on the ground. "You cain't set there and let us be throwed off the farm," Jud said. "Now git, afore I sting you with these here number-eight shot."

Fred saw the shotgun pointing toward him and he reluctantly trotted out front and began hunting again.

The doctor said, "He's ahead on covey finds, but if he keeps being unwilling to hunt he won't have a chance for even a second. Rap looks to be first sure."

"Well, we ain't whupped yet," said Jud mysteriously.

The course made a sharp turn, and for a few minutes neither dog was in sight. Then Rap appeared up front, having swung perfectly.

Jud waited a moment, and then said loudly, "That dog of mine he rambles so far I may have to shoot to make him hear me." He turned the mule out of the gallery and spurred him, and across the cornfield they went, Jud's legs and elbows flapping. Now out of sight of the gallery, he reached the thicket of a branch head, and crossed it, knowing exactly where Fred had gone. And there in the lespedeza he found him, again on game. Fred was lying down, pointing with a complete lack of enthusiasm.

"Now if you ain't a pretty sight," Jud said, tying the mule.

He put two shells in his old double-barreled gun and kicked the grass in front of Fred. At first nothing happened, and Fred watched scornfully. Then the covey erupted from the grass.

Jud's gun came up, and with the first barrel he tumbled a cock. He swung back, saw two birds crossing, pulled the second trigger, and both of them fell.

"Don't never again look at me like I cain't shoot a shot gun," Jud warned, blowing the smoke from the barrels.

Surprised to see any birds fall, Fred upon command sprang in and retrieved them with happy animation.

It was a different Fred that Jud brought back onto the course. When they overtook the gallery, Fred swung on out in front, running full speed. The spectators looked at one another, wondering what could have so invigorated the dog they thought had grown tired.

"Had to shoot to make him hear me," Jud explained to the judges. He pulled a quail from his pocket. "And durn' if a funny thing didn't happen. Unbeknownst to me, this here quail was a-setting in the tree I was under, and when I shot up in the air he fell right out."

"I hope we won't have another miracle like that, Mr. Lee," said Mr. Roe, the owner of the plantation.

"Ain't likely," Jud said. Then: "Judge, look way up yonder on that ridge. They's a dog a-pointing, and he looks like that old fool of mine."

Fred was pointing again, and behind stood Rap, backing him. They rode to the place, and both handlers dismounted. This time, as Jud walked past him, Fred's eyes held keen anticipation, and Jud, noting it, paused. *If sump'm don't fall, that butt-headed scoun'l will think last time was a accident.*

As he hesitated, a sudden thought occurred to him, and he drew one of the dead quail from his pocket. Concealing it, he walked in and flushed the covey. As the birds swept over the sedge tops, he threw the dead bird into the mass of them and fired into the air. Fred noted the falling bird with satisfaction, and retrieved it promptly and then sped on off in businesslike manner.

After that it was, they all agreed, as pretty a dog race as anybody could ask for. "Just gee and haw between 'em, and not a hobble for neither." After the heat was over, eight more dogs ran, but everybody knew Rap had taken first and Fred second.

It was only a few days later that the doctor had occasion to be in Jud's neck of the woods, and he drove up to the house about noon. It was somewhat warm for wintertime. Not seeing Fred under the porch, nor Jud anywhere, he wondered if they had gone hunting. But presently a head appeared at the window.

"Your father gone hunting?"

"Nope, he ain't," Jud's boy answered. "I'll fetch him."

Presently Jud came out on the porch and shouted jovially, "Come on in here, Doc, and lemme show you sump'm!"

"Kind of warm, isn't it?"

"Shore is. But I got just what'll fix you up. Ice water!"

"Ice water? At this time of year?"

Jud led him into the living room of the old house, and promptly pointed to the shining electric refrigerator that stood in the middle of the room.

"Chanced to stop in town after them bird-dog triles, and the feller sold 'er to me. Got the Ree to rig me up the electricity, and she's been a-going at it ever since."

"You mean the REA?" asked the doctor, weakly, opening the box. A light came on, revealing, on the shelves, four shotgun shells and a hat, nothing else.

The children clung to Jud's long legs and gazed at the refrigerator raptly. "Go git the bucket and let's mix up some ice water," Jud said. He pulled out one of the trays and shucked out the ice and threw it out the window. "We'll friz up some fresh," he explained. "That there has been in there since yestiddy. Sit down and rest easy. She'll be done friz it in thutty minutes."

"You bought this with your field-trial winnings?" the doctor asked finally.

"And that ain't all!" Jud said. "Come on!"

He led the doctor into another room, where there was a new bed of pure borax and lying asleep on it was the dog Fred. Jud explained, "If he's such all a moneymaker as that, I aim fer him to have a true bed and a room to hisself. And he don't eat nothing but the best water-ground corn meal and first-run pot liquor!"

Suddenly Jud cocked his head to one side. "Lissen. I hear a car. I'll be back later."

"Who are you running from?"

"That fellow from the bank, who you reckon? That's how come I was hid when you come."

"You mean you didn't pay the bank anything on your rent with that money?" demanded the doctor.

Jud was already out the door. "Tell him"—he called back—"tell him to come back next Tuesday, and I'll have the money shore!"

Mortgage on a Dog

Jud Lee lay hiding underneath the elderberry bush chewing contentedly on a sweet-gum stem when his small son came and said, "Pa! It ain't that little old fool from the bank this time. It's a big old fool with a revolver in his belt, and he's gittin' ready to load our stuff on his truck."

Jud stared incredulously. "If that bank has set the sheriff onto me just because I owe three years of rent," he said ominously, "I just be durn if I ain't goan git mad! They just keep worrying me and worrying me about that old money, and I ain't goan put up with it much longer."

The sheriff spoke to him pleasantly and the deputy nodded as he brought out a chair and put it in the truck.

"Sheriff," Jud said, "let's talk this over. If you put me out of here, my little family won't have nowheres to go at."

"You had the money after your dog won them trials, and you spent it, and the bank says for me to turn you out and that's all there is to it." He spoke to his deputy. "Keep the stuff coming, Alwin."

Jud watched his meager belongings being loaded. They were *really* going to throw him out.

From the interior the deputy called, "Sheriff, he's got a right nice bed in here, but there's a dog laying on it and he keeps growling at me when I try to git him off."

"Bring the bed on out, dog and all."

The deputy folded the mattress with Jud's bird dog, Fred, inside, and came stumbling out with it. He opened it up on the truck, and Fred looked around and then went back to sleep.

"Sheriff," Jud said, suddenly, "I've thought up sump'm. There's a doctor in town, and he's stuck on that durn dog yonder, and I bet I could git him to make a loan on Fred!"

The sheriff motioned to his deputy. "Just wait, Alwin." He said to Jud, "The bank said that I wasn't to listen to nothing you said, unless you happened to mention selling a valuable dog you had. They never spoke of mortgaging no dog, but if they git the money that's all they care about. Come on and we'll go to town. I'll go, and we'll take the dog."

THE RECEPTIONIST IN Doctor Ingram's office told Jud that the doctor was in but busy.

Jud said, "Shuh, he'll drop whatever he's doing when he hears it's about my old dog, Fred." And without waiting, he pushed through the door to the doctor's office before the receptionist could get up to stop him.

The doctor was examining a woman patient when Jud burst in. The woman gave a horrified scream. The startled doctor pushed Jud outside and shut the door.

"You idiot, you shouldn't have come bursting in there like that!" the doctor said angrily.

"Shuh, Doc, don't worry none. Stuff like that don't embarrass me. Let me tell you my proposition."

"If you've got a proposition, tell it to me quickly."

Jud's face saddened. "Well, the sheriff's out at my place a-fixing to turn my little fambly out into the cold."

"That's exactly what he should do. Goodby."

"Wait. You've always had a hankering to buy my dog Fred."

The doctor's interest quickened. "You mean you're actually willing to sell Fred to save your farm?"

"Not exactly. I figured to mortgage him to you until another one them trials, and then I would win the money to pay you back."

The doctor's eyes gleamed briefly. "Jud, the only reason I would consider such a proposition is because it may end in my owning the dog. I warn you about that. Now there's an open trial at Spencer this week end. I'll pay the bank sixty dollars—one year's rent, enough to stall them off for several months—and I'll put up the forty-dollar entry fee at Spencer, and I'll give you thirty dollars for transportation and expenses. Miss Monroe, please go with Mr. Lee to my lawyer's office and have him draw up an airtight lien on his dog Fred for the sum of one hundred and thirty dollars. I'll keep the dog here until you get back. Remember, Jud, next week bring either a hundred and thirty dollars or *my* dog Fred."

With thirty dollars cash money in his pocket and the bird dog Fred at his heels, Jud had started to the bus station to learn the bus schedule when he passed a used-car lot. At once it occurred to him that, if he was going to be traveling here and there following field trials, it would really be better to have his own car to drive. He got into conversation with the salesman, and went from one car to another, and finally, in the absolute back of the lot, they came to a vehicle the salesman was willing to let go for a cash down payment of twenty-five dollars.

The car did run pretty good, for the shape it was in, and Jud drove around town a couple of times, with Fred holding his head out the back window and grinning into the breeze. When he stopped, Clem Frisby, who had come to town to get some new calendars, approached him.

"Well, Jud, you acting mighty biggity, now that you got a car. Passed me right by while ago without a lift of a finger."

"I swear I never seen you, Clem, er I'd a-shore retched out and wove to you. Me and my money-making dog is all set to go win a field trial. Git in and go. We'll be back Monday er so."

"I'd shore like to see old Fred outhunt them city dogs," Clem said, "but right here at the end of the physical year when the stores is giving out new calendars, I ought to stay on the job."

"Git in. You got enough calendars."

Clem hesitated another moment, and finally unloaded his armful of rolled-up calendars on the floor of the back seat and got in. "Okay," he said with an excited grin, "let 'er go."

Spencer was a hundred and fifty miles away, and after a while the novelty of the ride began to wear off, and as night came Clem and Fred went to sleep. The car rocketed through the darkness, its one light blinking occasionally. For an hour the motor ran as smoothly as could be expected, and then suddenly began a rapid, hammering knock that grew in intensity until Clem roused up and Fred cocked his head inquiringly. Jud kept the accelerator pedal on the floor.

Finally Clem shouted, "Don't it sound to you like one them bearings is burnt out a little bit?"

"Yep. Sounds like it."

Clem went back to sleep. The knocking grew still louder. Clem woke up and said, "If that thing's going to keep up such-all a racket as that, let's stop and git it fixed."

The next town was fairly large. They were reluctant to slow down for fear the car wouldn't crank again, so they leaned out and yelled, "Where's a garage at?" but the few passers-by who were able to understand them above the clatter were too astonished to answer in time, so Clem said, "I'll hop out and get the inflammation and catch you coming round the block." Jud circled the block. Clem was waiting but missed him on the first round, and Jud had to circle him again.

Clem directed him to the garage, and as they drove in the whole night shift of mechanics came near and regarded the car interestedly.

"We want to git a bearing fixed, and we're in sort of a hurry," Jud said. "How much will it cost?"

"Can't tell, offhand," said the foreman. "Maybe you've busted a piston too. We'll take a look."

A half-hour later he said. "This repair job will cost you about fifteen dollars."

Jud said, "Fifteen dollars! You must think I'm made of money! Can't you fix up a bearing out of a piece of old shoe leather?"

"Not hardly," he answered. "Might as well git it fixed. You can't run like that—the burnt-out bearing driving the piston will wear your crankshaft down, and then you'll really be into it."

"Tell you what," Jud said. "Just take the durned old piston plumb out."

"You can't do that. There's another piston has to operate in rhythm with it. They'll be out of balance and she'll go to pieces."

"Then take the other piston out, too," Jud instructed.

The garageman argued, but Jud insisted. So they took out two pistons, crammed cardboard into the empty cylinders to keep any stray raw gas from leaking into the crankcase, and the job was done. When time came to crank up all the garage employees retreated to the other end. Clem stood down, too.

The motor started all right, and the four cylinders that had pistons fired fine; but there was a break in the roar when time came for the empty cylinders to fire. This caused the car to shake. Fred in the back, held his seat with difficulty, and his face took on an apprehensive look.

Jud cut the motor, and Fred, having momentary purchase for his feet, sprang through the window and ran to the other end of the garage, where he hid beneath a disabled car.

"You come here, sah!" Jud called. But Fred didn't come until Jud crawled underneath and got him.

Again he cranked up, and someone got in beside him, but the vibration of the car was such that his companion was just a blur.

"That you, Clem?" Jud shouted.

"Yep. That you, Jud?" Clem shouted.

"Yep."

Out on the road again, the tailpipe shook loose from the muffler so that part of the exhaust gas seeped up through the floorboards, and Fred presently sank to the seat in a grateful semicoma.

Jud said, "What's that clicking noise I keep hearing?"

"It's my false teeth hitting together," Clem complained. "I shore hate fer them to git all chipped up."

"Here," Jud said. "Just hold this old croker sack between your teeth."

Clem bit down on the croker sack and it worked fine. The next thing that bothered him was the heat that threatened to scald his feet.

"Suppose she catches afire?" Clem shouted suddenly.

Jud thought a moment, and then his face lit up. "She's insured, so the man says. Just before we git to Spencer, if she'd catch and burn up, it would be right nice. We'd be there, and git our money back too. Now if she catches, you grab your calendars, and I'll grab old Fred, and we'll git out and let 'er burn up."

"Reckon we hadn't ought to have a little fire drill?" Clem suggested. "I'd hate to forgit to save my calendars."

"Ain't a bad idea," Jud said. "After while, now, I'll make out she's afire, and we'll practice up."

"That's it, do it when I ain't expectant."

Presently Jud slammed on the brakes and shouted, "She's afire!" Clem grabbed his calendars, and Jud dragged out the torpid bird dog.

"We got it down, pat," Clem said with satisfaction. "What's the matter with Fred? He looks sorta sick."

"Just sulling," Jud said. "He'll be all right when he sees we're a-going bird-hunting."

Just before dawn, with the croker sack in his mouth straining Clem's snores, the car really did catch fire. Jud slammed on brakes and cried, "Clem, she's afire shore enough!"

Clem stumbled out, still holding the sack between his teeth. Jud, dragging Fred out, didn't see that Clem had opened the hood, and in his half-sleep state was throwing sand on the blazing motor. The fire quickly smothered.

"Well, I'll just be durned," Jud said in disgust. "Look what you went and done. You act to me like you ain't never had nothing insured before!"

With Clem chewing apologetically on the sack, Jud cranked up angrily and they drove on.

THE FIELD TRIAL ASSEMBLY was waiting impatiently when Jud's car drove up, stopped and backfired, causing Judge Rice's horse to rear. The field-trial judge was angry even before that.

"Is that the post entry Dr. Ingram phoned in last night?" he asked Jud, when Fred staggered shakily out.

"Yep," Jud said. "His name is Fred and he's raring to go."

Judge Rice bit off his words. "So are we, Mr. Lee. We've been waiting here ten minutes. You're in the first brace. Next time, be here when you're supposed to."

Jud said to Clem, "He sounds like somebody with a guvment job."

The judges rode out to the front of the gallery, and the secretary of the club announced, "First brace, Wildwood Jack and Fred. Bring your dogs forward."

Wildwood Jack was eager, jumping about and straining in the grasp of his handler. Fred trotted alongside Jud with a fatuous grin on his face. When they were out front, the big judge glanced at his watch. He started to say, "Are you ready, gentlemen?" but then looked at Jud and said, "Are you ready, men?"

Wildwood Jack broke away in quick jumps the instant of release. Fred strolled forward a few steps, then lay down and panted contentedly. The gallery, already impatient to get started, was forced to draw up to prevent running over Fred.

"Your dog," Judge Rice said elaborately, "doesn't quite show the drive we like to see in a class dog."

"Judge," Jud said worriedly, "somebody has tampered with that dog. Fred, you git going, sah!"

Fred wagged his tail briefly, and put his head on his legs.

"That dog ain't at hisself. He don't belong to lay there like that," Jud said, "and he don't belong to wag his tail."

Clem had gone back to the car, intending to follow in it as best he could, in company with the dog wagons and a spectator truck. Finally he got it cranked and underway. Fred, hearing the unmistakable racking noise of the motor, lifted his head in alarm. As the sound drew nearer, Fred got his feet up and started running.

With Fred on his way, Jud steered his horse to the rear of the gallery where Clem followed in the car.

"Something bad ails old Fred. Maybe I should have give him a through of medicine before we come," Jud said. "But it's too late now. Listen to me, Clem. If we can keep him out yonder in front, maybe he'll git back at hisself. He's took it into his head that he don't like our car, so if he tries to quit again, I'll raise up my head and you race the motor to beat all hell, so he can hear it."

Clem accepted this responsibility with pride. "We'll work in co-ornication and keep old Fred a-going," he said.

Wildwood Jack found birds. It was a small covey huddled in a hawthorne thicket, and when they burst out the other side, the dog was steady to wing and shot, and the gallery murmured in approval. Jack was sent away, and he raced along the fringe of the cornfield.

Fred had not been seen since the initial sprint which carried him over the hill and out of sight. On the right side of the course was a creek swamp, on the left beyond the broad and varying avenue of fields, a body of short-leaf pine woods. Jud began to wonder, worriedly, if Fred had taken it into his head to run away.

But presently, after galloping his horse hard, he found him. Fred was asleep in a patch of sunlight in the woods.

"I'm plumb disagusted at you," Jud said angrily. "Git up and go to work. Er do you want to do your hunting from now on with an old fool doctor that smells like sheep-dip?"

Fred made no effort to get going, but lay there looking up at Jud lazily. Presently, however, the gallery drew near. Jud moved his horse out into the clear and held up his hand to Clem. Quickly there came the racing and badly broken rhythm of the old car. Fred lifted his head in sudden alarm, and the next instant he sprang away and headed across the cornfield.

This second sprint cleared Fred's lungs somewhat of the gas, and instead of disappearing into the woods on the other side for another nap, he swung back out in front, far ahead of the gallery and gave the appearance of hunting. In fact, when Wildwood Jack found his third covey, Fred was in the vicinity and seeing his brace-mate on birds, honored the point.

"Well, I'm glad to find out the old fool will back," Jud said. "First time another dog ever found a covey in front of him."

Mrs. Terrill, who owned the hunting preserve the trials were being run on, drew her frothing horse alongside Jud and said, "Is that really so, Mr. Lee?"

"It's the truth, ma'am, and you know the truth will go from here to heaven."

"I do hope your dog is feeling well," she said.

"No'm, he ain't." He leaned slightly toward her and whispered, "I'm thinking he's been messed with."

Her eyes opened wide in horror. "Why, the poor thing! How terrible!"

But Fred was doing better now. He was covering his ground nicely, and Jud figured that if he could get him on birds a couple of times he might have a chance to be called back in the second series, even though Wildwood Jack had him beat on finds. But whereas Fred was now willing to hunt, his nose was badly off, and was proved a few minutes later.

Fred was seen to strike scent near a gallberry clump, then to turn, draw a few steps and point in fine style. Jud shouted, "He's got 'em, Judge, shore'n hell," and they rode to the place.

Jud dismounted, and with his gun in hand walked toward the pointing dog. Just as he got there, however, a sow with eight little pigs, to Fred's astonishment, emerged from the gallery clump and with offended dignity, walked away.

"Did you ever see the beat of that?" Jud demanded in amazement.

"I certainly did not," said Judge Rice coldly.

With ten minutes left to run, Jud became desperate. *I'm shore about to lose my old dog to that doctor.* Then Fred came in from a long swing out to one side, and just as he was about to pass the front of the gallery he wheeled and pointed. Every horse was drawn to a quick stop.

"Your dog is pointing straight toward me," Judge Rice was puzzled.

"You must be standing spang in the middle of the covey," Jud said. "Back up real easy like and maybe they won't flush."

The judge backed his horse, then drew him around to one side. But strangely, Fred slowly turned with the man, still pointing. The judge, perceiving this, moved all the way around the dog, and Fred kept moving with him, pointing.

"Lee," Judge Rice shouted, furiously, "your dog is pointing *me*."

"I'll be durn if he ain't! First a sow, and then you," Jud said. "Judge, you didn't eat quail for breakfast, did you?"

"No, I did not!"

"Judge, you right sure you ain't et no quail today?"

"I have not!" roared the judge. "Make that dog stop pointing me, Lee, and furthermore, don't ever run him in another field I'm judging, you understand?" He rode off.

After another brace had been put down and the gallery moved on, Clem and Jud were sitting on the running board, with Fred tied to keep him from running away from the old car.

"Well, I guess I've lost my old dog sure enough," Jud said, and tears rose in his eyes.

"I ain't never seen him zibit so many idiocentricities," Clem said. "It turned out to be a pretty good deal fer that doctor."

Jud straightened. "Clem, listen here! When I went up to see that lawyer, that doctor made me leave the dog in his office! You know what he done? He give Fred a dost of some kind of pizen, to make him act like that so I couldn't win!"

Clem ejaculated, "I just be durn!"

At this moment portly Mrs. Terrill rode back. "I couldn't go away without telling you how sorry I am that you lost, Mr. Lee," she said. "But I'm sure you must be wrong when you say someone tampered with your dog."

"No, I ain't wrong," Jud shouted, "and I've done figured out the very scoun'l what done it."

THAT AFTERNOON MRS. TERRILL'S big car stopped in front of Doctor Ingram's building, and out got Jud and Clem and the dog Fred, and Mrs. Terrill, and an officer of the S.P.C.A. and a policeman. They went inside.

Doctor Ingram, in a bright herringbone suit, looked at the assembly in amazement.

Jud spoke. "First thing is to give you your old money back. Here she is, a hund'ed and thirty dollars. Now you ain't got no more mortgage on my dog."

"Congratulations!" the doctor said. "Fred must have won!"

"You ain't fooling nobody with that made-up friendship. This fat lady here give me the money and took over the mortgage. Fred never won that field trial and you know how come!"

"What on earth are you talking about?"

The S.P.C.A. officer said gently, "Let us handle this little matter from here, Mr. Lee."

The outraged protests of the doctor got pretty loud, so Jud and Clem slipped out the door for quieter surroundings.

"It just goes to show you," Jud said darkly, "that you cain't tell who to trust in this world. I shore wouldn't a-thought it of that doctor."

"He shore turned out to be a wolf in cheap clothing," Clem said.

They walked on. Finally Jud said, "You know, Clem, I still think that judge had et quail for breakfast."

The Sometimes Dog

The fiscal manager of the Terrill properties looked up from his desk suddenly and said to Claude McLeod: "Now what is this? A past-due note for a hundred and thirty dollars signed by a Jud Lee, it looks like, and the security is 'one pointer dog, Fred.' A dog!"

"Well, Mr. Ryburn, you know how Mrs. Terrill is, softhearted. Jud Lee's a no-count cracker and he was about to lose his bird dog and she took his note. Never expected to get her money back."

"Of course not!" Ryburn exploded. "How does she expect me to put the plantation on a paying basis? Is that dog any good?"

"As good as I ever saw. He's worth twice the face of that note."

Ryburn's eyes sharpened. "Could you use another shooting dog on the plantation?"

"We can always use one like that. But I'd sort of hate to beat old Jud out of his dog."

"A note's a note, isn't it?"

JUD LEE, BEING CHITLIN'-HUNGRY, had spent the morning in search of a hog to kill, if necessary even one of his own. Behind him strolled the pointer Fred, now doubling as a catch dog. Having been instructed by Jud that this was a hog hunt, Fred knew better than to go running off bird-hunting.

But the hunt was unsuccessful unless you counted an armful of collards that Jud had got from Mr. Sidler's patch. "*Know* he wouldn't begrudge me a little old turn of collard greens," Jud thought. "And if he *is mean* enough to, it serves him right they was stole."

When he reached his house he found Claude McLeod and Mr. Ryburn waiting in front of his house in the car. Jud's children sat on the fenders of the car, motionlessly and silently, staring at them.

"Come in and set a spell," Jud invited.

Claude McLeod looked uncomfortable. He nudged Ryburn. "You got to do the talking."

"Lee, we have here your note to Mrs. Terrill for one hundred and thirty dollars, plus interest, with your dog Fred as collateral. Are you prepared to pay this note?"

"I shore as heck ain't prepared," Jud answered in astonishment.

"Then we'll have to take the dog."

"Why that old fat lady never aimed for me to have to pay that note!"

"The note is due, Lee, and I'm in charge of it."

Jud pleaded and threatened but he knew they had him. When they were gone and Fred with them, he squatted in the yard and tears came down his cheeks. The children leaned against the house and cried, and Ceely stood silently in the front door and covered her face with her old apron.

"I'll put a root in their yard," Jud said ominously. "Anyway, it's a satisfaction to know old Fred won't hunt fer them, ner nobody but me...."

A few days later Claude McLeod drove up to the house of the melancholy Lees. Jud rose to a sitting position, saw who it was, and called, "Little sister, fetch me my gun and a couple of them buckshot shells out'n that coffee can."

"Wait, Jud," Claude said. "I came to offer you a job. I was sure sorry about taking old Fred, but Ryburn's the boss, and he said the note had to be settled."

Jud didn't answer. "Little sister, what's a-keeping you?"

"Jud, listen. Fred won't hunt for me. Just mopes around and trots under the wagon. I told Ryburn the only way to get him to hunt was to hire you. He's set on making that deal work out, so he told me to come get you."

"What you aim to do," Jud said wisely, "is have me stay there until old Fred gits used to them Yankee ways, and then you'll git shed of me."

"We'll put it in writing. Set a time."

Jud thought a long time. Finally he said, "When I take a job," Jud said, "I like to settle down to it and stay with it. Make it two months. Er even three. I'll git my Sunday overhalls and my shoes."

But Jud had no intention of staying at Cedar Hill plantation two or three months. The idea was completely repugnant to him except as a possible position from which to get Fred back. Even the sight of the plantation, with its rambling white manor house on the winter-grass-green hill, the rolling acres of pine woods and fields, the wire and concrete kennel pens, the walking horses, and the huge and lazy Duroc swine failed to change his opinion of his job.

Only one thing impressed him—the speedy little gasoline lawn mower which buzzed rapidly across the greensward, piloted by a light-colored Negro in the bucket seat.

Down at the kennels fifty fine-looking dogs ran back and forth in their pens, yelping and barking until Claude shouted them quiet. Jud had never seen so many dogs. Fred lay in the sun, half asleep. He raised his head, manifested his recognition of Jud by yawning, and then dozed again.

"He don't look none too good," Jud said. "He's drindled down a right smart. Where you git your corn meal ground at?"

"We feed meat and prepared dog food," Claude said. "Fred didn't like meat at first but he's getting used to it. Now listen. We start in the morning at nine. You be ready. I want them to see old Fred hunt."

Next morning, Jud looked with astonishment at the hunting caravan. There were two handlers in white coats on clipped horses. Next, drawn by two huge matched bay mules, was a shining wicker brougham in which rode the four hunters—a shipbuilder, a woman artist, Ryburn and Mrs. Terrill—also in white coats. Behind them and drawn by matched chestnut mules was the glossy black-and-red dog wagon.

The Sometimes Dog

Claude McLeod had one of the Negroes bring Fred and another dog from the dog wagon. "Now make him hunt, Jud, or I'll be in bad around here after getting Ryburn to hire you."

The dog Fred looked at Jud to see if this was a hog hunt or a bird hunt, and Jud said, "Well, what you waiting on? Go at it."

Fred went at it. Claude relaxed in his saddle and enjoyed the sparkling and wise hunting. Presently Fred pointed. Claude shot Ryburn a look which said, "You see?"

Jud stood back and watched in curiosity as the shipbuilder and the woman artist finished their conversation and finally got down to shoot. The woman came on Jud's side and looked at him. He looked at her. She said, "Aren't you going to get my gun?"

Jud said, "Where's it at?"

She pointed sternly to the side of the dog wagon. But by now one of the Negroes got the gun from the gun box and came running forward and handed it to Jud. Jud handed it to her.

She said, "Why, you haven't loaded it!"

"If you don't even know how to load a durn' gun," Jud said, "you got no business fooling with it." He turned to his dog. "Fred, watch yourself when this skinny woman draws up to shoot."

Guns at the carry, the two shooters walked past the pointing dog with great stealthiness, as if threading their way through a mine field. Stooping between them went Claude, quirting the grass to flush the birds. The covey came up with a whirr, and the shooting commenced. Both guns boomed until empty and the woods echoed. One quail fell. Jud leaped against a tree in laughter. "Gosh a-*mighty*," he gasped. "It sounded like a war, and one little old bird fell." Ryburn told him to shut up.

The next development did shut Jud up. Instead of instructing Fred to go and retrieve the bird, Claude motioned, and the Negro on the dog wagon released two tiny, moplike cockers, who bobbled forward and raced for the bird.

"Aren't they sweet?" one of the women said.

When one of the cockers picked up the bird, it was more than the astonished Fred could stand. He landed upon the cocker in one rush. Mrs. Terrill screamed.

"Fred!" Jud shouted. "You come here, sah!"

Fred obeyed. He picked up the cocker, bird and all, and came trotting back to them.

"I guess maybe we better not let the spaniels retrieve while Fred's down," Claude suggested uneasily.

Mrs. Terrill mothered the shivering cocker in her arms. "Roy," she said to Ryburn, "you must get rid of that horrible dog immediately."

"Mrs. Terrill, we've got money tied up in that dog. You know I've got to do my job right. Maybe the spaniels should wait until another time to retrieve."

For the next two hours Fred went about redeeming himself, and he found six more coveys, to the other dog's one. Claude confided to Jud, "I feel a lot better now."

Jud said nothing, but he thought, "That's all right—just wait till tomorrow and you won't feel so good," and strolled down to the front terrace to watch the man operate the lawn mower.

THE NEXT MORNING it was Jud who got Fred from the dog wagon, and on the way up front, he said, in a low and stern aside to the dog, "Now you git behind me and stay there."

Fred obeyed. When the dogs were released, the other one shot busily away, but Fred strolled along beside Jud's horse, thinking it was a hog hunt. Claude and Ryburn looked at each other. "Make him get on out and hunt," Claude said.

"What ails you, Fred?" Jud demanded in mock impatience. Fred looked at him in a manner that returned the question.

As time passed, Jud appeared to get desperate. Finally he rode back to the wagon. Ryburn looked at him coldly.

"I might as well tell you the truth," Jud said. "Old Fred's just a sometimes dog. Sometimes he takes it into his head to hunt, and sometimes he don't."

"Well," said Ryburn with finality, "when he hunts, he's good enough to make up for his off days. We'll hunt him when he feels like hunting, and when not, we'll put him back in the wagon."

And for days that is the way matters stood. For the most part Jud kept Fred in, and after a few minutes each day Claude would resignedly order Fred put back into the dog wagon. But Jud sometimes got fed up with the inept and second-rate ways of the other dogs and he would say to Fred, "Well, go at it, then," and Fred would go at it. Every time he let Fred hunt, he reduced the chances of getting him back home, so he resisted the hunting impulse as much as he was able.

HE WAS BEGINNING to despair when an inspiration came one day at the kennels. He noticed that each of the dogs except Fred had a brass tag hanging from its collar. He asked the Negro kennel helper about this.

"Dem's rabies tags. Shows dey been nockerlated gainst goin' mad. Mr. McLeod say old Fred got to be nockerlated next time de vetinerest come out."

Soon after this the hunting party with Fred trotting lazily alongside traversed a course that paralleled a cornfield being hogged off by some of the famous Terrill Durocs. These were tremendous animals, some weighing six hundred pounds.

Jud saw an enormous sow and said loudly: "Whooeee! Look a-yonder what a *hog!*"

At the word *hog*, Fred shot away like a greyhound. He cleared the intervening fence in a soaring leap. The sow turned and looked at the approaching dog stupidly. In another second Fred had attached himself to her ear in a practiced and businesslike manner.

Instead of whirling like a flash and hooking at him with keen tusks, as any knowledgeable razorback would, the sow backed away with terrified squealing. Fred set his feet as a drag and held on.

"What's he *doing?*" Ryburn shouted.

"Stop him!" Mrs. Terrill demanded. "He's killing Suzanne of Ridge Row!"

"I never seen him do *that* before," Jud said.

"Well get him!" Ryburn demanded.

Jud rode to the fence and climbed over. For a few moments there was a flurry of action and then the sow was free, and she lumbered off like an outraged hippopotamus, breaking down cornstalks and grunting aggrievedly. In the melee Jud sustained a small cut on one hand, and a drop of blood fell from his finger tip. He put the happy Fred over the fence and rode back.

"What on earth was your dog trying to do?" Ryburn demanded, white-faced.

"I never in God's world seen such a thing," Jud answered solemnly.

"Does he do that often?"

"Never seen him do it before," Jud said. He visibly shuddered. "The day before you come got him, I recollect there was a little old feist dog come trotting by my place, acting sort of oddly, and old Fred was asleep, and this little old feist just reached out and took a bite at him as he went by—didn't even hardly more than wake him. I recollect I said to my old woman, "Ceely, you reckon that was a mad dog just bit old Fred? He was shore acting sort of oddy!" And she said, "Might a-been, and might not," and I let it go at that. But well—I reckon we know the straight of it now."

"What do you mean?" Ryburn asked.

"Folks, I hate to say it," Jud said slowly, "but our old Fred has done gone mad."

There was a stunned silence. They looked at Fred, who lay beside a tree with closed eyes, quietly panting.

"My heavens!" Mrs. Terrill whispered finally.

Claude McLeod said, nervously, "I don't hardly believe he's mad. I've seen dogs catch hogs before. I was going to inoculate him tomorrow."

"But he *hasn't* been inoculated," said Mrs. Terrill, "and he was bitten by a suspected dog."

There was another silence. Jud said, funereally, "There ain't but one thing left to do."

"What?"

Jud bowed his head. "I'll have to take old Fred down in the swamp and send him to meet his Maker."

Mrs. Terrill gasped. "Horrible! Can't we have the veterinarian chloroform him?"

"Well," Jud said sadly, "me and old Fred has been partners fer a good long spell, now. I sort of feel like he wouldn't want no stranger giving him no chloroform. With your permission I'll just take him on off now and git it over with. When you hear me shoot you'll know it's all over fer old Fred. Guess I won't come back—I'll ruther not have nobody around me but the good Lord."

"Oh, it seems so barbaric, but I suppose it's the best thing to do," said Mrs. Terrill.

Jud motioned to Fred, "Come on, old friend," he said sorrowfully, ""let's git it over with."

"Wait just a minute," said Ryburn. "There's no sense in shooting a perfectly good dog until we're sure he's rabid. After all, we've got a hundred and thirty dollars in Fred, not counting what we've paid Lee. We'll put the dog in solitary confinement for a few days and see what happens."

Jud swore under his breath. "I'm shore glad you thought of that," he said between his teeth. "I'm convinced in my mind that the poor feller's done fer, but I'm shore willing to put off the final day." He rode back to the carriage, slung a few drops of blood from his hand, and said, "Any you ladies got a piece of old rag with you? Old Fred made a mistake and bit me when I was a-pulling him offn that hog."

"Bit *you*?" exclaimed Mrs. Terrill.

Brag Dog and Other Stories

"Oh, tain't nothing much," Jud said.

"I know, but...but..." Mrs. Terrill said, "You must see a doctor at once!"

"Why, tain't nothing but a little old place. But I'll go if you say go."

NEXT DAY MRS. TERRILL made it a point to see Jud. Ryburn went with her. "Did you go to the doctor?" she asked.

"Yes'm. He said I hadn't ought to bother him with no such little scratch as that, and put some brown stuff on it, and charged me three dollars."

"But did you tell him it was a rabid dog that did it?"

Jud's face turned an angry red. "Lady, old Fred's got a heap of devilment in him, but I'll thank you not to call him no rabbit dog!"

"She means a mad dog, Lee," Ryburn said impatiently.

"I never mentioned nothing about that to the doctor, but he should a-known my own dog wouldn't a-bit me in his right mind."

"Oh, dear!" breathed Mrs. Terrill.

"I hardly think it's anything to worry about," Ryburn assured. "I stopped by Fred's confinement pen this morning and he seemed all right to me. Sleeping just as ever."

"You didn't notice no little froth around his mouth?" Jud asked, having gone to Fred's pen with shaving cream before daylight.

"Well," Ryburn said hesitantly, "yes and no. But there's nothing wrong with that dog. Just wait and see."

Next morning breakfast in the manor house was interrupted by the excited appearance of Lobie, one of the kennel Negroes.

"Mr. Ryburn!" he said.

They all stopped in surprise. "You know better than to come bursting in here," Ryburn said sternly.

"Yes, sir, but it's that mad dog Fred. Sometime last night he done chewed dat wire and got out—chewed through it good as you could cut it wid an ax—and headed for de hog field, and nearly run dem hogs crazy. We heard one squealing fit to kill about daylight, and went down there and Fred had him by de ear."

"Did you get him away?"

"Not none of us, no sir. Ain't goan touch no mad dog. We got dat Lee man and he went out and fotched him in."

"You and your hundred and thirty dollars!" Mrs. Terrill said angrily to Ryburn. "I hope you're satisfied. Penny wise and pound foolish! You never should have tried to take Mr. Lee's dog in the first place."

Ryburn said, hastily, "Lobie, tell Lee to come to my office in twenty minutes."

"He went back to bed, suh," Lobie said uneasily. "Said he was feeling bad. Said his bones and his jaws ached, and the thought of water made him choke. It sort of scared us, the way he acted."

There was a disturbed silence.

Somebody said, "We'd better call a doctor."

"Yes, and at once!"

The Sometimes Dog

At that moment the sounds of men's shouts and women's screaming reached them, and out of the spacious window that overlooked the lawn they saw people running in all directions, scattering like a covey of quail. One of them passed the Negro on the motor lawn mower and yelled something and kept going. A little boy tried to climb a tree.

Then appeared the cause of it all. Jud Lee, bareheaded, came toward the big house in a slow trot. His eyes were vacant, his jaw slack and wet, and his hair hung down on his forehead.

"Yon he come, and he done goan mad!" Lobie exclaimed in terror and fled.

"My heavens, what'll I do?"

"Perhaps somebody should go out and try to get him under control," Ryburn said nervously.

Outside, the Negro had thrown the lawn mower into neutral and, transfixed with horror, sat there watching the approach of Jud. Blue vapor puffed from the idling engine. When Jud was ten yards away, the Negro leaped and ran.

Jud's leaden trot brought him straight on to the terrace of the big house. On up the steps he came.

"Mercy, he's coming in here!"

They sat there, paralyzed. They heard the opening of the front door, then the fleeing footsteps of the butler. The curtains parted and in came Jud Lee, panting laboriously. The women screamed. Although Jud's vacant eyes had no look of recognition in them, his heavy-footed trot took him straight toward Ryburn.

"Wait, Lee!" Ryburn said, backing up. "Listen, old fellow—"

Jud appeared not to hear. A froth ran down his chin. His eyes were glazed, and he breathed hard. Ryburn turned and fled, and Jud followed, his trot quickening.

Through the Blue Room and the Mirror Room and the library and the Master's Den they went. A rug slipped with Ryburn and he went down, only to scramble up and run again. Every now and then he gasped out an agonizing remonstration, but Jud gave no sign of hearing.

Now they came to the hall, and for a space here it was a straightaway course. Jud's long strides lengthened even more. Suddenly he made a leap that covered the intervening distance and he landed on the other's back, and they went down. Ryburn screamed.

For a moment they rolled, then Jud's teeth sank into Ryburn's back. Ryburn fainted.

Some minutes later Ryburn regained consciousness and found the others gathered around him.

"Where did he go?" he whispered.

They looked out the front window. Down at the far end of the lawn they saw Jud. This time he was not afoot—he was riding in the motor lawn mower and going toward the highway. And behind him in a steady lope followed the dog Fred.

"He's escaping in the lawn mower," Ryburn said in amazement. "He's stealing it. He can't be mad if he's doing that! Phone the sheriff!"

"Let him go," Mrs. Terrill sighed. "Let him go."

Ryburn thought a moment, then said slowly, "Yes, let him go."

The man and the dog and the conveyance disappeared down the road.

The Hunting Fool

The horses' breaths fogged as Billy Brooks brushed their furry coats before saddling them. Jim could faintly remember when the problem of the Hart Kennels was to put a stop to Brooks' efficient market hunting on Hart leases. But Brooks was too smart. Jim's father would come in at night in one of his dread blue-faced silences. After his toddy and supper, he would turn the pages of *The Field* with heavy deliberation, and finally announce that the nigger Brooks had been shooting his birds again, and when he caught him there would be hell to pay. But they never caught him, and finally, in desperation, Jim's father hired Brooks, and that put a stop to it. Furthermore, he turned out to be the best Negro dog trainer they ever had.

The dogs saw the horses, and danced about the frosty kennel yards, yelping.

"*You* Red, *you* Joe, *you* Mac," Jim shouted. The dogs' barking subsided to eager whining.

"Who you hunting?" Jim asked.

"Old Snow, I guess," Brooks said, "and one the puppies." Snow—or as he was known on field trial programs, Diamond Robert's Rebel—was the kennel's brag dog, owned by young Drury Bowden.

"Why not Brains?" Jim suggested.

"If'n your Papa says Brains," Brooks said, with resignation, "hit's all right with me." This was another Bowden dog, liked by nobody but Jim.

Jim's father came out with his quirt hanging from his wrist. "Snow and Mike," he told Brooks; and turned to where Jim was saddling his own horse. "You off to school a-ready?"

"Yes, sir."

"It's right curious to me that I ain't heard you bellyaching none this year about going to school."

"I guess I've come to realize it," Jim said.

"I'm proud you finally did."

Jim gave the mare a nudge with his heels, and put his hands in his pocket, and let her take him to school in the swinging lope that could keep the dogs in sight all day, whether in the rolling red hills of Alabama or the flat chicken prairies of Saskatchewan.

The school house floors were clean-swept, chemical smelling. Two boys and a girl, country students like himself, were already in the classroom, standing around the hissing radiator. The girl had brought three yellow roses, and put them in a soda-fountain glass on Miss Hilton's desk.

He looked at his dollar watch. Twenty minutes to eight. She ought to be there before long. He started straightening out the mess in his desk, but gave it up presently.

Adele Hilton stood in the door a moment, talking to someone. Then she went to her desk. Jim's head felt light, the way it did when they were sewing up his hand after that dog from Huntsville got through with it.

She inspected the flowers. "They're nice. Who brought them?"

"Jim Hart," said Andy Barton, the pole vaulter.

That got a fine laugh. A girl between Jim and Andy inadvertently read Jim's lips and gasped in quite genuine horror.

"You didn't bring them, did you, Jim?" Miss Hilton asked.

"No'm," he said resentfully.

She gave him a funny little smile that he couldn't quite make out, and called the roll. He never missed a chance like that to look at her, to watch her mouth. Her hair was a sort of halfway blond—sandy, he guessed you called it—and she was small, with good legs and a smooth, graceful way of walking.

Everything worked out fine that day. When Study Hall came, he was the only student that had to stay in. There'd be just him and Miss Hilton. This was a wonderful break, and he was not embarrassed. After a few minutes, she laid down her grade book and came and sat on the desk in front of him, and put her feet in the seat. Her nearness was stupefying.

"Jim," she asked, "how is that you always have to stay in when I'm to keep Study Hall?"

"Mr. Logan caught me smoking in the basement, at recess."

"Did you make it a point to let him see you slipping down to the basement?"

"I guess he saw me going down, all right," Jim said.

"The only time you let them catch you doing anything is when you know it's my week to keep Study Hall."

"Seemed like I just had to have a smoke," he said.

She was silent for a moment. "Jim," she said, "how old are you?"

"Going on eighteen."

"I'm seven years older than you are."

"I guess you are."

"That's a big difference, seven years."

"Yes'm."

She stood up. "You'd better study some now."

NEXT DAY Miss Hilton went to the door, and said to Jim, "Somebody to see you, James."

Jim went out into the hall. Drury Bowden waited for him. "The Mantonville trials start the week before Christmas. The doctor says your father better not go. I came by to tell you you're to handle for me."

The Hunting Fool

You could see that he considered Jim a poor second choice. But that's the way Drury Bowden was, skeptical and sort of hard-boiled. Not a half bad fellow, though, in spite of it; and by far the Hart's best customer. He was one of the few local men who could afford a string of fine field-trial dogs. Dog training being the slow, painstaking work it is, Jim always found fascination in visiting the Bowden plant, with peanuts rattling in the blower tubes and the pecan bleachers grinding away and farmers unloading their cotton, and Drury walking about with his hat on the back of his head, and the teletype clicking busily with market reports, and one of the office girls saying, "We have Mr. Little in New York, now, Mr. Bowden; on the second phone," and Drury looking puzzled and asking, "Now what the hell did I want with Little? Oh, yes; tell 'em I'll talk in twenty minutes."

Now Drury asked, "Will your school be out in time for Mantonville?"

"Yes, sir. I'll be ready. I'll be glad to go."

"Okay. We'll take Snow and Mike and a couple of derbies maybe," he said. "Got to cull out my dogs before long."

Drury looked through the square glass into the classroom. "Who's that girl that came to the door?"

"Miss Hilton."

"She's a damned knockout," he said, reflectively.

They did fine at Mantonville, Snow winning the all-age without a run-off. Drury seemed to think the dogs succeeded in spite if Jim's handling, but, Jim thought, that's the way Drury was. When they got back, Christmas lights and Christmas crowds were everywhere, and Jim had fifty dollars in his pocket to spend on Adele Hilton's Christmas present. He bought her a watch, a beautiful little trick not big as a dime. He enclosed a card which boldly said, *"With love from J. Hart."*

Two days later he got a small package, insured, from her. The tissue-covered leather inner box contained a mans' white-gold wrist watch with a white pigskin strap. With excited fingers he drew out the card and read, *"Jim: The watch was sweet as could be, but I already have one, so I exchanged it for this, which is a Christmas present to you from yourself and from me. Miss Hilton."*

For a long time Jim stared at the watch, turning it slowly over and over and listening to its subdued ticking. Then he fastened it onto his wrist. "Dog take her sorry time," he muttered unhappily.

DAYLIGHT HAD NOT COME when Jim was partly awakened by a weird sort of squawking. He went back to sleep, and again some time later he heard the noise. Finally he dressed with sleep-fumbly fingers and went outside. There was Brains, having dug out and found a crippled outraged blue jay, which she for an hour had been casually carrying in her mouth while she trotted around on a tour of exploration. Jim would have felt better if she had escaped to go off on an early morning self-hunt. For Brains, in spite of her Proctor breeding and magnificent good looks, apparently had neither sense nor hunting instinct.

Jim had been taught to despise any bird dog that wasn't a good bird dog, but Brain's very foolishness endeared her to him. She was always carrying things around in her mouth. Maybe a pine cone, or a bottle, or a frog. She didn't carry it with her head and tail high, puppylike, with the air of having found something exciting, such as a possum carcass; she just absent-mindedly toted it around. Her food pan was with her constantly. When she got ready to sleep for an hour, she put the pan down. On waking, she'd pick it up again and walk casually to where she wanted to go.

Jim freed the jay bird and shut Brains up in a concrete-floored kennel pen. He looked at his watch to see how long before the first bell. School had become a form of torment since Adele Hilton and Drury Bowden got married. Of course she wouldn't teach any more after this year, but then if nothing happened, he would be graduating this year himself.

When the wedding trip was over, she had asked Jim to wait after school a moment, and said, "I wanted your good wishes, Jim."

He hadn't recovered from the sick shock of it even then, a week afterward, but he said, "I wish you good luck, ma'am. Don't expect I need to tell you what a fine kind of man you picked out."

She smiled slightly, and for a moment her mind was elsewhere. "He's awfully bullheaded, but I love him." She turned toward the door, "I do hope your father is going to be better."

"I sure hope so, too, thank you, ma'am." Outside, in the street, a flash of chromium indicated that Drury had left his pecans and cotton to come for her. But Jim said, "One more thing I want to thank you for, and that's for not ever laughing at me. To my face, anyway."

"I never laughed at you even to myself, Jim," she told him.

JIM QUIT SCHOOL FOR GOOD in March, when his father kept getting worse. Jim had just come in from working Snow when old Doctor Thursban blinked his glass eye at him and said, "You better spend what time you can with him from now on."

Jim's father was still in his right mind, and somewhat fascinated by the adventure of death. "I guess it's a heap more inviting to a man whose wife has done been gone on eight years," he mused. "You reckon she'll be there for me to recognize?"

"It won't be much of a place if she ain't," Jim said.

"I'll be glad to git several things straightened out in my mind about it," he went on. "They say that dogs is dead when they die, but human folks ain't. I don't see how come that should be so, when dogs is blood and bones and brains just like folks, and the life they got in them is just like the life we got in us." He smiled suddenly. "By God, I'd sure like to see old Buster again. You don't remember him. He was a drop, half pointer and half setter, and he was a sight to look at, with his short little old ears and a tail that bowed down'rds like it was broke in the middle. But when it come to finding birds he was a real man. Not as big-going as old Blue Davy, I don't guess, nor as bullheaded; Davy was six years old before we got him broke; he run like a fitified mustang till you took him up. Another dog I want to see is the little setter derby that died. I always put her down as one of the best prospects we ever had. She'd a-been another Snow, if she hadn't a-taken sick."

"You better rest some now, don't you reckon?" Jim asked.

"I imagine I got a sufficientcy of resting time ahead of me."

The Hunting Fool

ABOUT TWO MONTHS after Jim's father died, Drury Bowden and Adele came out to see the Bowden string from one end to the other. Some of the younger dogs Drury had never seen work at all. He made notes on their performances.

"Don't want any time wasted on plug dogs," he said.

"How can you tell the plugs from the winners, darling, in thirty minutes work?" Adele asked, with what seemed to Jim to be unnecessary pointedness.

"The good ones go."

"How simple," she murmured.

Jim noticed that her infrequent smiles had a queer tightness. Once when Drury and the Negro Brooks rode over a rise to follow the work of a puppy, Adele said, "I'm sorry you felt you had to give up school."

"You can't run a kennel at no desk," he said shortly, preferring not to talk to her.

"I hope you have luck," she said hesitantly. "Could you make a go of your kennel without Drury's dogs?"

"No'm. We got other dogs, but if Mr. Bowden moved his to another kennel, then folks would think something was wrong with me, and take their dogs away too. To tell the truth, it would just about ruin us."

She was pretty mad. "I told him that."

"You mean he's going to do it?"

She nodded. "Jim, sometimes I could kill him."

"I don't guess he wants to risk a young man like me with five or ten thousand dollars worth of bird dogs," Jim said slowly. "And maybe, from his side of it, he's right."

"Oh, of course he's right. He always is. It makes him almost unbearable."

Brooks had ridden out to get the two dogs in. Drury Bowden came back, his big red horse throwing lather.

"All right, let's have a look at Snow," Brown said. "And I see there's one other dog in there."

"That's Brains," Jim said.

"Brains?"

"Like you call a bald man Curly. She's a derby. We haven't done much on her."

"Put her down, anyway." Bowden was taking Snow out of the dog wagon himself. Snow as a small-boned dog, almost pure Llewellin, white except for three blackish spots on his left ear and some random ticking, with a busy tail, a laughing mouth, and enough hunting instinct for a dog twice as big. Drury lifted him down casually, without any petting or sweet talk. But somehow you knew that if anything had ever got an anchor on Drury Bowden's fibrous heart, this hustling little white dog had done it.

Snow leveled out straight toward a distant beggarweed patch, where one of his pet coveys stayed. His smooth stride was merry and unbelievably fast; he seemed a little white wraith flashing toward the horizon. Brains bounced around happily, barking at the horses.

"What kind of bird dog is that?" Drury demanded.

"She ain't quite caught on to it yet," Jim apologized.

Adele smiled. "I think she's a darling."

After a few minutes Brains wandered off into the woods, stopping occasionally to sniff a bush or to bite a flea on her back.

Drury said, "I hope you never told anybody that was my dog."

Before he had finished saying it, Brains pointed. She stood in good style, quite positive. Drury dismounted. But no birds got up in front of Brains. She moved forward, tail going, and pounced on something in the wiregrass. Then she swung away with the box turtle she had found. For a half hour she trotted aimlessly through the woods casually carrying the turtle. Jim was miserable.

Then, crossing a little woods road, Brains came upon another box turtle. In plain sight of everybody, she put the first turtle down, picked the second one up, and wandered on.

"I wish you'd look," Adele said, entranced.

"If you think she's through changing turtles," Drury acidly said to Jim, "you can take her up."

"Yonder's Snow, on point," Jim said, as they rounded a head.

Brains saw him too, and dropping her turtle, she ran toward him in great happy leaps.

"She's going to pop 'em," Drury shouted.

Instead, Brains launched herself straight at the immobile Snow, knocking him right into the middle of the covey, and as the quail whirred upon all sides, she squatted in the grass, wagging her tail at the stunned setter in an invitation to play.

"I want that dog disposed of," Drury said.

"You mean you're going to have her killed?" Adele demanded.

"Well, I don't care what he does with her. But I won't have an empty-headed fool like that."

"I'll bet Jim could make a good dog of her," Adele said, looking straight at him.

"It'd take a better man than Jim to do that."

"Drury!"

Jim's jaw muscles tightened angrily. But all he said was, "Brains ain't much."

A MONTH AFTER THE Bowden string was moved, the Hart Kennels had less than a half dozen dogs, most of them local shooting dogs being finished up. There was not one field-trial prospect in the yard.

"Don't see how us goan to git to the prairies this summer," Brooks said, warming his hands by the lightwood fire in the kennel house. Outside a mournful drizzle of ice-water rain had turned the earth into a mudball. Now it was stopping. "This'll be the fust year in the longest they ain't been some Hart-handled dogs on the Welbyton trials."

Jim was pulling on his old raincoat. He could see his father now, at Welbyton, standing in his stirrups with his cheeks red from blowing the whistle, his plaided mackinaw turned up about his head. Then his effortless hog-calling voice echoing across the rolling country, *"Ha-ay-oo, Jake!...hay-ay-oo, Jake!..."*

"Get on your boots and saddle up Kate, and then turn Brains out," Jim said.

The Hunting Fool

"That dog ain't wuth what-all you doin'," Brooks said. Jim slipped on his gloves, wondering grimly if Brooks was right. The night before he had traced Brains' ancestry and in *The American Field Stud Book* found a dog named Ready Dan, a pointer who had been a winner in the days when the setters had things mostly their way. Then in his father's old files of *The Field*, Jim at last found something about Ready Dan's character. Holding the almost shredded page together, he read: *"was disgusted with the pup's behavior, in fact I would have given the canine to anybody who asked. We have heard much of the pointer's vaunted precocity, as opposed to the setter, but Ready Dan was anything but precocious. He was two years old before he gave the first signs of being a bird dog. Would not even hunt. The only early development was his retrieving ability, which was uncanny. I would say that his..."* The rest of the page had deteriorated into illegibility.

Day after day throughout the winter Jim hunted Brains. She had not improved. She still trotted apparently aimlessly through the wood, often with a stick or a tin can in her mouth, sniffing idly at gopher holes, barking playfully at Jim, and fooling around in general—to a trainer absolutely the most hopeless and annoying sort of bird-dog behavior. On this miserable day, she jumped three rabbits. She watched the scampering flight of the first lethargically. The second, a few moments later, aroused her a bit. When the third flushed, she lunged forward after it with a determined yelp.

"S' git 'im gal!" Jim shouted, and the race was on. When she returned after while, panting heavily, he said, "Now you see there's fine sport to be had in these here woods."

Occasionally Brains would come upon birds, entirely by accident, and she would point. Her points were in beautiful style, and this was fortunate, because style is one of the many things that can't be trained into a bird dog. Jim was a deadly shot—a .410 was all the gun he needed—and she retrieved his birds perfectly, even with some animation. Then one day a crippled cock quail fluttered along just over the gallberry tops. Brains' ears lifted, and she gave chase. When she captured the bird and returned with it, there was a new look in her eye.

Rabbit chasing was still her favorite sport, though. She no longer trotted aimlessly—she scoured the woods with a merry, ground-eating pace. Every day she seemed to get a little faster. But she never got fast enough to outrun the rabbits she chased, and gradually her instincts led her to concentrating more and more on quail.

"You got a name for not having no sense," Jim observed, "but I notice it never took you long to find out you couldn't outrun them rabbits."

Because he was trying to develop her hunting instinct, Jim never disciplined Brains afield. She hunted as she pleased, and pointed what she liked, and if she flushed and chased a covey of birds out of sight, that was all right too. Only one thing was not tolerated—piddling. When she slowed up to sniff at something, and put her nose to the ground, Jim sent her on with sharp, impatient whistle blasts.

When the coveys began to break up and the bob-white mating call began to ring through the woods, dog training in the south was about over until fall. Billy Brooks went with Jim to give Brains one of the final workouts, and when they came in, he said," That ain't even the same dog, Mr. Jim. She's turnt into a true hunter and no mistake. I never thought she'd be no fast dog like *that*." Brooks stared at the dog with a puzzled frown. "They's something else, too. I can't quite study it out."

"Her personality's changed, looks to me like," Jim said.

"It sho' God has, now. She used to act like a absent-minded dog, without no sense. But she's smartened up. And just happy as a jay bird in a wild-cherry tree."

"I wouldn't take nothing for her," Jim said.

"The trouble about it," was Brooks' slow answer, "is that what's a drivin' you is wantin' to show somebody up, so people will laugh at him."

Jim's mouth tightened, and he said nothing.

"That ain't no proper use for no bird dog," Brooks said.

"What I want out of you," Jim said grimly, "is more work and less advice."

"Yes, suh, that's right," Brooks replied. He started to go out, but Jim stopped him.

"I got something to tell you," Jim said. "We're going to Canada."

Brooks eyes widened. "We *is*?"

"Me and Brains. I'm closing up the kennel. What money Papa left me I'm going to use to pay up the leases and taxes through next year. I'm even selling the horses."

"How you and that dog going to Canada?"

"First one way and then another. Ride when we can and walk when we can't."

"Mr. Jim, you layin' everything you got on that dog."

"I ain't got much to lay."

The Negro hesitated a moment in unhappy silence. "If'n I'd promise to keep my big mouth shut, you reckon you'd let me go along with you all?"

"I ain't going to have money to buy but one horse in Canada, and there ain't but one dog to work. You better be looking for another job."

"I reckon I'll sort o' hang around the place tillst you all git back."

"Can't yo' understand nothing, Brooks, for crying out loud? I ain't got no money. I can't pay you no longer."

"They's a right smart of down wood in the bottoms on the place. I could cut that into cordwood and make out all right."

"That's all right with me," Jim said, "if you ain't got no better sense."

"Yes, suh," Brooks said.

Jim went to the house with a bitter tightness in his throat. *Now he's gone and done something else. He's put the best dog nigger in the world to chopping cordwood.*

AFTER THEY HAD TAKEN a month hitchhiking to the Canadian prairies the first thing Jim did was to buy a horse with the forty dollars he had missed a good many meals to save. Then they started hunting. Jim hunted Brains upwind, whenever he could, so she'd hunt with head high and not let foot scent distract her. Sometimes he would see her on point a half mile away, and would sit motionless on his horse for fifteen or twenty minutes, so she'd learn to wait with her birds.

Brains pointed the first prairie chickens she came upon, but her tail moved nervously in a manner that told Jim she wasn't certain about her game at all, and when he flushed Brains was too startled at the size of the birds to even chase. The handlers rarely shoot chickens in Canada, but Jim made an exception in order to show Brains the

The Hunting Fool

nature of her quarry. After that, Brains pointed with great positiveness. Her points were staunch, but on the flush she went in with a lightning-like rush that was just too bad for any slow chicken. Jim said not a word at this kind of misbehavior, because it built boldness and fire into the dog. There'd be a time later for smoothing her up.

The days were fine, because Brains was nice company. At noon they'd stop in a bluff grove and have lunch. Jim would doze, while the indefatigable Brains trotted around with the empty sandwich paper in her mouth or annoyed the horse. At night, sometimes Jim would visit with the other dog men around there. But mostly he just sat in his cheap boarding-house room, staring at the night outside, thinking about other times in Canada, when they had all the dogs they could work, and a good house, and some of the dog men dropped in every night for a game of rummy. He thought about the kennels at home, empty, and the house boarded up, and the best dog nigger in the world splitting cordwood in the hot sun and selling it for three dollars and a half a cord.

And too, he thought a great deal about Adele Bowden. He remembered her small, not-quite-straight bottom teeth, her always neat sandy hair, her anger when some of the boys baited her. Jim guessed she wished she was teaching school again, now, instead of married, and he hated Drury Bowden for that, too.

One week before the first chicken trails, Brains got a taste of the force collar. When she pointed, Jim tied her trailing check cord around his waist, flushed the birds, and fired. Brains leaped after the bird.

"Whoa, Brains!" Jim shouted.

She paid no attention to him. The next instant she had hit the end of the cord, and the force collar grabbed her. She was abruptly thrown over, and the spikes bit at her neck. The dumbest dog in the world would have know that he had been treated that way because he didn't stop. Before many days, Brains was standing shot. But she still had a lot to learn about hunting.

Jim found that out when he entered her in the derby stake of the chicken trials at Rodenella. She went big, like a trial dog should, and she handled pretty well, but she didn't show on game enough to win anything. This was a disappointment to Jim, because he had hoped she'd take a third and maybe they'd have a little money to get home on.

But they got home eventually, broke and lean. Brooks was there, and four dogs romped in the kennel yard.

"A Mr. Wright lef' these dogs to be finished up. Said he knowed your papa. I told him you'd be back some time another, and he told me to go ahead to work on 'em tillst you got here."

"How you been hunting them?"

"On afoot. Here's the eighty dollars he give me for they first month."

That made Jim feel mighty good, to be with old Brooks again, and have dogs barking in the kennels, and eighty dollars in cash money.

"Any birds much?" he asked.

"I never seed the like of birds, Mr. Jim. They sho' is here, and that's the good Lawd's truth."

They were, too. And every day, Brains' gay stride found them, covey after covey.

"I think she's ready for Welbyton," Jim said finally.

"She sho' is ready for Welbyton, but I was hopin' you'd had a change of mind about all that, Mr. Jim. Let's skip old Welbyton, and go on them Georgia trials."

Jim's face darkened: "I ain't toughed it out this way only to change my mind. He's going to see what kind of a dog man I am, and what kind of fool dog this is he got shut of."

THEY WERE BOTH THERE, as he had known they would be. He saw them the night before the puppy stake, when he took Brains to the place where the dogs were kept. This was a vacant old store in which wooden pens had been built. Formerly a feed store, the place harbored an odor of meal and rats, mixed now with the smell of dogs and clean straw. At the far end was a lonesome puppy with his nose in a crack, whimpering. But most of the dogs were veteran campaigners, and stayed quiet.

"Hello, Jim," they said cordially, and shook his hand.

"I hear you've been in Canada," Adele said. "We missed you."

"You running any dogs?" Drury asked.

"I got a piece of one," Jim said, and turned away.

"Wait," Drury called, "How've you been getting along?"

"Just fine," Jim said sharply, and went on.

Drury shrugged, but presently Adele came down to Brains' pen.

"Jim, what's the matter with you?" she asked.

"Excuse me for acting that way," he answered

"I don't guess I blame you," she said slowly, glancing toward the front of the store where Drury was talking to some handlers. "I don't think I'll ever forgive him for what he did to you. Just when he and I begin to get along fine, I remember it."

Watching her face, Jim had a curious feeling. It was funny, but this was the first time it'd seemed that she was a woman and he just a boy. Not that it made any difference. His heart was running crazy, like it always did when she was around.

"That's a lovely dog you have," she said, absently.

"Yes'm," he said, startled to realize that neither she nor Drury would recognize Brains. "She's a derby. If she does pretty good I might run her in the all-age too."

She smiled. "In that case you might run against Drury and Snow. He's handling in the all-age. That would be something, wouldn't it?"

"Yes'm," he said grimly, "It sure would."

TWO DAYS LATER, in the derby, Brains got hot, and for the first time Jim's confidence in her was complete. She won first place among the two-year-olds.

"You're just a little old express train of a bird dog," Jim told her that night, as she bit imaginary fleas on his leg. "But tomorrow you got to hunt against the dad-blamdest setter you ever saw. And he handles like a circus dog, too—" he paused thoughtfully —"and that's because a mighty good man trained him." But Brains bounced away playfully into her pen, and peeped out at him, refusing to take Snow seriously. It was all just a game to her.

The Hunting Fool

In the last heat the following afternoon, braced with an erratic liver pointer, Brains again hunted well. Earlier, Drury Bowden's fancy-going setter had set the pace with five covey finds and perfect performance. That evening, the judges decided to let Brains and Snow run it off the following morning.

Drury Bowden said to Jim, "Bud, you've been mighty lucky with that two-year-old."

"It don't look like lucky to me," Jim said angrily.

"Where'd you get that dog, anyway?"

"A fellow give her to me. A fellow that don't know as much about bird dogs as he makes out," Jim said. "Not that it's a great deal of your business."

Drury shrugged. "I just asked."

As Jim was getting into the dog truck of another handler, a white-haired, leather-faced man came to him.

"That's a fine animal you're handling, son," he said. "I've been wondering about her breeding."

"Air Pilot's Rocket out of Lucy Nella."

"I knew it! The Nella dogs are straight down from the old boy."

"What old boy?"

"Ready Dan. Your dog's the spit and image of him. I owned Dan, you know. Well, maybe you wouldn't know—before you were born, I imagine."

"Yes, sir, but I know about Dan. Brains is a powerful lot like him, if what I read is true."

"Wasn't worth a nickel until he was nearly two years old. We kept him because he was the finest duck retriever you ever saw, from a puppy. Then, almost overnight, he turned into a bird dog."

"Brains is a stomp-down good retriever, too."

The old man went back to the cages, and stared at Brains, and even in the growing dusk Jim could see his eyes reddening as he talked, half to himself.

"By God it's him, born all over again, only turned bitch. I remember that ticked face, and that wrinkled forehead and ramrod tail. How are you, Danny lad?" Brains licked the fingers on the wire, then backed away as if to spring at them. The man turned to Jim. "He was that way, too, playful as a puppy all his life, or until he got too stiff to romp." He looked back at Brains, and said, "I'm not well-fixed like I used to be, son, or I'd buy this dog from you if she cost me ten thousand dollars. I can't offer anything, now."

Jim felt a slow shame spreading over him, watching this man's emotion, and remembering the true reason he had given so much time to Brains. For almost a year now he had planned how he would triumphantly hunt the dog Drury Bowden had thrown away. On impulse, Jim said, "She ain't for sale, sir, but I'd be honored if you would handle her tomorrow."

The man turned and stared at him. "I'll be glad to," he said quietly.

JIM LIFTED BRAINS DOWN from the cage, and snapped on the leash. She tightened it, and half-dragged him to where waited the judges and Drury and Snow, and old Colonel Jordan, the man who had owned Ready Dan, erect and silent in his saddle.

Somebody said, "That's a real dog, but she'll have to hump today."

"She'll hump, all right," someone else answered.

A newspaper photographer, almost disabled by three days in the saddle, hobbled around and took pictures of the straining, impatient dogs. Adele, slim and lovely in her field clothes, said, "Good luck, Jim."

One of the judges said, "All right, let 'em go!"

The two dogs broke like greyhounds, and for a second ran shoulder to shoulder. Then Snow swung off through the cornfield, moving swiftly, with a confident, businesslike pace. Brains kept straight, slashing happily through a thick terrace growth, then cutting across a fresh-plowed patch, her big, hurrying feet throwing clods into the air. Jim swung his horse off to the left, to be in a position to scout for Colonel Jordan. Now, far beyond the gallery to the right, he saw Snow make a competent circle, and he knew the dog well enough to expect birds. Then Snow had them; the little setter was one minute flying, the next moment motionless, head and tail up in a style so perfect it made a lump come in your throat. Drury dismounted and flushed the birds and fired, and still Snow stood as if frozen, until sent on. Jim felt a curious hollowness, watching Snow stand shot that way—his father had taught the dog that.

Brains kept driving, once slowing as if she had struck scent, then giving it up and hurrying on. Of the two dogs, neither seemed to have the edge on range. Both ran as wide as they could and still handle; neither gave any time to other than quail scent. Snow went swiftly and lightly, foxlike. Brains was a smasher, striking brush with a force that seemed to tear the root out. Snow was businesslike, experienced, and quietly competent; Brains was a puppy with a mature body and a choke-bore nose, happy as a squirrel and quite obviously aware that she was performing for an audience.

Jim was not sorry he had asked Colonel Jordan to handle Brains. The old gentleman was a capable and quiet dog man. And you could see that, for him, nobody else was there, just himself and Brains—Ready Dan born again.

Snow had found two coveys before Brains connected. She pinned them near a branchhead, without any hesitation, boldly, with a gay grin on her face that said, "Hey, folks, look what I've done!" When the Colonel walked into the point, the birds got up right under Brains. She made one lunge at shot, but held immediately at her handler's sharp command.

"That's good," Jordan said to Jim as he mounted. "She's young—plenty of time to shut down on her later. I like 'em a little anxious. That's the way the old boy was." He turned his horse back to the woods road, watching Brains, and again he was alone with the dog.

The first hour went by. Neither dog showed any weariness. Snow's gypsy inclinations took him out of sight and judgment for ten minutes. When they found him, he was on the course again, pointing.

Jim muttered suddenly, "The derby don't live that can outhunt that dog!" But perhaps Brains would make a good race of it, and that would serve Jim's purpose.

Brains found another covey. After the shot, she turned suddenly, barked joyously at Jordan, and streaked off again.

"Ain't she the doggondest fool?" Jim thought, grinning.

The Hunting Fool

Then, in contrast to Snow's sober competency, Brains' work began to border on the spectacular. With Snow cutting back in toward her, she came upon a scattered covey. She pointed, and Snow backed her flawlessly. Two birds got up. The dogs swung away, and Brains pointed again, and again Snow, now fifty yards to the left, backed. Three birds got up. Brains dashed down the rise, stopped abruptly, on game. Snow also stopped, immobile in all his superb dignity. This time one bird got up. When the shot was fired, Brains was sent on. Snow stood. Drury whistled sharply. The setter didn't move a muscle. "Point," called Drury, uncertainly. But he was right. Snow had the five remaining birds of the covey.

Brains' next stunt was to point atop a rail fence that she had been in the act of crossing. The photographer half-fell off his horse and took her picture. Then, just as Colonel Jordan started to climb over, Brains teetered, lost her balance, and fell spang into the middle of the covey. She stood flush, her expression one of amusement, as if the thing was a pretty good joke on her.

Then a half hour without a point. It was Snow who found birds again. And again. You just couldn't head him. And not one error did he make. Going through a fallow field, Snow scattered a drove of field larks without giving them a second glance. The larks circled, giving their foolish raspy whistle, and settled in a small sedge patch. A few second later Brains came by the sedge, whirled, and pointed.

"I'm afraid your dog has pointed those larks," Drury said.

"You handle your dog," Jim snapped, but he felt a sharp disappointment. After all, though, Brains was just a derby.

"Point," Colonel Jordan said, unhesitatingly.

He walked into the sedge. The larks fluttered up around him. He paid no attention to them, walked about in front of Brains rapidly, quirting the grass. And suddenly an enormous covey of quail erupted from around him, scaled toward the branch, and volplaned out of sight.

Jim turned to Drury with satisfaction. "Them larks make a lot of noise when they get up, don't they?"

But Drury was looking up the hill, to where the invincible Snow waited patiently with a covey of his own.

The judges looked at each other, conferred a moment. One of them said, "When you have fired, Mr. Bowden, you both can take your dogs up."

Then he rode over to Jim and Jordan. When Snow's point was proved valid, he said, "Jim, you've got a wonderful dog. But Snow knows a little too much for him yet. We're giving first to the setter."

"Yes, sir," Jim said, "I think that's right." And he meant it.

Back at the cars, Jim saw Drury and Adele coming toward him. He had waited for this moment a long time, knowing exactly what he would say to Drury. But now, strangely enough, he found himself watching Adele instead. She *did* seem like a woman instead of a girl his age. And abruptly his thoughts jumped to a girl in Welbyton he used to know, the hardware man's daughter. He wondered if she would be at home tonight. It was the first time he had thought about any other girl in a long time.

"Jim," Drury said, "I want to buy that dog. She's a bang-up pointer."

Without saying a word, Jim turned to the hunting wagon, and brought Brains out on a leash. He handed the leash to him.

"She's been your dog all the time. This is the one you wanted to get shut of. You said she was a fool."

They stared at him, remembering that day. Then Drury said, "She's a fool, all right—a hunting fool."

This was the end of the act he had planned. He turned and walked away. But Drury caught him. "Jim, listen."

"Well, what do you want?"

"I'm sending my dogs back to you in the morning. All of them."

Adele looked at her husband and suddenly, impulsively, she slipped her arm through his.

"You needn't to," Jim said. "I don't want 'em. I ain't going to handle them."

"I'm sending them anyway," Drury said.

"I'll send 'em straight back, too," Jim snapped. "Can't you understand nothing? I don't want your dogs."

"They'll be there first thing in the morning," Drury called, grinning.

"They better not!" He slammed the door. In a few seconds he looked around impatiently for the man who was giving him the lift. He was in a hurry to get to town and call Brooks, and tell him to get the kennels in shape, because the Bowden dogs were coming back.

A Dog for a Man

The dog had been pointing for some time before Jesse Clay noticed him. Jesse found a lightwood knot and ran stumblingly through the bull grass and sedge. Standing panting by the motionless Bo, the man searched the grass hungrily, looking carefully at every blade of grass. For five minutes he stared. Finally a quail's bright, frightened eye betrayed it. Jesse drew back his trembling arm and suddenly hurled the knot. It missed. The covey rose in a thundering whir. The dog leaped forward, eagerly sniffing the cover. The man stood in bitter, hungry disappointment, panting and shaking. He drew out a bottle containing about two fingers of lemon extract and drank the stuff, draining it, and threw the bottle away.

Jesse Clay sat on a log. The setter, Bo, a big half-starved black-and-white dog, lay down and watched the man. An hour passed. Finally Jesse mumbled, "I just got it to do," and he rose. He was a spare man about thirty, with brown hair gray at the temples; his clothes and beard were shabby, his eyes red-shot.

He started walking through the woods. The dog wanted to range out over the woods hunting, but Clay kept him in.

They found a branch head, and the dog drank. Clay smeared black mud all over the dog, rubbing it into his coat.

Later that day they came to an enormous plantation house, and walked around until they found the kennels. The dog man looked them over.

"I want to sell you this here dog," Jesse Clay said. He studied the kennel fence carefully. It was a high fence, about eight feet, but there was no inturned guard at the top.

"We don't use plug dogs," the dog man said.

"He'll outhunt any dog you got," Clay said, matter-of-factly.

"Beat it," the man laughed.

"I'll take three hundred for him."

The man stopped laughing. He shouted to a Negro man. "Get Kate out and saddle two horses."

When they came back in from an hour of hunting the two dogs, the kennel man said, "Where'd you steal that dog?"

"I don't monk' around with stole dogs," Jesse said. "I raised this'n from a puppy."

"You got his papers?"

"He's full-blood, all right. I had his papers, but I lost 'em. You want him or not?"

The man studied him. "Nobody going to come at us about him?"

"I told you he was mine. I can't do nothing but tell you. You want him?"

"We'll take him."

Jesse hung around for about an hour; until he got his check.

"What'd you say his name was?" the man asked.

"Joe. Don't leave him out," 'cause he'll be hell-bent on tryin' to follow me."

But when Bo was put into the kennel, he went quietly to the doghouse, sniffing and growling at the other dogs, and not once did he look at the retreating figure of Jesse Clay.

CLAY GOT SHAVED and cleaned up and bought new clothes. He drank a half pint of whisky and had dinner at the best restaurant in the Georgia town. Afterward he went to the poolroom. Several tables were busy, and young boys in shirt sleeves sat in the shoeshine chairs, watching. Clay took a fresh straight cigarette from his new pack, lit it with steady hands. After a while the manger, a short, fat man, came over.

"Hello," Clay said. "Anything going on in the back?"

"No."

"Tonight, I guess."

"Don't believe I've had the pleasure."

"I'm all right. Just a cracker lookin' for a place to spend some money."

"Well, I don't have nothin' to do with gamblin'. But you see that little fellow yonder with his hat on the back of his head? You talk to him."

"I sure thank you," Clay said.

SIX NIGHTS LATER Jesse Clay stumbled through the brush, running into bushes and even trees in the darkness. His coat and hat were gone, and his trousers were dirty; his face was hollowed out, unshaven, and his blear eyes burned dully. Some sober instinct seemed to guide him; finally he saw the white buildings of the kennel, and the smaller white doghouses. He stopped, panting, knowing if he went any closer the dogs would start barking.

Afterwhile he got his breath and gave a soft, almost inaudible whistle. He waited fearfully, but no dog barked. There was no sound. The moon came from behind a cloud, spreading a thin blue-whiteness over the place. In the distance he could even make out the dog-yard fence, but could see no dogs moving. He whistled again, low. He sat down to wait.

Presently he heard the sound of Bo's claws on the fence wire. Now he could see the setter, halfway up the fence. The dog slipped, and fell four feet to the concrete floor of the yard. Clay heard the thump. Bo started to climb the fence again.

Clay slept for an hour. When he woke, the moon had disappeared and the night was pitchy. Slight sounds came from the dog yard, where Bo was still trying to get over the eight-foot fence. The dog worked silently, never whining. Jesse Clay went back to sleep, trembling fitfully.

When he woke, the panting dog lay beside him with bleeding claws. Jesse Clay got heavily to his feet, and they started back through the woods. Somewhere a whippoorwill was whipping across the night air; a breeze riffled the canopy of leaves overhead. When they had gone about a mile they came to a creek.

"Come here," Clay said.

Picking the dog up by the scruff of his neck and the loose skin at his hindquarters, he threw him into the chilled waters of the creek. Bo swam out, shook himself and rolled in the dry leaves while Clay sat, his chin in his hand, on a pine log in which you could hear the borers grinding. Presently the dog was almost clean of the old mud Clay had smeared in his hair. He'd be hard to identify now.

They went on through the woods, Clay stumbling and running into things, and the dog walking patiently ahead of him.

CLAY SAT WITH HIS BACK against the wall of the boxcar and watched the countryside drift by, fields and pine trees with old blackened turpentine faces and distant unpainted shacks. He wondered if it was Mississippi, or still Alabama. He was hungry, so that his stomach ached as if it were overfull. Every now and then the dog would go sniffing around the boxcar, looking for something to eat, as if he hadn't searched it and smelled it a hundred times already.

The walls of the boxcar were of horizontal unpainted ceiling, and when your eyes were half-closed the cracks ran in a pleasant parallel pattern; there were shippers' cryptic, chalked numbers; addresses: "Rud Gainey, Marion Junction, Ala., going home at last." Wooden cleats and staples and nails with bits of shipper's cloth; wisps of metallic-shiny packing straw, white powdery stuff all about; and excelsior.

Clay stared out the opposite door. "I'm done with living like this!" he said suddenly, angrily.

The train started up a long incline, slowing gradually. The whistle echoed back, muted. On each side of the tracks were great pine forests. Clay saw a neat square sign on one of the trees. After a moment he saw another sign. They were too far to read, but he knew well enough what they said: POSTED.

Clay shoved the car door open a little wider. He leaned out to glance up the track; then, without hesitation, he jumped, rolling and bumping down the small fill. When he stopped and steadied his dizzy brain he saw Bo tumbling down the fill up ahead. The dog got up shaking himself, and trotted back to Clay. Now Clay could read the signs. POSTED. CHARLES HUDSON, OWNER.

The Hudson house was enormous, an unattractive red-brick square overlooking a winter lawn that swept down and down for acres to a grassy pond with little island clumps of dwarfed, mossy cypresses. The overseer's house, the dog man's house, the laundry and the kennels and the stables, all were a half mile north of the Big House.

Jesse Clay and the dog reached the kennels the day after leaving the train. The overseer's name was Woodall.

"I want you all to try out this dog," Jesse Clay told him.

"Take him to Peterson. He's the dog man," the old man said, regarding the unkempt figure suspiciously.

Peterson looked at the dog and then at Clay, and said what they always said, "Where'd you get that dog?"

"Raised him myself."

The dog man wasn't very interested. "Can't tell nothing about a dog's looks. What would you want for him?"

"You try him out. Then we'll talk price."

"Oh, all right. Miss Marie and I are trying out another dog in a minute. We'll take yours along."

"Well, listen. I ain't tryin' to bum nothin' off you, but if you want to see Bo at his best, you might let one of your niggers feed him a little something. He ain't et in three days."

A woman said, "You let that dog go three days without eating?" She wore well-cut but old riding boots, undistinguished riding trousers, a suede jacket. This was Miss Marie Hudson; she was a bit on the big side, and not what you would call pretty; but there was something about her you liked, even when she was getting madded up about letting a dog go hungry three days.

"Bo don't mind, ma'am," Clay said.

"How could you do it?"

"Couldn't help it. I ain't et either."

Miss Marie said, "While we're trying your dog, go up to Mrs. Woodall's and ask for something to eat."

"You try out the dog, lady. I'll wait right here. I ain't powerful hungry."

They were gone a terribly long time. He walked around the kennels, keeping a continual uproar going among the dogs. He was going to play it straight this time, but from force of habit he studied the dog-yard fence. Bo would have a time getting over it, because it had one of those barbed-wire guards turned inward at the top. The fence that separated the kennel pens, though, had no barrier, and a brainy dog might climb to the top of that and clamber over the barrier of the outside fence. But then, Clay guessed that no dog would think of that; not even Bo. The thought comforted him. He had to play it straight this time.

He walked around, examined the dog-food stove, the dip vats, the medical room, while a young Negro named Kaythod followed him watchfully. Clay wondered what was keeping them so long. Had Bo thrown a fit or something and run away?

Finally they came, Bo and the other dog, panting, with dancing, quivering tongues, the horses sleek with mild sweat. Kaythod took the horses away. Miss Marie and Peterson studied Clay acutely.

Finally Peterson said, "How much?"

Clay said, "Well, you know what he's worth. Not less than four or five hundred."

Neither of them said anything.

Clay said, "But what I'm after is a steady job. I'd do my very best to make Mr. Peterson good helper. If you all will give me a job, you can have Bo for a hundred dollars."

"Did you train this dog yourself?" Miss Marie asked.

"Yes'm."

"How did you teach him to stand shot?"

"Force collar, ma'am," Clay said. "I know you want to find out about me. But I ain't lying. I can teach a dog anything short of reading and writing. Just give me a try. I've been down, nearly to the bottom. I want a chance to come back up."

There was a trace of friendliness in Miss Marie's honest eyes. "We'll try you two weeks…Show him his cottage, Peterson."

The cottage Peterson took him to was small and compact. It was unfurnished; and the bareness reminded Clay of the boxcars.

"I'll have a bed and some stuff sent over," Peterson said, sitting in one of the windows. "If you get the job, Miss Marie'll advance you money for a bit of furniture of your own."

"She's sure nice, ain't she?" Clay asked.

A week later Clay was doing good work. Peterson looked at him speculatively.

"Look, bud. I don't know what's on your mind. But if you sure enough want to get on your feet, you come to a good place. I'm leaving here in a few months to go into field-trial handling. Woodall, the overseer, he's old. His job'll be vacant in time. If you're any account, you got a fine opportunity right here."

"I don't deserve breaks like this," Clay said slowly. "But I'm going to sure God work."

"Mr. Hudson—Miss Marie's old man—he don't come down, but a month in the winter. Miss Marie's the boss. She's no hard Yankee snob, either, for all the Hudson money. She's genuwine, bud, and you and me are just as good as God made, in her sight. Even better than some, I often think. Come on down to my house. I got some beer on ice."

"I ain't drinking anything, much oblige. But I'll just visit a minute before I fix that dip."

WHEN PETERSON LEFT, eight months later, Jesse Clay moved into his cottage. It was a fine little house, with thick ligustrum and tea-olive bushes shading the screened front porch, and a case of pretty good books.

Miss Marie came in, her hard boot heels clapping on the gray porch boards. Clay sat in front of the bookcase.

"Is that a book of poetry you're reading, Jesse, in heaven's name?" she asked.

"A little poetry won't hurt anybody," he said defensively. She looked over his shoulder and read:

Thus let me live, unseen, unknown;
Thus unlamented let me die;
Steal from the world, and not a stone
Tell where I lie.

She stood there, smiling. "I wouldn't have thought a person could change so much, Jesse. Nobody would know you were the same man."

"I'm not, ma'am."

She studied him appraisingly. "Look at him. He wears good field clothes. His face is smooth and his eye is clear. A touch of distinctive gray at the temples. And he reads poetry. Good, morbid stuff about dying unlamented," she said. "And I believe you know even more about dogs than Peterson."

"I've been around them a right smart."

"I'd like to know about your old life."

"I'd lot rather you didn't," he told her. "Look, Miss Marie, I ain't never said much about it, but you been terrible fine to me. I—I sure appreciate it."

"The good in a man is always waiting for a chance, don't you think?"

"Yes'm. But that's what the bad in him's doing too."

"Don't talk like that, Jesse," she said quietly, leaning against the mantle beside the yellow fire. "You interested in field trials?"

"Sure."

"Peterson told me before he left that you ought to run Bo in the Mississippi Open. That's next month at Mayfield. We usually let a handler pay his own expense and take the purse if he wins."

"I'd like to run the old fool, and that's the truth," he said. "I'm fixing to give him a workout right now. You want to go?"

"Yes, I'll go."

Bo was a fast, hard-going dog; his short-coupled frame lent his action a merry, snappy look. Yet he was big and powerful, and he ran like a horse, with thunder-drumming feet and pounding breath. He never went around anything he could jump over; therefore he seldom got lost, because no matter how wide his range, occasionally you'd see him flash in a white arc above the sedge and cover a mile away, jumping a five-foot lightwood stump that he could have avoided by swerving ten inches. His points were in the best picture-book style, legs apart and well planted, head well up, drinking the hot quail scent, tail erect; absolutely straight and absolutely motionless.

The day was good, clear and perfectly still and cold.

"Bo likes it cold, doesn't he?" Miss Marie said. "He goes his best when the air bites."

"I guess he'd do better in Tennessee than down here, the old Eskimo," Jesse said.

They rode side by side on the plantation horses; both watching the dogs. The horses' breathing fogged, and the hoofs crunched the thin clear ice. Presently Bo found game, and the young pointer circled over and honored nicely.

"You've done wonders with Little Red."

"I kind of thought you might like to run him in the derby," Jesse said.

"I'd love it," she said, sliding her cold twenty-gauge out of its stiff saddle scabbard. "Don't know whether I can shoot with half-frozen fingers or not."

They dismounted, rubbing their cold hands. "Now you old hard-head," Jesse said to Bo, "you're field-trial stuff. That means don't break shot; not any. When she shoots, you stand."

Miss Marie walked in front of the motionless dog, trim on her long straight legs and worn English boots, in her suede jacket which warmed her deep chest; she carried the gun carelessly, with old familiarity and capability. The birds whirred up, crossing and swinging back together, about fourteen of them.

A Dog for a Man

Bo lunged, and caught the rawhide whistle strap across his head for his impatience. The girl took her time. At the first barrel, a bird dropped, cold dead; at the second, a long shot, the bird wavered, dipped and tumbled to the ground.

"That was two cocks, all right!" Jesse said. Bo's tail had dropped, he shifted his feet nervously, watching the places where the birds fell. "Go get 'em," Jesse said.

Each of the dogs brought in a dead cock quail. Bo retrieved his by the head; Jesse pulled the bird and the head came off; that was Bo's reward, and he ate the head as he swung away at full speed again.

"You're getting pretty good on the cocks," Jesse told Miss Marie. "There's more of 'em than hens; you'll help your breeding stock."

"It's not as hard as I thought. You get the knack of watching for the white cheeks." She watched the hurrying dogs. "Bo broke a little, I noticed."

"I'll put a stop to that before the trial." He guessed Bo was still unsteady from the days when they had tried to kill birds with lightwood knots for something to eat.

PETERSON WAS AT MAYFIELD. "Come on down to Bill Stafford's room. We got a little fifty-cent draw game."

"I'll watch," Jesse said.

Most of the players were professional dog men, swinging round the field-trial circuit. Very few of them ever gamble or drink heavily. Only a little game every now and then as diversion from talk of the weather and judges and birds. A bottle of whisky was on the dresser beside the sweating water pitcher.

"You don't play poker?" one of the men asked Clay.

"Oh, I guess I'll take a hand. Just fifty cents, you said," Clay decided, sitting down nervously.

He won eight dollars. He went downstairs, exultant and confident. Miss Marie was in the lobby, talking to some of the millionaire dog owners' wives.

They ate together in the dining room. She made Jesse feel perfectly at ease. They weren't heiress and kennelman. They were two bird-dog people. Jesse knew suddenly that she as the kind of boss a workingman could just about trust with his immortal soul. He was sure lucky.

Afterward they went to the temporary trial dog kennels for a last look at Bo and the derby pointer, Little Red.

"You like working on the place?" Miss Marie asked suddenly.

"I sure do."

"I'll tell you something. Mr. Woodall wants to leave. He hasn't got much longer to live, and he wants to go to Florida, where his children are," she said. "You've proved yourself capable. When he leaves, you can have the overseer's job if you want it."

"You're mighty well right I want it."

"That's fine," she said.

DURING THE TRIALS THEY rode together except when Miss Marie ran Little Red in the derby, where the dog tied for third. In the open all-age, they both admired the work of a lemon pointer named Itching Heel.

"That son of a gun's a traveler," Jesse muttered, watching the dog running whippetlike along the far bounds of the course, a half mile away.

"He's marvelous," Miss Marie said, when a dog scout appeared on a distant rise, silhouetted horse and man and waving hat, to signal Itching Heel's fourth covey find; and in the excited half hush just before the horses were wheeled and spurred, the scout's small cry drifted down the rise: "Point!"

Bo's run, in the last brace, wasn't remarkable for game finding—he found two coveys and a single and his bracemate found none—but Bo got out and rambled, and his bold horselike speed impressed the judges enough to put Itching Heel and Bo in the second-series run-off with two other braces.

"Now listen, butter-brain," Jesse said to the dog that night, "any fool dog can run. You got to find game if you want to place in this to-do."

"Don't scold him," Miss Marie said. They were at the kennels, an empty store whose floor has been attacked by termites, so that it sagged in places. "There just weren't any birds on his course yesterday."

"He ought to've made some."

Next morning none of the four dogs in the first two braces distinguished themselves further than they had in the first series. The sun came up in a crisp sky; the weather held still sharp and cold when Bo and Itching Heel were put down. Bo's eager breath steamed as he strained against Jesse's brown hand at his collar. Beside them, Itching Heel waited, panting, muscles bunched under the smooth short hair, while his young handler gave him a quiet and intense and meaningless pep talk.

"Let 'em go!" said the starting judge, and both dogs broke like greyhounds after a rabbit. They split, Bo wheeling off to the right. He ran in a crazy, swift, drum-hoof, home-stretch manner. It wasn't a lope; it was a dead belly-to-the-ground run that took a man's breath away. Itching Heel was hell-bent for the horizon, going nicely with whipping tail and intelligent casts. But Bo swerved again, toward a five-foot fence.

"Damn his fool time!" Jesse swore. "He's going a quarter mile out of his way just to jump that fence!"

Bo's leap was a thing of incredible fluidity and grace; he cleared without touching, and when he struck the ground it was in a cold, flag-high point.

"Point!" Jesse shouted, and the judges kicked their horses into a run. Jesse dismounted and climbed the fence, gun in hand. Behind him he could hear the horses' hoofs thudding in the soft earth, and the crackling of old corn stalks. Bo waited motionless, erect, confident. Jesse went quickly into the brush ahead, kicking and quirting the leaves to put the birds up before they could run off and make Bo's point invalid. When they got up he fired into the air, watching the dog. Bo crouched eagerly, but he didn't break. Jesse seized his collar and lifted his front quarters off the ground and ran him off to a flying start.

Itching Heel found the next two coveys. Then Bo located again. And they were even on finds. Neither had any edge as to range; each ran as big as a dog could and still stay on the course. During the last half hour, Bo was out of judgment for a few minutes.

A Dog for a Man

"There he is!" Miss Marie said. Bo appeared far to the left, cutting back in toward the middle of the course, hunting hard. He glided over a barbed-wire fence.

"Dang if he don't like to skim 'em close," a man back of them said.

Itching Heel kept pushing. Presently Bo began to seem leg-weary; his range narrowed, and his characteristic dead run altered to a milder swinging lope.

"There he goes!" somebody in the gallery yelled. "No guts! He's had enough! Yonder's a setter dog for ye!"

Bo kept going at his tame pace, and once he looked like he was going to make game. But Itching Heel was as fast as ever, and when the judges told the handlers to take the dogs up, everybody knew the pointer had won.

Bo swung in at Jesse's sharp whistle blasts. When he was within fifty yards, they all saw dark blood drenching his quivering hindquarters. Jesse climbed down and found the six-inch barbed-wire gash that laid the inside of the left leg open. The dog's gums and inner lips were ghastly pale, which meant a lot of blood lost.

"Steeplechaser, ain't you?" Jesse said. "Good a-mind to leave you here to bleed plumb dry." He tied a handkerchief around the wound and carried the dog back to the dog truck, where a veterinarian waited with his needle and gut.

"Don't guess you all at Hudson's want to sell that dog," a man said to Jesse at the bar that night.

"Don't guess so."

"Too bad he had to go and cut hisself," the other said. "Might've won first. Of course, Itching Heel ain't no plug yard dog."

"Itching Heel's a real man."

"I'd be honored if you'd let me buy you a drink."

Jesse had thought he might risk a beer, but with the three-hundred-dollar second-place check in his pocket, he wanted something a little more like celebrating. So he drank a whisky; the almost-forgotten pleasant fire of it in his throat bewitched him.

"Yes, sir," the man said, "he's a lot of dog."

Another man had joined them. He had an old-fashioned glass in his hand. His face was vaguely familiar. "We used to have a dog sort of like yours," he said reminiscently. "Big, wide-going. Setter too. We bought him from a bum that showed up one day. It was kind of curious. But we lost the dog."

"I raised Bo from a puppy," Jesse said uneasily.

"It was our fault we lost him. The guy said the dog would try to follow him. But he acted all right the first night or two, so we quit chaining him. Then one night he got out, and that was the last we saw of him." He muddled the orange slice in his glass. "Wouldn't know the dog if I saw him, I don't guess. Just hope he didn't starve in the woods."

"I weaned Bo and raised him."

"Oh, I'm not thinking he's the dog," the man said hastily. "Sure wish he was, though. How about a drink?"

"Don't mind if I do," Jesse said. A strange scared feeling came over him. "No," he said slowly; "better not. Much obliged. No more." He walked out rapidly. Not that he couldn't handle another drink, he told himself. Things were different now. He was a new man. But he hadn't liked that foreboding.

Later, when they were back on the plantation, he remembered the strong way he had left the bar after one drink; and pride and confidence in himself returned.

"Think I'll go into town and see of I can run up on a little poker game," he told Miss Marie a short while after they got back.

Her eyes had a speculative and dubious look. But she said, "Why don't you?"

OLD MR. WOODALL came looking for Jesse Clay six days later, and finally located him asleep in the Mangum Hotel. Clay had a splitting head, his clothes were a mess, and he had six hundred dollars in cash.

Mr. Woodall persuaded him to take a shower and shave while his clothes were being pressed. Jesse's quaking razor nicked blood in a dozen places.

"I been showing the boys some poker," Jesse said. "Picked up fifty to a hundred every night. Did you send that boy for a pint like I asked you?"

"No. You've got to go back."

"Just wanted a drink for this bust-head." He spoke solemnly, profoundly: "You know, my luck sure took a turn for the better when I walked onto that plantation. Why, I can even win at poker!"

"We'll see how good your luck is when we get back," Woodall told him. "Personally, I wouldn't put too much store by that job until you talk to Miss Marie."

Jesse stared at him stupidly. "Is she mad?"

"Mad? No, 'mad' ain't exactly the word for it, son. Sort of stobbed, I'd say. She was right proud of the way you'd took ahold of yourself."

"Lord, I'd better see her right away," he breathed. He looked at the old man. "What has she heard?"

"I don't know what she's heard."

"I got to have a drink. I can't go up to her like this."

"You do like you please."

The drink steadied him a little, so that when he finally faced her in the big paneled living room his hands had stopped trembling and his headache had dulled. She wore a light-blue wool dress and she had on her glasses.

"Hello, Jesse." She smiled impersonally.

"Hello, Miss Marie. I guess I was sort of A.W.O.L."

"I guess you were."

"Well—" He hesitated, staring into the big log fire. "Is everything all right?"

"You mean your job?" she asked.

"Yes."

"You still have your job. But I wouldn't let this happen again, if I were you."

He grinned uneasily. "A man just goes on a little bust, sometimes, I guess."

He went down to the kennel and stared dully through the wire at the dogs that came rushing forward. Bo, the indifferent, lay beside the kennel house in the sun, watching Jesse. Jesse unlocked the gate and went in. Bo's leg was healing nicely.

A Dog for a Man

Jesse called one of the Negroes to saddle up two horses. They would work on some of the puppies, he said; and went to his house to change clothes and get a small sustaining drink.

As he was pulling on his cold boots, the phone rang.

"I wondered where you got off to," a man's voice said.

"I had to go back to work sometime."

"We got some more money for you—if you can get it."

"Keep it. I got plenty."

"What's the matter with you, anyway?"

"Nothing. I just got to work, I tell you," he said.

"A luck box like you don't have to work. Anyway, you don't work at night, do you?"

"No...Listen here, Alec; I've got to go out and run some puppies."

"Sure, boy. Go on. But we'll save you a chair tonight."

Jesse hesitated. If they had some more money, why not go on down there tonight? Miss Marie couldn't tell him what to do with his own time. Tomorrow he'd see about having the dove field plowed for the benne and Egyptian wheat, and she'd never know a thing about tonight. Not that is made any difference; it wasn't any hide off her back what he did on his own time, was it?

Lord, suppose his luck ran like it had last night? A pair of fives he'd held, with a jack kicker, and his two draw cards were a jack and a five, and he'd been afraid that nobody'd catch enough to bet on, and then Alec had rubbed his chin and laid down three dollars.

"Tell you what, Alec," he said finally; "I might drop down for a few minutes or so."

He was gone three days this time; he came back for a night and left again. Two weeks later old Mr. Woodall found him in the hotel.

"I guess you understand we couldn't put up with it plumb till Judgment Day," Woodall said.

Jesse's red-shot eyes glared at him. "All right; what?"

"I brought your stuff in. Don't come back on the place."

"You can't fire me now, Mr. Woodall! I'm down. I ain't got but twenty bucks to my name." He sat up in bed, groaning.

"That's too bad, son. Good-by."

"Wait! I'll see Miss Marie."

"She told me what to do."

"I'll talk to her."

"You can't. She left night before last for New York.

EVEN IN THE DARKNESS, Jesse Clay could make out the dim whiteness of the plantation houses where, three months before, he had worked. Stumbling, trembling, he got as close to the kennels as he could without alarming the dogs. Cat's-claw briers tugged at his trousers, but they were not good anyway. In the dim light he could see the doghouses; the metal posts stood bare, strung with fence wire that was not invisible.

73

At Jesse's third low whistle several of the dark blotches on the white-concrete kennel yard sat up and became alert. One dog, a big one, rose and came to the fence and stood motionless, listening. Then he backed off and jumped. The barbed-wire guard caught him, and he fell sprawling to the concrete. He tried again, and fell. He climbed, but got the guard wire and was stopped.

Jesse Clay watched for an hour and went to sleep.

Bo found that the fence between the kennel pens had no guard, but when he got over this he was in another pen of dogs.

It was getting on toward morning when he finally happened to stop on top of the inner fence; then he clambered over the guard and fell heavily to the concrete outside.

Just at daylight, Jesse Clay and the dog got into the boxcar. It had lately been used for shipping fertilizer, and at some time peanuts—a few hulls lay about the floor. The dog limped to a corner, turned around twice and lay down. Presently the car jolted and the train moved out slowly, headed for Tennessee. Jesse Clay went to sleep fitfully with the smell of guano in his nostrils.

Sis

I want to put it down just the way it was—not that I'd ever forget Sis.

I didn't know whose land I was on, but it was good bird land. Old Red found a covey, and I shot, and then we went after the singles. Red pointed again, and I tied the horse and kicked the bird out and shot it.

Then is when I saw Sis. She was standing about fifty yards away, watching us. She wasn't much to look at. She was white and lemon—pale lemon—a small and scrawny-looking pointer with a tail thin like a whip, and her bones seemed like they were made for a bird instead of a dog.

I wasn't in the mood to have my hunt ruined by some farmer's country dog. I said, "Git!"

She didn't git; her tail just moved a little. I mounted the horse, figuring that if she got in the way, a good stinging with No. 9 shot would send her home quick enough.

I never paid her any more attention. I just went on with my hunting and thinking. My thinking wasn't a great deal of enjoyment, because I was having a bad time. Just when I'd had the luck to be turned down for the draft because of my stomach, I lost my job. He was a damned old crank, my boss, but in wartime a man able and willing to keep a bird-dog kennel going is hard to find. Some way he found out I wasn't turning in all the stud fees from Rock Hill Dan, and he fired me. That's how come I was in those woods with nothing to my name but my horse and my nine-year bird dog, Red.

With all this on my mind, I never noticed this little bitch again until I saw her skirting a clearing way up ahead. The way she was going nearly knocked me out of the saddle. Did I say she wasn't much to look at? Mister, she was the prettiest-moving little thing ever turned loose in this world. She ran like she was born to run, and not to ever stop. And then she struck a scent, whipped out a quick circle, and pointed, and my throat was all of a sudden so dry I couldn't swallow.

I rode to her. You wouldn't have ever thought a little think like that could point with such style. She was cocked up like six o'clock, her head and tail high and her eyes bright. I stood beside her for a minute. She never moved. I walked in and kicked up the covey and shot a bird, and she broke and retrieved it. When she came to me, I got hold of her. On her collar it said, "W.E. Clarke, Jr." It wasn't a store collar, like a regular kennel would have, but made of harness leather, and the writing was scratched on a rough plate.

"A farmer's dog," I decided. I looked at her teeth. She wasn't hardly two years old! I hunted her another hour, and everything she done was perfect. Oh, she broke to shot a little, but only like a bold, young dog should. Slowly it began to come over me that this little bitch was the best dog I had ever seen. I didn't have no right to know it so soon, but I knew it just the same.

My first thought was to steal her. When I tried to steer her out of the woods, though, she'd stop and start home. Finally I turned around and followed her. If the man who owned her knew anything about dogs, she wouldn't be loose like that. I figured I could buy her for a fifty-dollar check, and be long gone before he tried to cash it. But one thing I knew for certain—she was the kind of dog a man spends his life looking for, and I was going to have her.

We ended up in front of an old, low farmhouse sitting under some big water oaks. There was a big man in overalls sitting in a rocking chair on the porch like he was waiting for somebody to come. The dog had gone up on the porch and was asleep there.

"Evening," the man said. "Get down and come in."

"That your dog?" I asked.

"Belongs to my boy, Billy," he said. "I hope she ain't been killing chickens or nothing."

"She came over there where I was hunting and I brought her back."

"Sis always goes to a gun. I just let her go. She don't get much pleasure with Billy gone. You have a nice hunt?"

"Well, she sort of messed us up, but it's all right."

The man looked around at the dog. "Ain't like Sis to cause trouble, more'n running all over creation. Billy, he sets a heap of store by her."

"Oh, she didn't bother me much," I said. ""Your boy Billy not here?"

"Nope." He reached and pulled at his cob pipe.

"When will he be back?"

"I can't rightly say."

I sat there, whittling on a straw, trying to figure out the situation so I'd know how to work the dog deal. I wished now that I'd just grabbed Sis up, in the woods, and rode off with her. Her belonging to a boy who "set a heap of store by her" wasn't so good. I had to move careful. I saw that. But I meant to have that dog.

"Where's Billy at?" I asked, finally.

"He's in the Marine Corps." He rocked slowly.

"Sort of puts a crimp into his bird hunting, don't it?" I smiled. "And leaves that idle dog there to feed."

"She don't eat hardly nothing," he shrugged. "And she's right smart company, to be so indifferent-like."

I looked up at a jay bird in the water oak. He would squat down and let out a big squawk, and from down in the creek another jay bird would answer him. I said, "My old dog yonder is about ready to go on a pension. I been thinking if I could find me a good, young dog to break, I'd buy him, if he didn't cost too much." The jay bird squawked. "Now that little bitch there, she's sort of small for heavy cover, and she breaks shot. But I believe with a lot of work I could make a pretty good dog out of her, if you're of a mind to let her go."

"She don't belong to me. She's Billy's."

"Surely he don't intend to just let her set out her best hunting years."

The man said, "I don't want to give you no short answer, but she just ain't for sale. Billy never told me not to sell her, and I don't hunt, myself, but I want her here for him when he comes back."

"Where's he at?" I asked, desperate.

"Well, somewhere out yonder in them islands, that's all I know. I ain't heard from him for quite a spell now. They said he helped when they took over that Tarawa island," he said, rocking. Then he added, "They got him listed as missing."

Missing for eight months. My heart give a little pound, because I knew I might get hold of that dog yet.

"You think he's coming back?"

"I figure he is," the man said.

I kept my mouth shut, waiting.

"Ain't no doubt in my mind about it," he said. He rocked forward and got up, motioning to me. "And when he comes, everything's going to be just the way he left it."

He led me into the house, and into Billy's room. There was a big feather bed, with a red bedspread on it, and a marble-top table on which was an oil lamp with a floweredy shade. Over the mantel there was a shotgun, fresh-oiled, resting on deer-foot racks. A dog whistle with a worn rawhide thong hung from one of the deer feet. There were pictures of women on the wall, mostly legs and breasts, cut from calendars and magazines. A wild-turkey beard was stuck to the wall; he must have been a big one, twenty pounds or more.

The man went over and straightened one of the pictures.

"When he gets back, everything's going to be ready for him." He nodded toward Sis, and added, "That little dog is his pride and joy."

I finally left, seeing I wasn't getting nowhere. All night I studied and studied, but I couldn't figure anything out. I knew if I outright stole the dog, old man Clarke would hunt me down like a chicken-killing possum. And it wouldn't be possible to run Sis in a field trial, with the word out that she was a stolen dog.

NEXT DAY, I WENT BACK to the same woods and fired my gun off, and after a few minutes, sure enough, here comes Sis. She stood there watching, waiting for me to start hunting. She was a funny-acting little dog, when she wasn't at work. She just stood still, never wagging her tail or acting excited or eager at all. When you'd pat her, she'd just stand there, polite, and wait until you got the patting over with. You could see she didn't really care a great hell of a lot about any man except one with a gun in his hand.

But I could tell she wasn't calm like she looked. The muscles in her hind legs trembled, and every now and then she yawned quick-like, the way a keyed-up dog does.

It was funny to see the change come over her, when she started hunting. She changed from a scrawny, little yard dog to a flashy fireball. And guts? Mister, she had guts. She was little, but cover didn't mean anything to her. If she couldn't smash through it, she'd go over in quick jumps. I've seen her hit a catclaw brier patch and never slow up, coming out on the other side with her tongue bleeding and thorns all over.

Well, I had to have her. Every now and then you see a man get that way about a woman—he's just got to have her, no matter what. But I wanted that dog worse than I ever wanted any woman. There's women everywhere, but there wasn't another dog in the world like Sis, and I knew I could make a mint with her.

But I had to play it careful. I had to stay in good with the old man. And yet, sometime soon, I had to convince him his son was dead. I had to play it careful and at the same time I had to play it fast, because I was about broke.

Old Man Clarke liked for me to hunt Sis. I quit tolling her to me with the gun; instead I'd ride right up to the house and get her. Generally he'd be sitting there on the porch, rocking and smoking. As soon as I'd come in sight, he'd stand up right quick, like I might be somebody else, then sit back down again when he saw it was just me. He liked me right enough, but it wasn't me he waited for.

BY THE TIME I'D BEEN around there a couple of weeks, I knew his schedule. He was in the fields by daylight, working, directing the Negroes, plowing. About eight he come in and eat the breakfast the old Negro woman had ready for him. Two places was always set at the table. If I happened to get there about breakfast time, as I often managed to do, a third place was set for me; nobody ever sat at that second place. After breakfast he would go out on the porch and smoke and rock until the mail carrier come. He'd hear the mail car long before I ever did. When he started knocking out his pipe, I knew the mailman would be along soon.

The mailman would drive up and stop at the box, and Clarke would just keep rocking until the car left. Then he would walk down to the box and take out the mail. A letter from a mail-order house, a circular from a store in town, the paper, a salve sample—stuff like that. Clarke would come back in, lay the mail on the table in the hall, and go back to the fields.

By the time I'd hunted Sis a half dozen times she was steadied down just enough. And she was right. One day we come in about midmorning. The mailman had come and gone, and Clarke had looked at the mail and not found what he looked for and returned to the field.

I opened up the paper and turned to the sports section, and there was a picture of a man and a bird dog, it said: "Robert Turnbull and his pointer Mustang to enter Ridgeview Open." I looked at the date of the trial, and it was next week. My hands trembled a little with excitement, and I began to figure.

Clarke came in at noon, took another glance at the mail and sat down, sort of tired and discouraged-like.

"You heard nothing from your boy yet?" I asked.

"Nope." He said it sort of slow.

I shook my head sad-like. "War is a bad thing."

He didn't say nothing, just rocked. And I knew that it wouldn't be long now.

In a few minutes I showed him in the paper about the field trial.

"I believe Sis might have a chance in that trial," I said. "It'd sure be a fine thing to have a field-trial winner for your boy, Billy, if he comes home."

Sis

It was easy. He didn't seem to care much, one way or another, and give me expense and entry-fee money, and off I and Sis went.

The Ridgeview Open was a one-course trial. A one-course trial isn't a real field trial, it's a city substitute, but it's better than no trial at all and it pays money to the winner. Instead of hunting native birds in their native woods, the dogs run a circular course. At the end of it is a bird field, where they've released a few half-tame pen-raised quail that half the time won't set to a point, won't fly, and liable as not will go running *chee-chee* right between your dog's legs. But, like I say, it's better than no trial at all, and the good handlers and good dogs come, and the trial pays good cash stakes, and that is what counts with me.

This Ridgeview course is in a rolling, rocky red-hill country with a little creek running through it. You could sit on the high hill and watch the whole business.

What I liked was the horses. They belonged to a cavalry outfit and they were big and able. There was a mare I liked, and a soldier was holding her for Roy Daney, but I told him Roy Daney had sent me for her, and got on and rode off.

It began to mist rain, right from the start. Cold, too. But they were tough judges, Adams and Eubanks, and they just turned up the collars of their slickers and never said a word about quitting. For two days it rained, off and on, and the little creek that ran through the course began to swell, and those red-clay hills got thick with mud, and every now and then a dog would decide he had enough, and would just quit. One little bitch made a long cast and disappeared, and when they found her, she was curled up in her pen in the barn, asleep.

But when it came Sis's first time to run, *she* didn't quit. She ran like she was just crazy about bad weather. She handled nice, and when we come around to the bird field I worked her in close and in a minute, bang, there she was a-pointing.

"Point, Judge!" I called, and drew out my blank pistol.

When I walked up beside Sis, there sat the quail by a little rock, without a speck of grass around it, and I saw Sis trembling like she couldn't stand it much longer.

"Don't you grab at that bird!" I said under my breath.

Then I said. "Shoo!" and the quail stood up, but instead of flying he began to run off, going *chee-chee*.

"There goes the bird, Judge!" I yelled, but Eubanks had judged over me before and he knew I was slick and he didn't take my word for nothing.

Anyway, there went the bird, slipping off through the grass and nobody knew whether Sis was telling the truth or false pointing. I stuck the pistol at the ground behind the bird and pulled the trigger, and *flurr*, that quail come out of there like a skyrocket.

They called Sis back for the second series. And the dog we drew to run against was Mustang, Turnbull's dog. When it came time, the weather just wasn't fit to be out in. But Adams and Eubanks just pulled their necks a little deeper into their slickers and said," Let's get going."

Sis was ready. And so was Mustang. When we let them go, they disappeared over the crest oaf the hill. Neither one showed up for a few minutes, and Turnbull and I rode along chatting away like we wasn't a bit worried. Then when we reached the next hill I saw Sis hurrying through a little short-leaf-pine grove. We made a turn to the left and in a minute there she was, already made the turn and out front again.

And before long the judges began passing little glances at each other. Maybe they had guessed that they were seeing as pretty and gutty a ground race as a dog ever run.

The cold stinging run even began to get old Mustang. Oh, he ran level enough, but not with his old-time punch. But Sis—you'd have thought it was blue-sky weather.

She ran along, merry as a squirrel and light as a feather, just about as far out as she could reach and still be seen. And moving fast. I don't see how she done it, with the mud soft and deep like that.

THEN WE CAME TO THAT CREEK, and it was all out of its banks, swollen and muddy. Before I noticed it, Sis had crossed the little wooden bridge and was well on up ahead, staying along the side of the small mountain. Now I didn't know what to do because before long the course turned back to the left again, and the ford she was supposed to cross back over would be four feet deep in rushing water. Of course I could cross the bridge myself and ride her down and bring her back across it—but she was making the best cast of the day, and that would spoil it.

"How can I get her back over, Judge?" I asked, for they had run several braces before that day.

"They all been having trouble," the judge admitted. "There's another bridge about a mile down beyond the ford. If a dog got over, they been using that."

I didn't like it a bit. Just when the final left turn of the course came, I had to go on another mile and get Sis and bring her the whole mile back. It would sure break up her race.

And I sure needed to win. I aimed to go back, finish convincing Old Man Clarke his boy wasn't coming back, and then pay him a hundred dollars—out of my win money—and get out of there with Sis. Now, though, it looked like I might not have any win money, and all because a little creek had gone wild—

The mare mucked along, bogging down to her knees every now and then, and we watched Sis sprinting across that hillside. She was a sight to see. Right about then is when that funny feeling began to come over me. All along I had been framing up a lot of talk to give old Clarke, working on him about Billy. But now I sort of wanted all that out of my mind, and somehow just watching that little dog run is what caused it.

Then the course swung to the left, and my dog was on the other side of the creek. I held my hand up so Sis could see me, and got ready to ride on down to the bridge and bring her across. I blew my whistle; I didn't see her. Then she appeared, right at the ford, and for a second she stopped there and looked at me across that boiling stream. And something in that way she stood there told me what to do. I stood in the stirrups and yelled, "Here, Sis, here!"

MISTER, MAYBE YOU WON'T understand this; but right then come the biggest thrill in my life. I'll even say this, right then my whole life took a sharp turn. I just couldn't go on being a sharper and a bum after what that dog did.

It wasn't much, in a way. She just jumped in and swam the creek. But all morning long not a dog had had the guts to try that torrent. They were all big and tough,

Sis

too—and Sis weighed thirty pounds. But when I called her, that's all she needed to make up her mind. In she went. I dug my heels into that mare, scared that I had drowned Sis. But just as I got there, out she climbed, fifty yards downstream. She gave herself a quick shake and was out ahead again, bird-hunting.

The dogs worked the bird field out and had a find apiece, but there wasn't any doubt as to who had won.

I was rubbing Sis dry with a croker sack when they told me she took first. And as they turned away, Adams muttered, "Damnedest little dog I ever see." And I thought I'd remember that to tell old man Clarke.

When I got back next day, although it wasn't time for the mail yet, Clarke wasn't sitting on the front porch. This was a puzzle, and I couldn't figure out what had happened. I went inside, and there he sat, staring at the fire. Had his old bedroom slippers on, and I knew he hadn't even been to the fields that morning.

"Here's your champion bird dog," I said.

He looked up, sort of vacantlike. "Billy always said she'd make a good'un."

In the kitchen I could hear the cook singing low.

I asked, "You—heard anything?"

He shook his head. "Ain't heard nothing. Ain't going to. I cain't fool myself no longer. He ain't coming back." Clarke went over and got his work shoes and put them on. He said, heavy-like, "I want you to take Sis. No sense in keeping her around here, when she could be an enjoyment to somebody."

Well, there it was. She was mine, free.

Right then I should have thanked him and turned around and got out of there. And yet, I'm not sorry for what I done.

I said, "Wait till you hear what I got to say. Up yonder, I run into Olin Brand. He's got a son in the Navy, and they wrote him up as missing, just like your boy. Well, Olin and his wife held on to hope for about six months, and then they give up. One day, up come Olin, Jr., like he had just been around the corner. Seems like he had made it to some little island, and the natives nursed him well and kept him right there until he was rescued. Olin says you can't never tell, in this war."

Clarke was staring at me. "Made it to an island!"

"That's what he said."

"Didn't have no way to let anybody know!"

"That's the way it was."

"They ought not to have give him up," Clarke said. "You cain't ever tell until you know."

"I figure it that way."

Like I say, I guess I was crazy. But I'm still not sorry. Anyway, I rode off, and when I took a last look back, there on the porch lay the best bird dog I ever blew a whistle over, and there *he* sat, rocking and smoking, and waiting for his boy to come home.

Field Trial

The room was very quiet. The only sound was the occasional creaking of leather whenever old Burns MacGregor shifted his great body in the big black chair.

The wood fire in the fireplace had almost burned itself out. The lonesome shadows, closing in, seemed about to smother the little glow that was left.

Burns crossed his legs and stared at his boots—he still had on his hunting clothes—and tried to remember when in all his sixty-five years he'd been so miserable.

Esca, his daughter, was at the country-club supper with Kelly Chapman, whom Burns half liked and wholly distrusted. That, ordinarily, would make him at least uncomfortable.

But he was more than uncomfortable tonight, and the cause of it was his friend of forty years, Charley Flint.

Somewhere within its waxed maple case the electric clock chimed. Twelve o'clock. Burns looked at the table across the room. The chessboard was there with the men all placed, just as the servant, not knowing anything had happened, had prepared it after dinner. Beside one of the chairs was the old smoking stand that Charley liked. But there were no ashes in it tonight.

Burns went over the whole episode again. Bojay had pointed. Charley Flint had said, "Your shot." Burns had walked in. The bird got up, flying low. Burns found it along the over barrel of his gun. Now that he thought of it, there was a faint recollection of Bojay somewhere in that picture—Bojay, who should have been back there stanch on his point. Then the detonation, and Bojay writhing in the brush with three tiny punctures in his neck just beginning to fill.

Within a minute, of course, the dog was up, eager to be hunting again. But during that minute they hadn't known he'd ever get up again, and the antagonism that had been growing for weeks reached its zenith. Recognizing the bitter silence with which Flint watched the dog handler examine the dog, Burns guessed then that he and Flint would never be friends again.

Always known as a fair man, Burns tried now to find that somehow he was to blame. He *was* a poor shot. But Bojay had broken on the flush.

Even as he tried to reason it all out, Burns knew that the shooting of Corduroy Bojay was only an incident that had crystallized the steadily growing unfriendliness.

The clock sounded again. Burns got up and put a piece of pinewood on the fire.

He heard the click of a door. Voices came nearer as Esca and Kelly Chapman approached by way of the four living rooms of varying degrees of formality that separated the entrance hall from the library.

They came in and talked to him while revolving in front of the awakening fire. Kelly's right palm was swathed with white.

"What's that bandage on your hand?" Burns asked Kelly.

"I got bit," Kelly answered.

"Bit?" exclaimed Burns, startled. "By whom?"

Esca said, "His dog, Jake, bit him."

"Some day that old badger's going to bite me once too often," Kelly said mildly.

"I'd think once would be too often," Burns suggested.

"Didn't you ever hear about the time Jake bit a man uptown?" Esca asked smiling. "The police had Kelly shut him up to watch for symptoms, but Kelly said if the so-and-so were rabid, then he was too, because Jake had bitten him a half-dozen times."

"I don't see why you keep a dog like that," Burns told Kelly.

"I don't either," Kelly answered. "The old son of a gun."

WHEN KELLY MADE ANOTHER revolution in front of the fire, Burns began subjecting him to the cold analysis of a watchful parent. Kelly was built like an oarsman, long-muscled and rangy. He was brown-haired, easygoing, and almost handsome.

If what one heard were true, he was inclined to be versatile. They said he was a crack bird shot, and that he played near-par golf. He was supposed even to have delivered a baby once. Out hunting, he had heard groans coming from a cabin, and found inside a woman in labor. Her husband had gone for the doctor, but there wasn't time to wait. So Kelly had delivered the child. The fellow, the said, could do anything.

Anything, that is, but work for a living. Kelly's livelihood was in writing outdoor magazine articles. That couldn't be called work, thought Burns, who before coming to Georgia had been a most energetic automobile manufacturer. He could see nothing, in fact, which proved that Kelly wasn't a fortune hunter. And still, money was far from Esca's only attraction.

Burns gazed upon her red-gold hair and straight teeth and chorus-girl figure. She was the type her mother had been. Nothing at all like himself; fortunately, for he was a great tenpin of a man, with huge shoulders, a size-eight head that was almost bald, and long, thin, big-boned legs. Undoubtedly Esca was lovely. Kelly might honestly love her. But there were other possibilities, and they had to be faced.

When Kelly had gone, Esca came back into the library. Burns saw something in her eyes that had never been there before.

"What's happened to you?" he asked immediately.

Esca's smile was slightly tremulous. "I guess I might as well get it over with. I'm in love."

"Chapman?"

"Yes."

Field Trial

Burns said, "Is it one of the reciprocal things, or the other kind?"

"He loves me."

"Talks marriage?"

"Yes."

BURNS LIFTED HIS BIG, top-heavy body from the chair and walked to the window. Outside, the night was opaque and a little ominous. Burns thought: Am I right about Chapman, or wrong? I may be wrong. But if I'm right, my daughter's in danger of ruining her life. Which would hurt her least—to lose a man she loves, or to marry a man who doesn't honestly love her?

Esca came to him determinedly, "Say something. I've got to know what you think."

Burns couldn't hold it in any longer. His massive head came up, and indignation amplified his voice. "Esca, I think Chapman would marry any acceptable girl with money!"

For a moment they looked at each other. Esca's eyes filled, but no tears overflowed. Burns realized then that she had never been sure about Chapman's sincerity herself. He felt very sorry for his daughter.

"I guess I could be wrong," he said gently.

"I wish I had some way of knowing that you are," Esca answered. She paused at the door. "Do I see him any more?"

"That's up to you," Burns said.

He put the chessboard and men away, and turned out the lamps. For a few minutes he stood there, staring into the flickering fire. Then he turned and slowly walked out to go to bed.

Charley Flint and Burns McGregor had often been pointed out as friends that would never part.

Burns had a sort of protective attitude toward Flint, like an older brother's. When they were vacationing together, Burns always insisted on doing the dirty work, and at parties he kept the servants hopping attendance to Flint. His attitude might have been due to the fact that Flint was only a normal-sized man, while he was a hulking fellow. Too, Flint had a couple of minor disorders. He was almost deaf in one ear, and when he was angry he stammered.

But no one could take better care of himself than the wiry, snow-haired Charley Flint. He had much of the physical vigor that had been with him in his Princeton days when he played what they called football then. As for his stammering, it was rarely heard. Rather than stammer, Flint would clamp his jaw in angry silence. He never had been a jocular man. When he shut up tight it was time to think back and see what you'd said.

Charley Flint's retirement from his publishing business had been voluntary. Burns, though, had retired on doctor's orders. He came to south Georgia one winter and stayed at Flint's winter home. Flint tried to interest him in hunting, but he never really got a kick out of the sport until one day a setter pup somebody had given him pointed his first covey of birds. That did it. From that proud moment on, Burns McGregor was a bird-dog man too.

Within a month, at a cost of two hundred thousand dollars, he had bought an estate which included a lovely, rambling white house of some thirty-odd rooms, and stables, laundry, kennels, a bonnet-bordered lake for ducks and bass, and ten thousand acres of Grade-A quail land. When the setter puppy died of distemper, Burns started looking around to replace him, and ended up by acquiring a string of fifteen high-class pointers and setters led by Beau Dupree's Iamonia Willie who, they told him, was as good a dog as Flint's famous young pointer, Corduroy Bojay.

Both men thought there was something poetic about their love of bird dogs and hunting. Now, in the afternoon of their lives they would reach the ultimate in companionship. But somehow it hadn't worked out that way.

They hadn't reckoned on the strange alchemy that takes place in a man's blood when he becomes a bird-dog owner, making him, where dogs are concerned, proud and prejudiced, and unreasonable beyond any understanding.

Within two weeks Burns admitted to himself that the afternoons he enjoyed most were the ones in which his expensive Llewellin outhunted Flint's pointer, and that he felt a fiendish pleasure every time Flint's dog made a mistake—which wasn't too often.

The two dogs were evenly matched. Bojay was a young dog. His virtues were speed and boldness. His slight unsteadiness and his tendency sometimes to false-point were young-dog faults; he'd outgrow them. Willie was a hard-working veteran; his experience made up for the extra bit of range that Bojay had over him. Willie would rarely make the error Bojay did that Monday afternoon, for instance.

The dog handler had come pounding down the woods road, waving his hat. "Point!" he shouted. "Bojay's got 'em near that rail fence by the benne field."

The two hunters spurred their horses. Presently they saw the big, keg-chested pointer frozen in his best picture-book point. Fifty yards behind him the point was being stylishly honored by Willie. A sight to make any sportsman's pulse rise.

The hunters took their fifteen-hundred-dollar overunders from the saddle scabbards and dismounted. But there weren't any birds. When they walked in for the covey flush a rabbit scuttled out.

Burns grinned. Flint saw him, his jaw muscles tightened, and he very conspicuously said nothing.

When Bojay pointed again thirty minutes later, Burns muttered, "I hope he's got birds this time."

Charley's lips moved twice before any sound came. "Don't worry. He has," he said coldly.

He did have. In fact, the rabbit point was the only mistake Bojay made that day. And he found six coveys of birds to the blue-ticked setter's three.

"Willie must not have been feeling right today," Burns conjectured, when their tired horses trotted through the purple dusk to the kennel house.

"They all have off days," Flint agreed, a little too magnanimously. "Then, too, Willie's not as young as he used to be."

Field Trial

"Why, he's just six years old—in his prime."

"I prefer a younger dog," Charley said calmly. "How about chess tonight?"

As the days passed, slurs like that began to be taken as deliberate insults. Antagonism seemed ever to lie close, appearing with increasing frequency.

Then came a dusk in which they returned from their hunting no longer friends. Twenty minutes before, Burns had accidentally shot Flint's dog.

At the kennel house they dismounted. Burns started to lift Bojay into the back of Flint's car, but Flint stepped quickly forward.

"I'll put him in," he said.

"Of course," Burns said. He turned away, then faced the car again. He'd make one more attempt at friendliness: "Coming over tonight?"

Flint didn't answer. Jaws clamped, he drove off.

Burns stood there for a moment, his finger tips twitching. Then he turned and stamped angrily into the kennel house.

The days that followed were bad. Occasionally Burns saw Charley Flint in town. They would murmur polite "hellos" and pass on. But the nights, of course were worse. For one thing, there was no chess. Nobody seemed to play chess nowadays.

Esca stayed home more than usual, and tried to pretend that she wasn't unhappy, but she was no actress. They weren't much comfort to each other.

Burns didn't see Kelly Chapman until the morning he and Esca went to the hunting lodge of Harry Ledyard, a Georgian friend, for trapshooting. Charley Flint was in the crowd, too, but so were a lot of people.

When they saw Kelly Chapman go to the station to shoot, Burns asked Esca, "Have you told him yet?"

Esca shook her head slightly. "I asked him to give me two weeks to decide. The two weeks are up tomorrow."

Kelly had begun shooting. Burns watched a moment. "It's going to be—My lord, he hasn't missed one! I think I'll go over and watch this!"

Esca and Burns separated. Later they met at a spot that was precisely, they discovered, in the path of Kelly Chapman and Charley Flint, who were on their way to the lodge for cocktails. Burns was still so awed by Kelly's shooting that he failed to realize that the meeting created something of a situation.

Kelly looked at Esca and said soberly, "Tomorrow."

"Yes," Esca answered.

"Young man," blurted Burns in honest admiration, "that was splendid shooting. I'd give a lot to be able to equal it."

"Would you?" Kelly said. "I'm going out with Mr. Flint this afternoon to see if we can't get the kinks out of his shootin'. Why don't you come along?"

Because of Esca, Burns knew it wouldn't be wise. "Thanks, I'm afraid I can't. You see—" At that moment, he caught Flint's cold smile. Burns thought: The old fool thinks it's because of him that I'm not going! He said, "Well—why not?" I *will* go along. It's nice of you, Chapman."

"My kennels, at two," Flint informed him stiffly.

THE HUNTING WAGON WAS ready to go when Kelly arrived at Flint's kennel. Burns and Charley sat on the kennel-house porch, smoking and talking about the weather with forced cordiality.

Kelly opened the rumble seat of his little old car, and a faded-looking yellow-and-white setter stood up in the seat, yawned nervously, and jumped out. He was far from a handsome dog. For a setter, his head was too blocky, and his chest was too short and round, and his tail had a slight upturn that suggested indifferent ancestry.

Burns and Charley both leaned forward in amazement.

"What is that?" Charley asked.

Kelly said, "That's my dog, Jake. Don't try to pet him."

Jake, making a stiff-legged sniffing tour around the kennel, was causing excitement from the twenty-odd dogs behind the fence. But beyond curling his tail even farther over his back and lifting his thin neck feathers, he paid no attention to the clamor.

Kelly opened the door of the hunting-wagon dog cage, where Willie and Bojay whined eagerly, and called Jake. Jake trotted over, lifted his lip in a soundless snarl at Kelly, and jumped into the open door.

"Meanest bird dog I ever saw," Kelly said, shutting the door.

He needn't have said it, because immediately Jake tangled with Willie in a whirling mass of dog flesh and white teeth, with Bojay backed up in a corner taking bites at whichever one exposed anything.

"Stop 'em!" Burns shouted with his boulder-like jaw outthrust.

Kelly was trying to stop them. "*You,* Jake! Down, sir! *Down!*" The fighting slowed, and Jake managed to lie down. Willie was glad enough to have it over.

"You'll have to git that dog outa there, Mr. Chapman," Collins, the dog handler, said. "Reach in and grab him."

"You reach in and grab him," Kelly said. Collins backed hastily away. Jake lay on his belly, licking his mouth, watching Kelly, and emitting little growling grunts. "Just for that," Kelly told the dog, "you'll walk. Come out of there."

Jake came out. A few minutes afterwards, when the wagon and horses started, he followed at heel, occasionally giving longing glances toward the piny woods on either side.

"He's a grouchy hound," Burns said.

Kelly agreed. "He hates everybody. Including me. Reckon I should've shot him long ago, the damned old fool."

Burns and Charley looked at each other significantly, their hostility set aside long enough mutually to acknowledge an undesirable situation. Some hunt this was going to be.

The dogs were put down. Willie and Bojay hit the ground running, and bolted straight ahead until they were out of sight over a roll of land. Jake made a wide cast to the right.

Afield, Jake looked a good deal more like a bird dog. His stride was smooth and fast. His tail straightened and whipped in rhythmic circles. And he seemed actually to be halfway friendly.

Jake located the first covey. They found him couchant, belly to the ground, in a thatch of bull grass.

"What's he doing?" Charley asked.

"He's just pointing," Kelly answered.

KELLY GAVE THEM SOME hints on wing shooting. During the three minutes of the discourse, Jake didn't move.

They walked in for the flush. There was the thunder of the covey rise. Burns picked out a circling quail, fired, and was properly pleased to see the bird tumble.

Flint had missed. Kelly, in order to watch the shots, hadn't fired.

Jake went into the pine saplings and pounced upon Burns' fluttering bird. When he retrieved it, Burns, on a strange impulse, reached out to stroke the dog's blocky head. Immediately Jake's good humor vanished. He drew his head back and snarled viciously.

"Don't pet him," Kelly said.

"Yes," answered Burns. "I see."

THEY MOVED ON AND Kelly called Jake in close to hunt the singles. Quartering conscientiously, with his tail-tip whipping those continuous circles, Jake suddenly pivoted, read the wind for a split second, and stopped. In a half-sitting position, he pointed.

Flint said: "He'd never get to first base in a field trial."

"That's right," Kelly said.

Not long after Jake had finished methodically pinning down the scattered singles, Collins came riding hard through the woods.

"Willie's got a covey over by the lake!" he called.

"Now," Burns thought proudly, as they lifted their horses to a gallop, "we'll see a real bird dog work."

But when they had followed the winding road around a grassy hill roll, the Negro wagon driver reined in the mules and motioned to them.

"That old yellah dog's got birds agin," he said, grinning. "See 'im laying' yondah in that broom sage?"

They took only the covey rise shot so they could hurry to the other point. But when they got to Willie something had happened to the birds. When the hunters walked in for the flush, nothing happened; and Willie began to move his head slowly and look around.

"The birds ran," Kelly guessed. "He'll relocate 'em though. Go ahead, Willie."

Willie circled through the brush anxiously. Bojay and Jake came in and began quartering. But the birds seemed to have disappeared.

Then the Negro chuckled: "Yonder he goes agin, a-pointin'. That Jake dog foun' 'em."

The other dogs saw Jake and honored. He had unraveled the vagrant scent and located the birds not a hundred yards from Willie's original point.

The dogs were all working nicely. Willie and Bojay had a tendency to range in the same directions, as if they didn't share the hostility of their owners, but Jake, ever independent, worked alone.

Jake was a hunting fool, and there was no longer any denying it. He began increasing his covey finds. To Burns it seemed that Bojay and Willie couldn't find birds themselves because they spent most of their time honoring Jake's crazy and invariably accurate points.

Burns and Charley were no longer listening to Kelly's tips on shooting. They were too engrossed in watching his dog.

Jake would range out of sight for awhile, then circle in to get the hunters relocated and veer away again with that smooth setter stride. If he didn't appear for fifteen minutes it was time to go look for him. The chances were that they'd find him crouching in a sassafras thicket, or sitting near a cornfield corner so rigidly immobile that he might be dead, except that no dog would pick out such an uncomfortable position to die in. He pointed sitting, standing, crouching, and some other ways words for which haven't been invented; but the points all were alike in one respect—they all meant birds.

Jake didn't seem to be putting on any Sunday performance—his attitude was that of a dog doing his job and thinking nothing of it. Only once did he approach the spectacular. Charley Flint shot a bird that fell on the other side of a gully. Retrieving the bird, Jake slid down the steep side of the ditch. Almost to the bottom he stopped. Practically standing on his head, a dead bird in his mouth, Jake did a surprising thing. He pointed.

Everybody stood transfixed. A lump of clay dislodged by Jake's foot rolled into the brush at the foot of the gully. Immediately a cock quail drummed straight up, leveled off, and volplaned to the woods, and not a gun was raised to shoot.

An inexorable conviction came over Burns. He wanted that dog, and he was going to have him.

"Come on," Kelly called. "That old ham-head is crawling through the bushes like he's hasselin' a bird again."

AFTER DINNER THAT NIGHT Burns was nervous and impatient. He paced the floor and smoked Esca's brand of cigarettes, which he disliked, without noticing it. Finally he said to Esca:

"I'm running into town to see Kelly Chapman about a dog. Want to drive me? I'll be only a minute. You can wait outside."

They wore overcoats and went in the long black open car. Esca drove fast through the cold, fragrant, white-shadowed night.

Kelly's house was on the edge of town. Esca brought the car to a velvety stop and turned off the lights. Burns got out and crossed the lawn. Jake lay in the middle of the porch.

"Hello," Burns said. Jake growled.

Burns detoured around him and knocked on the door.

Field Trial

Kelly was surprised to see him. He led him into the living room, where a card table held a ramshackle typewriter and what seemed to be reams of scattered paper.

Burns didn't sit down or take off his overcoat. He stood in front of the fire, and said:

"Chapman, I won't waste words. I'd like to buy that dog out on the porch. How much?"

Kelly said, "I don't guess the old fool is for sale, Mr. McGregor."

Burns forgot his bartering instincts. "Chapman, I'll give you two hundred dollars for Jake."

"No," answered Kelly, grinning.

"Five hundred. Yes, a thousand," said Burns.

"No." The grin was wilting.

Burns stood up and wobbled his great head the way he used to at directors' meetings when he was tired of wasting time and was ready to settle the thing. "Chapman, listen to me: three thousand dollars."

Kelly's face was white. "I'm sorry."

Burns stared and there was anger in his face. "It's robbery, Chapman, but I want that setter. Name your price."

Kelly said, "You haven't got enough money to buy that setter."

Burns sank into a chair. He wondered if Kelly Chapman knew how much money he did have, then decided that it probably didn't matter. Disappointment sickened him. He'd never doubted that tomorrow he'd own a bird dog that would out-hunt Corduroy Bojay seven days a week.

As he sat there, half listening to Kelly's efforts to make conversation, Burns remembered Esca, waiting in the car. A thought that had been trying to form itself in his brain suddenly crystallized. *This* was the young man he had advised his daughter not to marry. Had Chapman's attitude a moment ago been that of a fortune hunter? Burns thought not.

On impulse he wrote on an envelope: *"Bearer has my okay as a son-in-law. Don't let him get away. I warn you, he's stubborn."*

He folded the envelope, and said:

"Chapman, Esca's out front. Will you be good enough to give this to her, and wait for an answer, if there is one?"

Kelly was obviously puzzled, but he didn't ask questions. When he was gone, Burns went out on the porch and sat down. In the darkness somewhere near, Jake kept softly growling. A vague loneliness crept over Burns.

There was a flash of lights, and a blue limousine turned into the drive of Kelly's little house. Charley Flint appeared at the porch steps, blinked at Burns, and stopped.

"It's no use, Charley," Burns said.

"So you've beat me to him," Flint answered. His wiry old shoulders sagged. "I hope he bites your leg off."

"Kelly wouldn't sell the dog—at any price."

Flint came closer. "Say that again."

"It's the truth. He wouldn't sell him at all."

"I never heard of such a thing," Flint answered, mystified.

"No…I wish I hadn't seen that dog hunt," Burns said, sadly. "He sure made fools of our dogs. And us, too, Charley."

"I guess he did, at that."

BURNS MOVED OVER SO Charley could have the post to lean against, and Charley sat down. Neither of them spoke. A cloud slid across the bright moon. Burns watched its shadow spread over the lawn. Behind them, Jake grunted, rose, and walked across the porch.

Burns was glad somebody was there to be disappointed with him. He was wondering what Charley was thinking, when he felt a hand on his bony knee, and Charley said:

"How about a little chess?"

Burns' head came up. "You're on."

They walked to Charley's car. "Is there someone with you?"

"Yes," Burns answered, "but when two people are planning a future, you can't bother them with a little thing like a chess game. Come on."

TROUBLE'S CHILD

Joe stood in four feet of water, watching the shark. When the shark was close, Joe stabbed at him with the oar, furiously. The fish roiled the water and retreated, then came back with an angry rush, the dorsal fin knifing the brine. Joe stabbed, and the oar splintered, and when he looked at it all the blade was gone except a ragged, sharp-pointed corner.

"Come again," Joe rasped.

The shark was coming. Joe felt the oar go in, puncture the tough filelike hide, and this time the shark did not come back. Joe waded slowly back to the boat.

He sat on the empty seine deck, his anger passing and giving way to cold sickness. He had found the mullet and circled them with his gill net. Then the two sharks came for the mullet, like hungry wolves, ripping to shreds the old net that was Joe's only possession worth mentioning, and leaving him helpless in the midst of the best mullet run in years.

They were still running; he could hear them now as he sat brooding, and he could see them flash in the moonlight. Finally he started back to Palmetto Creek, paddling as best he could with the one oar. It was slow going. He thought of old Jules, for whom he used to work; the night his party boat burned, old Jules had to row five miles in, against a running-out tide. Jules was the best friend Joe had, but nobody would deny that Jules hated to row a boat. Smart, Jules was, but lazy as a yard dog.

Presently a light showed. It took Joe another hour to reach the boat, a trim, business-like launch that rocked placidly on its hawser.

"Hello!" Joe shouted.

"All right?" answered a voice. A door opened and the tall silhouette of a man came on deck.

"I ain't got but just one oar," Joe said hesitantly. He didn't want to tell about punishing the shark, and have the man think he was a fool.

"We've got extra oars. How about some coffee?"

"Well...don't care if I do."

There were three men. The one named Kelly was in dungarees, with a bare chest the color of canvas, and the build of a pole vaulter. The second was a small man in handsome silver glasses; his name was Ackerman and his eyes were bright and shrewd. The man who brought the coffee was a giant one-eyed Negro named Little Fred.

"Nice night," Ackerman said.

"Awful nice."

Silence. Then Joe said, "Guess this is the investing boat."

"What? Yes. To investigate the Pelican claim."

"She sure went down, by grannies."

"I think we've found her. I'm going down in the morning and take a look," Kelly said. "Only thing, we're a bit short of help. Our other man took sick in Panama City."

Joe said hesitantly, "You couldn't use just any old body, I don't guess."

"Oh, I don't know. The job's not hard. I do all the diving, and Ackerman does the microscope and such stuff."

A catch came into Joe's throat. "If you could use a hard-shell Florida cracker, Mr. Kelly, I'd work like a fool, long as the job lasts."

"Why, sure, you'd do," Kelly said.

Joe fought with the temptation to keep his mouth shut, but he had to say it. "Wouldn't be fair not to tell it on m'self," he said unhappily. "I'm hard luck."

Ackerman and Kelly looked at him.

"Soon's *I* start monking around with something," Joe said bitterly, "the trouble is bound to commence."

"That's queer," Ackerman said politely. "But we'll take a chance."

"Can you run an outboard?" Kelly said. "We'll loan you ours. Bring our mail with you tomorrow. I'll start diving about ten."

THAT NIGHT JOE STAYED at bleak Fiddler's Cove, in the palmetto shack that he and his father had called home. Since his father's lingering illness had ended in death, Joe often lay on his pallet transfixed with an empty loneliness; listening to the nightly march of the armies of fiddlers on the dirty beach outside. Tonight he had a new job; yet he couldn't let himself get happy about it until he saw how it turned out.

"You ain't no child of mine," his father had often said. "You're trouble's child."

It looked that way, too. The old man—he was sixty-one when Joe was born—could go out by himself and come back with the boat riding low and heavy with mullet and sea trout; but when Joe went the fish weren't there, or a tarpon got in the gill, or a squall came upon them. Joe knew it was because he was along.

After his father had drunk his last swallow of rotgut swamp moonshine and died, Joe left and went to town, to Palmetto Creek, job hunting. He remembered his first encounter with Nellie Barnaby, who worked in Crabflake Myers' store. Everybody took for granted she would marry Crabflake, sometime or other, and they said she was sure lucky, because Crabflake owned just about everything in town worth owning. Nellie was smart, like old Jules Barnaby; but that's about the only way she took after him. Jules was lazy and dried up, with a scrawny neck and thin, undershot jaw that was usually clamped on a sulphurous old pipe. Nellie, though, was hardworking; and there wasn't a handsomer girl on the coast—she was full-fleshed, ripe, with eyes and lashes so black they looked purple.

Joe had gone into Crabflake's store that time for some sardines and crackers—he hadn't eaten all day. Nellie looked at him and at his hair, which hadn't been cut in two months, and said, "That must be one of them new page-boy bobs."

He apologized, "Me and the old man gen'rally cut each other's hair, but he was abed fer two months. Last week he went and died."

"I'm sure mighty sorry to hear about it," she said.

Joe got his sardines and crackers and retired to the back of the store to eat. Nellie sold a fisherman some shear pins, and after a while she came back to where Joe was.

"I'm fixing to put in and try to get me a job," he confided.

"You ought to get some of that hair took off afore you go job hunting," she said. "When Crabflake comes we can go out back and I'll give you a haircutting."

"Shore Lord thank you, but I wouldn't put you to that trouble."

"Wouldn't be no trouble, not the first." She smiled. "Bet you ain't half bad-looking, with that hair off."

"Aw, foot," he said.

She did a good job, but he was glad when it was over. He had never had a pretty girl standing that close to him, and he felt a queer uneasiness, almost fright.

First place he went was Jules Barnaby's house, because he knew Nellie was not there and might be later. Jules came to the door and howled the yard dogs quiet.

Joe said, "Don't guess you want no wood chopped, ner your yard roke."

Jules took his old pipe from his compressed angular jaw, and looked at him with sharp, weather-squinted old eyes. "You couldn't be old Ned Bullock's boy, could you?"

"That's right."

"Well, now. Mighty sorry to hear old Ned went to his reward," Jules said, walking to the front gate. "Don't need my yard roke, bud, ner no wood chopped." He squinted at the sun. "You know anything about cleaning up a boat?"

"Never monked around a fine boat like the Pelican, if that's what you got in mind," Joe said hesitantly, "but I reckon the man that learnt had to try."

"It's about an hour o'sun. You got time to git started on her. Party fishing's been so poorly I took to mullet fishing 'er some. She stinks like a Greek sponger. Too danged lazy to clean 'er m'self."

THAT'S HOW JOE STARTED working for Jules. The pay hadn't been much, but then there wasn't much in party fishing, with the fish not running right. Sometimes Joe felt that he didn't help matters, being hard luck the way he was. Then one night Jules came staggering into the house doggone near dead from rowing five miles in against the tide, and said the Pelican had burned and sunk right in the river channel. That had ended *that* job.

Now, though, he had another one. Maybe he wasn't as hard luck as he used to be. He cranked the motor and started in to Palmetto Creek for the insurance boat's mail. The day was sharp and clear, and life moved in the green bay. Presently he saw frightened minnows jumping. Silver knives lanced through the water—mackerel. At last the mackerel had come! And Jules Barnaby's boat lay on the salt sand of the river bottom.

Brag Dog and Other Stories

Nellie Barnaby stood in the doorway of the store as he passed on the way to the two-by-four post office for the insurance boat's mail. She smiled and waved at him; he lifted one finger, smiled painfully and hurried on. She was still there when he came back with the letters, and she called, "Got a letter from your girl, looks like."

"Shucks," he said, "this ain't mine. B'longs to that fella Kelly, on the investment boat." He stopped a moment, proudly. "Got a job with 'em."

"Sure enough!" she said, frowning.

"Don't guess I'll hold on to it fer long, though," he said, cheerfully.

Nellie stood in the doorway, watching him in silence, still frowning a little. He had a curious feeling that he'd like the conversation to continue, that he was almost enjoying it.

"Well," he said, "guess I'd a-better be ramblin'." He stuck his toe in the sand and waited, but Nellie said nothing. He looked at the sun. Hardly eight o'clock yet. No hurry, really. But Nellie had quit talking altogether, looked as though. "Well," Joe said, "guess I'd a-better be ramblin'."

A man's voice said, "Busy, ain't you?" It was Crabflake Myers, sarcastic as always, who had come up on the porch with Jules Barnaby.

"Yes," Nellie said. "Joe's might busy. Got him a new job."

"Hey?" said Jules, jerking his gaunt jaw around. He was fretful and jumpy since his boat burned.

"He's helping the claim investigators," Nellie said.

Crabflake stepped down off the porch and confronted Joe. He was a big man, bulky around the shoulders. He was mad and his eyes seemed to give off sparks like an emery wheel.

"You working on that yonder insurance boat?" he demanded.

"Shore am," Joe said, wondering at their anger. "We start a-divin' at ten er so."

Jules clumped down and joined them. "How come you done it, bud?" he asked.

Crabflake glared. "Him and Judas Iscariot. Two of a kind."

"I got to earn my bread," Joe argued.

"Fine way to earn it, after what all Jules has did for you."

"Shucks a-mighty," Joe protested. "It ain't like Jules went and fired his boat a-purpose."

A look passed between Crabflake and old Jules. Jules said, "Them insurance companies don't send men around to see if they can find cause to pay out more than was asked, bud."

"They always look about when somebody gets burnt out," Joe protested.

"They'll be dang glad to find excuse not to pay me."

Joe shifted uneasily. "Hadn't though about it that-a-way, Jules," he said slowly. "It'll just about put me into bankrupture, but if you say so I'll give the job plumb up."

"What you do is strictly your own lookout," Jules said acidly. "It don't matter to me; not none. See?"

Joe saw; saw that he had hurt his old friend deeply. But, anyway, he would take the mail out to the insurance boat, and tell them he was quitting. Maybe that would make Jules and Nellie feel better toward him. He didn't care what Crabflake Myers thought.

He stepped up on the store porch and started to go inside, remembering that he would be late getting back, if he had to row in. He would need some food.

"Wait," Crabflake growled. "Where you think you going?"

"In here."

"No, you ain't. You keep out of my store."

"I was going to buy something," Joe said. "Don't you want my business?"

"Not no Judas business," Crabflake said, and Joe couldn't help thinking he saw approval in Nellie's eyes. "Come on, git right on out of there."

"Ain't no call to git horsy," Joe said, feeling that Crabflake was perhaps within his rights, but still not wanting to be bossed around. He began to get sort of mad, like he had when the sharks tried to run right on over him and tear up his gill net.

Crabflake stepped up on the porch. "You goan git out, er not?"

"I ain't ready."

"Well, you're goin', ready er no!" Crabflake's big hands seized him, and the next thing Joe knew he was sprawling in the rough white shells of the road. Crabflake was on the porch, glaring down on him. Jules was gaping, pipe sagging. Nellie was at the doorway, holding both hands to her mouth.

"Guess I had it a-coming," Joe said, painfully getting up. "But some day I may have me some property, and if I do I shore hope to catch you on it just once."

Crabflake snorted. Nellie turned and disappeared into the store.

The sun was bright upon the water when Joe arrived. Maybelle, the insurance launch, had swung on her anchor with the incoming tide. The fellow named Kelly wore bathing trunks, and the giant Negro, Little Fred, worked among the hose and valves of the diving apparatus.

Kelly greeted him with none of the cordiality he had shown last night: "Why didn't you tell us you worked for Barnaby until the boat sank?"

"It never once come to mind," Joe answered.

"Kid," Kelly said ominously, and Joe saw that he could be very tough when necessary, "if you got some fast stuff in mind, you come to a bad place."

"All I wanted was a job!" Joe said.

"Okay. But you watch your step, boy. And when I'm below, *you* keep away from that pump, see?"

Doggone it to hell, Joe thought, now it's *them* a-rantin' at me. Indignantly, he said, "You-all act like you think Jules fired his boat hisself."

"Being suspicious is what we get paid for," Kelly said, harshly. "And this time it ain't hard to be suspicious. When a man's broke and hard up, and his business ain't getting any better, a big fire can come in mighty handy. Especially when ten thousand in insurance money would put him on top of the world."

"Jules never burnt that boat up!"

"Well, I hope he didn't. But we'll see. Meanwhile, bud—be careful."

Ackerman fastened the helmet around Kelly's shoulders and Little Fred began pumping. Kelly, in shorts and the helmet and leaden shoes, held a watertight flashlight in one hand. A hand ax was strapped around his waist. He climbed over the gunwale onto the rope ladder.

Suddenly, from somewhere, there was a sharp, flat echo. Kelly's helmeted head fell against the gunwale with a heavy clunk. His hands clutched weakly, slipped, and he slid down into the water. Ackerman grabbed the helmet lines and held him afloat. Little Fred jumped to the side of the boat, his one eye wide in fright.

"Keep pumping!" Ackerman yelled at him.

Joe and Ackerman hauled the weak figure aboard and removed the diving helmet. A red hole, bubbling with blood, was on Kelly's smooth, tanned back.

"Get the cabin between us and that north shore," Kelly said weakly.

They did that, and Ackerman yelled to Little Fred, "Haul that anchor in!"

"Wait, Ackerman," Kelly said painfully. "That slug missed my backbone, else I'd be croaked. I ain't bleeding at the mouth or nose, so maybe it didn't hit a lung either, some way." He winced as Ackerman daubed the wound with antiseptic. "The Maybelle ought to stay right here, over the boat Barnaby burned. Anyway, that twenty-two-horse outboard would take me in faster."

His hard, cold blue eyes fastened on Joe.

"This guy can run me in."

"You damn' fool," Ackerman said, "don't you know he's the one that tipped them off when you would start diving?"

"Sure," Kelly said. His hand lifted Ackerman's big automatic from the holster, and Joe saw the hideous muzzle swing toward him and stop. "Put me in the boat facing stern. I'll handle Mr. Bullock!"

Big Fred lifted the heavy motor as if it were papier-mache instead of steel, and fastened it onto the stern piece of the small boat. They laid Kelly on a mattress in the front of the boat, facing stern.

"All right,' Kelly said between his teeth, holding the gun steadily on Joe.

Joe turned on the gas, primed the carburetor and pulled the starting cord. The motor spat, then broke into a drumming exhaust hum, and the boat began skimming along the top of the water.

So now, Joe thought miserably, both sides thought he was a traitor.

"Listen," he said, 'I guess it was me told them, all right, but I shore never meant to start nothing like this."

Kelly, lying on his side with a pillow under his head, was pale. But those ice-blue eyes didn't waver. Nor did the automatic. He said nothing.

"I come out this morning with my mind sot to give the job up," Joe said above the motor hum. "But I ain't aquittin' now, after the way they're a-doin'."

Kelly's lips moved. Joe saw what he said, although he couldn't hear: "You're quitting, all right."

"Well, put that gun down. I ain't goan bother you."

Kelly's lips moved again: "I'll keep it."

Then his head sagged, and fell forward. The pistol slid to the bottom of the boat. Joe retrieved it, and put the pillow under Kelly's head.

"Hard guy, ain't you?" Joe said.

It was night when Joe got back to the Maybelle, floating fitfully in the moonlit water. The silhouette of Ackerman rose on the deck. Something ominous shone in his hand.

"Who's there?" he asked.

"Me, Joe."

"What is it?" he asked. "How about Kelly?"

Joe climbed aboard. "He's in the hospital at Tallahassee. The doctor said the bullet busted a rib and grazed his barnacle tubes. Said he would be gittin' along tol'able well fore long if didn't no information sot in." Joe handed him a piece of folded newspaper. "I brung you this."

Ackerman opened the newspaper and turned a flashlight on the piece of lead that lay in its wrinkles.

"Did that simple ass trust you to bring this bullet back?" Ackerman asked.

"Not exactly. The doctor fetched it out of Kelly. Kelly didn't know I got it. Kelly didn't know nothing at all, after we left here. He cold-out fainted a mile up the river. I could've fed him to the stingarees easy as not, if I was the outlaw you-all make me out."

Ackerman stared at him thoughtfully. Finally he said, "That is so, isn't it?" He seemed relieved to be able to trust Joe. His spectacles beamed briefly. He beckoned Joe into the cabin, where a muted radio played Hungarian gypsy music.

"What I puzzle about," Joe said, "is like this: if Jules' boat went down plumb natural, how come anybody cares a durn if you-all take a look at it?"

"Sure, that's it. The answer is that the Pelican was burned for the insurance," Ackerman said grimly. "But how the hell am I going to prove it with Kelly piled up in a hospital for a month?"

"If it don't take a man with a big lot of sense," Joe said, "I'll go down in that there helmet outfit."

Ackerman looked at him eagerly. "If you feel that way, you can try tomorrow," he said. "Looks like now you might find out something pretty ugly about Jules Barnaby."

"If Jules is the kind of man to sink a boat, and shoot an honest man doing his job, looks like it might just as well be me that finds it out as anybody," Joe said.

THE LIGHT OF THE morning sun filtered down through twenty-five feet of water to where Joe walked ponderously around the blackened remains of the Pelican. His first uneasiness at using the diving helmet had passed, and he had almost got used to the rubbery, unnatural smell of the air that Little Fred sent pulsing down the hose.

Overhead, a twelve-foot sand shark cruised, his cat eyes staring in uneasy curiosity, before he disappeared in the murkiness. Joe's foot struck something. Half imbedded in the sand was a fire ax. He recognized it as the one that had been in the Pelican's cabin. How had it got outside the boat?

Then he saw how. In the Pelican's once-graceful bow, a crude hole gaped. A hole hacked open with an ax. Joe felt a deep shock. There wasn't any doubt now—Jules Barnaby had sunk the Pelican.

Dazed, Joe made his way aboard the charred boat. Even in its unnatural blackness, he felt a funereal familiarity with the vessel that had once been the pride of the Palmetto Creek coast. There was a scarred corpse of Jules' four-horsepower outboard motor that had towed many a skiff of Georgia fishermen about the grassy trout flats. The great bass spotlight that would pierce the coast darkness no longer had a polished sheen but perched dully, its curved shell burned into a nobby lump. Upon the floor, by the place the dresser used to be, lay a brownish something that he recognized as Jules' ponderous old watch.

Joe went outside and found the ax. Evidence—on Nellie's father. He got ready to ascend, but a certain uneasiness came over him. Something was not just right. He had overlooked something. He groped for an idea that would not materialize. Finally he walked around the boat again, puzzled.

It was on this march that he stepped on the sting ray. His only sensation was a sudden numbing pain just above the knee, a shocking pain. He could almost see the four-inch filthy brown barb embedded in his leg, and the sting ray swerving away into the darkness.

Joe was startled, and the pain already throbbed; but he was not surprised, because when you're just naturally hard luck you take misfortunes for granted. More than anything else, he was mad, because he figured he had been on the point of discovering what it was about the Pelican that he had overlooked.

Now the leg was hurting, and it was hard to think of anything else. He ought to hurry to a doctor and get the barb cut out. But that would mean several days in bed—the barb *could* cost him a leg if he wasn't careful. By that time the thing that had been rising in his mind would have sunk again, irrevocably. He just had to keep tugging at it.

When Ackerman lifted the helmet, Joe kept standing waist deep in the water, so they couldn't see the blood or the sting-ray barb.

"How about getting me my old slicker?" he asked. "Sort of coldy."

Ackerman helped him get his arms into the sleeves. "Where'd you get that fire ax?" he asked.

"Outside the boat." Joe swallowed hard. Now it had to come. "They was a hole in the hull. Cut from the outside with an ax."

"So," said Ackerman, eyes narrowed. "Get on your clothes and come below."

The leg wasn't bleeding much, but the flesh was slightly blue around the brown nub of the barb. Joe split a handkerchief and tied it just below the wound, to absorb the slight bleeding. Then, he painfully dressed and went below, still trying to remember what he had seen under water that didn't seem right.

On the apron of Ackerman's microscope lay the misshapen lead bullet that had been in Kelly's back. Ackerman said, "You know anybody that's got a .30-06 rifle around here?"

"A .30-06?" Joe asked, startled. Then he heard his voice say, "Jules used to have one. Don't know whether he's still got it er no."

There was a silence. Ackerman wiped his glasses with his handkerchief. "Come on. You and me and the sheriff are going to have a little talk with Jules Barnaby."

THE TALK TOOK PLACE in Crabflake Myers' store, where they found Jules. Crabflake was there too, and Nellie. Nellie looked at Joe only once, and her glance was hostile and deeply hurt. Jules' face was a dull red under the salty tan, and occasionally he glanced at Joe angrily as he talked:

"And like I say, she caught from that plague-gone gas stove in the galley. I never seen the fire till too late, being alone and at the wheel. I done the purely best I could, and finally I seen it weren't no use."

"Then what?"

"Like I told you. I got in the rowboat and rowed five miles home, against a running-out tide that near wore my arms out."

Ackerman went out and got the fire ax. "How come you threw this overboard?"

Old Jules licked his lips. Crabflake stared at the ax with bulging eyes. "I—I—" Jules muttered.

"Where'd that ax come from?" Crabflake demanded.

Ackerman said, "Joe found it near the bow of the boat. He also found what the ax had been used for—to knock a hole in the Pelican's hull!"

Jules glared at Joe, his gnarled hands trembling in a furious anger. Joe thought he was going to spring at him, but he didn't.

Jules said, finally, "All right. Now that our young detective has gathered his evidence so good, I'll explain how it was. I seen the boat was a goner, unless I done something drastic. Excited like I was, I thought I might sink her and put out the fire. Be cheaper to raise her than buy a new boat. Only, when I busted that hole in her, she still didn't go down. Afterward, I happened to think how it would sound to the insurance company, that hole knocked in the hull, and I decided to keep my mouth shut about that part. I didn't know an insurance company would go paying a young smart aleck to test an honest man's word!" he snapped, scowling at Joe.

Joe waited until a tremor of electric pain in his leg passed, then said, "What honest man went and shot Mr. Kelly in the back?"

"Done what?" Jules gasped.

Ackerman said, "Where's that .30-06 rifle of yours?"

Jules mumbled, "I sold it."

"To whom?"

"Try and find out!"

Ackerman shrugged. "You're not helping your case any. Your story would hang together better if Kelly hadn't been shot. Sheriff, I think we're going to have to ask for a couple of indictments for this man. And if you'll find the rifle, I'll prove it's the one that fired the shot."

"We'll fight it in court!" Crabflake yelled. "He's due that money, every cent!"

"Wait a minute," Ackerman said. "What's your ticket in this?"

"You won't cheat Jules Barnaby out o' that payment, not if I can help it!" Crabflake said, his little eyes red with anger.

A queer feeling came to Joe above the numbing throb in his leg. There was something that they had missed. Then, abruptly, it came to him, all in one piece.

"If you want to arrest somebody," Joe said. "Crabflake Myers has got Jules' rifle. I remember, now that Crabflake starts yelling about money. Crabflake took the rifle as part interest on what Jules owes him."

"You shut up!" Crabflake screamed, launching himself across the room at Joe. Joe stuck out his good leg and let Crabflake rim himself on it good and hard, then while Crabflake was still gasping, he stood up, balanced himself precariously on the good leg and loosed a solid left fist at Crabflake's bulldog jaw. Crabflake stumbled back against a counter.

Before anything else could happen, Joe's whirling brain tried to interpret a strong pressure of bare cool arms around him, then Nellie's voice: "Leave Joe alone! Can't you see he's taken sick?"

"Daughter," old Jules quavered angrily, "unloosen yourself from around that."

Nellie obeyed, but stood beside the wavering Joe, steadying him. The sheriff likewise steadied the dazed Crabflake. Ackerman studied Joe, and said, "What's the matter, Joe?"

Joe sat down heavily and answered, "Let me finish, first." They were all looking at him. "I got it all straightened out in my mind, now. Jules owes Crabflake two thousand dollars he borrowed a long time ago. Crabflake knew he'd git paid if Jules collected the insurance money. That's how come he shot at Kelly, I guess."

"He's crazy!" Crabflake said.

"You got Jules Barnaby's .30-06 rifle?" the sheriff asked ominously.

"Yes, but I wasn't tryin' to hit that feller, just scare him. We knew that insurance company would try to squirm out of payin', if they found that hole."

"I don't blame 'em," the sheriff said, snapping the cuffs on Crabflake.

"Well, I wouldn't be too sure," Joe said slowly. "I got that sort of figured out, too." He drew a misshapen piece of metal from his pocket. Jules' watch. It was this watch and the outboard motor, he knew now, that had stuck in his mind. "Look at that watch. I found it in the boat. Jules' granddaddy used to own it. You wound it with a little key. Jules was sure proud of it."

They all stared at him. Ackerman said, impatiently, "Well?"

"Don't look to me like a man planning to burn up his boat would 'a' left a prize watch like that aboard," Joe said. "Looks to me like Jules was telling the truth about the boat."

"He could have just forgot the watch," Ackerman said.

"I guess he could," Joe said. "But knowing how bad Jules hates to row a boat, I don't believe he forgot that there outboard motor I seen on the bottom. Smart as Jules is, if he'd been planning all along to burn the Pelican he'd've found reason to have that motor on the skiff. Five miles of rowing against a tide ain't Jules' idea of fun, ner mine neither. But Jules was too busy trying to put out that fire to wonder about gitting home. Don't it kind of look that way?"

Ackerman looked startled. "Maybe we better look around a little more."

Nellie gave Joe's arm an excited squeeze.

Joe stood up and his leg trembled and buckled, and he fell. "Fell down," he said apologetically.

IT WAS SEVERAL WEEKS later when Joe broke the news to the boys down at Mullins' fish house. Joe walked with a stick.

Trouble's Child

"Looks like I just naturally ain't hard luck any more," Joe said happily. "Getting me a wife that can do nigh anything, from cutting bait to cutting hair, and gitting a job on Jules' fine new boat. Yes, sir. Goodby, trouble."

He limped out, hunting for somebody else to tell.

"Shucks a-mighty," one of the fishermen said. "He thinks his troubles is over, and him just 'fore a-gittin' married."

The Sounds of Geese

The wild geese flew over high, the November sun momentarily glinting on the white of their chins and tails. Joe Bullock looked up from his painting and watched them briefly. "Them's late gitting here," he thought. Three skiffs passed the Pelican II, the gill nets piled on their stern decks. Without breaking the steady rhythm of their rowing, the men nodded as they moved by, partly to Joe, but mostly to Nellie Barnaby.

The fishermen turned in at Jules Barnaby's fish-house dock with their catch, and Joe said, "Nellie, I been thinking."

Nellie Barnaby sat on the rail of her father's party-fishing cruiser boat and watched a niggergoose feeding under an overhang of bay brush.

"Nellie," Joe said, "ain't no sense in you marrying me."

"Ain't it?" she said. "How come?"

"You don't want to marry no old hardluck somebody like me."

"Thought you said you wasn't hard luck no more, after gitting me promised to you," Nellie said. "You ain't backing out, are you, Joe?"

"No. Ain't nothing like that. It just looks like everybody's making money but me. Party fishing's plumb done, you might say, until spring er so."

"You could go gill netting."

"Ain't got no gill net."

"Pa'd let you have the loan of one."

Joe shook his head. "Ain't fishing with no borrowed net. Hard luck the way I am, a shark'd git in it, er a sawfish, and then I wouldn't just only be broke, I'd be into debt. Then I couldn't never build you no little bumbalow."

"The way the fish are running now," Nellie insisted, "you could pay for a net in one night."

"I'm scared if I went gill netting, it'd put a stop to the whole dadgone run, and then wouldn't nobody catch no fish. Be dog, if that ain't the truth. I ain't got the heart to mess up everybody's moneymaking."

"Ah, foot, Joe," Nellie said in disappointment.

Joe's brush smoothly spread the paint over the scars the Pelican II had received in the September storm, when the water had been knee-deep in Crabflake Myers' store. Joe didn't look up, avoiding the hurt in Nellie's dark eyes, until Walt Minton called him.

Walt Minton was the preacher and the best red fisherman in town. He stood below them on the pier, with his little outboard resting on a croker-sack pad on his shoulder.

"Let me have a skiff, Joe," he said. "Them reds is going to be hongry out in the mouth of the river. I aim to harelip a few." Noticing the downcast manner of them, he said, "What ails you-all? Ain't had no disagreement, I hope."

"Everybody's making money but us," Nellie said. She nodded toward her father's fish house, where the latest catch was being weighed.

The preacher had been worried during this period of prosperity, for the jooks were getting too much business. He said, "Too much money is like a rattlesnake."

"Is that the truth?" Joe asked.

"The Lord's own sweet truth."

"We don't want too much," Nellie said. "Just some."

"Ain't you working for Jules, Joe?"

"Yes, but he cain't afford to pay me nothing much, except when they's fishing parties er goose hunters to take out. Trout and reds, they've come into the river now and don't nobody need a guide to find them. As for goose hunting, ain't many folks got the guts for that."

"Guess old John Ulm was one of the few shore-enough goose hunters, rest his soul," the preacher said, tightening the outboard's clamps on the transom of the skiff. "Just come from a visit to his widow's. I been mighty proud of Miss Gussie. Took her sorrow bravest I ever seen. Held up fine, to now. But I'm afraid she's done sagged a mite, last few days. I guess Crabflake Myers has been a comfort to her—he's been solacing her every time I visited her."

"She got the insurance money yet?" Nellie asked.

"Nope, she ain't, and it's just too bad. Everybody knows poor John is dead, rest him. But you cain't blame the insurance company for wanting some kind of evidence. Guess Miss Gussie'll have to wait a few years, till John's declared dead, legal."

"I hope Crabflake Myers won't be neglecting his Christian attention to her when he sees the money ain't coming for a spell," Nellie said, thoughtfully, after the preacher had motored away from the dock and downriver.

"That ain't no way to talk," Joe admonished.

"I hope you don't think Crabflake's visiting that mean cat of a Miss Gussie Ulm for fun."

THEY SAID JOHN ULM had known as well as anybody that September was no time to go sailing off to Cedar Keys in that little sloop of his, but they figured that he had got another bait of listening to Miss Gussie and took off for a rest, and that he'd rather risk a good many afternoon squalls than stay home with his wife on one of her quarrelsome spells.

But the way it turned out, it wasn't just an afternoon squall that came up. A real storm cut loose, with a seventy-mile wind that blew the shingles off houses like scales off a fish.

On the afternoon before the storm, John Ulm's boat was sighted from Gar Head Point, below the mouth of the Aucilla. And that was the last time it was seen. John

The Sounds of Geese

Ulm was dead, and everybody knew it. But the company that carried his ten-thousand-dollar insurance policy—with a double indemnity clause that made it now worth twenty thousand—understandably declined to pay off until some sort of evidence of John's wreck was brought to light. Even a piece of the boat would be sufficient, they said.

Weeks passed, and no sign of John or his boat could be found. Finally, Miss Gussie offered five hundred dollars for part of her husband's wrecked boat. This, it turn out, was Crabflake Myers' suggestion. Not that the offer did any good. The fishermen kept looking, but John's boat wasn't found.

"Don't make no difference," Nellie said, "if Crabflake's got his mind set on it, he'll figure some way to git that insurance company to pay up."

"Sh-sh," Joe said. "Yon he is, right now."

They watched Myers striding across the shell road that led to the Barnaby office. He was a big, slightly stooped, slightly bald man. He was good at figures, especially those preceded by the dollar symbol. He wasn't well liked, but nobody wanted to be enemy to someone who could foreclose on them at will. "Shucks," Joe once said, "before I'd have folks scared of me like that, I'd rather be in bankrupture."

Myers went into the office of Jules Barnaby. Presently old Jules stuck his head out of the door and called Joe.

"Come here."

Joe went into the little kerosene-warmed office. Nellie went too.

"Is it *him* you goan send me goose hunting with?" Crabflake demanded.

"He's the best they is," Jules said.

"I believe I'll take the next-best this time," Crabflake said angrily, "and git somebody else."

"That's plumb up to you," Jules said.

Crabflake started toward the door; then, apparently struck by a new thought, he turned and said, "I don't know Jules. If you say he's a good hunter, I'll tolerate him."

Joe shook his head. "Ain't no use going goose hunting today."

Nellie nudged him sharply. Jules spat in the sand box under the desk, and said nothing.

Crabflake said, 'How come it ain't?"

"The wind ain't right. On a quiet sunshiny day like this, them geese most generally just lay offshore, squonking and feeding. They ain't goan fly, not none."

"I'll chance it," Crabflake said. "Git moving."

Joe shook his head. "Ain't a bit of use."

Nellie's elbow punched him again. "I'll help you get your things together."

"You going er not?" Crabflake demanded. "I'm paying for it, and if I say go, we go."

"Nope," Joe said. "I wouldn't feel right in my mind about taking no man's money fer guiding on a day like this. Now you take a day when they's a good breeze of southwest wind, we can have some luck."

"Joe," Nellie said incredulously, "you goan refuse to go, bad as we need money?"

"Nellie, I just wouldn't feel right about it."

"Well, for gosh sake!" Crabflake exclaimed angrily. "I guess I can get somebody else to go!"

"I expect you can," Joe answered, "but you ain't goan kill no geese."

Before long, Crabflake was back, his face red with anger, a touch of color even showing through the thin hair on top of his head. "Bullock," he said, "I'm good a-mind to brad your nose! Cain't git *nobody* in this place to take me goose hunting. They all said that if you said weren't no use going, they didn't care to try it either. You've messed me up good!" He drew back his fist, cocked and ready.

"Let 'er go," Joe said firmly. "Just pile right on in."

But Crabflake noticed the size of Joe's fist, and he thought better of punishing him. With an angry grunt he turned and slammed out.

Old Jules took his vaporous pipe from his bony jaw, and said, "Joe, you got to learn that the customer is nearbout always right."

"I ain't taking nobody goose hunting on a day like this. I'm hard luck enough when conditions is right. A man would sit a long time on his behind, waiting fer geese to fly today."

"Joe," Nellie said, and he saw that she was crying, "you're just no-'count, that's your trouble. You make out to be hard luck, but you're just purely trifling! I don't want nothing more to do with you, Joe. You hear me?"

Jules said, "You ain't quitting him just because he won't go goose hunting with Crabflake, Nellie, for gosh sakes?"

"No. I've learnt something about him, that's all."

Joe sat down, because he felt sick. Finally he said, "Guess I knowed from the first you wouldn't never come right out and marry me. I couldn't expect no good luck like that to happen to me."

THAT NIGHT THE WIND changed around to the southwest, and blew in a good high tide, and brought flying foggy rain. With daylight, the cabbage-palm fronds rattled and glistened wetly, and the water in the river carried a surface of broken suds; and droves of restless wild fowl moved up and down the coast line.

Joe had stayed awake most of the night, grieving about Nellie, so that when he did drop off he overslept, and daylight was almost there by the time he got dressed. Then he heard somebody calling for him from below, the voice muffled by the blow of the wind. He went down from his room over Jules' boathouse, and found Crabflake Myers waiting for him.

"*Now* what's wrong with the weather?" Crabflake asked.

"Drizzly."

"I mean for goose hunting."

Joe admitted, "She's a pretty durn' good goose day."

"Well, what's your reason for not going with me today? Got a bad cold or something another, I reckon."

"No, my health's tol'able good. But this goose hunting—it takes a right smart of a man to tough it out, in weather like this."

"I been goose hunting before!" Crabflake said angrily. "You going er no?"

The Sounds of Geese

"I'd just as soon," Joe said finally.

They loaded their guns and shells and a few cans of beans into Crabflake's little launch, the Kingfish, and presently shoved off down the chopped water of the river. They had forty miles to go down the coast, to the vast juncus-grass sea marsh beyond tiny Limestone Island.

Here, on calm days, the great rafts of Canada geese fed in the shallow water. Joe had lain on shore in the smelly muck, hidden by needle-pointed juncus grass, watching them paddle contentedly about, upending themselves so their long necks would reach down to the tender bottom shoots. For hours, while he waited for them to drift in close enough for a shot, he had listened to their satisfied squonks and mutters, with an occasional full *ah-honk* from a sentinel gander.

But on days like today the tide was too high for them to feed on the bottom, and they had to keep swimming constantly to prevent being blown to shore by the wind. So they flew. Some headed back toward the hammock and lit in the tiny fresh-water ponds, where it was possible for a good woodsman to stalk them. Others kept beating nervously up and down the coast line, fighting the wind, and offering an occasional flight shot.

They were flying when Joe headed the boat into Rock Creek. In spite of his sadness because of Nellie, Joe's pulse moved fast, seeing the magnificent birds flying in bunches of eight or ten, and listening to their honks above the wind. Ducks were flying, too, and once, not far offshore a thousand scaup flew over Limestone Island in a scurrying cloud. As Joe maneuvered the Kingfish past the rocks of the creek, he was curious about Crabflake, who lay in the cabin bunk chewing his cigar. For a man so hell-bent to go goose hunting, he was strangely unexcited by a coastal scene that should stir the blood of any wild-fowl hunter.

"He sure don't act much like a goose hunter," Joe mused. "Maybe he is, but till he proves hisself he's goan be on prohibition with me."

They anchored the boat near an island, and Joe went ashore and climbed a scrub oak. From this vantage the marsh now took on another dimension, and he could see numberless winding creeks, and the round ponds like silver dollars in the sea marsh, and areas of salt flats. None of the ponds now held geese close to the coast. Joe climbed down, and they started to the next island inland.

Slogging across the marsh, the stinging gusts of rain at their backs, pushing through the thick, stabbing juncus, Crabflake showed little enthusiasm for the hunt.

"How come we cain't sit on a point and try for a flight shot?" he demanded finally. "Ain't no use to kill ourself just for a few old geese."

"They might fly over you on a point, of you're lucky," Joe said. "I ain't lucky, so I most generally go to my geese, instead of waiting for them to come to me."

"Tomorrow I'm goan sit on a point," Crabflake said.

Joe shrugged and kept walking, pushing through the rank grass. He wished John Ulm hadn't gone and got himself drowned. He and John, now, on a day like this, would stalk the ponds and when night came they'd have all the geese they could stagger out with.

John had been a fine hunting partner. He hadn't ever wanted to go back home, because his wife, Miss Gussie, was a pretty severe letdown after a good goose hunt, or even a poor one. Joe was usually the one who had made the motion to go home....

They reached an island he and John had named Bell-Cow Island, because a rattlesnake—John called them bell-cows—had almost got him one warm day last season. Joe climbed an oak he had used many times, and from the top of it the marsh flattened out beneath him. Then Joe stiffened. On a little pond about a quarter mile away were seven Canadian geese, quietly feeding.

"Okay," he said, climbing down. "Git ready to crawl on your belly like a rat pile."

Part of the distance they walked in a crouch. As they drew closer, Joe motioned to advance on hands and knees. The last hundred yards they slid on their bellies, Crabflake protesting in angry whispers that the mucky water was soaking him to the skin. But Joe didn't heed, and crawled on, inching through the grass. He listened. Above the wind rustle of the grass he heard *pum-pum* as a goose flapped its wings in contentment. They were close.

Joe peered through the grass. Now he saw them. Five of the geese had their heads under water. One gander picked serenely at his wing feathers. Another gander held his head up in semialertness.

"They're right up ahead," Joe whispered. "Git ready to shoot."

"Where?" asked Crabflake, and raised his head to look.

At once the geese rose from the water, honking noisily.

Joe exclaimed fervently, "Dog take the luck!" and fired at the lead gander. At the first shot the big goose wavered, then fell with the second load, striking the water with head under, and paddling in convulsive circles. Crabflake finally recovered enough to fire a couple of times, but the geese were out of range.

"I got one!" Crabflake said, seeing the dying goose on the water.

"If you hadn't stuck that bald head up we'd a-had four or five," Joe said disgustedly. "If that's your goose out there, wade out and git him."

"I ain't the guide. You wade out and git my goose."

"Yes, sir," Joe said, and stepped out into the water.

THAT NIGHT JOE LAY in his bunk, thinking about Nellie and listening to the faint honking of the geese, like the barking of country dogs in the distance. Once he dimly thought he heard Crabflake get up, then he went back to sleep.

After breakfast they started out again. Here and there small flocks of geese headed back out to sea.

"We missed our chance yesterday," Joe said as they came to a small creek. "But maybe we'll git a shot or two before they all go back outside."

He waded out into the creek, and Crabflake followed. Joe started to step up on the opposite bank when his foot struck something. He thought it a rock, and gave it only a passing benediction; but a glance showed that it was a piece of wood, imbedded in the soft mud of the creek bottom.

"Hey, look," Joe said. He loosened the wood and finally pulled it free, and it was a piece of sailboat rudder, splintered near the upper end where the tiller would have been. Two pieces of brass strapping, discolored with verdigris, bound the flat surface of the rudder.

The Sounds of Geese

"That's the rudder of John Ulm's boat!" whispered Crabflake. "I'd know it anywhere. I sold him that brass on there."

"It sure looks like it," Joe said. He washed the mud from the rudder.

"Boy," Crabflake said, "you've sure stepped in luck this time! That's five hundred dollars you stumped your toe on!"

"If this turns out to be John's rudder, and Miss Gussie pays five hundred dollars for it," Joe said, "half the money is sure yours, by rights."

"No, sir," Crabflake said. "You found it, and the money belongs to you. I ain't goan try to horn in on your luck. Let's git on back to the boat and take that rudder home."

"Ain't no powerful hurry. We might git two or three shots. We can deliver the rudder tomorrow."

"Today's better," Crabflake said firmly. "Come on."

Crabflake's impatience was understandable to Joe, because if this was really John Ulm's rudder, Miss Gussie would get the insurance money. But, as they made their way back to the boat, the thing that puzzled Joe was Crabflake's generosity regarding the five-hundred-dollar reward. It just wasn't natural for him to waive his share in a claim like that.

The tide was low and there was no getting out of the Rock Creek for two hours. While they waited, Joe studied the rudder they had found. With his knife, he scraped it to examine the grain of the wood. Finally he said:

"I hate to tell you, Crabflake, but this ain't no rudder off'n John's boat."

"How come it ain't? I'd know that rudder anywhere."

"Nope. This un's pine. John's rudder was oak. I helped him plane it smooth. And one time me and him harpooned a shark that turnt and tried to bite the boat. His teeth marks was in John's rudder," Joe said. "Come on, let's go after them geese."

Crabflake walked back and forth nervously. Suddenly he said, with a wise smile, "Won't nobody but me and you know it ain't John's rudder. You can git that money right on. I ain't goan let the cat out of the bag."

"I'd feel sort of guilted about pulling a trick like that," Joe said. "We better git started if we want to try the geese."

Crabflake exploded. "I swear, I don't believe you got good sense!"

"Me and you just don't think like each other," Joe said. "You coming er not?"

Crabflake subsided abruptly, and said, "You go on stalking. I'm tired of wallowing in that muck. I'm going out on one them points and set down and wait for a flight."

While Joe hunted that afternoon, he figured the whole thing out. Crabflake had decided to use him as a guide because people knew they weren't friends, and wouldn't suspect the two of them of conspiring together. Probably Crabflake had made the rudder a while back, and exposed it to weather and barnacles. Some of the green touches on the brass looked a bit like green paint. Then last night Crabflake had planted the fake rudder on their trail, so Joe could find it. Yes, Joe thought, he had all the steps of the scheme figured out.

All, he discovered, except the next step. For when he got back with three geese to Rock Creek just before dark, Crabflake Myers and his boat, Kingfish, were gone.

"Hey!" Joe shouted, thinking at first that Crabflake might have simply moved the boat around a bend for some reason. But a half-hour of searching and shouting convinced him that Crabflake had gone and left him.

Joe stood there by Rock Creek with night falling around him, and realized that he was alone on the sea marsh, fifteen or twenty miles from the nearest settlement, with a half-dozen rivers and creeks between. Crabflake had gone home to report finding John Ulm's rudder, and to tell of Joe Bullock's getting lost. Possibly he would get the insurance money for Miss Gussie and then come back to find Joe.

"Or maybe he figures just to let me parish to death out here," Joe figured. The unfairness of it overwhelmed him, and he said angrily, "It shore ain't no way to do a fellow!"

Joe made his way to the nearest island and prepared to spend the night. With dried palm leaves and cedar and pine sticks he built a fire, and while it was catching up he used his pocket knife to cut green cabbage-tree fronds for his bed. He roasted the livers and gizzards of the geese and ate them. Finally he went to sleep, shivering in the cold.

Next morning he set out for the hammock, leaving the dead geese, for they were heavy and he had a lot of rough walking and swimming to do. *"He's plumb mistooken if he reckons I'm goan to set here and parish to death,"* Joe told himself.

Now the tide was out and the creeks were low, so that only once or twice did he get wet all over. The sun came out, and the dogflies attacked him in hordes that left blood flecks on his face and hands. He went on, wading and walking and pushing through the grass, thinking, *"It ain't no way to do nobody."*

He stopped to rest before wading the last creek short of the hammock. A flock of ibis sailed overhead. Joe leaned down to tie his boot and saw the broken mast of a boat. For a second he stared at it, puzzled. Then he started searching.

Before long he found what he was looking for. He found all that was left of John Ulm. If they had thought about it, they'd have remembered that in the storm the water had covered the marsh.

A heavy sadness weighed upon Joe, here beside the bones of his old friend. He sank to the ground and leaned back against one of the palm trunks and closed his eyes. A gull flew lazily above, looking about inquiringly; from the hammock came the scolding bark of a gray squirrel. A breeze rattled the palm leaves pleasantly.

A new thought gradually came upon Joe's consciousness. This was no place for sadness; this was a place of peace. John Ulm had lived a full life, and now—away from woman's sharp tongue—he rested on his beloved marshland; where the wild fowl flew, and the raccoons hunted, and where, even now, far off, came the honking of wild geese....

Joe fought the hammock that afternoon. Bamboo and prickly ash cut him and tore his clothes, and cypress knees tripped his stumbling feet. Joe thought, *It just ain't no way to do a fellow."* But now, if he ever got out, he had Crabflake Myers where he wanted him. For he could easily prove that the rudder was a fake, and then never mention that he had found genuine evidence of John's death. Of course, he'd lose the five hundred dollars Miss Gussie had offered, but he was willing to do that to get even with Crabflake.

Still, it seemed inadequate revenge. What he wanted was something permanent. And next day as he reached the high palmetto flatwoods beyond the hammock, he knew the terrible thing he could do to Crabflake Myers....

JOE BULLOCK WAS SPREADING his gill net—the one he had bought with part of the five hundred dollars—on the grass to dry, and Nellie Barnaby was watching him, and Joe said, heavily: "Nellie, I been aiming to tell you: you ought not to marry me."

"Why not, Joe?" she asked. "You've proved you'll work, since you got that net."

"Well, I hate to say it, but something's been heavy on my conscious. I ain't no kind of man for you to marry. I pulled a powerful dirty trick on a fellow. Dirtiest I ever heard tell of," he said in remorse.

Before she could inquire about this, Preacher Walt Minton came down the dock with his outboard motor, going red fishing. Joe was glad he came, because now he could confess to his girl and to his preacher at the same time, and have done with it.

"What's the trouble with you-all?" Walt asked.

"I pulled a dirty trick on Crabflake," Joe said. And he told them what he had done. "At first I wasn't going to tell about finding John. Then I remembered what you said about too much money being like a rattlesnake, and I thought about Miss Gussie, and I knowed the worst thing could happen to Crabflake was to have to live with Miss Gussie Ulm and all that money the rest of his life. If I'd a-just shot him it wouldn't a-been so heavy on my mind."

Walt thought a minute, and finally he said, "Joe, it ain't for us to know the workings of the All-Mighty. Maybe it's in His book for Crabflake and Miss Gussie to be married up, and you had to git mad and make things come out right. I don't know about that. But I'm plumb positive that John Ulm wouldn't a-wanted all that money he had paid in on that insurance policy to go to waste. It was Miss Gussie's money, and Crabflake don't concern us, not none. Maybe you had the wrong idea, all right, but Miss Gussie was shore due her money," Walt added. "For all we know, maybe the Lord caused all this to happen, just so John Ulm's widow could get what was coming to her."

"You reckon so?" Joe asked hopefully.

"Like as not," Walt said firmly. He clamped the motor on a skiff.

Nellie smiled at Joe.

"I guess it's like the good Book says," Joe sighed. "The Lord moves in mischeevious ways."

Jumping-horse Man

Somebody shook me and I woke up. It was dark outside the window—Farn had said we were starting early. Farn's face, usually so slick, was stubbled with a two-day beard, and his suit was a mess. I wished Sadie could see him. Sadie was so particular about the way her men looked.

Farn glanced down at himself. He had slept in his clothes, and had made me do the same. "Don't I look like a rube?"

We went down and got in the rented old car and started into the back country Farn said held more bastard thoroughbreds than you could count. The country was rolling and the sun was hot, but now I felt better and I forgot being mad with Farn and Sadie for making me come along. Sadie was my stepmother—thirty-two, I guess she was, the kind of woman the men sort of gather around when her husband's out on the track or down at the stable. Not that she had encouraged them especially, because Pop had been quite a cocky lad to look at, and front was everything to Sadie. When Mrs. Milburn's chaser pecked and ended over, though, and Pop spent the rest of his few days in the bone house, Sadie began to meet Farn.

That was even before Pop died, and that's why I hated her and why I'll be hating her the next time you ask me. I guess she thought I wasn't old enough to know what was going on. So the reason I had not wanted to go with Farn to find a jumper was because it was Sadie who asked me to. "You go with him now, like he says. Sort of follow along behind like a farmer's boy, and keep your mouth shut," she told me.

We visited a lot of farms before we found what we wanted. When I saw this horse, the skin on my hands turned cold, like when I used to watch Pop take a water jump. Oh, he was a horse! You wouldn't've thought so, unless you happen to be a jumping-horse man. He wasn't a sleek-curved fancy-dan horse; he was a big, raw-boned brown colt. He had the shoulder, and he had the hindquarters—and the clincher was the mark of a hobble on his hide. I got so excited I forgot to play dumb.

"Look, Farn!" I said, pointing to the hobble rub.

He gave me a look that would have frozen a grapefruit, and then calmly walked over to a chestnut mare near by, and said, "Yep, bub, she's a nice 'un, ain't she?" He walked around and around her. He didn't give the brown colt another glance.

"How much for this mare?" Farn asked, finally.

The farmer pulled at his mustache. "Well, I don't scarcely know what to ask for that horse."

"I couldn't pay a big price."

"It's hard to say," the farmer kept muttering. But finally he said, "I ought not to do it; but if you want that mare you can have her for two hundred dollars."

Farn looked unhappy, and said, "That's too much for a poor man to put into a horse. Much obliged for letting me look. Come on, bub."

The farmer pointed to the brown colt and said. "How you like that 'un?"

"That gawky 'un?" Farn said.

"He'll fill out a right smart. He ain't but four. I got more horses than I can feed, and I'll give you a pretty good price on him, if you can use him."

When it was all settled, and the colt belonged to Farn, we drove off. Farn didn't say a word, and I kept watching him. But watching him didn't help. When he got around a bend, he stopped the old car and gave me a hard one with the back of his hand.

"Next time keep your trap shut," he said quietly.

"Okay," I said, spitting blood from my mouth.

When Pop had seen he was on his way out, he had called me in and said, "Jerry, kid, I got a couple of things to say. When I'm gone, you stick with Sadie."

"I'm sixteen. I can look out for me."

"Maybe it's her I want looked out for."

"Maybe she don't want me."

"You stick anyway, until you know she can get along."

"One more thing now," he said. "What you want to make out for yourself?"

"I hadn't thought about it."

"I'd like you to be a lawyer, or a radio man, or something like that, if you feel like it. You got no bug to be a chaser jock, have you?"

"I don't know. You never let me jump a horse."

"And with reason. If you ever took four and a half feet on a good strong horse, you'd never be satisfied doing anything that would make you any money. I ain't going to say yes or no about it, but my advice to you is never ride a jumping horse once. That's all I got to say."

He left me two hundred and fifty bucks at the bank, and told me not to use it until I needed it. He hadn't been long gone before I knew I'd need it soon. Farn, with his flashy show horses, his hundred-dollar coats and deep-shining boots, had taken Sadie over—or at least as much as any man could take Sadie over. It was odd man out, and the odd man was me. I was in Sadie's way, and I was a nuisance to Farn; so I figured I'd be leaving soon.

On Tuesday the brown colt, Benjie, arrived. I was at the barn when he came, and he walked down out of the truck as calm as if he rode trucks all the time. Sadie and Farn came down presently. Sadie stayed sort of near the door, for she did not like stable smells.

"Saddle him," Farn said, "and let's see how much of a jumper we've got."

Farn left the stirrups long, for he was a gaited-horse man, not a jumper really. But he did know enough to trot around a bit to warm up the horse's muscles. At first

Benjie was lazy; the only thing he did was throw his head a little after Farn's heavy hands began to hurt his tender mouth.

Meanwhile Perk and I set up the jump. We put the bar at two feet, like we had been told. The jump didn't have any wings. Sadie watched Farn, not the colt.

Benjie looked at the bar with some curiosity as he trotted toward it, but no fear. Farn tried to make him gallop, but Benjie wouldn't bother. He didn't need to—he went over the bar as pretty as you ever saw.

"So far, so good," grunted Perk.

"Put it up to three," Farn said.

"A whole foot?" I asked.

"You heard me."

Again Benjie came trotting leisurely, his ears forward. He was lazy, all right, or perhaps not feeling very peppy after his truck ride. At any rate, he carelessly struck the bar with his hind foot. When he did it the second time, Farn jerked Benjie's mouth angrily.

"Get my whip," he said.

Perk nodded. "A little slashing is just what that horse needs."

The first time Farn's whip cut into his belly, Benjie jumped in astonishment. Farn kept laying it on. I turned my head away, but I could still hear the *whup, whup, whup*. Sadie called, "I wish you wouldn't do that in your good clothes."

Benjie tried to run, but Farn kept him tight-checked, so that he could only wheel and dance frantically and perhaps wildly wonder what he was being punished for. But, of course, he wasn't being punished; he was simply being given the standard horse-show methods for keying up a docile horse. Farn liked keying them up that way.

Then he turned him toward the jump, cut him again sharply with the whip, and loosened the reins. Benjie shot away and cleared the jump by a foot. On landing he tried to bolt, but Farn hit him hard with the curb and brought him around in a circle and stopped him sharply.

He jumped him several times more, even to four feet, and Benjie never touched. But he was scared and nervous and wouldn't be still between jumps. I remember hearing Pop say, one time, that a scared horse isn't a safe one. I don't guess there's anything more scared than a scared horse.

"Well," Farn said to Sadie when he was through, "it looks like I've added a jumper to my string. Let's go to the Palms and get a drink on it."

"With you looking like that?" she said disdainfully. "Not me. I'll see you later."

I cooled Benjie off, and put him up. He wouldn't eat anything at all that night, and drank only in short, nervous draughts. I tried to talk to him and get him calmed down, but he couldn't get used to the strange new and apparently hostile life into which he had been thrust.

"Some day, boy, I'll even up with him for today," I muttered.

Next morning he was better, and he ate. I hung around his stall and gave him a carrot and tried to make him forget the day before. But there didn't seem to be much point to it, for I knew many days like that one were coming for him.

And they did come. Farn would phone down to the stable and tell Perkinson to get the jumping horse ready, and Perk would put a light blanket on Benjie to keep from cutting his hide, and then lay on to him with a rubber hose until the colt was fit to go crazy. Then Farn would arrive, mount, and put him over some jumps.

With Farn in the saddle Benjie was hardly a sane horse. His jumping went from bad to worse. Whenever Farn headed him for a jump, Benjie would bolt wildly toward it; sometimes he would clear by a foot and sometimes he would knock the bars flying.

Perk said, finally, "Looks like we've bought a fool."

"I knew that damned farmer was a crook time I saw him!" Farn said angrily. "Well, keep your mouth shut about this horse and maybe we can unload him on somebody."

Having given up on Benjie, Farn didn't bother with him, and day by day the horse got quieter, and ate better. But all Farn had to do was walk up to the door, and Benjie would start getting jittery. "A fool," Farn said in disgust. "But we'll stick somebody with him."

One moonlight night I led Benjie from his stall and saddled him. He showed some nervousness as I mounted, and if I had raised my hand he'd have tried to bolt. But I sat very quietly paying no attention to his restless turning. After a few minutes I nudged him slightly, and he sprang away in a short, stiff-kneed, sideways gallop. I reined him in to a stop, and then started him again. Finally I was able to get him to walk away, and that was what I wanted. For an hour I walked him, and when I put him in the stall he was as quiet as a kitten.

EVERY NIGHT, NOW, I rode Benjie, and eventually I was convinced that, away from Perk and Farn he would be a quiet and dependable horse. "Before long," I said, "we're going to be checking out of here. And some day we'll come back." I knew that Benjie could be bought, and that he was a good horse. I'd never really thought of jumping him, because I figured that, in his mind, he'd always connect the jumping standard with the pain Farn had inflicted.

But on this night I happened to ride near the jump, and instead of shying from it, he threw his ears forward and seemed waiting to see if I was going to send him into it. I took him around the training ring again, and this time I headed him straight for the jump.

The bar must have been at about four feet, but I was afraid that if I stopped to lower it I'd lose my nerve. I don't remember passing over the bar. I just remember taking off, and a feeling of being way up in the air, and then the ground rushing up in that terrible moment of descent. Even as Benjie's front feet struck, I had a quick fear that the crushing downweight would crack his leg bones. And then we were down, and Benjie was galloping easily around the ring. My hands were still nerveless on the reins. Finally Benjie slowed and stopped, and began grazing at the fringe in the center of the ring. Many minutes passed before my heart stopped pounding. And then a hot fire seemed to grow in my chest, and from that moment on I was a jumping-horse man.

Jumping-Horse Man

Two days later I waited impatiently at old John Stewart's filling station. What clothes I had were in a bundle inside in the corner by the air compressor. Finally old John drove in and put his car under the greasing shed. He had been a friend of Pop's and now he was being a friend to me.

"You have any customers?" he asked.

"Three. Did you get him?"

"I guess you collected their ration coupons and all."

"Sure I did. Did you get him?" I demanded.

"Yes, I got him," he answered, and handed me a ten-dollar bill. "He's a hard trader. This is all you have coming back."

"That's okay. I still got a bargain."

Presently John's Negro, Robert, came down the street, and he was leading Benjie.

"Well," John said. "There's your horse."

Benjie knew me. He smelled me, gave me a little push with his nose, and then looked indifferently around at the town. *My* horse. My horse Benjie.

"I'm glad to help you, Jerry," old John said. "When you leaving?"

"Now," I answered.

"Good luck, son. Find you a good job and stick to it. And listen, there's a lot of stuff behind you now, and you want to forget it."

"No," I answered. "I ain't forgetting a thing."

I stopped at a little crossroads Florida store, for some sardines—with my last dime—and when I came out a car had driven up. It was a coupé not old but pretty well banged up, and the driver was a brown old guy with a big hat, and beside him was a girl, his daughter I figured. She had a flowered handkerchief or something around her hair, and she was sure pretty.

The man said, "Son, will that horse work cattle?"

I said, "Yes, sir, he sure will."

"He's might long and gawky-looking for a cow horse," the man said. "You out of work?"

If the girl hadn't been there I guess I'd have told the truth, but I said, "Not exactly. I'm on my way to Miami to enter the horse show."

"I didn't know about any horse show in Miami," the man said, puzzled. Then he seemed to catch on, and he said, "I'm short of hands, and we've got a lot of work coming up. If you got time to stop off a while, and if you think your horse will work cows, I can give you a job."

So that's how I got out to this cattle ranch, and that's how I met Betty, the ranchman's daughter. That's where I first knew Billy O'Day too. Billy was short and tough and simple-minded. He was a little out of shape from getting tossed off bucking horses and Brahmas, for every year he left to travel a couple of months with the rodeo.

It soon was plain that Benjie wasn't a cattle horse. He caught on to chasing steers, and for his size, even got pretty quick at cutting and turning. But when I tried to whirl a rope off him he nearly went out of his head. It was too much like Farn's whip.

They kept me on, though, because they didn't have enough hands as it was. In the afternoons, late, I'd take Benjie out in the pasture and jump him. I've known a lot of jumping horses since then, but honest, there never was another like Benjie. Chasing cows had been good for him, for now all he needed to liven him up was a touch of a spur. And he loved to jump. He tried to jump anything I'd aim him at, no matter how high.

"When they start gitting the rodeo together, Jerry," Billy O'Day said, "you ought to go with me, and take that horse."

"He ain't no rodeo horse."

"They got all kinds of acts, gosh a-mighty. Trick horses and a lot of stuff. We'll git you up an act. I'll tell you what, I'll lay down on top of my horse and let you jump over us. I could lay on my back on the horse like I was a-laying up in my bunk, smoking a cigarette and reading a funny book, and you could come along and jump over us."

"You must be crazy," I said.

Betty must have heard about this, because she was down at the pasture one day watching me jump Benjie, and when I stopped she said, "Are you going away with Billy?"

"I got to make some money someway."

"I wish you didn't have to go," she said. She looked at me, and finally she asked, 'What is it you carry on your mind all the time, Jerry?"

"I don't carry anything on my mind."

She said, "If you ever come by this way, stop in to see us. Maybe you might even write us a postcard sometime."

"Sure I will."

"Look," she said suddenly. "Why don't you enter Benjie in the Florida Southern show? Dad says they've got a big jumper stake. He goes down every year to see that show."

"I'll sure try to make it." But I didn't know where I'd be when that show came off.

The rodeo manager looked at me and then at Benjie, and he said, "A lot of horses can jump."

Billy O'Day said, "Not like this one, Mr. Donly."

Donly nodded at me. "Let me see something special."

I mounted and wondered what I could do that would seem special. Then I noticed his car over by a tree; it was a convertible with the top down. I touched Benjie with the spur, and headed him straight for the automobile. I held him straight, gave him a little more spur, and he surged right over it.

"That's okay," Donly said. "But not new."

"I ain't come to the main part," I said. I dismounted, took off the saddle, bridle and everything, and Benjie didn't have on anything but the shoes on his feet. Then I squirmed up on him, put my belt around his neck to steer him with, and started him toward the car again. He jumped it as slick and as calm as anything you ever saw, and I neck-reined him back to where Donly and Billy O'day stood.

"Now you're talking!" Donly said, and Billy winked at me.

It wasn't as hard as it looked. A car with the top down, these days, isn't more than about four feet high, and a horse naturally gets some breadth in a four-foot jump. Staying on without a saddle is easy if you've got balance and a little grip in your legs. Of course without a bit, Benjie could have turned out if he'd wanted to, or run away after landing; but jumping was what he liked, and he was too lazy to run away without he had been scared or something.

One night we were in Dothan, Alabama, and it was dusty and those Brahmas were just mean as hell, and Billy O'Day got tossed right quick. It looked to me like the Brahmas stepped on him, but in the dust you never can tell. I went around behind the chutes, and they had pulled Billy's boot off. The cowboys and cowgirls were standing around him, bright-colored in their red and yellow silk as they waited for the horseback quadrille and one of the girls spat angrily and said, "That old Brahma stepped on Billy's foot."

The doctor took us up to his office, and while he worked on Billy I looked at the papers and magazines. Then is when I saw this picture. It was a man and a horse taking a jump, and the words at the bottom read: FAMOUS PAIR TO APPEAR IN JUMPER STAKE AT FLORIDA SOUTHERN SHOW. *Rudolph Farn and his sensational new jumper, Altimeter, will be among the stars performing next week at the horse show which annually attracts horse owners and riders throughout the South.*

The picture of Farn sent a cold shudder of anger over me, and for a moment the picture blurred out. But that horse looked good; he was jumping clean, and clearing by just a fraction, the way a good horse does. His mouth was open, and I knew Farn's tight rein was doing that. He looked to be brown, and about Benjie's size. I wondered what kind of disposition he had, to survive Farn's training methods.

I took the paper into the office, and Billy was lying on his back with his hands behind his head, telling the doctor how he'd once seen a Brahma tear down a wire fence he'd got hung in. I held the picture in front of Billy.

"I'm going to that show," I said evenly.

"Okay. I might as well go too. I won't be able to do nothing with this foot," Billy said. "Durn, that's some horse, ain't he? Read me what it says—I forgot my glasses."

I read it to him—Billy can't read, but he doesn't like for anybody to know it—and when I got through he said, "You know that feller?"

"Yes, I know him."

"You sort of sounded like you did."

It was sure a spangle of a show. In the stall next to the one they gave me was a golden five-gaited stallion that kept moving and squealing and occasionally kicking at the boards that separated him from Benjie. On the other side, a woman was washing a pure white walking-horse colt that was entered in the mare-and-colt class. The place was full of horses and horse smells and horse talk. People strolled by the stalls, and they admired the stallion and then the colt, and they stared at Benjie and asked one another what a horse like that was doing at a horse show. From the ring the amplifiers rattled and croaked and finally said something or other. Benjie stood at the door and looked at the scene with indifference.

But his indifference vanished when Farn appeared. I'll tell the truth—if it had occurred to me that Benjie would have remembered Farn, or that Farn would try to be so clever, I don't believe I'd have come. My only thought had been that I'd show Farn up by jumping so high he'd lose his guts or either bust his neck; but I wasn't even sure of doing this after hearing about that horse, Altimeter.

I was picking Benjie's feet when Farn and Sadie came. Benjie stiffened, and he threw his head up, and stood there like a buck scenting danger, and when I turned around there they were, Sadie looked like a movie actress, and Farn, with his neat-cut blond mustache and his tweed riding coat, had enough front for even Sadie. I later found out they had got married two weeks before.

"Hello, Jerry," Sadie said. "Why did you go off without telling anybody?"

"I just left," I said. I was watching Benjie out of the corner of my eye. He still hadn't moved a muscle; I guess he was trying to place Farn.

"It wasn't very grateful of you, after all we'd done for you," Farn said reasonably, tapping his boots with his riding whip. He was watching Benjie, too.

"Such as what?"

Suddenly Farn leaned forward and pointed the whip at Benjie and shook it in his face, and said, "Isn't that the horse I used to own?"

Benjie jumped straight backward, banging a board off the back of his stall, and his eyes rolled white. Quickly I slipped a stirrup iron off a saddle, and holding it by the leather I stepped outside and shut the upper half of the stall door behind me.

"Get away from here," I said.

"Sorry," Farn said smoothly. "I'd forgotten that horse was so—eccentric."

I went back in and began trying to quiet Benjie. He settled down quicker than I did; for I was still sore when somebody else stopped at the door, and I whirled and there was Betty. She wore dark glasses, and that kerchief thing around her hair like when I first saw her, and right away I began to forget about Farn.

"I'm so glad to see you, Jerry!" she said.

I shook her hand and forgot to turn it loose. I hadn't ever had a girl, not a real girl of my own, and now all of a sudden I knew I had one and it was Betty, and the feeling was like that night when I rode Benjie and headed him for the jump for the first time, a sort of choked-up, half-scared excitement. Now she was telling me about coming down with her father and everything, and all I could say was, "Well, I declare. Well, I declare."

FARN'S HORSE, ALTIMETER, WAS everything they had said. I saw that before the bar got to four feet. The crowd had overflowed the bleacher seats and boxes and were packed three deep around the rail, and all of them were keyed up the way a jumper class always gets them.

Altimeter had been talked about a lot, and they gave him a big hand every time he went into the ring. After seeing him jump a few times, I knew why Farn hadn't been able to ruin him. Altimeter was a hot horse—he was born fiery and excited, and instead of needing keying up, he had to be held in. When he saw a jump ahead, he tried to go for it wide open, and it was all Farn's heavy hunting pelham could do to hold him in until he got there. Then Altimeter would sail over as pretty as anything you ever saw.

Jumping-Horse Man

After the bar got past four feet, horses began dropping out. Each horse had two tries, and then it was goodby. Neither Altimeter nor Benjie had even nicked. Farn had not spoken to me, but I kept my eye on him. As the bar approached five feet, and Benjie was still going over easy as jumping a log, Farn began to look at us like he hadn't noticed we were there.

First thing I had done was to spot Betty, sitting with her father, and every time I finished my jump amid the clapping, it was her smile that was my applause. Benjie had grown applause-conscious long ago, in the rodeo, and he ate it up. He always did better in a performance than in practice. I was sure proud of my horse this day, there seemed no limit to what he could do. Altimeter was going nicely, too.

The bar had passed six feet before either of us had to use his second jump, and it was Altimeter who missed. He cleared on his second try; and Farn brought him around while they moved the bar up.

I must have been watching Betty when it happened. All of a sudden there Farn was beside me, and Altimeter, whirling and dance as if unmanageable, crashed into Benjie. Farn shouted at Altimeter, "Here, you, sah!" and while we were jammed up together he struck his spur into Benjie, and swished his whip overhead. At once Benjie reared and fell away in fright, and then bolted toward the rail. I got him turned just before he would have jumped it and landed in a crowded box. I couldn't hold him with that snaffle, but I drew him around in smaller circles until finally he stopped and stood there with feet apart, trembling. There was a hush over the crowd.

"Are you ready, Number Eighteen?" blared the amplifier.

I wasn't near ready, not with my horse half out of his head, but I couldn't wait. It was my time to jump, and I had either to try or get out. So I worked Benjie into the ring and got him headed right. He shot wildly toward the standard, not seeming to feel my sawing at his mouth. There were four bars—he sent the whole bunch of them scattering.

"Now look what you did!" I scolded him. Knocking the bars off seemed to get his mind off Farn's whip for just a moment, because that was a new experience for him. While this was still on his mind I brought him around again and by that time the attendants had put the bars back. We came in fast—too fast—but this time Benjie was rating himself. I don't know how high that bar was, but it was sure up there. Benjie took off, and the ground seemed miles below. I heard one of his hind feet tick the top bar, but when I looked back it was still there and the crowd let out a roar.

I rode straight to where Betty sat, and I pointed to the kerchief on her head.

"Loan me that," I said, "for luck."

She gave it to me and said, "It should be a glove, really."

I don't know what she meant by that, but I took the kerchief and ran it under Benjie's bridle and over his eyes, so that he was blindfolded, yet with one snatch I could pull it away.

"What's that for?" the ringmaster asked.

"To keep him from getting dust in his eyes," I said. "Monkey dust."

Altimeter ticked the bar and it slid to the edge of the peg and stayed. That's the way the crowd liked them, close. Farn came riding toward me, laughing loudly and talking to me as if we were having the friendliest kind of competition.

"Keep away!" I told him.

But he rode right straight to me and laughed, "They're making us really jump, are they, Jerry?" and slapped his thing with his hand—the hand that had the whip in it. The whip passed within six inches of Benjie's head. Benjie didn't see it. Benjie didn't move. I walked him out onto the ring, headed him toward the jump, and leaning forward, snatched the blindfold away. Then I saw how high the bar had got, and my throat froze. But rather than let the horse sense how scared I was, I gave him my heel. We took off, and for one long moment seemed to hang over the bar. I felt Benjie's hindquarters turn sideways to clear, and next the ground rushed up like on a roller coaster and we were going down and down and then we landed and when I looked back, not a bar had moved.

"Benjie," I said, all choked up, "My horse Benjie."

Farn had been trying to hold Altimeter and now he eased off and the horse went into the jump. I saw that he was going to miss from the way Farn tried to sort of lift him off, and Altimeter's front hoof struck. It was the first really bad jump he had made, and Farn was furious.

All the way back around for his last try, Farn nagged Altimeter with the bit, and the horse began fighting him and that made Farn madder, and suddenly he cut Altimeter under the belly with his whip. The horse jumped in fright and astonishment, learning for the first time the meaning of the thing his rider carried in his hand. The whip on Altimeter was a mistake and everybody knew it as soon as they started toward the jump. I remembered what Pop had said, "A scared horse is never a safe one"—and Altimeter was scared.

Let me make one thing clear. I didn't want this. I had plenty against Farn, and I'm sure he had it coming to him, but I hadn't asked for anything like what happened.

What happened was, Altimeter hung his front feet on the top bar, one on each side, scissorslike. Farn went off, sort of sideways, but still holding the reins. They came down in a sprawl. And when they struck, Farn was on the bottom.

A gasp went up from the crowd, and then Altimeter got to his feet and trotted off with the saddle under his belly. Farn lay there on his side, unmoving, and a woman screamed and I knew it was Sadie.

The crowd forgets quickly. The final class had come, the open five-gaited, and the horses were racking around the ring with manes flying when Billy O'Day came to where Betty and I were sitting and said that Farn's pelvis was broken. Betty said that would get well, wouldn't it, and I just told her yes. I didn't tell her that Farn's self-assured walk would now be more of a sideway shuffle, and I didn't tell her how his wife, Sadie, liked front. I didn't tell her how Sadie had lost interest in Pop when he got his, and how Farn had taken her over.

"Did you notice how much Altimeter and Benjie are of a size and color?" I asked presently.

"Yes," Betty said.

"I guess Altimeter will be for sale," Billy said.

Jumping-Horse Man

"I might try to buy him," I said finally. This is what I have in mind, and I think it would make a fine act for the rodeo. Instead of jumping the moving car with one horse, suppose I jump it with two horses at one time, standing up with a foot on each one? That would be a real sight, especially with Altimeter and Benjie matched up so well.

I think it would be a fine act. Billy O'Day thinks so too. Betty doesn't think so much of it.

Trial by Marriage
(Two of a Kind)

Part I

Duff lay in the cold leaves, concealed under an alder. Again he held two fingers against his throat, and a yelping sound came from his mouth. Then he listened.

A redbird whistled in a tulip tree. Out of range across the bottom on a piney hill, a buck stood with raised head, unmoving, then grazed on. A flight of robins passed overhead, above the tall trees.

Then he heard the answer. Beyond the screen of underbrush, a wild turkey replied to him. Duff noiselessly slipped the safety off the shotgun with trembling fingers. He swallowed. Not in two days had he eaten. He could have killed small birds; but he only had three shells left, and each one of them should provide him with at least two days' food. That meant a deer or a turkey, or a covey of quail on the ground. The second day of hunger, he had found, was always the worst. The third day was bad, too, but by then your stomach had begun to get used to being empty. After the first few days a sort of amused lunacy crept over you, so that even cutting your own throat could be regarded as a diverting little trick, of no more importance than burning your girl's initials on your arm with sulphuric acid as some of them had done in the high-school laboratory. He sometimes wondered what had been his mother's state of mind when she shot herself. Undoubtedly she had been in some "accelerated"—as they had said—mental condition; that afternoon she had played the piano with a stormy genius that would have astonished those who knew her as a self-conscious, complaining, thumb-fingered music teacher, then had gone upstairs to stick the muzzle of the old hammerless revolver in her mouth and blow off the top of her head. Afterward there had been some whispers of murder, because the trigger of the old revolver was almost more than a man could pull, certainly more, they said, than fragile Mrs. Webster could have pulled.

At the inquest, the coroner's wife and several other women were asked to pull the trigger of the revolver, but not one of them could snap the gun. Duff's father, who at the time had been out quail hunting as usual—leaving the run-down little drugstore to the care of the sixteen-year-old soda jerker, who habitually put a third of the scanty receipts in his pocket as they came in—finally had risen heavily and picked up the revolver. Thrusting the muzzle of the gun in his mouth to demonstrate, he showed she had probably pulled the trigger with her two thumbs instead of the right index finger, and they had seen the truth of it.

Now Duff heard the sound of the turkey's scratching behind the screening thicket. A calf, lost from his mama, bawled. Duff held his breath. The turkey began going *putt! putt!* nervously, as the calf kept up his bawling.

The calf stopped bawling, perhaps having been rejoined by its mother. Duff yelped again. After an almost interminable time, the turkey answered.

Suddenly the young gobbler stepped up on a log, in full view. The sun glistened on his burnished neck; his purplish-red head was alert. Duff raised his gun with an excruciating slowness. The turkey relaxed and ruffled its feathers. Duff's gun was almost level; he could feel the nerves in his left wrist jumping. A leaf crackled. The turkey's head went back up, and the disarranged feathers lay quickly down. The turkey went *putt!*

Aiming at the head, Duff pulled the trigger. The turkey leaped over backward and flopped and kicked spasmodically in the damp leaves. Duff jumped up and ran, almost stumbling in his eagerness to reach the dying bird.

When the last feeble kicking passed, Duff leaned his gun on a log and picked up the turkey by the head, just as a man in brown leggings stepped from behind a tree with a Colt .45 in his hand.

"Stand right there, and don't move that gun," he said. "Didn't expect to yelp up no warden, did you?"

Duff stared at him.

"Them 'Posted' signs, buddy, wasn't put up just for looks," the warden said.

Duff tried to speak, but his voice stuck.

"Now come here, and bring that turkey with you."

"I got to have him," Duff said simply.

The warden looked at him curiously. "You see what I got here in my hand, don't you?"

Duff knew that if he leaned over to pick up his gun, he would be shot. His gun was something he needed badly, but there wasn't any choice. *He may have more pistol there than he can handle, unless he's an old army man.*

Duff turned his back and began walking away, leaving his gun on the log. He slung the turkey over his shoulder.

"Hey! You wait!"

Duff kept walking, as if he hadn't heard.

"You better stop!"

Duff kept on, stepping unhurriedly over a bush. If he started running, he would be shot instantly. But even the toughest warden would have to heat up a bit before firing at the back of a man calmly walking away.

"You hear me? I'm fixing to shoot!"

Duff shifted the turkey to the other shoulder. He paused to look interestedly at a wildcat scratch-mark on a chinquapin tree, then continued.

"You better stop!"

Then there was a momentary silence, followed by the crash of the automatic. A two-inch dogwood limb abruptly broke and fell above Duff's head, and now the time to run had come. He shoved the turkey under his arm and jumped away, putting as much cover between him and the automatic as he could. The bullets were crashing like cannon balls now, but none of them came close.

Trial by Marriage

At first the flight exhilarated him; then he began to tire, and once when he stopped he found that his breath was coming with such agonizing swiftness that he was almost suffocated, and his fingers could hardly keep their grip on the dead turkey.

The shooting ceased, and after a long time Duff heard the rapid thud of a horse's hoofs. The warden had gone back to where he had tied his horse and now was coming to try to head Duff off. Duff crept quietly under a bush.

Presently the horse came by, moving more carefully as it felt its way across the litter of the bottom, regardless of the warden's angry kicks. Duff could hear the animal's windy breathing; the hoofs passed close by, not fifteen feet away. The sound of them gradually faded.

Duff lay still. An hour passed. Again and again the warden coursed the woods, searching. Finally dark came, and with it silence. Duff crawled out, stretched, and started the long blind walk to the fence that marked the outer boundary of the plantation.

After he reached the road, he walked four hours down it, and finally stopped in a creek swamp and began preparing his turkey for roasting.

When the turkey was finished the next day, Duff didn't eat again until Tuesday.

Without the gun he felt helpless. Traveling aimlessly, sleeping under bridges, and avoiding farmhouses as if he were a fugitive, he gradually developed a certain self-sufficiency. One warm day he happened upon a big diamondback that had come out of the land-tortoise hole that it had pre-empted for the winter. Basking peacefully in the sun, the rattlesnake had neither the energy nor the inclination to glide back into the hole, but drew its head back and sounded a dry warning. Duff killed the snake with a lightwood knot, and that night roasted the pink-white flesh over oak coals. Lightwood knots and sticks, because of their hardness and compactness, became weapons. He grew proficient at seeing rabbits huddled in the brush, their bright frightened eyes betraying their camouflage, and at smashing their skulls with one quick throw. He learned to watch for puddles and small sloughs left by a falling creek, and to muddy the water so that the trapped small fish would seek the surface, whereupon he would flip them out. One day while he was stalking a heron, a red-tailed hawk plummeted out of the sky upon a woods rat, just in front of where he lay; and while the bird was occupied in dispatching its prey, Duff killed it with a lucky throw; and he had both a hawk and a rat for supper.

But it was only infrequently that he had luck like that. Most of the time the quarry flushed too soon, or his throw was bad, or he found no rabbits. Most of the time he was hungry.

Then one day he came upon a dead half-grown pig, so freshly killed that the buzzards had not even found it. Duff carefully looked around. The gentle slope of the Alabama hillside was spaced with young pines; at the bottom was a gully of sedge and bramble. Beyond was a brown cornfield, at the far end of which a Negro and a mule were plowing, just beginning to break ground, the new furrows gray-black upon the straw-colored field. In the distance, perhaps a mile away, was a water-oak grove, and almost concealed within it, a farmhouse. In the morning stillness, Duff heard the far, faint sound of several dogs barking. He wondered if the Negro plowman could see him that far away. Finally, crawling backward on his hands and knees, he began dragging the hog behind him.

Only after he had reached the woods, and sat there panting and admiring his prize, did he wonder how the pig had met his death. Satisfied that the trees would conceal the smoke, he got a fire started; and while the sticks were catching, he examined the pig. The only marks were holes behind the head, and a small amount of dried blood in the dark bristles. When he turned the pig over, its head dangled loosely; and Duff perceived that something had bitten the pig behind the head so savagely that its neck had been broken.

Next day he went back to the hill and lay in the sunshine. When his stomach was empty, he was too absorbed in the problem of filling it for introspection. But now that it was full, his dissatisfaction with himself returned.

IT USED TO BE A JOKE around Hattiesburg to say, "I've been downtown all morning helping Duff Webster," which meant doing nothing. And the old ladies around town said, "Guess Duff's taking after his papa."

And this, he supposed, was partly true. For the good days that he remembered were the ones when his father had been a professional horseman, and then a field-trial man. Some of his earliest memories were of helping his father put their five-gaited mare's tail into the tail set to make it arch, and of firing her with ginger root to make her lively and flashy. But Duff's mother despised horse-show life and horse-show people, and kept nagging Troy Webster until he gave it up. In his youth he had trained dogs, and now he returned to it in a professional way, and got hold of a good setter, a dog he won over two thousand dollars with the first year.

Then for several years they had lived the nomad life of field-trial people. From November until March they traveled to the big-time Southern trials, thence up east for the one-course trials on pheasants, until late spring, and finally the twenty-five-hundred-mile trek to the summer training-grounds on the prairies of Manitoba. Duff remembered this part of his life with a faint pleasure, even in spite of his mother's attempts to turn him against it.

"Might as well be gypsies," she complained bitterly. "Not a chance to live a normal, Christian life, or to appreciate fine things."

Before long she had ceased accompanying Troy, and had kept Duff at home, where she could play the piano to him and read poetry to him and try in every way possible to counteract the influence of his earlier life. Eventually she persuaded Troy to give up field trials, and to buy the little drugstore. At the moment Troy thought he was tired of being a nomad, but after a few months of trying to sell hot-water bottles and Dr. Pierce's Pellets for Pale People he lost his enthusiasm for it. He had been a fairly good provider before; but as a merchant he was shiftless and indifferent. Duff's mother began teaching music to help out, and to try to shame Troy into working harder. But Troy didn't shame easily.

"The trouble with me," Troy had said one afternoon when he and Duff were on the lake, duck hunting, "is I was born a hundred years too late. God never meant me to be no drugstore man. I get sick of just smelling that damned drugstore. On the other hand, horse manure smells pretty good to me. Listen. When I was a boy, the neighbors used to come get me to track down their strayed cows, I was so good at it; and getting lost in the woods is something that just ain't in my book. I've killed ducks flying with a twenty-two rifle; I can sneak through the woods quiet as a cat. Why, if I'd been born far enough back, they might have statues to me instead of to Davy Crockett and them! But my kind ain't in demand any more. Now you got to be good at selling stuff, or banking, or singing on the radio. You take a man who knows how to blow in a hound dog or make a horse swim a creek or head off a crippled deer—he ain't nobody now, just a loafer or a poacher or maybe a game warden."

But Troy didn't really worry about it. And that was the difference between him and Duff. Duff thought maybe his mother might have had something to do with it, because all his life she kept telling him what a great man he was going to be, possibly a musician or a painter. She tried to teach him piano until she discovered he was tone-deaf.

When he was younger, she used to read high-minded poetry to him. He had rebelled at these forced feedings of inspiration; he would never forget the memory of her somewhat nasal voice as she put "expression" in the readings. He exasperated her by preferring *Barrack Room Ballads*. Often, now that he was a man, he wished he remembered more of the other poems. And he found that he fully expected to be, if not a great man, at least one capable of making a living. So it was a surprise to find that his ambition was no greater than his father's. At the beginning of each promising job he would goad himself fiercely—only, at last, to lose interest in it.

NOW HE FOUND THAT no work in his life absorbed him like his fight for survival. Each hungry night he lay by his fire planning his hunt for the next day. The problem of how to capture one of the soft-shelled turtles in a slough fascinated him. He was inordinately pleased to discover that there were mussels in the river, after noticing their trails here and there on the white sand of the bottom.

But the problem of the dead pig was not solved for several days.

On a morning that he thought might be Sunday, because the birds were singing, he came upon a freshly killed goat, a big ram with a fine spread of horns. Exhilarated by this good fortune, he felt the animal's still-warm neck to see if it was broken as the pig's had been.

There was a bloodstain in the goat hair back of the shoulders. Grasping one of the thick horns, he raised the head off the ground, and the goat seemed to break in the middle. Duff stared, his hunger forgotten. Again he lifted the goat's head and again only the front half lifted.

Duff had an impulse to drop the goat and run. Slowly he knelt down and felt the animal's backbone, the still-damp blood staining his hands. The backbone was broken. *What could have done that?* he thought uneasily.

Near by, a woodpecker worked his way up a tree, rattling the dead bark. Duff looked at the goat. With a queer nervousness, he opened his knife and made a shallow slit down the back of the animal, then pulled the skin back so he could see the injury. On the smooth pink flesh were blood-filled holes—teeth marks.

Just then he heard a sound, and he turned with a start. Standing there watching him was a dog—a big, straight-legged pointer dog with a chest like a well bucket, and wide-sprung ribs, and a lean belly. The dog's head was like something cut from stone;

it was black with a white blaze, and the rest of him was white with black ticking; his eyes, instead of being deep brown, were light, almost yellow. He stood watching Duff unemotionally, gently panting; and Duff suddenly knew it was those exposed capable teeth that had broken the goat's back.

"Hello, pup," Duff said, relieved.

The dog lifted his lip in a soundless snarl.

"Take it easy, boy." He moved slowly toward the dog. The big pointer gave a warning growl.

"Ah, come on. Don't try to be tough. You're not so bad—just a goat-killer."

The dog jumped then, straight for Duff's face. Surprised, Duff jerked backward, and the dog's jaws chopped shut, loud in their nearness. He shoved the dog away, only to have him spring again. This time Duff struck blindly at him with his fist, turning the dog half around in the air. On the second swing, Duff lost his balance and fell, and instantly the dog's jaws closed on his thigh. Duff rolled over, and the dog was upon him again, this time going for his stomach, but on that flat surface he could get nothing in his mouth but clothes. Duff seized the dog's neck and slung him to one side. As he tried to rise the animal came again, and Duff kicked him away.

For a moment they paused, the dog standing in a crouch, with his head down, ready. Slowly Duff rose to his feet, his face ash-gray with weakness. Then, as if bored with the fight, the dog turned and went away.

Duff's leg began to throb, and the spit was dry in his mouth. The strength was gone from him, as if his ligaments had been cut, so that only by great exertion of will could he close the fingers of his hand.

Overhead, a crow flew, the bright winter sun glinting off its back. The borers worked steadily and noisily in a pine log near by. The morning grew. Finally Duff crawled over and began skinning the goat.

EVERY NIGHT HE SAT UNDER the creek bridge with his increasingly inflamed leg throbbing and stared into the fire and tried to figure some way to get even with that outlaw dog. His mind conceived many shrewd snares and traps, none of which worked. Finally he saw the pointer ranging the countryside. From the tree into which he had painfully pulled himself, he could follow the dog's swift coursing. Even above his hatred, he suddenly felt a strange kinship for this dog. They were both misfits, outlaws. They were two of a kind.

He saw the dog head out toward a cornfield. From a blackberry patch, something broke cover—a litter of half-grown pigs. The dog swerved and effortlessly overtook one of them and, almost without slowing, killed it and flung it aside. By the time the sound of the terrified squeal drifted to Duff, the pig was dead, and the dog was out into the field.

Halfway out in the cornfield, the pointer checked his flat, blinding run and swung at right angles. With his head high, as if he were looking over a stump, he trotted swiftly and unswervingly across the field for a good hundred yards and then, without creeping or drawing, stopped cold. For one electric second, the dog stood in a high, breath-taking point. Then he sprang, snapping at the covey of quail that erupted all around him. The quail streamed over the rise with the pointer hot behind them.

Trial by Marriage

THREE DAYS LATER the dog was trapped, but not in a contrivance of Duff's making. He caught a hind leg in a fence. Duff chanced upon him, apparently not long after it happened. The dog was not yelping; silently he writhed and twisted as he hung there, trying to get at the imprisoned leg and chew himself free.

Nervously Duff looked for a club heavy enough to be of protection. Finally he found a piece of fence post, from which he knocked off the rotted sap until a solid bludgeon of pine heart was left. He limped back to the dog, not sure, now that he had him, what he would do.

The pointer had ceased struggling to watch, his front feet braced against the wire. Duff touched him gingerly with the end of the club, and immediately the dog's jaws closed upon it. Duff twisted it free.

The dog watched him, his lips fluttering with a measured, rattling growl.

Duff's eye fell upon the dog's collar. A brass plate was upon it. He could see one word: *Reward*.

Duff cut a limb from a black-gum tree with his knife and trimmed it to four feet, the thickness being that of a broom handle. Working patiently, he bored a hole through one end of the stick with the point of his knife, and through this he ran a strand of wire twisted from the fence. He removed his torn coat. With one hand he prodded the dog; when the animal's quick jaw seized the club, he instantly threw the coat over the dog's head. There was a short struggle as the dog fought the coat, but at last it was fast on him, with the sleeves tight around his head.

While the dog was preoccupied in trying to bite his way out of the coat, Duff quickly twisted the loose strands of the wire around the collar. That done, he had the dog fast on the stick and therefore under his control, so that he could neither attack him nor run away. The plate on the collar read: *Reward. Amos Hawthorne, Tafton, Ala.* He raised the dog, taking the pressure off the bound hind foot and releasing it, and snatched the coat loose.

The dog's first move was to leap at Duff. In spite of the fact that he only hurt himself by trying to jump against the stick, he kept at it, circling and charging time after time. Finally he tried to get away, but Duff braced himself and held on against the dog's incredibly powerful pulling. At last the dog became reconciled to his capture and stood watching the man and softly growling. When Duff started walking the dog wasn't inclined to accompany him; but Duff jerked him a couple of times, and finally he reluctantly followed.

WHILE COLORED JOHN WESLEY DAVIS and his son Paul were putting the dogs in the wagon, Lucie Sullivan gave her horse an extra bit of grooming. Wearing old riding-breeches and briar-scratched boots, she strapped him and picked his feet and adjusted the bridle. She loved the horse and liked to touch him and work on him herself. He was a bay gelding, four years old, a somewhat small, good-chested animal; still too nervous and full of colt foolishness to be a first-class dog-training horse.

The first time she had ever got on him the bridle broke, and he bolted. As he ran the saddle began to slip; holding onto the mane, she had managed to keep easing higher on the horse so that the saddle went on over without her, and eventually slipped off completely. When the horse finally tired of his gallop, Lucie was still there, without saddle or bridle. They had put an item in the *Tafton Weekly Times* about that.

The horse moved about impatiently, turning his ears toward the sounds of the eager dogs and the Negroes. John Wesley spoke to the dogs with a natural familiarity, as if everything he said was completely understandable to them. "Okay, Mike, you gits another tryout today; only recollect we's pointing patidges and not stink-birds, if you don't mind. Look out dere, Nat, better not pick no argument with old Friendship, if'n you want to live to flesh mo' coveys."

Paul, his son, was a quiet, morose type. As he harnessed the dog-wagon mules, he sang:

> "I want to die easy when I die,
> I want to die easy when I die,
> Shout Salvation as I fly—"

Lucie stopped brushing. She was a rather plain girl, with light hair and coloring; she used no make-up, which she figured was just as well. But her teeth were even and dull white, and her figure was good, and her gray-blue eyes were animated by an Irish love of life.

"For gosh sake," she said. "I don't call that dying easy."

The Negro boy stopped singing. He had a deep and pleasant voice, and had studied at Tuskegee Institute.

"What's the call for that?" Lucie asked.

Paul straightened and looked at her. "I guess it's just the nigger in me."

"Why can't the nigger in you sing about God's chillun having shoes or something, huh? It's too early in the day to be dying easy." She looked at him again. "What's the matter with you lately, Paul?"

"Nothing."

John Wesley heard and looked worried. "Yes'm, Miss Lucie, something's wrong wid dat chile, Lawd knows. He's troubled in his mind."

Paul looked at his father angrily and went back to fastening the harness.

"Miss Lucie," John Wesley said, regarding his son with puzzlement, "he say he gwine away."

"You're leaving, Paul?"

"Yes, Miss Lucie."

"Where? North?"

"I guess so. I wish Papa hadn't said anything about it."

Lucie had known long ago that Paul wasn't meant to be just a dog trainer's man, although sometimes it seemed that he liked handling dogs even better than John Wesley did. She had known this as far back as high-school days, when the white boys had got Paul to work their algebra homework for them.

In those days, she recalled with a rush of memory, she had been going with Charley Bedlow. That was before Delia Phillips had appeared. Charley had taken her to her first dance, in his old car. On the way to the pavilion the car stalled, and she had to get out in her new long dress and push; but she had tied the dress up around her hips in the dark and thought nothing of it. At the dance Charley drank several bottles of home brew. She tasted it once, which was enough, and thereafter watched with awe as he let it flow down his throat with hardly a gurgle.

Until that time she had considered kissing immoral, so when Charley caught her off guard and gave her a thorough one on her horrified mouth, she responded with her fist—which, in his home-brewed happiness, he considered not worth getting sore about. Later, in bed, she reviewed the incident and found the memory of the kiss not at all disagreeable. Next day she apologized to him and asked him to please let her know in advance next time so she could be ready. "Next time," she said, "just knock."

For a while, then, she and Charley were doing what was known as "going together." This was more his idea than hers, and before long getting rid of him amounted to a problem. And then it was that Delia Phillips arrived upon her awareness. For Delia, to Lucie's gratitude, stole Charley away.

Delia's swift and positive acquisition of Charley Bedlow, Lucie recalled, was the first indication of the power of this female electromagnet. Delia then was only a sophomore, which is low in the high-school caste; and it soon developed that few boys interested her at all. But when one did interest her she threw the switch, and whoever it was in the magnetic field was drawn inexorably in, and held fast there as long as she saw fit to keep the current on. "It's interesting to watch her work," one of the girls had said, "as long as it's not your boy she's working."

Charley Bedlow—soon dropped by Delia—failed to graduate, for, not caring to face Lucie, he quit visiting the kennels for aid from Paul. "Don't know as it matters much about Mister Charley not gitting by," Paul concluded. "His I.Q. ain't none too high anyway."

DRIVING OUT—THEY LIVED in town so as to be away from the noise of the dogs, and drove the four miles out to the kennels every morning—Amos Hawthorne had complained that his morning eggnog had slipped up on him, so Lucie decided not to worry him with the matter of Paul's going away. The dogs saw him coming, an erect, six-foot-three man of seventy-odd, and they let out an excited, deafening chorus. For a moment he tried to talk against the noise, then whirled, as if hearing it for the first time, and squalled:

"Wha-a-a, you!"

There was instant silence, and the kennel pens emptied magically. Presently here and there a head appeared; a bold dog or two tiptoed out of houses into the pens, and before long most of them were out again, standing up on the heavy wire and whining to be carried afield that day.

Abruptly all the dogs began barking furiously, their attention now at the gate, where Duff Webster and the dog had turned in from the highway. Duff walked slowly; his clothes were unkempt, and one trouser-leg was split to the knee, so that his calf was exposed.

John Wesley said, "Here come a tramp. And, look ayonder, Mr. Amos," he added suddenly, "if dat ain't ol' Judas he got with him!"

All of them stopped what they were doing and watched the approaching ones curiously. Lucie's horse snorted and moved restlessly.

Duff said, "I'm looking for Amos Hawthorne."

"That's me," Amos said, leaning forward to squint at him.

Duff licked his dry lips. His eyes were red-shot, as if with fever. "I brought your dog. I thought you might be glad to get him back."

Amos snorted. "That dog? He ain't no good. Been loose two weeks. Every farmer in the county's gunning for him—with my permission."

Duff hesitated. "It says 'Reward' on his collar."

"All my collars are the same. He ain't no good, just an outlaw dog. Just a mean, hard-headed bolter."

"Well, it said 'Reward,' " Duff said disappointedly.

"Well you ain't gonna get a dime out of me. We was taking him to the vet to chloroform the day he got away. You go git you another money-making scheme."

"Pay him something, Squire," Lucie interrupted. "It says it on the collar. He probably earned it, getting Judas onto that device he's fixed there."

"Lucie, I ain't paying no tramp no reward for no goat-killing dog. Paul, you got my horse ready?"

"Yes, sir."

"Paul," Lucie said, handing him a key, "go get my pocketbook out of the car. I'll pay the reward out of the grocery money, and let the old tightwad eat maypops and branch water for a few days."

"Yes'm."

John Wesley then spoke with deliberation. " 'Scuse me, Miss Lucie, but dat man's sick. Look at dat leg!"

They looked. An angry purple showed on the veins of his exposed calf.

"What's wrong with your leg?" Lucie asked. "Did that dog bite you?"

"Yes, he did that, all right. Were you going to pay me something for catching him?"

"Yes," Lucie said finally. "Here's five dollars. My advice is to spend it in a doctor's office."

He steered the dog Judas toward the kennels. "You want me to put him in here?"

"Not in there!" roared Amos Hawthorne suddenly, so that Lucie's horse jumped. The dog nearest the gate was a liver-and-white pointer, now somewhat fat around the shoulders, with graying muzzle, and his growl at Judas showed yellowed teeth. "For Pete's sake, Wesley, take that Judas dog and shut him up in that empty pen. You going to stand there and let him put that dog in with Sam?"

Duff folded the bill with a preoccupied deliberation, creasing each fold with thumbnail and forefinger. His fingers were trembling, and the simple act seemed to take hours.

Lucie said, "Thanks for bringing our dog back."

"That's all right."

While the Negroes loaded the dogs into the dog wagon, she watched Duff as he walked toward the gate. He went slowly, with a careful tread, as if he were drunk.

"All right, Lucie," her grandfather called.

"Just a minute," she said. "Let's see if he's going to make it to the road or fall in the yard."

Amos came back and watched, too, suspiciously.

Trial by Marriage

"Them tramps and hoboes like that, they got all sorts of tricks. Being sick and needing medicine is old as me, and God knows that's old. Your ma, now, in her day, she used to fall for any crazy story."

"Sucker, wasn't she?" The man reached the gate and now crossed the cattle-gap, stepping from one pipe to another. "I imagine they were glad to get a sucker like her in heaven, to elect her chairman of the board or something," Lucie said. "Look, he's made the road. Now he's the county's responsibility, huh? Takes a load off my mind, I have my doubts."

"Just drunk, likely as not." The dogs were barking, and the two Negroes were waiting.

"They sort of get me, Squire, these derelicts on their way to sunny Florida," Lucie said meditatively. "Who are they, and where do they come from, and what's the matter with them? You take our friend about to fall on his beard yonder; I know it sounds funny, but there's an outside chance that, under that front, there's a brain and a heart and capacity for work and love."

"If them fellows was any account," Amos said impatiently, "they wouldn't be in that fix."

"I guess that's true part of the time," she said, leading her horse forward so she could see the man in the road. She turned back. "There he goes. Wesley, go to your house and tell Sarah to have some sort of bed ready, then come down to the road and help us."

When she got to the road, Duff was sitting on the bank, head in his hands, with his feet in the ditch. He didn't look up until the horse stopped beside him. He stared at the girl for a moment, his eyes fever-bright.

"Who are you?" he asked.

"Lucie Sullivan," she answered. "What's your name?"

"Duff Webster," he said. "That's a nice horse."

"Look," she said, "now that I've got you in a confiding state of mind, when did you eat last?"

He pondered a moment and finally said, "Recently."

"How recently?"

"I forget."

She dismounted and stood in the road, holding the reins, and she talked to him while she waited. "Let's talk of something you might remember, then. When did you work last?"

"What's that got to do with it? I didn't come here and I'm not going to leave." Rubbing his hand across his mouth, he gently fell over backward, but his bright eyes remained open. When he talked his lips barely moved, so that what he said was almost indistinguishable. "On Saturday nights, late, even after the barbershop has closed, then's when you scrub the fount, and the ammonia chokes you and makes your eyes run, and I looked up and there stood this—and what it seemed he had in his hand seemed like a—a gun—and I thought he was somebody just playing a, you know, a—the twenty-nine dollars he took out of the cash drawer was the most of any Saturday night except then my eyes kept running water and he thought I was crying and I let him have the glassful of ammonia and blinded him and he shot down a row of Peruna—"

"Listen, you haven't been shot? Is that what's wrong with you?"

"I'm fine—"

"Oh, sure. Don't take me out, coach, I'm all right," Lucie said.

TEAGUE MCGINNIS, on his way to the Free-for-All, stopped by to see Amos Hawthorne. McGinnis was a Texan, a small, pleasant, hard-riding, hard-working dog man not long ago moved to Alabama. His face was weather-burned, though not of the brown-parchment quality that generations of sun and cold and wind had imparted to old Amos's. McGinnis drank almost nightly, always in small, frequent swallows straight from the bottle, without any chaser except a deep, appreciative intake of breath; the liquor apparently had no effect at all on him, unless to make him even pleasanter than ever. His brag dog was Hotfoot, a fiery-going young pointer, somewhat small-headed but, as Amos said the first time he saw the dog run, "He's got more style than a sheep's got guts."

"Lucie's at the picture show. When she comes in," Amos said now, "you-all can ride out and find a pen for your dogs. We'll put you up, too."

"Be sure you got room. I don't want to cause you trouble," Teague McGinnis said. "I aim to give your dogs hell, same as ever."

"Young fellow, you sleep on my bed and drink my liquor, and welcome; but when we turn the dogs loose, we'll run 'em till the hair slips, right on."

"Don't believe I've had the pleasure of meeting your granddaughter, Lucie."

"She's a good hand, though being a woman she ain't got a good squalling voice for a field-trial handler," the old man said.

"I hear your eyes are going back on you some," McGinnis said sympathetically.

"Good as yours," Amos said sharply. "Better, maybe."

McGinnis mumbled in embarrassment. Then: "Glad you've retired old Sam. He was always hard to beat," McGinnis said presently. "One grand dog!"

Amos looked at him levelly. "McGinnis, Sam ain't retired, as you'll find out at Grand Junction in February."

"Why, that dog's over ten years old!" McGinnis said.

"Yes, and I'm seventy-odd; but you better pray you don't draw against the old folks in the National!"

After Lucie came in and they had talked awhile, Amos said, "Take him and his old plug dogs out to the kennels, Lucie. I'm going to bed."

"I wanted to see our patient anyway," she answered. "Doc's going out."

They rode the four miles out to the kennel farm in Teague McGinnis's pick-up truck. The dogs were in their cages in the back.

"The Squire's some guy," McGinnis said.

"He'll be okay when he matures. He's just at the awkward age now," Lucie said. "If you're from Texas, you'll have to see my horse."

"I'm all for looking at anything that'll keep me out with you a little longer."

She looked around at him. "That's okay with me. Although I never thought I'd put up with any man wearing those high-heeled cowboy boots."

After they put the dogs in an empty kennel pen, she led him to the barn, and held the flashlight into the stall of her colt, Pete. McGinnis took the light and went over the horse slowly.

Finally she said, "Well, say something. What's wrong with him?"

"He's okay."

"Just okay, huh?"

"He's all right," McGinnis said.

"Just all right, huh?" she answered, laughing. She took his arm and steered him toward John Wesley Davis's house. "That horse is a bit fresh. Tomorrow we're going to hitch him to a plow and let him work off a little meanness. Think he'll object? He's never been put to a plow."

"All I can tell you is don't hitch him to any plow you want to use again," McGinnis said. "I'm sorry I'll be leaving too early to see that."

Dr. Phillips was at the house when they got there. His handsome daughter, Delia, who sometimes acted as nurse for him, opened the old black pill case. Duff Webster was in Wesley's company bed, his head rolling. Two fever spots were on his cheeks and he made incoherent noises.

Delia looked at him. "It wouldn't surprise me," she said speculatively, "if under that beard there was a pretty good-looking face."

Lucie thought, *Uh oh; that from Delia ought to revive him.* She asked Dr. Phillips, "How is he now?"

"Two years ago," Dr. Phillips said, rummaging in his case, "a case of septicemia like this would have called for a lot of desperate treatment and transfusions; and he'd've kicked off anyway. Now we just shoot the sulfathiazole to him and, bingo, he's okay. I'm trying to get his fever down right now. But there's no question about his living, although I will say that he ain't greatly enthusiastic about it."

Duff's head gradually slowed in its twisting, and he said:

> "The earth is iron, and the skies are brass,
> And faint with fervor of the flaming air
> The languid hours pass—"

Lucie listened in amazement. "That's poetry."

"He *been* talking like that, Miss Lucie," John Wesley said, in the morose tone that had overtaken him since Paul left to go North. "Yere dis morning he speak a piece give me de trembles. Talk about down to de devil."

"He must have been a schoolteacher, sometime or other," said Delia Phillips.

When they were outside, Teague whistled softly. "Yow! Who's that girl in there?"

"Hey," Lucie said, "what is this? You saw me first."

"I'm just curious."

"Yeah, I know. Just curious. Well, I'm happy to say that you didn't register on Delia's voltmeter. Else I'd be hitchhiking home."

IT WAS APPARENT THAT the colt did not like the looks of the equipment they were draping around him. The more they put on him, the more nervous he became; and when finally John Wesley hitched the plow to him and said, "Giddup, Pete!" the colt went forward just enough to feel the encumbrance behind him and then reared, perpendicular, hoofs pawing the air. Again he reared, only this time without reservation;

he went on over backward, and fell in a mess of chain and leather. They hastened to extricate him, avoiding the threshing hoofs.

Amos shouted, "He won't git away with that!"

"Let's skip it," Luce begged. "He'll kill himself."

"Listen, child," Amos said. "That horse has got to be worked hard and regular. If you won't let nobody else ride him, he'll have to be plowed. Wesley, put him up until tomorrow, and maybe by then he'll learn a little sense."

When Lucie went in to see the sick man, she found him shaven and awake. She stood in stunned silence, seeing for the first time what he looked like. His burned skin clung tight to the bone. His chin and mouth were chiseled into lean lines, his nose was thin and almost Roman, his eyes were black as his eyebrows and hair; his eyes were boyish, but there were no laugh wrinkles around them.

"Hello," she said. "You must be feeling better."

"I reckon you'll be glad to have me off your hands," he said.

"Oh, not especially. Our dog bit you, after all."

Next day he was propped up in bed, and could see them having their trouble with the colt and the plow. He got painfully up, slipped on his old clothes, and limped out to where they were harnessing the snorting horse.

"Look," Lucie said. "Lazarus has risen."

"The doctor say you could git up?" Amos asked.

"I forgot to ask him," Duff said, supporting himself on the fence. He paused. "It's not any of my business, but you're liable to hurt this colt. If you'll hitch him up again, maybe I can make him behave."

"He's had enough for today."

"I believe I could make him behave."

"What are you going to do?"

"Hitch him up and let me show you."

They hitched the colt up again. He was so wild they had to hold him by a twist on his nose.

"All right," Lucie said to Duff, "what now?"

"Turn him loose."

They released the twist from the horse's nose. He lunged forward, felt the plow catch in the earth, then reared, and went over backward like some sort of mechanical tumbling toy.

"God dammit!" Amos said. "Git him loose, quick!"

"No, leave him alone!" Duff said, hobbling forward.

He reached the struggling colt and fell upon his head. The colt's struggling ceased. For thirty minutes Duff sat there on the colt's head, holding him down.

"Now let's straighten him out," he said, "and see."

They straightened the gear, and Duff got up. The horse came up with a leap and shook himself.

"Giddup," Duff said.

Pete danced for a moment, as if he were about to rear. Then he seemed to think better of it, and went forward into the collar with a smash, and the gray earth began to up-spill over the smooth moldboard of the plowshare. John Wesley had to get into a trot to keep up.

ON THE DAY DUFF was dismissed by the doctor, Lucie asked him, "Where to now?"

"Down the road is all I know," He answered, ill at ease.

She said, "Look, before you go, would you help me saddle Pete? Everybody's out now, and sometimes he acts up."

He followed her into the yard and to the tack room. It was a cold, somewhat windy day, and the moving air howled softly against the corners of the barn; the dogs stood shivering in their kennels, watching them. She noticed that he brought the bridle holding the mouth of the Pelham bit in his hands to warm it; he saddled the horse deftly and tightened the girth gradually, one hole at a time, unhurriedly. Pete stood still.

He led the horse out past the kennels, just as a delivery truck from town drove up with a dog crate in which a young setter lay disconsolately.

When the dog had been unloaded, she said, "He's from Indiana. A Derby prospect. Good head on him."

"Looks like Sport's Peerless stock," Duff said.

She glanced at him sharply. "That's a son of Sport's Peerless."

"Anybody can see the resemblance."

"No, not anybody. Only somebody that knows bird dogs. Look," she said directly, "do you want a job?"

"Why, you don't know anything about me."

"More than you think," she said. "We lost a hand last week. Do you want the job or not?"

Duff felt suddenly trapped. What he had thought he wanted was to go his own way, alone, to return to the animal life that he had found. He was suspicious of his overwhelming gratitude to this friendly, generous girl. And yet, from somewhere there was an urge to stay.

"Well?" she said. "You want the job?"

"I don't exactly know."

"Where could I find out?" she asked.

Later, when it was all settled, Lucie said to her grandfather, "Squire, you needn't look any further for a helper to take Paul's place. I got one."

"Who?"

She tilted her head toward Duff. "Him."

"That tramp? You ain't hired *him!*"

"Squire, he knows something about dogs, or he'd never've got that Judas here. But even if he was raised in a shoe store, he can clean out kennels and stuff."

"You don't know nothing about him."

"He mentioned that."

"I ain't goan hire no tramp that comes into my yard!"

"Squire, look. He wasn't begging—fine place to come, if he was. And if he doesn't suit us, we'll let him go. Okay?"

"He don't suit me! Not none. Let him go right now."

"I guess we lose the advance pay I gave him to get him some clothes," she lied.

"*What!* You've done give him money? Well put him to doing something then! If you cain't find nothing else, have him pick the fleas off them dogs by hand." He shook his mud-gray head and looked toward Wesley's house angrily. "Durned if I ain't done sunk mighty low, having to git a something-another like that to feed my dogs."

Afterward Duff went to the kennels and came to the pen of the black-and-white pointer Judas, drawn to the dog by some strange kinship that transcended their enmity. For they were both, he felt, misfits, outlaws. The hostility of Amos Hawthorne hurt him, stifled the quick admiration that he felt for the old trainer. The girl was certainly friendly enough, but then being friendly was stock in trade with girls. He disliked them all in advance, knowing that they were all subject to the metamorphosis of marriage, emerging from the ceremony as something quite different from what they had been or seemed to be. "I don't know what it is about them words a preacher says," Troy Webster had once confided, "but a woman ain't the same any more after they're said." Only with this wild dog did he feel at ease.

"Hello, Judas," Duff said.

The dog rose and walked stiffly toward him. He bared his teeth and growled.

"Don't worry," Duff said. "You're liable to get another chance at me."

EVERY MORNING DUFF walked the four miles to the kennels from Tafton. Leaving before daylight, he walked rapidly in the cold early morning. At first he had simply helped around the kennels, saddling and tending the horses, and caring for the dogs.

" 'Tain't like de old-timey days," Wesley said, the day they were worming the dogs. "Us used to have a whole yardful of dogs round here. Didn't have no empty pens. Now we got just twenty er so dogs and most of dem just shooting-dogs to be trained for folks. De field-trial owners, dey recollect bout Cap'm Amos gitting to be eighty or ninety years old, and dey just naturally send dey dogs to somebody else. 'Oh, dere never was a better one dan old Amos, in his day. De beat of him didn't live,' dey say—and send dey dogs on to somebody else. Dey don't see dat Cap'm Amos ain't no common soul; he's a miracle de Lawd done passed. He can cave in a hoss wid dem old long legs right today, and blow a bulge in a dog whistle.

"You see dat old Ambling Sam dog yonder, sitting up dere grinning in de sun, wid his eyes closed like he thinking bout sump'm? He all we got dat can win. But dey ain't no better dan him never been turned loose. Some says old Crazy Mary Montrose was better, and some says Sioux, and some says Comanche Frank, but I seen 'em all go, and old Sam'l he would a-jest naturally run 'em into a gopher hole. It ain't happened for him to win at Grand Junction in de National yet, but dat's jest de way de numbers fell. He goan be de next National Champion just as sho as de Lawd loves de trufe.

"Old Sam, he de banker-man. He furnish de cash, right on, one year to de next. 'Old Sam, he too old to do nothing dis year,' dey say. Den he come trickling right on along and he take a fust here, and a second hyar, and befo' long we done made out another year.

"But he de last. Wen he pass on, it's goan be bad. Old Sam, he gits good puppies, but dey sends dem to somebody else to train, now'days, 'scusing dat old fool Judas."

"Judas by old Sam?" Duff asked.

Trial by Marriage

"Right straight by him. Cap'm Amos, he say he some kind of throwback. I'm got dat old devil's toofs printed from my head to my tail. He ain't got a brain in his head. Turn him loose and he just don't come back. Kill hogs er calves er anything git in his way. He bit a man's bull one day, befo' de Lawd he did! How you goan train a dog when you can't catch him, and den when you catch him you cain't touch him?"

Duff wiped his hands on a croker sack.

"What they going to do with Judas?"

"Feed him till he dies of his own meanness."

"They told me they were taking him to a vet to be chloroformed."

"Dey was taking him, but dey took him before. At de last minute, dey ain't got de heart. Dat's one of old Sam's puppies. Cap'm Amos, he s'posed to be hardhearted, but he don't fool nobody. He love dat old Sam dog, and I guess he got a little left over for any o' Sam's puppies. But won't nobody ever break dat Judas."

When the trainers were gone, and the dogs left behind had tired of their unhappy howling, Duff went to the pen where the dog Judas was kept alone like some wild beast. Judas was standing at the wire, watching the departing horses, but he made no sounds of disappointment, nor raced up and down the run in the frenzied manner of his neighbors. He turned and looked at Duff unemotionally, yellowed-eyed. Duff stared at Judas. "I wonder if I could break a black-hearted old devil like you?"

DUFF WORKED HARD at his job, expecting every day that his interest would lag or that Amos would fire him. But so far he found his interest mounting instead, and Amos paid no attention to him, except to grunt curtly at him. Tafton offered little diversion except a movie or a pool game. At night he was usually ready to go to his boardinghouse bed. The boarders had accepted him immediately; most of them were young men, mechanics, drugstore clerks, filling-station attendants.

Sometimes they had a nickel poker game; on Saturday night it might be a quarter game, and a little whiskey with it. Other Saturday nights most of the boys would Lava-soap the grease from their hands, put on their best blue suits, and off to the bright lights of Montgomery they would go. Monday they would go to work stoically—red-eyed, heavy-headed robots; by nightfall they would have recovered, and at supper there would be some laughter again. Usually there had been some incident that made the trip memorable, with one of them having been the goat, and this would be good for comment for weeks and maybe even months afterward.

On Sunday mornings when the boys were away, Duff would sit on the porch, occasionally reading a book from the tiny library over the shoe shop, or planning his campaign against the dog Judas, while the people went by in their Sunday best on the way to church. Old Mrs. Townsell, who ran the boardinghouse, would pass often by the window inside, ashamed to be seen in her working-clothes at church time, commenting about people who passed.

"That's Mr. Mylick, owns half of town, tight as the bark on a tree, tighter even than your boss-man, Amos Hawthorne, I reckon. They say one December he opened his pocketbook to buy his daughter a package of gum for Christmas, and a June bug flew out'n it. That's his daughter with him. Cute, ain't she? They say there's a high-yellow gal in town is the spit'n image of her. I wouldn't know about that, though Mr. Mylick was a pure case not so many years back. *Mamie, don't let them greens boil over.*"

"No, ma'am," the cook answered, "dey ain't. I just put my hand on my nabel and dey stops."

"Look," Duff said suddenly, when Mrs. Townsell returned for another glance through the shades, "who's that yonder in the car?"

"That's Delia Phillips. She was elected prettiest in Tafton school, her senior year. Her pa's Doctor Phillips, cured you of blood poison. Ain't she pretty?"

"Sure is," Duff admitted.

"And got the sweetest voice. Sings in the Baptist choir," Mrs. Townsell said. "Why don't you go to church sometimes, Duff, 'stead of sitting around staring at nothing all the time? Won't kill you. Wisht I could go Sunday mornings, when everybody's all decked out and cheerful. Evening church is always sort of mournful."

"I believe I will go to church for a change," Duff said, rising, still looking at the departing Plymouth. He hurried upstairs and changed to the suit he had bought for a dollar a week.

The Baptist church was on the other side of town, past the colored boys with their shine-chairs, and the old courthouse with its *Keep off the Grass* signs, and the myriad sparrows chirping loudly in the water-oak trees, and the depot where the town cripple sold Sunday issues of the *Montgomery Advertiser* and the *Birmingham Age-Herald* from an express-company truck, and the store windows of shotgun shells and ladies' ready-to-wear, and the corner drugstore now closed because it was church hour.

They were singing "Beulah Land" when he got there; someone handed him a book turned to the right page. And there she was in the choir, where he could get a good look at her.

"I'm dwelling on a mountain
Underneath a cloudless sky;
I'm drinking from a fountain
That never shall run dry;
Oh, yes, I'm feasting,
On the manna,
From a bountiful supply,
For I am dwelling
In Beulah Land!"

The last chord of the piano died away, and the minister prayed long and earnestly and repetitiously. Finally the sermon began, and Duff was able to concentrate on the face of the girl. She was every bit as beautiful as she had seemed at first; her hair was very dark brown, her mouth and nose just right, and what he could see of her figure entirely proportional and adequate. Once he looked up to find her gaze squarely upon him. He wanted to smile or something, but his face froze; she looked away.

After the offering was taken, Delia rose and sang. She was tall, and her voice was clear and pleasant. Then followed the benediction, and afterward the preacher shook Duff's hand at the door; he was fiftyish, earnest, friendly. Others spoke to

Duff. He waited impatiently, until finally Delia came out, smiling as she talked to a gray-haired woman in a cherry-covered hat. He watched her; her legs were good, and her walk was good. "Do come again, won't you?" someone was saying. Yes, he'd come next Sunday.

Now her father joined her, and as they passed, Dr. Phillips looked at Duff and said, "Hello, Webster, didn't recognize you at first. Glad to have you with us at church. You've met my daughter, Delia."

"I don't believe so."

"Oh, yes," Delia said, looking at him squarely. "Well, you *were* delirious."

"I'd had some hard luck. I guess I was a pretty sorry sight," Duff mumbled. He felt himself sweating.

"The reason the good Lord puts hard luck on us is so we can lick it," Dr. Phillips said wisely. "When you got nothing to do, boy, drop by to see us."

"Yes, come by," Delia said, smiling at him.

Duff opened his mouth, but said nothing.

"Well?" she asked, looking at him directly. "Are you coming?"

"That'll be fine," Duff muttered. *No,* he thought uneasily, *that's something I sure better not do.*

Sunday afternoons reminded him of his home-town and high-school days, when the boys hung around his father's drugstore and played the phonograph and stood out front watching the few passing cars that came slowly by—cars with families, and the kids wrestling on the back seat, a vacationing Ole Miss student, with a strange girl, making his father's car go *chak-a-chak-a,* and seven laughing Negroes in a bucking, boiling Model T. He could remember Art Gillam, the Whispering Pianist, singing, "Baby, please don't be angry, for I was only teasing you," remember sitting out on the back step, smoking a forbidden cigarette and watching the flies buzz around the empty ice-cream churns in the sun. It was the same now, here in Tafton, except the phonograph was a multicolored juke organ, and the record was of a colored girl singing, *"I'm gonna change my way of livin', and if that ain't enough, I'll change the way I strut my stuff—"*

Duff walked out to the kennels with the sheepskin coat he had bought from Alex, the mechanic, for two dollars on the night of the last poker game. As he passed Wesley's house he identified himself with a shout and went on back to the pens, where the dogs woke from their siesta to bark happily at him.

The sheepskin had got too hot while he was walking out, but now he put it back on and went to Judas's pen. The big black-and-white pointer looked at him levelly with those yellow eyes, growling when Duff's hand touched the gate hasp.

"I'm coming in, mister," Duff said, "and if you don't kill me I'm going to keep coming in. I guess you might as well get used to it."

He opened the door. Judas's growl rose a note, and he stood up stiffly. The moment Duff stepped inside, the dog leaped at him. Duff turned sideways, thrusting the heavily padded arm quickly into the dog's open jaws. Judas's teeth closed on the inch-thick sleeve savagely. Duff shook him loose, and again let him grab a mouthful of coat. The dog hung there on the man's side like a panther, trying to bite through. Duff seized him by the back of the neck, close up behind the ears, and pulled him loose and held him, wriggling and snarling insanely, in the air.

"You'd kill me, wouldn't you?" he demanded without anger. "Yes, sir, you sure would." He propelled Judas toward the back of the kennel pen. Stepping out the door, he shut it just as the raging dog came rushing after him and struck the wire.

"Hello," said Lucie, coming into view. "What's all the racket?"

It was the first time he had ever seen her in a dress. She wore her light hair loose, and her hands were in the pockets of her tweed coat; her gray eyes watched him in amazement. "I drove out to take a look at my horse—haven't seen him since yesterday afternoon, and that's too long. I thought it was a kennel fight. I hope you didn't try to go in there with Judas."

"I just came out."

She looked at him. "In a hurry, too, I'll bet. Had you left something valuable in there, like the Kohinoor diamond or possibly somebody's mother?"

"I went in there to see if he could bite through this sheepskin coat."

She stared at him. "Why?"

"I think maybe I can break him."

She pointed at the dog, who now stood with one foot on the wire watching Duff intently, growling softly. "You're going to break *that?*"

"Well, maybe."

"You're going to make him point, and back, and stand shot, and hunt to the gun?"

"I hope to," he admitted.

"How?"

"I haven't got all of it figured out yet," he said.

"Oh, I see," she replied, with friendly scorn.

He shrugged out of the coat, and looked at his arm. The dog's teeth had come through in two places, scratching the skin and starting a tiny flow of blood.

"Just a little sulfathiazole and a couple of transfusions and you'll be all right," she murmured. "Look, why don't you try love and affection on Judas? That's what they do in books and things. You can win him over with kindness, and in the end he will be old dog Tray, and save your life a couple of times. I can see him now, swimming out in the whirlpool to rescue your young son, and barking to wake up the neighbors when the house catches on fire." She motioned. "Come on. I've got to see that horse."

As he followed her neat-cut figure to the barn, she said, "It's okay with me if you want to try to make something out of Judas. But we tried and gave him up as an outlaw."

They turned the gelding out into the corral, and sat on the fence and watched him run, with his tail arched. Presently Lucie said, "What did you do this morning?"

"Went to church."

"No fooling."

"What's wrong with that?"

"What did you go for?"

"Well, to look at that girl," Duff admitted.

"Who?"

"Delia Phillips."

Lucie turned around a bit and faced him. "I needn't have asked what girl. Look, you're a funny guy. Tell me about you."

"There's nothing to tell."

"Say me some poetry."

"I don't know any poetry."

"Oh, no— Look at him; isn't he a horse, though?"

"He sure is," Duff answered.

"Does septicemia make one break out in a poetic rash? I'll have to ask Doctor Phillips about that. Delia's father."

"Oh, you know—" he said. "Haven't you had to memorize a lot of poetry all your life, in school and places? I can't recite it, but sometimes little snatches of it pop up."

"I guess I'm nosy. But you fascinate me. The Vagabond Poet and Wild-Animal Trainer. I never had to memorize anything about down, down, down to the devil, not in the school I went to."

He said nothing. The January sun glinted in the enamel of her white teeth, and came through the loose strands of her hair, making them golden instead of sandy-colored.

"Listen," Duff said, with an effort. "There's not much to tell, but here's what there is. My father runs a drugstore on the edge of Hattiesburg. He owes everybody in town. My mother wanted me to be somebody, but I couldn't. For three or four years after I finished school I worked in sawmills, drugstores, tobacco barns, insurance offices, and a lot of other things, never very long at a time. Last month she shot herself—not on account of me, something else, I guess. We didn't have much in common, but the way she went sort of got me. I decided to leave then. I lost my gun in Georgia, when a plantation warden nearly caught me. That dog tried to kill me when I came up on him right after he'd caught a goat. The doctor fixed me up. You gave me a job and that's as far as I know."

She said, "Do you think you'll stay here long?"

"I don't know. Mr. Hawthorne doesn't like me. He might kick me out any time. But I'd like to make good—for once."

"Maybe this is what you were meant for, huh?"

He looked toward the kennels. "I'm staying till I break that dog, anyway."

"Then you'll be here quite a spell," she said. "I'll tell you what. Tomorrow you will go afield with us and I'll show you a bird dog."

Nine years before, a farmer came to old Amos and said, "I've got a young dog I want to sell you."

"What kind of dog?"

"He's whatever kind of dog you want. He'll hunt quail, deer, squirrel, or fox."

"That ain't the kind I want," Amos said shortly.

"Well you take him and see. He'll find more birds than any dog you got in any one of these coobs. Best squirrel dog in Alabama, and he'll run with a hound pack. Damnedest dog you ever heard tell of."

"I was just goan say that," Amos said. "I got all I need."

"You ought to at least try him."

"Well, hell, leave him here."

Amos had the dog put in one of the pens and forgot about him. In two days the farmer called and wanted to know how he liked him. Amos told him he had been down in the back and hadn't been able to try the dog, and to call again sometime soon. That afternoon, he told Wesley to take the dog out.

Wesley came in with his eyes bulging. "Cap'm, where you git him? Dat's a *vappin'* dog. He done traveled six hund'ed miles dis evening, fum one hill to de nex'!"

"What after, deer or fox?"

"No, sir, patidges!"

"Don't give me no stuff, now," Amos warned. "Didn't find no birds, did he?"

"Ten coveys, suh. He sho' did!"

Amos's old eyes narrowed. "Took 'em out, I reckon."

"*Pointed* 'em! Stood up yonder like he was some kind of bird-dog God A-mighty, wid his tail straight up'ards as a willow stick. I shot a bird, and he broke to fotch him, den he went down and nail dem singlings one de time like an old brood bitch, den gone fum here again!"

Amos went out with them next day, and again the dog Sam ranged on the horizon and found covey after covey, and incidentally treed two squirrels. When they came in at noon, Amos said, "Now I wonder where that farmer Ben stole this dog? Wonder if it was far enough away so's nobody'd find him with me?" He made inquiries in the neighborhood of the farmer; one man said, "That Sam dog? Shore I know him—Ben raised him. I seen that pup the day he was born. They wasn't but two in the litter and the other'n he took sick and died. Me and Ben was hunting that dog when he wasn't four months old—had to lift him over logs. I've brung him home in my old hunting-sack, many a night. You aiming to buy him?"

"Ben wanted me to give him a tryout," Amos said carefully.

"Well, Ben's a friend o' mine, so I won't tell nothing on his dog."

"Wouldn't want you to do that," Amos said, hopefully. "If the dog's fitified or something, I'll find it out."

"Oh, he's a beastly scoun'l; healthy as a buck hant. 'Tain't that," he said. "See here, you just take him out and try him; you'll see, first off. That's all I can tell you. Ben's the best friend I got in the world, and I wouldn't do nothing to hurt no deal of his."

The following day was Saturday, and Amos knew the farmer would be out to see about his dog. And just at noon he came, driving a brightly polished Model A, and dressed in his best town clothes.

"Well," he said cheerfully, "you done give Sam all the tryout you want?"

Amos studied a moment. Then he called, "Wesley, didn't we take out that dog of Mister Ben's the other day?"

"Yas, suh," Wesley said dolefully. "*You* remember dat dog," he added meaningfully.

"Why, what'd he do?" asked the farmer, looking from one of them to the other. "You got to remember he ain't but little over a year old. You understand how a puppy is. A man that knows dogs like you do, he understands to make allowances for a young dog's puppy ways."

"I ain't said nothing against the dog," Amos said, searching the bottles of medicine on the shelf in the kennel house. "Oh, Wesley, git Mister Ben's dog fer him and put him in the car."

"Look," Ben said, "you a dog trainer. I ain't. With just a little work, you could fix him right up so anybody could handle him. And you see he healthy. He's had copperas onct a month since he was born. Not a worm. in him. What would you give me for him right now, cash?"

Trial by Marriage

"Ben, I tell you the truth. We got more dogs around here now than we got feed fer. And you know I ain't young as I used to be. Cain't spend no time working on just any kind of dog," Amos said. "Wesley, turn that back seat up. You want that dog to git the car all dirty?"

"Tell you what. I'll sell that dog to you cheap. I got a bad knee—mule kicked me last summer. Curious sorta thing, she hadn't never done nothing like that before, gentle as a cat, then of a sudden, *wham,* she done it. Look," he said pulling up his trouser-leg, "see that scar?"

"Where?" Amos asked, squinting down.

"Right there. Can't see it so good now, but in rainy weather she turns plumb red."

"We been a long time without rain, ain't we?" Amos said.

He glanced toward the car, then went back to searching the shelf. "Maybe you better tie him in, Wesley, so he won't jump out."

"That's all right, he ain't goan jump out, not that puppy. Got more sense than any dog I ever seen," the farmer said. "Since old Kate kicked me, I ain't been able to do much walking. Fact is, she just about knocked me out of huntin'. Only reason I'd sell old Sam. But I guess I'll have to let him go. Cheap, too."

"What's cheap to one man," Amos said idly, "might be higher'n a cat's back to another. What you want for that dog?"

The farmer glanced at him quickly, then halfway turned to the car, minutely inspecting a pine knot on the side of the house. He touched his finger to a drop of resin that stood on the knot, rubbed his thumb to it, then smelled it interestedly. "Well, I don't rightly know, to tell you the truth. He's such a pet around the house. If the wife and kids knowed I even mentioned selling old Sam, they'd just about quit me."

"I wouldn't want to buy no kid's pet dog, Ben."

The farmer rolled the turpentine off his hand. "Well, I tell you, Mister Hawthorne, they just maul him around and plague him until I don't see how the poor dog stands it. It just ain't right for no dog to have to put up with such. The other day I told Verie, I said, 'Them young'uns is goan drive that dog crazy; I swear the first good man that offers me fifty dollars, I'll let Sam go, just to p'tect him from them young'uns!' "

Later that afternoon, Ben appeared at the F. Mitchell Horse and Mule Company barn, where the boys were sitting around with their chairs leaned back against the wall. They asked him why he looked so pert, and he cut a corner off his plug, stuck it in his mouth, and said:

"Well, boys, they say old Amos Hawthorne knows a whole heap about bird dogs, but me and him tied up in a trade this evenin', and I cold rammed it to him. Lucifer, you know that combination puppy was such a stomp-down'un fer a while, then kept gitting wilder and wilder, till we had to tie that ten foot of trace chain on him to keep him in sight? And we'd wear out our feet looking fer him, and him pointing a mile away somewhere? Well, that's the dog. I guess I ought not to tell it on the old man— I like old Amos, and I don't want to hurt his reputation none. Don't want this to go no further, mind you—" He leaned forward. "Boys, old Amos Hawthorne forked over forty cash dollars for that wild dog!"

They named the dog Ambling Sam. Amos, who had never bothered to learn to write—"That's how come I keep on living; don't never worry about no notes I've signed at the bank"—had Lucie, then in high school, write various people in an effort to trace the dog's breeding, and they finally got enough data to register him.

The farmer had told the strict truth about Sam's being a combination dog, and that was his main trouble. There weren't many deer to bother them, but Sam never went through a creek bottom without making a couple of whipping circles for squirrel scent; and when he treed a squirrel he would sit down and wait until Amos rode up. For a long time Sam just couldn't believe that squirrels were no longer to be hunted. Amos would ride past him, ignoring him completely, while Sam danced excitedly around the tree. When Amos kept on going, Sam looked at him in perplexity. He would follow a way, anxiously, then return to the tree. Finally Sam would give up the squirrel tree and somewhat unhappily head out on the scent of his trainer. After a few of these treatments, he abandoned squirrel hunting.

Jack rabbits, though, were another matter. That summer when they got up to the chicken prairies of Saskatchewan, Sam indicated at once that these swift animals were his preferred game. Most young dogs chase jack rabbits for a distance, then give up in despair and go back to hunting prairie chickens. But not Sam.

"Dat Sam, he de only dog I ever see could make one dem jacks lay his years back and put dat other foot down," Wesley said.

That was the first year Paul had been taken to Canada. He was fourteen then, strangely capable, being quiet and even-tempered, and the animals liked his solemn singing around the barn. Then he was used as a wagon driver, and he watched old Amos and his father having their troubles with Sam and the jack rabbits.

One day they were in the village; Paul was told to get some corks, and while the Frenchman in the little store was trying to understand what the Alabama Negro meant by "jug stoppers," a wheat farmer came in cursing the chestnut mare that had brought him to town. "Pullin' all the dom time, wears your dom arms near out, she ought to dom well be on a bloody race track!" Paul took one look at the horse, and went to find Amos Hawthorne. Amos bought the mare for sixty-one dollars and a half.

Next day Paul rode the little mare with the hunting caravan, holding her in by main force until Sam, swinging in front, struck his first jack rabbit of the morning; then Paul loosened the curb pressure on her mouth and nudged her with his heel. The mare jumped twenty feet, then flattened out in a dead run across the sage, over gopher holes and buffalo wallows, and finally Paul headed the dog off. For weeks that went on daily. The mare got so she would jump forward every time she saw Sam flush a jack rabbit. Sam got wise, too. After a few days of having those hoofs come thundering behind him, and then a taste of the whip, he would glance quickly back to see how much start he had on the horse before pursuing a rabbit he had flushed. Finally he perceived that it was a losing game, and after that would glance interestedly at jack rabbits but never chased them again.

They taught Ambling Sam steadiness to wing and shot, and from that time on he was known as the cleanest-broken dog in major trials. At the end of the summer, he ran unplaced at Moose Jaw, but won at Pierson, Manitoba, paying Amos seven hundred dollars. From that time on Sam was a winning dog; whenever a handler arrived at a new trial, his first question was, "Is old Amos here with that Sam dog?" Sam won on prairie chicken and Huns and quail and pheasant. He won every championship—except the one old Amos wanted most, the National Championship at Grand Junction.

When the farmer, Ben, learned of the dog's exploits, he said in annoyance, "Aye, dammit, if I'd a-knowed he was goan turn out to be such a dog as all that, I'd shore never let old Amos jew me down from fifty dollars!"

THE FIRST MORNING that Duff went out with the trainers they put old Sam down without any ceremony, as if he were just a dog. Now Amos rode out front on his gray horse, oblivious of everything but the ten-year-old pointer far ahead. Regularly Sam would look back; old Amos would point his whip to the right, and the dog would go to the right. This almost visible affinity between dog and handler had caused Sam to be known as a mechanical dog, or "whip-runner." But Sam didn't depend on Amos; he knew how to hunt.

"I mind the championship of 1912," Amos had said once. "Them days, wasn't a dog handler behind every sassafras bush, ner a championship fer every dog. Me and Jim Avent and David Rose and Beazell and Ed Garr and Er Shelly and Jake Bishop and a few others. Setters was the dog then. They don't grow them no more like La Besita, and Avent's Sioux, and Geneva. La Besita—Bee, they called her—now, before God, there was a bird dog! A little ball of fire she was, weather didn't make no never mind to her, she'd run when the ice was on the ground to cut a dog's feet off, er when the sun would addle your brains. Then, yonder she'd be, cocked up on point fit to knock a judge's eye out. She was a bird dog, that little bitch. Sometime I think even old Sam would a-had to hump to beat that little Bee.

"But this was earlier, before Bee's time. Avent had three dogs entered in 1912, Mobile, Momoney, and that lemon-and-white setter, Commissioner. He figured to win with Mobile er either Momoney. But Mobile he cut his throat with his birdwork, and he was out of it. Come time to run Momoney, Jim said to me, 'You watch me, I'm goan run that Monora plumb out the county.'

"They put the dogs down, the judges told 'em to let 'em go. But Jim held Momoney just a second, and then shot her right in behind Monora, and away them dogs went, over the hill and yonder, with Martin, Monora's handler, yelling and whistling and trying to turn his dog. Wasn't no bird hunt, it was a bitch race. Old Jim he just rid along, not saying nothing, waiting for Momoney to come back and go to hunting and take the stake, while Martin was off trying to git his dog back on the course. After while, a dog come back; but it wasn't Jim's dog—it was Monora. Jim stuck the spurs in his horse and he went dog hunting hisself. But he never found her until too late. Wa'n't often Jim messed hisself up like that.

"But Monora she went on and cut her throat too, and Jim he had his last chance with Commissioner, the dog he hadn't figured on. The race had done simmered down to him and Cord's Lad of Jingo, Ed Garr's pointer. He was a stomp-down bird dog, that Lad. Better'n Commissioner, and Jim he knowed it good as anybody. And Ed Garr wasn't never classed as nobody's fool. So it looked like old Jim was goan take a whuppin'.

"That night before they run, me and Hochwalt and one or two others, we went up to see how old Jim was taking it. He was laying up in the bed, propped up atop two pillows, with his hands behind his head, looking at the wall. He never said nothing, and we knowed something was going on in his brain, and we sat down to wait it out.

"Finally, Jim said, 'I'm goan take that yellow dog and win that race tomorrow,' meaning Commissioner.

"Nobody said nothing, because it was hard to keep from laughing. In a minute I said, 'Garr don't know nothing.'

"'Ed ain't nobody's fool,' Jim he admitted.

"'That pointer, he's just a plug dog.'

"'You just watch. I'm goan make him look like a plug.'

"'How you aim to pass this miracle?' we asked him.

"'You mind now, we been running dogs on this here course three weeks. I figure them birds done got tired of being rooted around every day. They've done shifted out. You know I can send that dog into any corner I'm a-mind to. I'm goan have him out on the hills and run him from one covey to another. Garr'll have his pointer busting the course right down the middle.'

"Next day, that's what he done, shore enough. Garr's dog run as nice a race as you could want, but he couldn't find no birds. Jim Avent he would wave his whip, and old Commissioner would hop from one hill to another, out wide. He never had half the steam that pointer had, but every time you turned your head he'd be jammed into another covey of birds. Garr nearly went crazy. Come taking-up time, wasn't nothin' fer the judges to do but hand it to Avent and his whip-running dog."

THIS MORNING THEY had ridden only twenty minutes when Ambling Sam, after a prodigious cast, was seen to stop far out, a tiny spot of white at that distance.

"Point, Cap'm Amos!" Wesley said.

The old man rose in his stirrups. "Where?"

"Right on up yonder. Straight behead of us."

They galloped toward the point. Wesley shouted at Duff, "Dis place, hit's plumb *illuminated* with birds. And old Sam, he just cold find 'em."

Sam stood erect, with his stiff tail slanting up, his feet solidly planted and somewhat stretched, his mouth open in a confident grin.

As Amos swung lithely down with his .410, Lucie turned to Duff and whispered, "Okay?"

The birds got up. Sam's tail dropped slightly, and his ears rose, but he did not move forward. Amos fired twice, and two cock birds fell from the whirring covey. He clucked, and Sam streaked toward the first dead bird. When he retrieved the second bird, Amos let him pull off the head and eat it.

"Eyes gittin' bad, hell!" Amos grunted after he had sent the dog on and returned to his horse. "I can still see down a gun bar'l."

Suddenly he stared at Duff, apparently realizing for the first time that he was along. "Who told *him* to come?" he demanded, looking at Wesley and Lucie.

"Me. What's wrong with that?" Lucie said.

Waving his head from one side to the other, Amos answered, "I ain't goan have no tramp riding my horses!"

"It ain't much of a horse," Duff said amiably, thinking that Amos had been joking, "even for a tramp." Instantly he froze, for he saw his mistake.

Amos took his foot out of the stirrup and walked around to Duff's side and pointed the dog whip at his face, looking along it, and said, almost in a whisper, "Bud, you make just one slip and you're goan be bumming it down that road again, you git me?"

Lucie said, "He hasn't done anything."

"He ain't got to do nothing. I don't like him. I don't like the way he looks, ner acts, ner smells, ner nothing. And that's all that makes any difference, 'cause I'm still the boss-man around here." He looked sharply at Lucie. "Er ain't I?"

Lucie looked at him angrily, but said nothing.

Duff, trying desperately to rectify his mistake, helped his standing by demonstrating an uncanny instinct for finding a lost dog, and for seeing dogs at incredible distances. And when a setter named Smoky Joe had a running fit and streaked out through the woods crazily, it was Duff who overtook him, and herded the sick dog like a maverick calf back to the dog wagon.

"The Squire doesn't like you," Lucie said afterward, "and that's for keeps. But he knows a dog man when he sees one, and so he'll tolerate you. You did okay."

Part II

AT LEAST ONCE A DAY, Duff went into Judas's pen. Formerly they had fed the pointer by throwing a piece of meat to one end of the pen and setting his pan of food inside the door when he went after the meat. But now Duff put on the sheepskin coat and simply stepped into the pen with the dog pan, in the hope that Judas would finally begin to welcome his entrance. After a week or two, though, it became apparent that to Judas hunger was secondary to his desire to get a man's throat, preferably Duff's, between his jaws. For one period Duff let him go three days without eating, then entered with a pan of raw hamburger—only to have the dog spring at him, knocking the meat in all directions, and grab the heavy sheepskin coat upturned around Duff's neck.

"Man's best friend," murmured Lucie as she helped brush the bits of meat off Duff's clothes.

"Maybe we ought to lay him out with a shot of Nembutal," Duff said patiently, "and then pull his teeth."

"That wouldn't be no help. I'd as soon be chewed to pieces," Wesley said, "as gummed to death."

Saturday night Alex Prin, the mechanic, drove up in front of the boardinghouse, and instead of walking in crying, "Deal! Deal!" as usual, he called Duff out to his car, the motor of which was still running.

As Duff approached, Alex said confidentially, "Boy, I've got an idea that will knock you for a row. Come here."

Duff reached the car and laid one hand on the door, and immediately an electric shock almost knocked him down. Alex collapsed over the steering-wheel in merriment. Alex had rigged an arrangement that enabled him to short the ignition onto the body of the car at will.

"Damn your hide, Alex!" Duff grinned.

"Ain't that hot?" Alex said happily. "I just knocked the sheriff for a loop, uptown. Git in and let's ride around and have some fun. There's the bottle, in that pocket."

Duff thoughtfully watched the frantic backward leaps, the eyeglasses jumping off, the surprised eyes; and when he came home he had bought a hotshot battery, a Model T coil, and a big spool of small-gauge copper wire. While the poker game went on that night he sewed a crude pocket on the back of the sheepskin coat into which he fitted the battery and coil, then brought the thin threads of copper wire around, sewing them down on the outside of the coat. The switch he placed inside the pocket.

Before he entered Judas's kennel Sunday, he walked around outside, making threatening gestures and slapping the fence until Judas was in an angry frenzy. He opened the gate and stepped inside. Judas leaped, hitting him on the shoulder with fury, then recoiling from the electricity so violently that he landed on his back in the middle of the pen. He rose, shook himself, and sprang again, only to fall away the instant he touched the coat.

Now Judas stood off, growling and watching Duff in puzzlement. Duff took a step forward. The dog retreated a step. Duff turned his back, but Judas did not advance.

Duff went out of the pen and took off the coat and came back, now watching the dog sharply. Judas again retreated.

"Okay, pardner," Duff said with satisfaction. "Now we're getting somewhere."

After that, in spare time, the lessons progressed—always in the absence of Amos Hawthorne, of course. What Duff wanted was one day to present the old trainer with Judas broken and tractable. Certainly that would remove the hostility that bore on Duff night and day.

Duff borrowed a shoat that Wesley was about to slaughter—"I may get him killed for you right quick"—and rigged up an electric harness for it, with two wires leading outside to the battery and coil and switch. He shoved the squealing pig into the pen with the dog, and Judas was on him like a jaguar. In one second Judas struck the pig and missed a vital spot; the next second he had leaped frantically away. Duff left the pig for a while, but Judas made no further attempt to kill it. When the pig, looking for a way of escape from the pen, came toward him, Judas growled and jumped on top of his house.

One afternoon not long after that, Lucie saw Duff getting ready to feed Judas.

"Wait, Mr. Beatty," she said, "you forgot your coat."

Duff opened the gate and stepped inside, while Lucie watched in fearful expectancy. Judas stood in the middle of the pen and allowed Duff to put the pan down. Duff took a step toward the dog and caused him to retreat.

She stared at him, then at Judas. "Can you also make water come out of a rock, like Moses did?"

"Never tried that," Duff said.

The old trainer had not ridden that afternoon. Lucie was waiting around front in her car when Duff got through. Dark had almost come. The motor was idling, and the heater sent a warm billowing of air through the car. As Duff got in beside her, she gave him a sudden, direct smile. Already buoyed up by his progress with Judas, her smile gave him a feeling of warm companionship. He realized that this girl came nearer to being a friend to him than anybody he had ever known.

Abruptly he said, "You've been pretty nice to me."

"Sure I have," she said lightly.

He suddenly reached over and kissed her on the cheek.

"Hey," she said. "That's sort of all right."

This time he kissed her mouth instead.

"Whoa," she said, pushing him away. "What's happening here? Let me think."

"No," he said urgently, "don't think."

He kissed her again, and presently felt her move closer, almost crowding him, and her breathing quickened.

"My heavens!" she whispered, gasping. "I think I must be dying. Feel my heart. Wait—no more, thanks. Tomorrow, maybe, or next week I'll have recovered sufficiently. Listen. Tell me, was all that *gratitude?* If it was, I'm liable to be trying to do you favors all the time."

As she started the car off, Duff could say nothing. Many words came to his mind, but none to his lips.

AHEAD, A RABBIT RAN out of the brush along the ditch into the glare of the headlights, then bounced down the road and crossed over. Lucie and Duff approached Bill's Tavern, Tafton's lone juke, a cheap frame structure with a bright blue neon border around the eaves, and a red sign *Eat,* a place of many humors where sometimes several couples from town would come and play noisily, where an old man with a wet, slack mouth watched the whirling cherries and lemons and plums as his nickels clinked into the slot machine, where once in a while far into some Saturday night there would be trouble, with an ice pick or even a gun coming into view, where girls hopped cars or served tables or danced with whoever asked them, simple girls with a matter-of-fact worldly wisdom brought on, perhaps, by an unfortunate early marriage and a child farmed out with a relative.

Bill's Tavern was like a business or a government or a legislature or a world—whether it was good or bad depended on who dominated it at the time.

"How about a beer?" Duff said finally.

She turned the car in and blew the horn. "Let's don't be too long. Teague McGinnis is coming over tonight."

"Maybe we better go, then."

"Oh, no," she said, pinching his leg.

He said, fascinated, "You're a sort of fresh girl."

"Refreshing, you mean."

The waitress came out, an almost-pretty girl in cheap slacks. Inside the juke organ began playing and the notes emanated from the loudspeaker under the neon eaves and spread over the calm Alabama countryside.

"Some day," Lucie said thoughtfully, when the girl had gone, "I'm going to find out what's behind that mask you use for a face."

"You won't find much, I'm afraid," he said.

She smiled at him in that sudden, honest way of hers and said, "Maybe I will."

The girl brought the beer and hooked the tray on the car, and went in a little sliding dance step, snapping her fingers to the music.

"What I like about you," Lucie said, "is your superior brand of conversation. Duff, listen. Are you coming to see me or anything?"

"I don't guess I ought to."

"Sure you ought to. I'll have to think of something, because the Squire would bust a gusset if you came to the house. He's not crazy about you."

"I don't want to cause trouble."

"Duff," she said seriously, "I want to see you. Honest. I'll fix it. You wait and see."

Lucie proved to be expert at duplicity. She told Amos that she was going to a show, or to play bridge. Sometimes Duff simply came to the house after nine, which was Amos's invariable going-to-bed time. This night they drove to the bluff that overlooked the amber river. The night belonged more to May than January; across the river a light showed dimly in a farmer's house, and she speculated that they must have a sick baby, because no farmer would be up that hour of his own volition. Her forehead was against the side of his neck, and her hand was under his coat against his shoulder in her friendly intimacy that he found so fascinating.

"We could go down to the bank. There's pine straw to sit on, and it's not cold," Duff said.

She shivered a little and tightened her arm across his chest. "Tell me something nice, Duff."

"I don't know how."

"Maybe I just don't affect you that way."

"You know better than that."

"Yes, I guess I do."

He tried to explain. "I try to say something nice, but when I've got you like this, there's so much rises in my heart that it gets all bottled up in my throat and none of it will come out. Do you see what I mean?"

"Oh, Duff, of course I see," she said, holding him tighter. "You don't have to say anything."

He shifted his cramped long legs. "Let's get out."

She hesitated, close against him. "Duff, I don't know."

"What's the matter? Come on."

"Duff, if we get out, something's going to happen."

"What?"

"Something."

He stared at her. "That's always up to you."

"No, Duff. Not this time."

"Well, hell, you can say you better not get out."

"Oh, you're crazy. I better not, all right," she said. "Only, Duff, it'll be new to me." She looked across the river. "Look, it's gone out. I guess they got him to sleep."

"What?"

"That light's gone out."

"What light?"

"The one in that house across the river. Duff, get out."

Afterward, she was staring solemnly at the sky overhead, and there was enough moonlight that he could see her face. She had never seemed so solemn. Yet the unnatural soberness of her was not disturbing for it was not of remorse or doubt, but serenity. He lay beside her on his back, staring with her at the sky, her arm linked through his, and the emotion that filled him was transcendent. It was a singing, upsurging thing that hurt because of its fullness, and he touched her with wonderment and even some reverence, as if she were a perishable thing of immeasurable preciousness. Now he rose upon one elbow and held her hand against his cheek.

"Lucie?"

"Yes."

He hesitated.

"What, Duff?"

"I'm so full I can't talk."

"Why?"

"Because I love you so much."

"Oh, Duff, I love you so much, too."

He struggled to say the things that swelled within him, but his tongue could not manage them. This inarticulateness almost maddened him, and he unknowingly squeezed her hand painfully, until suddenly, as if it were an explosion, he said,

"A belt of straw and ivy-buds
  With coral clasps and amber studs:
  And if these pleasure may thee move,
  Come live with me and be my Love.
  Silver dishes for thy meat,
  As precious as the gods do eat,
  Shall on an ivory table be
  Prepared each day for thee and me."

Now Lucie's face was against his, and he felt the dampness of her cheek. But then she said, lightly, "Sounds okay. When does all that start?"

"From this minute."

She smiled at him and said, "You know what I said I was going to find out?"

'No."

"What's behind that front."

"Have you found out?"

"Yes, darling, I've found out. This is you—outside, strong and silent and almost tough. But inside, sensitive and kinder than all get-out, and a lot of other things."

"Shucks," Duff said.

"Isn't that right?"

"If you say it, Lucie, it's right."

Below them the river flowed noiselessly. A dim light lay upon it. There was a long silence.

"Look, what has Delia Phillips got that I haven't got—besides an artist-model face and a soprano voice?" Lucie finally said. "She's not for you, Duff. *I'm* for you."

"Who said anything about her?" he wished Delia hadn't been mentioned.

"You went to church just to see her, didn't you? But let me tell you about me. I'm full of pep, just bubbly as I can be. That's what you like about me, because I keep you from having the mullygrubs so much. And I'm not bad to look at. My face is sort of plain, but anyway it's not dished-in or anything, and when you get more in love with me you may even think it's pretty. And my figure is—well, I think it's doggone good. Or isn't it?"

"It's okay."

"Just okay, huh? You're crazy."

"What else about you?" he asked interestedly.

"Well, I can sit a running buck on a cold-jawed horse and worm a dog and lots of things Delia can't do. Cook and everything."

"You must be quite a gal," he said, smiling in the dark.

"Sure I am. Duff, listen. Think what it'll be like, raising the puppies and breaking the dogs and campaigning the circuit. Summers we'll be on the lone prairie, with the coyotes howling just like in the song, and the wind blowing fit to lift the mortgage off the house. And the grasshoppers eating everything green—Jake Bishop said they even ate a green tire-cover off his car one time. Oh, we'll do fine. Maybe you'll even break Judas and win with him, and that'll give us a reputation, and I'll sort of flirt with the owners and get them to send their dogs to us and—"

"That'll give us a reputation, too."

"Oh, you know, just sort of tease them. I know how to do it," she said. "Stop laughing. I'm not kidding."

"I know it."

"Honey, look. I love you and you love me. I don't know about that ivory table and stuff, but it'll be fine whether you can arrange for the ivory table or not. Don't you see how fine it'll be? Huh? Don't you?"

"It *sounds* fine," he admitted.

"What's wrong with it?"

Duff said slowly, "I'm no bargain, Lucie. And Amos Hawthorne will find plenty wrong with it."

"Well, I'll tell you about him. The Squire was born with a quota of three changes of mind per lifetime. He changed his mind once when he was forty-three, once eight years later, and the final time when he was sixty-nine. He's used them all up. He wouldn't believe in you if you were the Apostle Paul. But, look, he doesn't have to. I'm the one. And I do. You've changed since you came, even. Don't you *feel* different?"

"I feel all right," he said.

"Well, tell me you love me again."

"I do, all right."

"Do what?"

"What you said."

"Well, my conscience, say it!" she said, punching him.

"Lucie, I love you," he said warmly, kissing her. "But what are we going to do about it?"

She mused, "'Silver dishes for thy meat, As precious as the gods do eat, Shall on an ivory table be Prepared each day for thee and me.' Yes, sir, that'll be okay. I guess the precious meat part means some of that steak Mr. Merrick had last week," she said. "Duff, I tried to tell you about the Squire. We'll have to wait."

"Wait? Do you want to wait?"

"We can't run away and leave him. It's hard hiking these days for the Squire. The owners just can't believe he's the man he used to be. They send their dogs to young men like Teague McGinnis or Jack Harper or Earl Crangle. Of course as long as we've got Ambling Sam we'll get some fifty-dollar stud fees, but Sam can't be campaigned much," she told him. "The only thing about the Squire, I think maybe his eyes aren't any too good any more. He's too tight to go to an eye doctor, but I caught him trying on glasses in the dime store last week. I'm some help to him, I guess, but I can't really handle a hardheaded young field-trial dog. I haven't got a voice for making dogs come to me. But *men*, now—"

"Hell, I'm nobody to talk of marrying you, broke as I am," he said morosely.

"A belt of straw shouldn't cost much. Look, the baby's awake again. Probably got earache, poor thing. I bet I could fix him up. Don't you bet I could?"

"Sure," he said. "Come here."

Although since the lessons of the electric coat Judas no longer made unprovoked attacks, Duff became convinced that the day would never come when a man could lay a hand on the dog without being bitten. A light leather muzzle seemed the answer to this, but the dog then spent his time fighting the muzzle instead of hunting. Finally Duff left him in his kennel, muzzled. After two days of clawing and rubbing, Judas resigned himself to it.

"I think I'll take him out tomorrow," Duff said on Saturday night.

"And lose him?" Lucie said.

"Well, I'm going to let him pull a drag."

"I don't know who's the most buttheaded, that dog or you."

"Maybe that's what this contest is about."

"You know," she said, "that buttheadedness is something you've acquired since you came. Maybe determination is a better word, huh? I guess that's what makes a good dog man. The Squire's like that. And Teague, too, some."

"What's *he* got to do with this?" he asked curiously.

"Nothing."

"What's he to you, anyway, Lucie?"

"Now stop it," she said. She picked up his hand in that little way of hers, and kissed it quickly. "Please stop it, Duff. I love *you*."

"There wouldn't be anything boring about life with you, I can see that." He smiled, in spite of himself. And it was this that frequently worried him. There were moments—an increasing number of them—when he wondered if, instead of being honestly in love with Lucie, he were not simply fascinated by her light impudence and overwhelmed with gratitude for her generous friendliness.

"Hot ziggety, that's some recommendation," she was saying. "Recipe for a full life. A boss like the Squire, a dog like Judas, and a girl like me. Happy days."

THE NEXT MORNING, Sunday, when Duff and Lucie got to the kennel, John Wesley waited for them with three horses saddled.

With an eight-foot chain dragging behind, the muzzled Judas was released. He spurted away in great plunging leaps, the heavy chain jumping and dancing behind him.

"Take the right and I'll take the left," Duff said to Wesley. "Lucie, follow the course."

Now Judas was swinging out to the left, followed by a small dust cloud. Afield, he seemed to lose his sullenness, and ran with a snap and sparkle that gave him almost an air of gaiety. His tail whipped merrily, a sign that he was bird hunting and not just running. Apparently hardly burdened by the trace chain, he skirted a sedge field, then crossed a weed area on a long diagonal that ended in a lespedeza patch in a scrub-pine woods. He made two quick whips through this, then came out into the field again, still speeding. He was away on a busy, industrious race; but it was his own race. Not once did he look back to keep the riders in view. He was not concerned with the direction of the course—he laid his own course.

But Duff had his horse in a lope, and stayed a couple of hundred yards behind Judas. After fifteen minutes, Judas's pace had not slackened.

"Is he going to pull that chain like that all day?" he mused incredulously.

At ten o'clock Judas was still going, hunting wisely, but with a country-wide abandon, running completely wild as far as his handlers were concerned.

"Dat's what I'm feared of," Wesley panted once when they lost him temporarily, "is you won't never break him of dat wild-hog go-yonder bescattlin'."

"But if I ever do," Duff replied, "I'll have one almighty stem-winder!"

Now Judas appeared up ahead, whipping in a shortening circle, hot on bird scent. Suddenly he stopped, a picture in suspended motion as he hung there with his body stiff and slightly forward, his head lowered in the exact position it had been when the scent got strong, his ramrod tail pointing at the pine-tops.

"Whoa, now!" Duff yelled, and, drawing closer, slid from his saddle and walked rapidly but unobtrusively toward the pointing dog.

Judas still had not moved, except to open his mouth and close it again, as if to swallow some of the hot scent that welled up to him. When Duff got within fifty feet, the dog took one step, then froze again.

Judas's tail-tip quivered slightly. Then, like a projectile, he catapulted forward, and the covey erupted around him as he tried to get his muzzled jaws on a flying quail. The covey streaked away, with Judas in futile pursuit.

"There'll come a day," Duff said, unruffled, "when you'll stand there and watch them bust loose all around you, and hear me shoot, and you'll know better than to move until I say move."

Presently the burden of the chain began to show in Judas's range. He became limited, and instead of casting in long diagonals cut more sharply across the front, and once they saw him check back after hearing Lucie's clear call. He found five coveys and also flushed and attacked a farmer's guinea flock, a hog, and a milk cow, but since he was muzzled the principal damage was to the cow's nervous system.

Next time they ran him, he again pulled the chain for what seemed an incredible time before shortening his distance; and then again he seemed to begin showing a slight regard for the direction of his handlers. On the third Sunday, Duff waited until the chain had tired the dog down, then he spurred his horse and caught him.

When Wesley and Lucie came up, he said, "I believe we can try him without the chain now. But if I'm wrong it's going to take some hard riding to keep from losing him. So get ready."

Trial by Marriage

With Judas growling and trying to get his muzzled jaws on him, Duff unfastened the chain, and Judas made a line for a distant oak scrub. They rode on, waiting for him to cut through the scrub and come out ahead. But Judas didn't come out ahead. He bolted.

At night they gave up their search and went back.

"I guess we'll have to tell the Squire," Lucie said. "That's going to be bad."

Old Amos's eyes glinted when Duff told him. "You mean you been working them horses every Sunday when they due to be a-resting, runnin' that pea-headed, fiti-fied, no-count Judas dog?"

"I thought to break him," Duff said slowly, seeing his idea for winning the old man's friendship collapsing.

"Before God," Amos said, his breath whistling, "I hope I drop dead if ever I let a road tramp into my kennel yard again! You listen to me—don't you think I know a little something-another about bird dogs? Hah? That dog cain't be broke, er I'd a done it long ago. If he's gone now, it's good riddance. Maybe you can mind your own business now, *and leave them horses be except on work days!*"

These weeks the attention of the whole kennel was directed toward readying Ambling Sam for the National Championship. This, mainly, meant careful conditioning. A few days before the trek to Grand Junction began, an ancient car stopped outside, and a young man in overalls climbed down and approached them where they sat on the front steps of Wesley's house.

"Mr. Hawthorne," the young farmer said, "have you lost a dog?"

Amos looked past him and saw, sitting on the back seat of the old car, the dog Judas, tied by a piece of haywire around a window post.

"No," Amos snapped, "I ain't."

"He's got your name on his collar."

"Must be a collar I give somebody. I ain't lost no dog."

"If you'll bring the dog in," Lucie said to the farmer, "we'll be glad to pay the reward. That's our dog. He's just joking." She went around the house and called Duff. "Here's your wandering boy come home," she said.

"I ain't paying out not one more copper cent for that dog," Amos said with finality. "Take him on back with you, bud. You can have him instead of the reward."

"Him?" the farmer asked. "I don't want no dog like that, Mr. Hawthorne. He's a mean 'un. That dog'll kill somebody. I ain't particular about no big reward, just a little something for the trouble he put me to, gitting him here. Figured I was doing you a favor."

"Not nair penny," said Amos. "Take him on home and shoot him, if you're a-mind to."

"How'd you catch him?" Duff asked the farmer, as soon as he got there.

"He came galloping after some of my turkeys, and I sicked my catch dog on him. Durned if I didn't have to go pull *him* off *my* dog, and him muzzled. I seen he belonged here, and I know he was one of Mr. Hawthorne's valuable bird dogs."

"I ain't paying one penny for him," Amos said.

"You live around here?" Duff asked curiously.

"I live thirty miles below Tafton. He were a long way from home, all right. I figured he must a-jumped off a truck or some such. Don't guess no dog is no such powerful rambler as all that."

Duff said to Amos, "Listen, you better take that dog back. Some day I'm going to have him broke."

"Hah!" snorted Amos. "The only broke will be me, from paying out rewards, and hog money and goat money and turkey money for them critters that has the unlucky fortune to git in his fool way."

"I'm going to break him, though."

"Well, why don't *you* pay the reward? You pay for him, and you can have him. If he's such an all-fired pistol ball, gitting him fer five dollars ought to be some bargain."

"To a man working for you, five dollars is a pile of money, but I'll pay it. From now on, he's my dog."

Amos's old mouth split in a grin, showing stubs of teeth like snags in a creek. "I ain't goin' to forget he's your dog. You can keep him in that kennel fer one dollar a week and you furnish his food. But he ain't to be run on none of my hunting-leases, ner from none of my horses. And if he gits loose and kills some farmer's calf, remember he's *your* dog, not mine. You'll learn not to be so crazy about him." Then he added suddenly, "First thing you do is take off that damn collar with my name on it!"

ANYBODY WHO HAD A connection with Ambling Sam, Tafton's national figure, amounted to a near-celebrity, so Duff Webster's social standing never was in question. He had always avoided bridge parties, the town society's main diversion, but Mrs. Ott's invitation caught him unawares. So he went, thinking that, after all, it might not be so bad. This judgment was confirmed when he drew his tasseled tally card from the ornate silver platter to discover that he was Table 1, Couple 2, and Delia Phillips was his partner.

"Hello," she said, her brown, direct eyes smiling in a friendly way.

He murmured a greeting, annoyed by the ringing in his ears that came when he looked at her at this point-blank range. Most of the players were older and married, which gave him a warm feeling of comradeship for his bridge partner. She seemed to share this feeling, for between hands her manner was almost as if they were alone in the room.

But during the play she did not smile; she played with a close earnestness, almost like a cat stalking a quail brood, and he understood that she would not like to lose, no matter how social the game. The first two or three hands Duff could hardly make his eyes stay on the cards, so conscious was he of the presence across the table, and his bidding was half inaudible, not according to Culbertson, and once or twice out of turn. Luckily the first hands were dominated by the opponents, so that Duff's job consisted mostly in following suit. During the dealing of the fourth hand—their opponents had made one game—Duff suddenly remembered that partners at head table don't change, which meant that he could keep Delia for a partner as long as they could remain at head table. Now he forced his cards into focus, saw that they included six hearts with ace, king, and jack and satisfactory support. Delia responded to his bidding and gave him a good dummy, and after losing two tricks, he made five and game.

"That was nice," Delia said, looking at him.

From then on he played seriously, and by drawing good cards and being lucky on certain wild finesses and having the really skillful help of Delia, they remained at head table the whole evening. While refreshments were being served, he heard himself saying casually, "If I had a car I'd offer to take you home."

"I live right across the street," she said. "You can walk over with me if you like."

He would not have believed that the prospect of escorting any girl across the street could have put his nerves into a numb tremor. But there was no denying her appeal. Her hair was dark, only slightly darker than her eyes; her lips instead of being thin were full, with only a small amount of pale lipstick, the effect being one of positive, lasting beauty. But her principal attractiveness acted on other senses than the eye; a powerful animal magnetism that pulled at him as if with silk-covered steel cables.

"I've wondered," she was saying, "why you hadn't come to see me. You said you would, I seem to remember."

"Well—"

"Oh, well. Maybe I didn't make such an impression on you. You're here now, anyway."

"I've been pretty busy."

Delia said, "I've an idea whom you've been busy with."

"I mean busy training dogs."

They sat in Delia's living-room. She said, "What's it like, following field trials?"

"You start in Canada and just go from one place to another, until the National Championship at Grand Junction, that's all. We go to Grand Junction before long."

"I've always wanted to travel, but you can't do it on what a country doctor makes. I remember in school, the teacher used to get Lucie Sullivan to tell the class about some of the places she'd been, romantic-sounding places like Saskatchewan and Vinita and all. I was so envious I could've killed her."

Duff said, "You wouldn't think some of the places were so hot."

"Some day, though," Delia said, "I'm going to see them. Maybe you'll take me, sometime."

"Me?" Duff said in astonishment.

"Maybe," she said, her eyes crinkling in amusement.

Duff said, for lack of anything else, "Perhaps Amos will hire you in my place. He doesn't think I'm so hot."

"There's been talk about that," Delia said. She looked at him thoughtfully. "You'd be surprised at how few secrets you can have in this town."

There seemed to be some special meaning to this, but when Duff asked what she meant, Delia talked of other things. She talked about her plants, the tiny wild growths that she found in the woods, and presently rose to get one of them to show him.

He watched the easy grace of her legs as she returned with the small pot, and when she sat down beside him the perfume of her reached him delicately. She held the little plant in the cup of her two hands, close to her face. Duff could not see the plant for seeing her face so close to it.

"It's pretty," he muttered. "What do you call it?"

"I don't know. I haven't found out. It's got an odd smell. See?" She moved the plant toward him, and moved her face toward him at the same time.

Deliberately, Duff took the pot from her hands, set it on the coffee table, and then swept Delia into his arms. Her mouth unhesitatingly met his in quick and profound passion. Presently he felt himself floating drunkenly on a swelling emotional flood. Her fingernails bit into his back, and now her breath came in fluttering gasps.

"Stop now," she whispered urgently, and buried her face against his neck. The ornate clock on the mantel ticked distantly, the cherubs hanging to its sides in tireless sweetness, and the long hand jumped ahead a minute, rested sixty seconds and sprang again.

Finally Delia straightened and said brightly, "Hello."

Duff stemmed the rush of thoughts that sprinted through his brain; and the main one of them was about Lucie, and he said, "Look, it's time for me to go."

"What's your hurry, Duff?" she asked.

"I have to get up early—before day."

She moved a little closer to him and looked at him and said quietly, "Don't go, Duff."

So he stayed longer. Presently, abruptly, he stood up. "So long."

"Wait a little longer, Duff."

"Can't you understand anything?" he asked, most of his anger being at himself. "I've *got* to go."

She rose and stood beside him and put her arms gently around him. "When will I see you again? Soon?"

"Sometime," he said desperately.

"Soon?"

"No, it better not be soon."

In her bedroom, after he had gone, Delia undressed in front of the red-coal fire in the iron grate. Humming softly as she stepped out of her underclothes, she pirouetted in front of the mirror, briefly admiring her chorus-girl figure, then let the warm silk of her gown slide down over it. She turned on the little pink-plastic radio beside her bed. Presently there came an outpouring of music. She left each station on only for a few minutes, preferring to travel from one place to another.

For now she was in another world. She was *in the beautiful Walnut Room of the Hotel Bismarck here in Chicago dancing to the suave music of Tommy Tucker and his orchestra* and now she was *in the Waldorf-Astoria here in New York listening to the Latin rhythms of Xavier Cugat*...and now she was *in Birmingham, where we are broadcasting the election returns of the*...She turned the radio off, for her father was knocking at the door; she was in Tafton, Alabama.

Dr. Phillips came in. "I'm afraid you'll wake your mother with all that racket," he said.

Delia watched him as he held a pine splinter in the fire to get a light for his stub of cigar. The firelight shone redly on his spectacles and the old ashes and dandruff on the coat of his unpressed blue suit. "I'll play it down low," she said.

"Floyd Sheppard come by while you were at the party," Dr. Phillips said. "He sat and talked with us some, when he found out you weren't here."

"Oh, well. I don't care if I did miss him," she said.

He looked at her in surprise. "What's wrong between you and Floyd?"

"Nothing," she said absently. "Maybe I've got somebody else on my mind."

Dr. Phillips looked at her in perplexity. "I think Floyd's sort of got it in his head that you're going to marry him. Makes hisself pretty much at home here, anyway."

"Well, I don't think I'm going to marry *him*," she said lightly.

"You know your own mind, and I ain't trying to change it. But how come you're so down on Floyd, all of a sudden? I bet he makes more with his store now than I do."

"You mean collects more."

"Delia, a doctor has to heal the sick, whether they can pay or not. Let's don't get arguing that again," Dr. Phillips said heavily. "Floyd's going to start remodeling next week. Going to have a big opening and everything."

Delia said, "There's a grocery store in Montgomery covers half a block, air-conditioned and everything. Floyd wouldn't be such a big shot anywhere except in Tafton." She looked at her father thoughtfully. "Are you still going out to the pond fishing tomorrow afternoon?"

"Unless somebody decides to have a baby before I can get off."

Delia sat down at her dressing-table and began rubbing cleansing cream on her smooth-skinned face. "Why don't you ask Duff Webster to go with you? I know he likes to fish, because I heard him talking to the boys tonight, and asking if there were any bass around here."

"Where did you get that idea?"

"He's new here, and all. He doesn't know where to go or anything. It'd be nice for you to do, don't you think?"

"Well, sure, I'd be glad to take him. I'll call him tomorrow morning."

"Don't tell him I had anything to do with it. He might resent it."

Next afternoon when Dr. Phillips came home for his fishing-tackle, he found Delia in slacks, with her hair done up in a bright red ribbon. She told him that she had decided to ride out to the pond with them, and while they were fishing she would look for moss and holly. Duff, too, seemed surprised when he came out of the boardinghouse to find her in the car. She explained that she didn't fish, and that he needn't start worrying about having a dumb woman along, because she wouldn't bother them at all.

Dr. Phillips had brought an extra rod for Duff. They went in two boats, and in opposite directions. As he fished, Duff's Negro boatman gave him an account in detail of his family, of his son who was farming in Georgia, and of another son who was a waiter in Selma, and of the daughter who had left home eight years before and never been heard from since. But Duff was inattentive, thinking as he was, not of fishing, but of Delia on the shore.

Duff fished for an hour and a half without a strike, and he said, "We might as well go in, Michael. They're not doing anything."

"Le's don't go in yet, boss. Dey belongs to go at it jest before dark. Doctor Phillips, he catches most of his fish atter de sun done gone down."

But Duff told him to paddle on back to the landing anyway. There he found Delia, having gathered her leaves, waiting in the car.

"Not quitting, are you?" she asked.

"They're not doing anything," he said.

"I'm glad you came out! I was beginning to get lonesome," she said. "Did you think of me last night, after you left, Duff?"

"Yes, I sure did," he said vehemently.

"I thought of you, Duff," she said softly. "Aren't you going to kiss me?"

"Your father might come in and see us."

"Kiss me," she chided, "and hush."

Later, when her father did come out, with four bass, she said to Duff, "When we get home, you might as well stop by the house and have some supper with us. That is, if you don't mind cold chicken."

NOW BY DAY DUFF drove himself tirelessly, trying to rid his brain of the thought of Delia. But she followed him as he rode through the Alabama countryside and no matter how hard he resisted he was always remembering the hot burn of her mouth and the cool smoothness of her skin. He avoided Lucie these days, out of pure guilt. But because everybody was so intent on Ambling Sam's preparation for the National Championship she didn't seem to notice it.

Some nights Duff forced himself to go to a show, or to the poolroom, in order not to be drawn to Delia's house. Then, next day, a call for him would come to the boardinghouse, and it would be Delia. Why hadn't he come around last night? And he would be angered by the eagerness with which he heard her voice.

"I must be losing my power," Delia would say lightly.

"I wish you were," he would answer fervently.

"Ah, now, Duff. How could you stay away last night, when you know I wanted to see you?"

"Well, I had some things to do, and all—" he answered. And then he would hear himself say, "What about tonight?"

"Not tonight—now. Come now," she answered.

And he would go.

The night before they were to leave for Grand Junction, Duff finally steeled himself to say the things to Delia that he knew he should have said long ago. When he got ready to go home that night he stood up and said:

"Delia, this is our last night. I'm not coming back."

She smiled languidly up at him. "Ah, you're joking, Duff."

"No. I'm not joking. Listen, and try to believe me and understand me. I'm supposed to be in love with somebody else—you know who—and I'm supposed to be engaged to her—"

"But you're in love with me!"

"Who said so?"

"Nobody *said* so."

"Well you're too rich for my blood, I know that. I can't keep coming to see you and kissing you and thinking about you all day, when I'm supposed to be thinking of somebody else. It isn't fair, Delia. I don't know how I'm going to stay away from you, but I'm going to do it."

She was silent. Then she stood beside him and held his hand gently. "Duff, I understand. I'm going to miss you—oh, I'm going to miss you so! But you know what you want to do. I think it's fine of you to feel that way, to be so loyal. Maybe sometime—" She dropped her hands. The clock ticked. "Oh, well. Let's put an end to it if you want it that way. Will you kiss me good-by?"

"If I kissed you, there'd be no good-by. I'll have to just tell you."

Dr. Phillips came in immediately afterward, and he found Delia seated on the footstool in front of the fire, staring thoughtfully at the smoke from her cigarette.

"I passed Webster. He's leaving earlier than usual."

"Yes, he's gone," she said slowly.

Her tone arrested him. "For good?"

She smiled thoughtfully. "Oh, no. Just for a while."

TRANSPORTING HORSES BEING the trouble it is, Amos Hawthorne, like other handlers, usually took a chance on getting good horses from the uncertain hodgepodge of for-hire animals offered at the field-trial grounds. At any trial this motley herd consists mostly of lazy, uncomfortable horses, but also inevitably includes a few kickers, buckers, pullers, and stumblers, as well as a sound, sensible horse or two. But the chances of getting hold of a good horse are not encouraging. The National Championship, while no harder to win than two or three other stakes like the Free-for-All and the Quail Championship, outclasses every other trial in prestige. "Lost that damn stake in 1937 because my scout was on a plug horse and couldn't keep up with the dog," Amos said. "I ain't running the risk of that again."

The three older horses walked up into the truck with hardly a lift of their ears; but Lucie's young horse, Pete, was something else. He snorted and backed away. Duff tried riding him in, and he reared and turned off. Blindfolding proved no good; a twist of his nose caused him to stand rocklike instead of following the lead in; a chain tightened around his bottom jaw only made him wilder. Finally they constructed a makeshift loading chute, got Pete headed into that, and then touched his shining bay rump with the wires of the hotshot battery; Pete jumped all the way into the front end of the truck in one leap.

Amos Hawthorne and Lucie left at eight, with Lucie driving and old Ambling Sam peacefully dozing in the trunk dog crate. Wesley and Duff followed in the truck, heading west until they hit the Mississippi line and the Meridian-Tupelo highway, when they turned north and settled down to two hundred miles of monotonously straight and smooth driving. They left the pine belt behind, and the country became wide open and rolling.

"To me," Lucie had once said, "half the fun of field trials is the word-of-mouth competition. Some talkers, those dog men. The owners talk about their own dogs. The handlers talk about the dog that won at the last trial. If he left a point to relocate moving birds, he's a blinker. If he ran independently and was hard to bend around, he's a bolter; but if he handled with noticeable ease, he's a whip-runner. In any event, no matter what he did, he had no business taking the stake. Oh, winning in the field is just a small scimption compared to getting a unanimous decision from those Lobby Judges.

"The handlers don't brag on their own dogs. Not in public anyway. They may admit to their wives that Ben is hot as a match, but when the gang is sitting around trying to worm something out of each other, all they get is poor-mouth. Ben's not himself, his shoulder's stiff, his feet are raw, he's off his feed, got a speargrass barb in his cheek, he just ain't right, don't know what's ailing him. My, it's pitiful. Then young Ben goes out and runs like a million, and the handler, with that quiet, satisfied look on his face, and nothing at all to say now, sits around and waits for the judges to give him the check.

"Some of the handlers, like the Squire, have practically no education at all; others have been to college, but they speak the same language. Sit around and listen to some of the near-insults they dish out to one another under the name of kidding, and you'd think the fighting ought to start any minute; yet any one of the boys will lend another one a bale of hay if he gets caught short.

"They're pretty cold-blooded about their dogs; to them a fine, affectionate bird dog is just a money-making machine. At least that's the way it looks. Only, on the other hand, they wouldn't be spending their lives with dogs if way down deep there wasn't some kind of love for them."

GRAND JUNCTION IS A quiet village whose only pretensions to anything grand is the fact that it is the best-known field-trial center in the world. For about three hundred and fifty days a year, the village is almost dormant; then field-trial week approaches, and the municipal pulse steps up. The housewives put their spare room in shape to take care of the visitors, and begin collecting groceries for lunches to be prepared, and the men start arranging for horses from surrounding farmers.

The druggist, whose storeroom is used as a clubroom during the trial, looks to his stock of Coca-Cola syrup and orange juice, and arranges his floor space to allow for the prolonged bull sessions. On days when the weather is too rough for dog running, men in boots occupy all the tables, the fountain stools, the counters, and most of the standing-space, and it is an achievement to walk in and buy a roll of gauze and come out the same half hour.

The drawings were held Sunday night at the hotel in an atmosphere of tobacco smoke and bird-dog conversation. Duff came late, entering in the silence that accompanies the announcement of the pairings. Lucie gave him a wink; she was sitting between Teague McGinnis and Ralph Skown, the young sportsman owner of Hotfoot, and Duff did not wink back.

"In the first brace, Maybelle Mazie with Rider's Willie," the secretary called, as he drew from the hat containing the names of thirty-six dogs, twenty-nine pointers and seven setters, all of whom had necessarily won a recognized trial previously. "Second brace, Medallion with—Hotfoot. Third brace—" Ambling Sam was called for the sixth brace, with a bold young pointer called Ticonderoga. That meant the afternoon of the third day of running.

After the drawings, the handlers and owners and wives and reporters resumed their talk. The handlers began drifting off first, to be sure their dogs were well quartered for the night. Since the running would take more than a week, a good many of the dog men in the lower heats got ready to go back home, to return later.

Lucie was a center of considerable interest, and Duff had a hard time saying to her privately, "Let's blow."

"Gee, honey," she said, "I haven't had so many men to play with in a coon's age. I think I'll stay and give my eyelashes a little exercise."

Later Teague McGinnis said, "I wouldn't have hardly known Webster."

"He's doing fine now."

"So I saw when he came in and you gave him that wink."

She said, "Yes, he's doing *all* right."

Teague looked toward the door, and said, "Well, he sure seems like a nice fellow."

"My conscience, Teague; you're no help," she said.

He looked at her in surprise. "What's the matter?"

"Let it go," she said.

Outside, a thin filtering of snow had begun, falling in tiny whispers past the bare limbs of the trees as Duff walked, feeling the chill of it against his face, seeing it sift down past the corner street lights, stepping upon the thin cushion of it on the sidewalk concrete. He wondered if his dog Judas was well bedded and warm, back in Tafton. In front of the house where he was boarding, he paused at the gate, then went on past, his coat turned up, walking slowly, aimlessly. He kept wondering where Lucie was, and whom she was with. He hadn't thought he would mind her being out with someone else, but he did. The feeling that held him was not of anger, but of lonesomeness.

The worst part of it was that her going out with somebody else was tacit permission for him to do the same. She had removed one of his principal weapons for resisting the silken pull of Delia Phillips.

Once summoned, the image of Delia persisted. He remembered the afternoon in the car, when he had held her chin in his hands, and he could still recall the perfumed smoothness of her skin. For a few steps he even imagined that she was walking beside him in the snowfall, her arm through his arm and her warm hand folded in his fingers inside his overcoat pocket.

The snow did not last the night, and in the cold early morning the field-trial gallery assembled on the Hobart Ames plantation near the little branch, amid the confusion of cars and men and Negroes with horses calling, "Try dis'n, cap'm; yere de one you want, best horse in Lardemore County, genuwine Tennessee walker." Men working with saddles, horses squealing, a car in the ditch. Sky overcast, wind out of the east. The two handlers brought their dogs up front, where the three judges sat silently waiting—on his big, mannerly horse with the bleached tie rope around its neck, Hobart Ames, who had ridden every brace of the stake since 1897 except one in 1908, when Ed Garr won with Count Whitestone II, and little Benton King, in his mackinaw and rubber boots, and Nash Buckingham, who wrote *The Shootin'est Gent'men*.

The handlers held their eager dogs. Mr. Ames looked at his watch. Time, 8:47.

"Ready, gentlemen?" Dr. King asked.

"Okay," the handlers said.

"All right, let 'em go."

The men unsnapped the leads, and the two dogs bolted away like whippets. For two hundred yards they stayed locked in a dog race, then Rider's Willie swung off through the soggy cornfield and began bird hunting. Maybelle Mazie made a turn-off somewhat to the right, too, and disappeared over the rise.

The application of neither dog, said the Field report later, was impressive. When the turn into the low country was made, Willie made several tentative points in the open, stabbing forward, then dashed on without game being seen. A bevy, the first of the day, was observed on the ground at a honeysuckle thicket. When the second road was crossed, Willie searched more diligently; he subsequently proved a hard-running dog with a penchant for finding game. He had an unproductive point in edge of cotton field at a fringe of bleached grass near plum thickets, stanch if not stylish on this, but thereafter he piled up an impressive bird score albeit the bird work was not inspirational in quality...Willie frequently contacted game; four bevies were cleanly handled if not with a plethora of style; two bevies represented stops to flush, another bevy he pointed, then roaded too close...

Maybelle Mazie and Rider's Willie finished the three hours somewhat weary; neither had run anything like a championship race. But the gallery was pleased with the morning; the first brace had proved the birds were there.

One of the handlers looked at the sky and said to Teague McGinnis, "You beat that snow and you couldn't ask for a better afternoon."

The judges and three or four others had lunch in the magnificent old Ames house. Everybody else ate outside, picnic style; after lunch the first day, there were few strangers.

At 12:57, Teague McGinnis stood with his hand under Hotfoot's collar. Medallion, the other dog, whined and rose eagerly on his hind legs, in his handler's grasp.

"Now, boys," said a man in the gallery, "if you want to see a traveling bird dog, just watch that Texas dog go."

Teague McGinnis didn't come from the great open spaces; he was born in the marshes of east Texas, on the edge of the Cajun country. His father was a rice farmer, and when rice farmers were making their killing he spent his money on good saddle horses and fine foxhounds. After rice turned out to be just another way to lose your shirt, the McGinnises lost their shirts, and then found oil on the land. They sold out and moved to Houston, and Mr. McGinnis built a hundred-thousand-dollar house in the country, full of intricate gadgets controlled by push buttons, in which he imperturbably lolled with his Stetson hat on his head and nothing on his feet.

Six high-class dogs had a room on the second floor, dogs young Teague ran in various amateur trials about the country. He and one of the dogs flew to an amateur championship at Albany, and won second. But Mr. McGinnis got restless with his marble staircases and his indirect lighting and his fancy garden, and he began speculating in oil leases, and that was the end of prosperity; he ended up back in the marsh country, trying to make a living rice farming. Sometimes he would tell his friends about the big house he used to have, and the way you could push a button and a machine would wash the clothes and dry them and iron them; it was as if he were telling them about a trip he had taken, a place he had visited and liked but where he had never really belonged.

Teague didn't mind being broke again, either, except that it interfered with his bird dogs. So he became a professional trainer and handler. There was a lot of difference, he found, between a carefree amateur trial and an open trial against hard-working professionals who eat or starve by the performance of their dogs. For a long time he himself was of the category of starving professionals, existing by the aid of shooting-dogs left with him for training at twenty dollars a month. The dogs he had won with in amateur trials found birds and performed well, but they didn't have the extra degree of fire it took to win in fast company.

Trial by Marriage

One day a letter came from Ralph Skown, of Houston, who sent Teague shooting-dogs for training occasionally.

Dear McGinnis:

Today I shipped you a Wahoo—Kentucky Babe puppy. He's a healthy dog and might make us a good dog. You might worm him and give him distemper shots. Let him run and hunt like he pleases before shutting down on him. I haven't named him, I'll let you do that.

Sincerely,
Ralph Skown

The puppy was only four months old when he arrived. The usual young dog on being shipped away from home and transported by a noisy, unsettling conveyance amidst strange people and odd smells, emerges from his dog crate unhappily, cringing before unknown feet and wetting the ground nervously. But this puppy came out in one exuberant leap, made a couple of joyous circles around the yard, then attacked Teague's Negro's trouser-cuff ferociously, pulling and growling. The Negro, Hansel, lifted his leg, and the puppy held on until all his feet were off the ground. Next he jumped halfway up to Teague's face in an effort to lick it, then started his mad circling again.

"He goin' so fast," Hansel laughed, "he goan burn his feets up!" After that the dog's name was Hotfoot.

When Hotfoot's puppy days were over, and it was time for him to steady down and quit chasing everything that ran before him, he broke easily. He had two wins as a Derby, one on chickens and one on quail. As the dog's reputation grew, McGinnis's fortunes rose, and by the time Hotfoot was an all-age dog, the Texan's kennels held all the shooting-dogs he could train and two or three first-class field-trial dogs. When he moved to Alabama, Hotfoot ran better than ever.

RUNNING IN HIS FIRST National Championship, Hotfoot found six coveys, five of which he handled cleanly, pointing positively and loftily. *The American Field* later reported: *He ran with sparkle, as if he were having the time of his life, and in the opinion of many would have sewed up the stake if he had negotiated the treacherous Hell's Forest with more ease. Even so, it was generally granted that the pace he set was a fast one. Several of the other handlers evinced discouragement at their chances, though, of course, not openly...Medallion having been out of judgment for thirty minutes, Hotfoot's race toward the last was against the snow. He lost this race, but turned it to victory when in the last eight minutes he meritoriously pointed a huddled bevy in a sumac thicket, with the big flakes now falling in almost blinding profusion. That point was something to remember...*

Next morning the bare Tennessee countryside was white-covered. Shortly after eight o'clock the call came from the Ames house to Frank Swift's drugstore: "There will be no running today."

Now was the time to talk about old races and duck shooting and night fox hunting and guns and walking horses. Some of the men got up a dime poker game. But most of them, during the day, stayed around the drugstore. Outside the snow fell intermittently; and inside they recalled the time Jim Avent was disqualified for running as a Derby—under two years old—a dog with worn teeth, and the way old Comanche Rap would steal points, of which his handler, Joe Crane, said, "Well, you don't win stakes backing," and the bill the late Al Hochwalt got from the Negro taxi driver who carried him in the trial grounds which itemized: *Three comes and three goes at four bits a went—three dollars.*

"A dog I won't never forget," said Amos Hawthorne, "was old Joe Cumming, an Antonio setter. You talk about your dogs with sand in their craw, well, this setter was one of 'em. Guts? Aye, damn, he had a full belly of 'em. I mind that championship he run in, believe it was 1899 or thereabouts, not no time recent, anyhow. Him and another dog, I fergit his name, was the hotshots, and in the first heat it was just gee and haw between them, both of 'em running and finding and not a bobble. That night some says Joe won, and some says this other dog—Dave Earl his name was. But the judges, as usual, wasn't so quick to come out with a say-so; and the upshot of it was that both dogs was called back for the next day.

"Next morning they hadn't no more than cast them dogs off when this Joe setter he begin to run on three legs, and anybody but a fool could see he was plumb lame. Well, Titus he stopped the dog and took a look, and there wasn't nothing to be seen to cause all that limping, and so he decided to let Joe go on, thinking it might be just some kind of stiffness. Joe he was willing, too, and away he went, three-legged as a milk stool. Before terrible much longer, yonder we seen him, froze up on birds. Titus flushed 'em, and shot, and Joe stood there grinning at him; and then away he went again. The other dog he was running good, but he wasn't finding no birds much, and it looked like the more Joe run the better he got. Before long we seen he was letting that lame foot hit the ground every now and then, and when the second hour come he had done forgot all about being lame and going hell-alickety, with one foot as good as another. He won, too.

"Well, seemlike that's all there was to it, until next day. They had old Joe in the living-room—fixing to draw his picture if I make no mistake—and somebody begin fooling with him, petting him, feeling around his foot to see what had ailed it the day before. Come to find out Joe had rammed a inch-long locust thorn plumb through his foot; the pad had done closed over it at the bottom, and it didn't quite come through on the other side. They got a knife and opened 'er up a little so they could git holt with a pair of pliers, and then pulled it out. That dog had got so bird-happy he just forgot he had a sore foot."

Somebody said, "Best foxhound I ever seen didn't have but three legs. Lost one on a trap."

Another said, "I like guts in a dog, but I like brains, too. Take Alford's John. Remember him, Mr. Hawthorne?"

"He had a head on him, all right."

"You could nearly 'bout see him thinking. I recollect one time there was a trailing dog in behind him, a fast 'un; John was anxious to shake this dog off his tail. Finally he seen he couldn't outrun him, so he found him a good high fence, and over this he went, and the other dog couldn't make it, and had to go off by hisself. I guess old Mary Montrose was a hell of a dog, but I'd like to see her tie in with Alford's John just one time. Wasn't never no dog he run a heat with ever placed over him in a trial. That's going some."

"Well," somebody said, "I never seen John run, but if he was better than that pointer bitch, Mary, he was a power. Me, I'll stick with Mary. I saw her win the National Championship when she'd just turned two years old, hardly more than a puppy. Then she came back and won it twice more, and won at bench shows in between."

The great old dogs lived again that day in the drugstore—Rip Rap and Baby Ale and Comanche Frank and Count Gladstone and John Proctor and Eugene M; and the young men sat and listened. Duff leaned forward and said nothing, but he didn't miss a word. *Some day,* he thought, *they'll have another dog to talk about and remember—a traveling, black-hearted devil named Judas.*

"Well," someone said finally, "you can name all them dogs and take your pick. But I don't believe one of them could beat Amos Hawthorne's Ambling Sam, in his day."

"What you mean, in his day?" Amos demanded, and the others grinned.

"I mean when he was younger."

"Let me tell you something," Amos said coldly, "Ambling Sam's day, mister, is next Thursday."

FRIDAY NIGHT, SOMEWHERE about twelve, Teague McGinnis's black coupe moved slowly along the wet road. The radio played softly. *"Maybe you'll ask me to come back again, and maybe I'll say, 'Maybe.'"* Teague sat deep in the seat, one foot propped on the handbrake lever.

"That's a good song," Teague said, lazily humming it.

"Yes, it's pretty good," Lucie said. "Teague, do you know any poetry?"

"Poetry?" He looked at her puzzled. "I know some dirty limericks."

"So do I. I mean real poetry."

"I guess not. How come?"

"Nothing."

"You know," he said, "a lot of times I don't get you. I guess I'm dumb."

She laughed up at him. "You are sort of dumb."

"I get along," he said tolerantly. "Don't have to make my living reading women's minds." He opened the glove compartment and brought out a bottle of rye whisky. While Lucie held the wheel, he took a small swallow, screwed the cap back on, and replaced the bottle.

"You know," he said, thoughtfully, "I can't get over that heat old Sam run yesterday."

"I believe you. You've talked about it enough."

"It just ain't possible for no ten-year-old bird dog to get out and run for three hours, and then have to be rid down to catch him when taking-up time come."

"Are you worried, Teague?"

"Me? I tell you what's a fact, Lucie, if I could see what I seen Thursday every time I entered a trial, I wouldn't much care if I never took a stake. Honest, everybody expected to hear old Sam had waked up dead this morning."

"You know what you are? A sportsman. I've heard of them, but I'd given up ever seeing one."

"Lucie, if old Sam hadn't messed up on that last covey so bad, be dog if I don't think they'd 'a' give it to him without a runoff. Hot damn, I'd like to see 'em give it to the old Squire anyway. Everybody's been taking such pity on him. He told 'em he could still handle and his dog could still run, and wouldn't nobody believe him, including me. But if they make Sam run again, it'll be bad."

"Why?"

"He can't run another race like that."

"Teague, you're a funny one."

"Well, if he runs like that again, I just want to see it that's all." He took another swallow of whisky.

"Teague " Lucie asked, "what do you think of me?"

"You know."

"I mean, what is your opinion of me? You think I'm on the level, straight, no fooling, and that sort of stuff?"

"As straight as any woman."

"You're some gentleman."

"Who said I was a gentleman?'

"Why don't you attack me, then?"

"I ain't ready."

"When will you be ready?" she asked interestedly.

"About Sunday night."

Again she was silent. She changed the radio. Then said, "Teague, that about Sunday night sounds nice, but I don't think I'll go with you any more."

"Don't you want to, or what?"

"What do you think of me, honest?"

"I think you're plumb straight."

"Well, if I'm plumb straight, I ought to quit seeing you. You're okay and it won't be easy. Look, why don't you be a heel every now and then to help me out?"

"I ain't that much of a sportsman."

had turned good, and every morning two dogs ran, and every afternoon two more ran. All of them were fine bird dogs, dogs with a heart for hunting. Some of them ran big, and handled well, and found birds, and stood them right. A few had streaks of pottering or ran wild or found no birds or handled what they found sloppily, all of which even fine dogs will sometimes do. But Duff Webster figured that so far not a heat could touch those of Hotfoot and Ambling Sam.

When the last brace was taken up, the judges rode off a way and dismounted. The gallery dismounted, too, and stood around talking, speculating, lighting cigarettes. The horses stood quietly, in contrast to the first day; the foolishness had been ridden out in nine hard days—you could have crawled between the legs of the meanest horse there. Now the judges called R.H. Scott, the club secretary. He joined them and listened to what they had to say. The judges came back and mounted their horses and rode away, while Scott said:

"The judges request the handlers of Hotfoot and Ambling Sam to have their dogs on the morning course at eight forty-five a. m. tomorrow."

Trial by Marriage

Some of the handlers had their dogs loaded, and some of the followers had made business appointments for the next day; but hardly a man left town. The old phone in the drugstore was kept busy until after ten o'clock.

…*Hello, Mr. Jones, I'm ready with Nashville…Hello, Mr. Vestal, I'm ready with Memphis…ready with Holly Springs…ready with West Point…Hello, Jim, hello. This is Arthur…listen to me…get in your car and come to Grand Junction tonight…You want to see a stomp-down dog race? …Ambling Sam and Hotfoot…I don't give a damn if he's twenty years old you ought to seen him Thursday…*

The morning was a good one, with only a slight mist hanging over the still-muddy grounds. Several amateur photographers and two newspaper photographers floundered in the mud, squatting, squinting, clicking, adjusting diaphragms, changing shutter speeds, winding films, flipping out burned, clouded flash bulbs. In sepulchral silence sat the judges. Hotfoot walked on his hind legs, in McGinnis's grasp, and whined and jumped about.

Ambling Sam stood quietly, not moving; nobody held him or touched him. Amos Hawthorne had told him to stand, and had mounted his horse, and Sam stood. There was gray about Sam's muzzle, a suggestion of fat on his shoulders, and his eyes did not have the bulging brightness they had had when the stud booklet to prospective breeders was written.

But, of course, the stud booklet was written six years ago… *With superb breeding, individuality, brains, and remarkable field quality, this dog stands at the top as a stud animal,. His conformation is ideal, tall and racy, yet has plenty of strength; he has the setter shoulder that we all try to breed; his running-gear is perfect—long, free and easy stride that takes him over the ground at a tremendous rate, yet light as a fox on his feet. Ambling Sam has a clean cut head of the bench-show type, with a neck that is long and clean and never will become throaty. He stands straight on his tiptoes, legs straight and well under him, and has the best of feet; with an arch back of great strength and endurance; his tail is straight and tapering, set on at the right place. As to his field-trial quality, all dog men know what he has accomplished…* That was six years before, and now the setter shoulder that we all try to breed had a suggestion of fat about it, and the long and clean neck that will never become throaty had become somewhat throaty.

Dr. King looked at his watch. Time, 8:51. Sky clear, wind out of the northeast. "Gentlemen, are you ready?"

Teague McGinnis, wrestling with Hotfoot, said, Hell, yes, he was ready; and the gallery chuckled nervously. Amos nodded.

"All right, let 'em go."

Amos said, "Git, Sam!" and Sam shot away as Teague McGinnis released Hotfoot. The dogs ran shoulder to shoulder in the customary race for a few seconds. But Sam had run in too many trials to be diverted from the main object. He turned off, and even as he ran you could see him sizing up the country. Ahead were open fields, and a dog that wanted to do some line running could bust the fields wide open. To the right were the woods, and a dog that wanted to find birds might skirt them. Sam headed for the woods. Duff turned his horse out toward the edge of the course. At 8:55 Sam checked his fast flight, and took five quick steps, without any drawing or hesitating, and suddenly there he stood with his tail up and his head high, and the only moving thing about him was his tongue over his discolored old teeth as he grinned and waited.

"Point!" called Duff, who was scouting.

Amos Hawthorne rode up and dismounted, and drew his gun from the saddle boot. He walked out in front of Sam, far ahead in case the birds were running, and began quirting the grass with his whip, then came in closer. There was an explosive *whirr-r-r* as the birds burst from the sedge and grass; Amos turned toward Sam, catching his eye, and fired the gun into the air.

Sam lifted his head and ears and watched the flight of the quail interestedly but he did not move in his tracks until Amos lifted him by the collar and thrust him away. Now Sam was gone again, keeping away in that snappy, short-coupled puppy-dog stride. He skirted the field edges, the plump thickets, the locust groves, the fallow ground. He stayed ahead, not once back-casting or road-running. A man who knew bird country would stand in his stirrups and say, "'There ought to be a covey yonder, and yonder, and yonder." And those were the places Sam went—and he found birds.

But that was no surprise to anybody. They knew Sam could find birds, for nobody doubted his choke-bore nose, or his near-human brain that had ten years of bird hunting to refer to. The surprise was that he could now still grind away the swift miles, and smash through the swamps and leap the red-clay gullies.

"I'll swear, I believe old Amos has rung in a young dog on us. That pistol ball yonder cain't be ten years old."

"I wouldn't put it past old Amos, except I don't believe he could turn up a young dog that's got as much sense as that gentleman topping the hill yonder."

"Boys, you listen to me," said another. "I've bred bitches to that Ambling Sam for six years and I'm gonna keep breeding to him as long as they got him at stud. You think I don't know every mark and tick on that old dog's hide? I've sat and watched the puppies pop out, and soon as the bitch would lick them clean, I've said, 'That'n's got Sam's tail spot, and that'n's got the same spot over the ribs.' Some day, if I keep at it, and if my money holds out, I'm going to get one that's just like him in every way and I'm going to have me an Ambling Sam born all over again," he said. "That's Sam out yonder, boys. You take my word for it."

"Well, if that dog is ten years old, about thirty minutes of that kind of running is all you'll see out of him."

...The dog is old Ambling Sam, grizzled veteran of more than ten years, showing the telltale gray about his muzzle, the flabby fat of age about his shoulders and quarters, the fading eye of passing time—but under that exterior there still beats a great heart which has carried him through many a battle from the prairies of Saskatchewan to the plains of Texas. The fires of youth have burned out, but there still remains that spark of genius just as it was in the days of his prime. No one expected Sam to go out and do more than a turn or two, and perhaps even Amos Hawthorne felt that same way when he led him out before that vast audience. But Ambling Sam's big brave heart beat true, and mayhap it was more than instinct that led him to do the deeds he did; but whatever it was, reason or instinct or unquenchable courage, Sam ran a race like in the old days. True enough he did not go as fast as his fiery young opponent, but he went as wide and he searched out the birdy places with the mature intelligence born of the long experi-

ence that he has had. He did not tarry anywhere that was not inviting; he handled perfectly and he always stayed out ahead. But Sam made two errors that morning, one heroic, one tragic...

Hotfoot made errors, too, that morning. They were errors born of exuberance and boldness rather than bad nose or faulty training. Twice he smashed into birds, knowing they were there and going to them like a falcon, but stopping one split second too late, to see them rise in confusion around him spilling their surprised droppings upon the frost-bitten grass. But Hotfoot stood there, his tail half up and his ears relaxed in disappointment, and waited for McGinnis to shoot and send him on. The rest of the time Hotfoot was jumping, from one hill to the next. McGinnis rode nervously, watching; presently a distant moving spot of white would show, and he would say, "Yon he is, judge!" Then another disappearance, and McGinnis getting nervous again, only to have the flash of white that was Hotfoot streak from a far-away locust head. "Yon he is, judge!" And finally, the spot of white stopped, and McGinnis's scout rode out holding his hat up to signal the point, and when they arrived, there stood Hotfoot, rammed up in a point fit to knock you out of your saddle.

When the gallery got past the out-jut of woods on the right, they saw Duff riding out also, and his hat was up, and yonder stood Sam, and he had birds, too.

"You wait. Ain't but an hour gone yet. In another hour that old Sam dog will be trotting behind Hawthorne's horse—or dead."

Now the second hour wore on. Some said Hotfoot was ahead, some said Sam. They were about even on birds, anyway; the rest of it was conjecture. Hotfoot had an inner fire that seemed to drive him like a demon, and when he pointed you had to swallow the lump in your throat to see such cocky perfection; he seemed to be posing, trying to lift his head higher than his tail, a living thing turned to cold granite; when he pointed he was no longer a dog, he was a statue that no sculptor could have chiseled.

At first glance he seemed truly immobile, for he never allowed himself to pant, mouth open, or to tremble. But if you watched closely you could see his upper lip shake with the exhalations, and you could see the hide stretch tight over his flaring ribs as he breathed, see the slow movement of his eyes as he looked slightly back to see if McGinnis was coming. Ambling Sam made up in handling and bird-wisdom what he lacked in youthful fire. When Hawthorne wanted Sam to turn, he squalled and lifted his whip; and Sam, a half mile away, turned as if he had a string tied to him and the old handler had pulled it. As Duff rode the fringes of the course, he was not seeing Sam, but his dog Judas. *If I could ever get that old fool of mine to handle like that I'd have the best damn dog in the world.*

The judges had expected to reach a decision within an hour and a half. But at that time the only way to choose between the dogs would have been with a coin. Toward the end of the second hour, Ambling Sam began to slow a bit; his casts were shorter, and more often he turned back in to see Amos, and in the gallery the wise ones smiled knowingly and some shook their heads a bit sadly.

Then old Amos stood in his stirrups and sent a mighty whistle blast across the hills, and old Sam heard it and jumped as if stung with birdshot. And he kept jumping. Every now and then—not too often—Amos would hit him with that whistle, and Sam would drive.

After his next covey, Sam went even wider. He was running with animation, as if with the quail scent he had inhaled youth.

He ran like a Derby dog. They couldn't believe he was an old dog; and even Sam forgot it. For when he came to one of those Tennessee gullies, he thought he had the power to clear it. Sam jumped, trying to clear a twenty-foot chasm. He was five feet short, slamming into the side of the red bank and rolling to the bottom of the gully. Duff saw it and spurred his horse. But Amos Hawthorne was the first one to reach the brink of the gully and see at the bottom the still dog. Amos was on the ground before his horse fully stopped. He started down the steep red-clay side, only to lose his balance and go tumbling head over heel to the bottom.

Afterward, most of them said that Amos Hawthorne never got over that fall. Others said it was the sight of his dog Ambling Sam lying like dead at the bottom of that deep gully that Amos never got over—even though Sam, with only the wind knocked out of him, the next minute got up, sucked in his breath hard as if he were choking, then shot up the steep red side of the ravine and headed for the distant sedge patches.

But it was Sam's second error of judgment that they never forgot. The Time, 11:18. Sky overcast, temperature rising, increasing northeasterly wind. Hotfoot had just found his sixth covey of quail—two less than those found by Ambling Sam. Sam had not been spotted for four minutes, and Duff Webster could occasionally be seen riding the outward woods, searching. Presently Amos turned his horse out, too, and began looking for his dog. Then somebody up ahead saw Sam on point. Several people called to Amos, but the now-gusty wind blew their calls away.

Nash Buckingham said to one of the idle dog men, "Handle Sam, please."

The handler, Bill McCrory, rode up behind the dog and dismounted. While he was reaching for his gun, Amos Hawthorne returned, having finally been made to hear. But now, before either man approached, Sam stirred, then turned and left his point, streaking away on a new cast.

"You see the way that old dog corrected?" somebody asked. "A dog's nose fools him every now and then, but old Sam don't let his'n fool him long."

And that would have been the end of it, with credit to Sam, but Duff, having been signaled to come on in, and seeing the gallery move forward, cut in sharply to catch up. Duff came galloping straight across the place where Ambling Sam had pointed, and when he got there, an enormous covey of birds got up at precisely the spot where Sam had been looking—the spot that Sam had left. Everybody saw the birds. There was an immediate, stunned hush; horses were reined in, and men looked at each other significantly.

Sam suddenly broke his stand and deliberately went off to the left. Judges and others followed along the roadway, giving Sam credit for a correction. But unfortunately, Hawthorne's scout, Duff Webster, who has won for himself considerable praise for his astute and seemingly prescient dog-finding ability, came galloping in to rejoin the gallery and crossed the spot where Sam had pointed. There to the amazement of all, he rode up a bevy of quail. Much can—and will—be said about this occurrence. Up until now Sam was perhaps the National Champion; but after this incident even the rankest novice knew that the honorable Sam had cut his own throat.

Trial by Marriage

Blinking—leaving a valid point—is the unpardonable crime of bird-dogdom. The judges, unfortunately, must go by what they see, not what they know.

The judges know that a ten-year-old dog doesn't suddenly turn into a blinker; they probably suspect that the rising wind took away from Sam the vagrant scent and that he had, rather than show indecision, moved on. It is also unfortunate that Webster, who had not seen the original point, happened to ride through the exact terrain, and therefore be the direct contributing factor to the losing race of Ambling Sam. But in site of the disappointment of Ambling Sam fans, Hotfoot proved himself one of the best dogs of the decade, and no one has any call to be ashamed of the new National Champion...

LUCIE AND AMOS drove back to Grand Junction slowly, the tires crunching on the wet gravel. Lucie, at the wheel, tried to keep her head slightly turned so her grandfather would not see the silent tears that ran down her solemn face. But Amos wasn't looking; he slumped forward, his jaw slack and his eyes staring at the instrument panel.

"I never thought I'd ever see that head hanging," Lucie said finally.

Amos shifted, and said, "Where's that Webster, that rode up them birds right in front of every damn body?"

"Squire, listen. He didn't see that point."

"Yes, he did. He rode up them birds on purpose."

"Oh, you're crazy!"

"Where's he at?"

"He's riding in with the horse truck."

"You pay him off and tell him he's fired. And if he ever puts a foot on my place again, he'll wish he hadn't."

Lucie turned the car onto the pavement. "Don't talk like that. Sam ran a good race. Nobody's going to hold that point against Sam."

Amos rubbed his hand against the instrument panel absently as if feeling the smoothness of it. "Aye, dammit," he said, presently, "they said we couldn't go three hours. Well, we shore went it."

"Yes."

"Next year—" he muttered. "Just wait till next year. We'll damn shore win that championship."

PART III

When they got back to Tafton, it was apparent that, after seventy-odd years of youth, age had suddenly overtaken Amos Hawthorne. His hand, only last week stone-steady, had become trembling and uncertain. Coming back from Grand Junction, he had to stop and visit rest rooms frequently; his step was no longer strong and light-footed, his mind at times turned childish, and his sight was plainly failing. "He can see just a mite better than a mole, and that's all," Dr. Phillips said. "He's through riding. Maybe he's through walking. You keep him in a half-dark room for a couple of weeks, and if he makes out to get better, we'll let him up."

Lucie had persuaded Amos to let Duff stay on a few weeks longer—"Until you're able to be up," she had said, knowing that time wouldn't come.

"Lucie," Amos said shrewdly, "you don't want him here fer no reason beside dog training?"

"No. That's silly," she said uneasily.

"I'll allow him to feed my dogs, and to ride my horses a spell longer," Amos said, almost whispering in his fierceness, "but, child, if you ever allow him to make up to you, I'll have him to kill."

That night they sat in the car by the bank of the river again, and it was late. Lucie had told Duff what Amos had said, and Duff had heard her in morose silence.

Now she rested quiet in Duff's arms and listened to the faint sound of a car rumbling across the bridge around the bend of the river, perhaps returning from the big dance at Zurich. This was the same place they had come the first time, and there was again a light in the farmer's house across the river.

"Duff?"

"Yes."

"You see that light? You remember that first night, weeks ago, when we came here? I heard today that there is a sick child there. They're afraid it's polio."

"That's too bad," he said heavily.

She sat up. "What's the matter, Duff? You're so moody tonight. You got the mullygrubs again?"

"Yes, Lucie. I've really got them."

She kissed him. "Hey, stop talking so solemn. Listen. Answer me. What's the trouble?"

"Lucie," he said finally, "I'm leaving."

"What?"

"I'm quitting the job."

"But why? What's wrong?"

"Oh, hell, everything's wrong. I keep thinking about riding up those quail that Sam blinked, and causing him to lose the championship. That old dog had run his heart out, and then I had to come along and show the judges the only mistake he made. I can hear those birds flying up around me now. Sometimes I think I've got a sort of reverse Midas touch—everything I touch goes sour."

"You got to worry about something that couldn't be helped, for conscience's sake?"

"Well it could have mighty easily not happened," he said desolately.

"That's no cause to leave."

"There's not much reason to stay."

"I'm a reason, Duff; stay for me."

Duff waited a moment. "If I could get a job somewhere else, maybe they'd let me work on Judas in my spare time. He ought to be worked hard," he said. "Old Amos hates me and the dog both. It's hard to get out and labor for a man that hates your guts. It's all right for a while—you can hate back. But before long it begins to weigh you down. I don't like to keep a job a woman holds for me."

"Oh, you're just plain crazy. Look, we need you. Wesley can't break all those dogs, and I'm not much help."

"They're the old man's kennels, and he's the one wants to be shut of me."

"Can't you understand anything, for crying out loud? I'm the one who's got to make the kennel pay."

"I'm not going to leave you in the lurch. We'll get another trainer maybe."

"Well then," she said presently, "what about us?"

"Who?"

"You and me, and the ivory table and all that stuff."

"I'm coming back for you."

"Listen, Duff. You can't say it that way. I'm in love with you, don't you know that?"

He said, curiously, "*Are* you in love with me?"

"How can you ask that? Don't I show it? Huh? Didn't I go off the high board for you?" she demanded. "Let me ask you something. Do *you* love *me*?"

"Sure."

She mused, "Tell me this, don't you really wish I didn't love you, so you wouldn't feel—well, a responsibility?"

He shifted, suddenly uncomfortable.

"Don't you?" she insisted.

"No," he lied.

"If you feel that way it'll spoil everything."

"Why will it?" he asked.

"It just will. You'll think I'm tied onto you."

He stared at the dark river and the light beyond it. He said nothing.

"Duff, your chivalry's fine, and I like it. You remember that night I said I'd figured out what was behind your cast-iron front? Well, I saw some of that chivalry stuff, and a few other things. All okay, too. But you save the chivalry for another time; I'm twenty-one and then some, and if necessary I'll flash a birth certificate to prove it. And nobody shoved me out of the car that night. I just opened the door and stepped out. Even if I knew I'd not ever see you afterward, I'd do it again. Only next time I wouldn't step out—I'd jump."

He laughed abruptly.

"Hey," she said, pleased. "That's okay. I never heard a real laugh come out of you before. Is there another one inside somewhere?"

"You're a crazy girl."

"Didn't I tell you? See, every time you get to worrying about something and get all mullygrubbed, I'll say something snappy and *bing!* It's gone," she said. "Now, look. I'll do something for you." She kissed him. It was a good kiss, the kind that leaves shortness of breath, but not exhaustion.

She turned to look at him. "Listen to me, Duff. You don't have to marry me. I'm not ruined or anything; I'm good as new. Better. Can't you understand that, huh?"

"Honey, listen, I want to marry you."

"But you'd marry me whether you wanted to or not."

"I reckon so."

"Oh, Lord, Duff." She sighed. "This is a hell of a come-off. Why did I have to fall for a guy like this? You can't tell where his love ends and his conscience begins. Look, I want to be married on my merits—and don't ask me what they are, either, because you know I'll tell you."

He kissed her ear. "You're okay."

Presently she said, "Okay, I'm okay. We better go."

As they crossed the bridge, they saw the headlights of a car coming out the little road that led from the farmer's house. The car waited at the highway to let them pass, and the lights flashed in their faces. Duff turned on the radio. Distantly overhead came the drone of the airliner on its way to Birmingham, and presently its wing lights were visible, a red speck and a green speck hurrying across the tar-paper sky.

Next day Amos complained of pains, and Lucie got Dr. Phillips on the phone. Amos lay almost as if in a coma, his brown leathery face gaunt and sunken, when the doctor came. Delia Phillips, in the nurse's white uniform she wore when helping her father, came with him; she began efficiently and quietly taking Amos's pulse and temperature, and checking the medicines on the night table.

Finally Dr. Phillips leaned back and lit his pipe and said thoughtfully, "Don't believe it was nothing but a temporary setback, Lucie. He'll be all right."

Amos looked from one of them to the other, trying to identify the blurs. "I'm hungry," he complained.

"Your dinner's coming," Lucie said.

Delia was shutting her father's pill case. She turned to Lucie. "How was the dance at Zurich last night?"

"I haven't heard," Lucie said.

Delia turned and looked at her. "Didn't you go?"

"No," Lucie said. "I didn't."

"Why, Dad was out visiting the polio case about three this morning, and he said on the way back he saw you and Duff corning from the dance at Zurich!"

They caught the sudden frightened look on Lucie's face, heard Amos rise on his elbow in the bed. Dr. Phillips coughed uneasily and said, "Now, Delia, I said I *reckoned* they'd been to the dance—I mean—I said, *looked* like it was them. But of course it wasn't, since she said—"

"Lucie," Amos said ominously, "you been out at three o'clock with that Webster?"

"My heavens!" Delia whispered. "What have I done?"

"Plenty," Lucie snapped.

"You answer me!" Amos demanded.

"We'll talk about it presently, Squire," Lucie said angrily, "when our friends have gone."

On the front porch Delia said, "Lucie, I'm so sorry."

Lucie said, "It'll come out all right." *Sure, it'll come out all right—I think not,* she mused, watching them get into the car. *It'll come out fine—thanks to friend Delia. Dammit, I wish I knew whether that break was accidental. I just wish I could be sure.*

Holding the wall for support, Amos groped his way around the room to the closet, and opened the door. His trembling old hand slipped familiarly around the balance of the double-barreled shotgun that leaned against the wall. He explored the shelves blindly until he found a paper box, on which was a picture of a bright red deer leaping over a bush. On the side of the box was printed: *12 ga. 3½ drams. 0 Buck— 12 Pellets.*

Amos slipped two shells in the gun, closed the breech, and found his way back to the bed. He slipped the gun under the cover and felt it lying cold against his leg. For a few seconds he lay there panting. Then he called, "Lucie!"

Trial by Marriage

She came in, very pale. "Yes, Squire?"

Amos said, "When Webster gits in this evening, tell him to come here. I want to see him."

"What about?"

"About the dogs; what you reckon?" he said.

"Oh," she said, relieved. "All right."

"You be sure and tell him," Amos said. "I want to see him."

DUFF READ THE note Lucie had sent out to him at the kennels.

Duff:

I won't be out today as the Squire's not feeling good. He wants to see you when you come in. So do I. Hell's to pay.

Lucie.

`While he was puzzling over the note, a boy came out of Wesley's house and walked toward him. It was Paul, Wesley's son, returned from the North.

"Mister Duff," he said, "I'd like a word with you."

"When did you get back?" Duff demanded.

"Today."

"How come you left up North? I thought you had got ambitious."

"Well, I decided to come back. That's been my trouble, I guess. I've been too ambitious." He spoke with resignation and hopelessness.

"It's all right with me about the job, if it's okay with Miss Sullivan. You can go out with me this afternoon."

Duff was glad that the young Negro had come back, because he was a good hand with dogs, and he used his head. But there was an unnatural melancholy about him that was contagious. He worked satisfactorily, though, and his manner was more than offset by his instinct for scouting and finding lost dogs.

They ran a harum-scarum puppy that had an overflowing love of hunting, boundless energy, and a head as hard as a lightwood knot. Amos Hawthorne often said, "You take one of them hardheaded dogs that just grins at you when you rip a streak of hide off him with a whip, and then turns around and does the same thing again, you got a dog you can make something out of. He'll near drive you daft till you break him, but when you git him like you want him you can name your price fer him. Them kind that crawls around and whines and cries, they're twice the trouble and half the dog."

They were working some cutover pine land when the puppy pointed. Paul saw him first and waved his hat. Duff spurred his horse as fast as he dared over the pine tops and junk butts.

"Whoa, boy," he cautioned as he dismounted.

Then the dog broke, his first leap landing him spang in the middle of the covey. The birds came up in a thunder, one or two going off back over Duff's head, the remainder reforming and heading for the thicket at the drain of the two hills. And the puppy, although he knew better, was right in behind them.

"*Whoa!*" squalled Duff, but the puppy didn't heed. Out of the corner of his eye, Duff saw Paul's horse cut around sharply and then sprint after the dog, leaping over logs and swerving around the dead brush of sawed pine trees. Before they got to the bottom, the Negro had cut the dog off, and, still going at a dead run, he turned the dog back with a shout above the thudding hoofs. Then the horse swerved sharply to avoid a hole, and struck a log with his flying feet and went down.

By the time Duff got there, the horse had risen, and held his right foot off the ground. Paul lay in the wiregrass on one elbow, his face a contortion of pain. Duff quickly kneeled beside him and ran his hand along the Negro's upper chest. A lump stood out near his neck.

"You've busted your collarbone," Duff said.

"Is that horse's leg broken?" Paul said between his teeth, sweat running down the brown skin of his throat.

Duff made a quick examination. "No, I guess not. But he's stove up for a while, all right." He stood up for a moment, considering their predicament. They were at least five miles from the kennels, and they had only one horse, a horse that refused to carry double.

"Get up on that stump," Duff said, "and I can ease you over into the saddle."

"Mister Duff," Paul said uncertainly, "it's five miles to the kennels. That's a long way for you to have to walk."

"You remember about that next time," Duff said, "when you get to thinking you're Wild Bill Hickok."

"Yes, sir."

Duff got him into the saddle and, leading the dog and the injured horse, started the long walk back home.

LATER, AS HE LAY WITH his arm strapped against his chest, Paul said to Duff, who had come to see about him, "Mister Duff, a lot of people would have made a nigger walk in from that fall."

"Maybe it's what I should have done," Duff said.

"Yes, sir, I guess that's the truth. When we come near anybody, I was wishing you had. It didn't look right, you walking and me riding," Paul said uncomfortably. "The trouble with me, I guess I better tell you, is I'm too conscious of being a black man in a white man's world. That's why I went North, because I thought things were different. A colored man can ride beside a white man on a streetcar, and sit anywhere he wants at a picture show. Ain't no hesitancy about voting—they come ask you to vote. I thought I could get somewhere, because I got a fair singing voice, or I could teach school, mathematics or something. But I found out there's lots of good singers looking for jobs, and you got to have a degree to teach. It wasn't that, though, that made me dissatisfied; it was finding out that I was still black anyway. I could go into some restaurants, others I couldn't; I couldn't stay in downtown hotels—they were full, they told me. What they do up yonder, they concede the colored man a little more here and a little more there, but he don't ever forget he's a colored man. Somebody'll remind him, by a look or a word, every day. You can make money, but it cost you more to live, and anyway I got to wanting to see some bird-dog running, so when it all added up I just came on home."

Trial by Marriage

"You got your mind on the wrong things," Duff said.

"It ain't that I want what they call social equality. It's just that I couldn't get away from the feeling that I was unclean, untouchable, or something. That's what I've been running from all my life, the feeling that I'm a filthy animal of some kind. That's why I worked so hard at school and tried to read and learn, so I'd feel superior, but it didn't do any good. Maybe you don't know it, but when you put your hand on my shoulder, feeling for the place, you did something a lot of people wouldn't do, even if I had been dying. When we were going home my shoulder was hurting, and I was embarrassed to be riding while you walked, and my thoughts kept running around in circles, and I remembered how I used to think about that verse they read in church, something about 'as much as ye have done it unto the least of these, ye have done it also to me,' and I used to wonder if they read that in the white folks' church. But I just want to be sure I'm human. I appreciate what you did today, Mister Duff."

"Next time I better let you walk, if it's going to put all that in your head."

"No, sir, I don't believe you'd let me walk. And it helped get a lot of stuff out of my head, is what it did."

"Well, hurry up and get well, then. We've got dogs to break."

DUFF WENT ON TO town and Amos Hawthorne's house, in response to Lucie's note. The house was quiet, and he guessed that Lucie had gone out for the moment. It was after dark, and the light in the hall was on. Duff went in, wishing that he could see Lucie and find out what the note meant.

"Lucie?" called old Amos from his bedroom.

"It's me," Duff said. "I heard you wanted me."

"Come in here."

Duff stepped into the sickroom. Amos had hunched himself up to a semi-sitting position, his head thrust forward as he tried to see.

"Lock the door, Webster," Amos ordered.

"What for?" Duff asked curiously.

"I want to talk to you," Amos said. "Private."

Duff turned the key in the door. Behind him, he heard the old man say softly, "I see you now. I can make you out. Look around here slow. Don't make no quick move."

Duff turned and looked into the gaping muzzle of the double-barreled gun Amos Hawthorne held dead on him.

"Look out with that thing!" Duff said, alarmed. "What you think you're doing?"

"Don't move, Webster, just don't move. I can make you out plain enough to blow you in two."

Duff stood frozen, his back pressed against the door he had locked. "What's got into you?" he demanded.

"You was out with her last night. *Late.* Three o'clock," said Amos, with cold anger.

"No," Duff said.

"Doctor Phillips seen you. And Lucie done admitted as much."

Now, suddenly, Duff remembered the automobile headlights that flashed in their faces as they crossed the bridge. So that had been Dr. Phillips, returning from attending the poliomyelitis case. With his left hand behind him, Duff felt for the key, saying, "No, there's something wrong."

"Ain't nothing wrong," Amos snapped. "You better git away from that door. Take two steps to your left. Not but two. This gun's loaded with buckshot."

And you intend to use them, too, Duff thought, moving two steps from the locked door.

Amos said, "I know what you and her was doing, out till three o'clock!" His voice had a bitter, vengeful note.

"You're crazy!"

"I ain't crazy. That's what you thought—thought I was crazy, and you could git away with what-all you been doing! *But now you see you didn't quite git away with it!*"

"Wait a minute. Put that gun up," Duff said, sweating. "Let's straighten this out some."

"Too late for talking, Webster! I warned you and you never listened. It's just too late for talking!" Amos said, his breath whistling fiercely. *"Now it's time to—"*

Duff dived to the floor, near the foot of the bed, just before the gun roared. A splintered, fist-sized hole appeared on the wall where he had stood. A glass fell from the mantel and broke. The thin haze of gunsmoke hung suspended, and the sweetish smell of it reached Duff on the floor where he lay trying to hold the sound of his breath from Amos's listening ears.

The bed stirred. "I see you, Webster," said Amos "And I got another barrel."

Duff lay motionless, waiting for someone to come and investigate the noise. Nobody came. He dared not move, for he knew the hypersensitive ears of the old man would catch the faintest rustle of clothes or creak of floorboard. And that Amos would shoot at the first sound.

"I see you," Amos repeated. "Lying there on the floor. You might as well git up."

If you saw me, Duff thought, *you'd be shooting that other barrel, not talking.*

Two courses seemed open to him. The first was to crawl to the door and try to unlock it and get out before Amos shot. Next to impossible, that course. The other was to crawl around to Amos's side and touch off the second trigger of the gun. The trouble was, if one board creaked he would be as good as dead.

This thought induced another one. With excruciating slowness, Duff drew his right leg up and painstakingly untied his shoe lace. He took off the shoe. Then, taking a deep, hopeful breath, he tossed the shoe to the other side of the room.

"*Hah!*" Amos exclaimed triumphantly, swiftly swinging the gun toward the sound. The gun roared, and Duff's shoe jumped, the leather of it in shreds. Duff sprang up and unlocked the door.

He was opening the front gate when Lucie drove up and got out, her arms full of groceries.

"Hello," she said brightly. "How long—Why, Duff, what's wrong? What's happened?"

"Look," Duff said, holding her wrist, "Paul broke his collarbone this afternoon. When he gets well enough to ride again, I'll really have to be leaving. There will be trouble if I stay longer."

When he told her what had happened in the house, Lucie began crying, and finally she said, "Yes, I guess maybe you had better go. I guess it's the only thing to do."

She looked into Duff's eyes. "Please try to forgive him. He's stubborn and unreasonable and all. But he loves me, Duff, and that's why he did it."

NEXT DAY, AMOS revived somewhat from the relapse the incident with Duff had left him in. He lay still, his harness-leather face and mud-gray hair and dark glasses raised on two white pillows.

"How's things at the kennels?" he asked.

"Fine enough," said Lucie. She was pale. "Wesley's been trying to find us a boy to help until Paul can ride."

Amos said, "Webster gone?"

"Yes," she lied.

"Didn't skip out with nothing wasn't his, did he?" Amos asked sharply.

"No, Squire."

"It's a wonder." Presently he said, "How's Sam?"

"Fine."

"You ain't letting him git fat?"

"Not a bit of it."

"They seeing to his feet?"

"Look," Lucie said suddenly, "why don't you let me bring Sam in tomorrow? He'll be company. Okay?"

Amos snorted. "I don't want no dog in this house. It's plenty enough to work all your life trainin' 'em and feedin' 'em and runnin' 'em, without bringin' 'em into your bedroom like one of them little dish-faced Pekingeses."

But Lucie brought Sam into town anyway, and led him into the old trainer's bedroom. Amos heard the dog's toenails clicking on the floor, and he demanded, "Lucie, have you brung a dog into this house?"

"Just Sam," she said.

"Aye, dammit," he began, "it's gittin' to where—"

His long skeletal fingers went over the dog's head and slid down his shoulder. Sam's fine-cut head was slightly raised as he scented the medicinal taint on the old familiar hand. The dog relaxed, grinned, and stood there while Amos's fingers inspected him. "Gitting to where—Lucie, he's got fat on these ribs."

"Just a touch. Tomorrow I'll have Wesley put him in harness and road him a while," she said.

Then she added, "If you're through with him I'll take him on out."

"Wait a minute," Amos said, "I want to see—" He kept sliding his hand over the dog's back and neck, as if looking for some sign of improper conditioning. Lucie went out and shut the door.

Next day she forgot to bring Ambling Sam into town.

"Where's Sam at?" Amos asked.

"Out at the kennel," she answered.

"What's the matter with him?" he demanded. "Why don't you want me to see him? He been on one of his fighting sprees?"

"Why he's fine. Nothing wrong with Sam."

"Yes, it is! You cain't fool me."

"No, Squire! He's okay. I'll bring him tonight and show you, huh?"

Amos relaxed, muttering, "Well, all right. But you be sure he comes in. I ain't goan let a valuable dog like that go down without my knowing it."

After that, Ambling Sam spent part of every day in Amos Hawthorne's room, and a ritual developed. On being brought in, Sam would trot with restrained pleasure to the bedside, and Amos then went into his act of pretending to feel the dog's shoulders and legs and even the pads of his feet; and when it was over and he was through surreptitiously petting Sam, the pointer went to a corner and went to sleep.

The dog's presence in the room always called for discussion by Amos's occasional visitors, for Ambling Sam was the pride of the town. Because Sam was a pointer, the status of setters in that section was low. But Amos, who remembered his love, La Besita, never got as critical of setters as some of his pointer-men contemporaries.

"Wasn't so terrible long back they just wasn't nothing, pointers wasn't, and once they even had separate stakes for pointers so they wouldn't have to buck up against setters. When a fellow run a pointer he done it sort of sheepish, near-bout apologizing when he brung him out the crate. But long time ago I seen old Rip Rap run, and I knowed some day another the pointer men wasn't going to have to keep apologizing. And it was the dogs that come down from old black-and-white Rip that seen to it. Fishel's Frank and Alford's John was two of the best been put down, and they give the pointers the big boost. Fishel's Frank he was just so full of himself it looked like sometimes he was just goin' to bust open fer eagerness, and the way he could crack that tail was a sight to see; and Alford's John he could think just like a man. Well they nicked John bitches to Frank dogs and before long, look what happened—Comanche Frank, DeSoto Frank, Mary Montrose, John Proctor, Ferris's Jake, Muscle Shoals Jake, Air Pilot's Sam, and now Ariel and Luminary. All right straight on down. And these days it's the setter handlers that's got to apologize and act sheepish.

"But if it hadn't been for W.J. Baughn, the setter might still be top dog. Baughn, he sold a couple of setter puppies to C.H. Foust, the way Hochwalt told the story to me, and Foust, before long he decided he had him a couple of powerhouses, and he writ to Baughn to come see if he didn't have two field-trial dogs. Baughn he come, and they hitched up a buggy and went out. This was in Warren, Indiana; and on the way out a pointer puppy took it into his head to go along with him. His feet they was too big, and his joints was the size of biscuits and he looked like he might trip on his ears.

" 'What's that following us?' Baughn he asked.

" 'Ain't nothing but a fool pointer. Belongs to the druggist in town. Any time he spies somebody that looks like they might be going a-hunting, he trails along. But he don't hurt nothing,' Foust said. 'Now, you watch these two setter puppies go.'

"Well, they put them setter puppies down and off they went. Hunted sort of pretty, too, but Baughn he soon knowed they wasn't field-trial dogs. He kept watching 'em though, sort of dutiful-like, until he seen a white streak away yonder outside the setters. Pretty soon he made out what it was, that pointer puppy that had followed them out. They'd plumb forgot about him. Well, yonder he was just running all over the country and every now and then flash-pointing a covey of birds. But Baughn he

Trial by Marriage

didn't say nothing. Not then. That afternoon he said, 'I want to take another look at them dogs before I tell you what I think.'

" 'Okay,' Foust said. 'Ain't they the slickest dogs you ever seen, though?'

"So next morning they went out, and sure enough when they come through town that pointer just naturally joined up with 'em again. This time Baughn he never paid no attention to the setters, he just kept his eye on the pointer puppy that was jumping along a half a mile away.

" 'Well,' Foust said after thirty or forty minutes, 'what you think about my setters?'

" 'You want a shore-'nough field-trial dog?' Baughn asked him.

" 'Shore I do. How come you think I bought these here dogs?'

" 'You just better forget about them two puppies I sold you. They ain't got what it takes. You see that pointer puppy lighting out yonder? You buy *him*.'

" 'That knobby-kneed hound? Why I wouldn't have him if Alford give him to me!'

" 'You git him, if you want a field-trial dog.'

"Well Foust he cussed and fumed and finally went into town and asked Alford, who run the drugstore, if he wanted to sell the dog, and Alford he come right out and told him Yes, the dog was too fast to be a good bird dog, and he would sell him for twenty-five dollars. Foust he didn't want to pay that much for *no* pointer, so he come back at him with a proposition to board the dog and run him in the trials, and they would split the prize money, if they lucked out and won any. Alford he told him okay. And he shore made a good deal when he done it, because the first trial they popped young John into, he won first place in the Derby!

"From then on he won from one end to the other. Some of them that knowed him say his equal ain't never been seen. Anyway, he was truly a good one every time I run against him. It turned out his sons they didn't do so much, but when John's daughters was put to Fishel's Frank blood something happened. The puppies took old John's sense and old Frank's fire, and, by God, after that the setters just naturally had their feet to the stove all the time! But if W. J. Baughn hadn't gone down to Foust's and happened upon that puppy, I guess we'd still be apologizing when we took a pointer out of a dog crate."

One visitor listened to Amos's field-trial talk for a while, and finally he said, "I went to a field trial once. Didn't see a hell of a lot to get excited over."

"A good many folks likes 'em," Amos said.

"Yes, and why I don't know. They told me the trials were colorful, but I found out what the colors are—black and blue. The first thing you do is get on a strange horse, not knowing whether he's going to throw you or bite you. Then they turn a couple of dogs loose that streak away like they were chasing a cat, and in a few seconds they're gone. You ride along, trying to see the dogs, but you just get a glimpse every fifteen minutes or so. Nobody else seems interested in the dogs, or maybe they know they can't see 'em anyhow, and they ride along and talk and kid each other, or say, 'Did you get a good horse?' or 'You going to Holly Springs next week?' I noticed each one of the handlers had about two men sort of sneaking through the woods on each side, helping keep up with the dogs without seeming to, and finally one of the fellows rides out way over yonder nearly out of sight and waves his hat. Then we all have a horse race to see who gets there first, and all of us beat the judges. When we stop we see the dog standing up like he thinks he's the only dog in the world that ever found a covey of birds.

" The handler says, 'It was a stop to flush, judge, the birds have gone.'

" 'Hasn't he got a fine style?' somebody whispers.

" 'Looks like a million dollars,' somebody else agrees.

" 'Well broke, too. Hasn't moved a muscle since the birds left.'

" 'No use to stand there, though,' I said, 'after he's flushed the birds,' and they give me a cold look.

"Well, that went on and on. I tried to amuse myself by thinking how sore I would be next day, and by counting the birds we rode up that the dogs hadn't seen. Every now and then I would see a dog a mile or so off, but it hurt my eyes to try to keep him in sight, so I gave up on the dogs. They found a couple of coveys apiece in the hour they ran.

"Next brace, there was a dog that stayed where you could see him pretty well, and I began to take a new interest. Furthermore he found birds all over the place, one covey after another. I got pretty excited, and told my nearest neighbor, 'Now there's a real bird dog,' and he said, 'Him? He's got no business in a big-time trial like this.' I said, 'You wait and see who they give the first prize to,' but he just looked disgusted. Well, they give the first prize to a dog that was in sight about fifteen minutes' total of his hour, he found two coveys, stopped to flush on another, and had a false point. The dog I picked had found six coveys, been in sight almost all the time, and hadn't made a single error. He had found more birds than any other dog in the trial. I just couldn't understand it, so I privately asked the judge if he would explain what was wrong with that dog's run, maybe I had missed something. 'Oh,' he said, 'he's a nice dog, very stylish although a little too birdy, but he's just in too fast company in a trial like this.' On the way home I stopped at a stream to water my horse, and he lay down and rolled in the water, with me on him. I don't care for field trials."

ON THE SAME DAY that Wesley's new handler showed up for work at the kennels, Ambling Sam got in one of his fighting moods. Sam's usual disposition was fairly peace-loving, but occasionally he became irritable and took offense if any other dog brushed against him or even walked too close to him. On this day a puppy in the same pen tried to play with him and jumped up on him, and Sam turned on him with a lightning savagery, throwing the younger dog against the kennel wire and biting him from one end to the other. Lucie and Wesley came running, shouting at the dogs without effect. Wesley grabbed the water bucket and drenched the snarling dogs, and that ended the fight.

"For an old grandpa like you," Wesley panted angrily at Sam, "you sho' does act puppified sometimes!"

"Alf," said Lucie to the new colored boy who stood outside staring, "take this old fool and put him in that empty pen and let him cool off for a few days."

The new boy, Alf, led Sam down toward the end of the kennel yard, in the direction of the empty pen Lucie had pointed out to him.

"Ain't you shame yourself, a-fighting and a-fussing like that?" he asked the now quietly panting bird dog.

Trial by Marriage

There were two pens in which no dogs were in sight. Alf hesitated momentarily, then chose the end pen because it seemed to have more warm sunlight. He opened the gate and Sam walked in.

For a while Sam stood at the fence and watched the preparations for the morning hunt. Now the horses were saddled and the hunting-wagon was being loaded with the dogs that would be worked. Finally the caravan pulled out, Lucie and Wesley going in one direction, Duff taking the new boy with hint to the north.

With only a faint interest, Sam inspected the punishment pen into which he had been thrust, sniffing one post after another and following the usual ritual. Finally he entered the kennel house; instantly his manner became one of challenge, for the dog Judas lay asleep in one corner. Judas stirred and raised his head, then was on his feet instantly, and there was no father-and-son love between the two dogs.

Sam advanced stiff-legged, tail and hackles up. Judas came to meet him. No preliminary argument took place; one moment later they were whirling in battle. Half-locked, they rolled out the door into the yard. They now fought silently, not growling. Blood spread its red stain upon them and upon the ground. In silence the to-the-death combat went on. Sam's teeth closed on Judas's upper jaw, some of them stabbing the roof of his mouth. Judas swirled, flung the older dog aside, and struck quickly at the back of Sam's neck.

From that moment on Ambling Sam was dying, but he kept fighting. Finally he could not rise. Even as the life went out of him he was trying to get his jaws onto Judas's foot. Then the muscles relaxed, and his hemorrhage-paled tongue slid out of his mouth and lay on the pink earth, sand particles clinging to it; and his glassy eyes slowly closed. A few blowflies with their ghoulish instincts found him and were humming around him almost before he stopped breathing. For a few moments Judas stood at the scene of his patricide. Then he limped to the kennel house and began treating his wounds.

He was still engaged in his first-aid work when the tragedy was discovered. When Lucie came she gave a sharp, deeply painful gasp, and fainted. Alf, the innocent cause of it all, ran away.

They buried Sam down in the piney-woods pasture, where, before long, the quail would start their spring whistling; laid him under without ceremony; but afterward Lucie quietly returned with a vase of blue flowers. Before she reached the place she heard a voice, and knew that Wesley had come back ahead of her. She saw him there on his knees, not satisfied to bury Sam without some sort of funeral speech. Wesley was saying:

"...And he was jest a dog, Lawd, but such a dog as ain't never been on dis-yeah green earth. 'Scuse me, Lawd, please recollect he was a Christian-folks kind of a bird dog, didn't have no bad habits 'cept a little foughtin' now and den, didn't suck eggs, didn't bite nobody, didn't bark at white folks, didn't never loaf on de job when he was workin'. Well, here he come. It ain't for no common field hand like me to know what kind of 'rangemints you got up yonder, and maybe dey ain't no allowance made for dogs and such. But in time I heard bird-dog folks say you got a plantation leased up yonder, and it's a thousand miles long and twice as wide, and dey ain't no briers ner rattlesnakes, and it ain't never hot and ain't never ground-froze, and de birds is golden birds with sapphire eyes and dey don't run and dey don't flush wild, and ain't no night to spoil de hunt, and no whistle to call de dogs in; and dat's where de good dogs go when dey die.

"Well, Lawd, if you got de huntin' rights on such a place as dat, now you got a true good bird dog to turn loose on it. Though 'scuse me for tryin' to tell you, 'cause if old Jingo and Crazy Mary Montrose and Sioux and John Proctor and such as them is up there, you don't need nobody to tell you what a good bird dog is. But, Lawd, some day when you git fed up wid looking down here and seeing de world wranglin' and sinnin' and a-ruckusin', take old Sam out and run him against de best you got up dere, and see if you don't have a Jesusly-fine dog race. I thanks you, Lawd. Amen."

That afternoon Amos said to Lucie, "Where's Sam at?"

"He's—they're running him this afternoon," Lucie said unhappily.

The rest of the day Amos was nervous and fidgety, and nothing pleased him. The following day Lucie had to think of some other lie, and she told him that Sam had been taken to the veterinary.

Amos rose portentously to a sitting position. *"What ails him?"*

"Nothing," Lucie said. "He's just being checked over, sort of."

After that, Lucie and Duff and Wesley held a conference.

"Somebody's got to think of something," Lucie said. "If the Squire passes another day without seeing him, he won't be fit to live with. Not that he ever was."

Since Amos was practically blind, the decision was to try substituting another dog for the dead Ambling Sam. After considerable study, they selected a five-year-old dog, named Piggot's Red Devil. Lucie said it was an outright sacrilege to let Red substitute for old Sam, for he was a loafing, gopher-digging, brainless bird dog; but his size and conformation were about the same as Sam's—which, now, were more important than hunting ability.

On the following morning Wesley brought Red into town, and handed the leash to Lucie. She patted the dog nervously and led him into the house. Outside Amos's room she hesitated, changing the leash from one hand to the other. Red stood indifferently, his tail wagging silently.

"Gee," Lucie whispered to Wesley, "I wish it were only a couple of leopards or something in there."

She took a breath, then turned the knob of the door. A chemical, sickroom smell drifted out; the shades were down, the winter sunlight breaking through one or two holes in them, to be caught in the dotted-Swiss curtain Lucie had made. Amos was dozing as the table radio reported farm prices from Montgomery.

"Hah?" Amos said, stirring.

"Squire," Lucie said, wetting her lips, "here he is."

"Who?"

"Here's your dog."

Red now moved forward, sniffing the sheets and the table of medicine bottles. Amos's groping hand found the dog and slid over his shoulders slowly, caressingly. Lucie watched in agony, thinking: *The voice is Jacob's voice, but the hands are the hands of Esau.* After a seemingly interminable time, Amos said, "He ain't got as much fat."

"Better, huh? We've been roading him, like I said."

Amos grunted, and there was nothing in his face to indicate whether or not he was suspicious. After a while, he grumbled, "A house ain't no place for no bird dog."

"Want me to take him out?" she asked hopefully.

Amos's brown hand tightened against the dog. "Might as well let him stay, since you brung him," he said.

When released, Red made a tour of the room, sniffing at every strange object. "What's the matter with you, Sam?" Amos asked, listening. "You act like you ain't never been in this room before, walking around sniffing and acting curious. Ain't nothing changed since last week."

"He's just looking around to be doing something," Lucie said.

Amos said absently, "Yeah—yeah. Well, go on about your business. Don't like to have nobody just hanging around me all the time."

Outside, Wesley waited for the report, tricklets of sweat on his neck. "Did we git by wid it?"

Lucie clicked her tongue. "Like a breeze," she said.

THE DOG JUDAS LAY tied to a tree, and his alert yellow eyes followed the movements of jays in the pine trees on the slope, and he saw a sparrow light on a sprig of sedge and press it down to get at the seeds. Occasionally his ears tilted nervously toward the sound of the voices of Lucie and Duff Webster, who had run him for a half hour with the chain on his collar, and who now sat near their tethered horses.

Lucie leaned back on her elbow in the warm winter sun, with a tiny bow of ribbon in her loose sandy hair and a cigarette in her mouth. She said, thoughtfully, "Where'll you go, Duff?"

He drew a clipping from the *American Field* from his pocketbook.

Wanted: First-class dog man and plantation kennel manager. Must be young, hardworking, intelligent. Apply: Osceola Plantation, Zurich, Alabama.

"Oh, it'd be fine if you get that job," she said. "Zurich's only thirty miles. You could come down to see me."

"That's right."

She murmured, "My, what enthusiasm!"

"I don't like the way we have to sneak around. Do you, Lucie?"

"No, I guess not," she admitted. "I could choke that Delia for blabbing it right out in front of the Squire!"

"How could she know old Amos would raise so much hell?"

"Something tells me she knew, all right."

"That doesn't make sense," he said sharply.

She glanced at him in surprise. "Gee, you don't have to get mad. Let's don't fight about that. Let's fight about when you're coming back to see me."

He said nothing. With his pocketknife he cut the rough edges off a piece of pine bark.

"Duff, listen to me," she said finally, sitting up. "Let's get things straightened out. How do we stand, you and me and the ivory table? Huh?"

"There's more to it than that, Lucie. There's Amos Hawthorne."

"I'm not forgetting him. But I'll wait for you, Duff—a hundred years, if that's what it takes. Now, you tell me how you feel about it."

"You don't have anything to worry about," he said; "I'll come back for you."

"That's a fine way to put it," she said angrily. "All I've got to worry about is whether you're in love or just chivalrous. And I think I know."

"Of course I love you," he insisted.

She gazed out over the rolling brown countryside for a long moment. Then she took a deep breath and said, "Duff, I'm going to tell you something."

"Okay."

"You won't like it."

"What is it?" he asked curiously.

"I wasn't ever going to tell you, but the way you're acting, I'll have to prove you aren't beholden to me."

"Why not?"

"Well, because of what happened at Grand Junction between Teague McGinnis and me."

He turned quickly. "What do you mean? What happened?"

"Well—something."

"What?"

"Something."

He stared at her. The piece of bark dropped from his fingers. Finally he said, "Oh."

"You see?"

"Yes," he answered slowly. "I guess I see."

Some crows found an owl in a sapling, and they dived at him and cried loudly and excitedly. Others, far away, heard the scolding sounds and answered, and flew to join the attack. They came in twos and threes, and lit in the sapling and in other trees near by. The owl stood it for a while, then in dignity flew away. The crows followed, diving at the owl from behind in an angry frenzy. Gradually the bedlam faded into the distance.

"Duff, please say something."

He stared blankly. A spider crawled down his arm and out on one of his fingers, then dropped to the ground on a silver thread.

"Duff, aren't you going to shout at me or something?"

"No."

"Well, say *something*."

"Why did you do it?"

She shrugged, and two tears spilled over and ran down her cheek. "Don't know, Duff. Just did it," she said. She thought: *Oh, Duff, it's not true, not even half true. I'm lying because you'd always think you were roped in. You'd never quit thinking that, and we'd never have a chance. There's nobody but you and never will be.*

WHILE HE WAS WAITING for the bus, Duff went to the poolroom and drank a glass of beer. Oblivious to the sound of billiard balls and the talk and two men next to him arguing about tractors and mules, he watched the bubbles of beer foam burst. Duff

Trial by Marriage

made a design on the frosting on the curved glass with his thumbnail. Behind the counter were several elaborately painted signs: *In God We Trust—All Others Pay Cash. Liberal Credit to All Those Over Eighty—When Accompanied by Their Parents.*

His emotions now, he realized bitterly, were quite different from what they had been immediately following Lucie's confession. After recovering from the first numb jolt of what she had said, he had felt a half-pleasant release. But as soon as he left the Hawthorne kennels the full hurt of it struck him like a maul between the shoulder blades. In trying to understand why he should be affected to such an extent, he finally concluded that it was his pride that had been so severely damaged. Now his only thought was to get away, and to be free forever of any thought of Lucie.

He gazed at the beer, wondering if enough of that would anesthetize his brain for a while. If necessary he could wait until tomorrow to see about the job. No, alcohol wouldn't be much help. The only difference in his thinking would be still darker thoughts and more of them.

The shine boy's rag cracked rhythmically. One of the pool players missed a shot and swore feelingly.

He finished the beer and looked at his watch. Still thirty minutes before the bus to Zurich came. He wandered out, and gazed dully into store windows.

"Oh, hello, Duff," said Delia Phillips, coming out of the drugstore.

"Hello," he said.

"How've you been?"

"All right," he said. The afternoon sun gave her skin a lovely translucent quality; and the curve of her mouth fascinated him.

"Duff," she said worriedly, "come here and let me talk to you a moment."

Her father's car was at the curb, and they got in and she said, "I've wanted to tell you how sorry I am about the other day. I had no idea Mr. Hawthorne minded your going with Lucie. I feel terrible about it."

"It's okay. Maybe it was for the best."

"But it was so unnecessary to even bring the subject up. I know it caused trouble."

"It did, all right."

"Well, I'm just sorry, that's all." She looked at him. "How much trouble did it cause?"

"Plenty. I'm through out there. But maybe that's the way it ought to be," he said unhappily. "Let's forget about it. I'm not sore at you."

"I do hope you aren't, Duff," she said. "What are you going to do?"

"I'm waiting for the bus. I'm going to Zurich to try to get a job with James Lampley, at Osceola Plantation."

"I'll tell you what—I'll drive you up. Dad's gone fishing with Allan Prince, and won't need the car."

"I couldn't let you do that."

"It's only thirty miles. And I want to do it."

"Well, sure, that'll be fine," he said, instantly sensing a lift in his spirits. And he knew, abruptly, that here was the relief he had wanted. Delia was exactly what he needed.

She backed out and turned the car north and onto the broad, red-clay highway to Zurich. A rust-colored cloud rose behind the car.

Duff lit a cigarette. "How are things coming along for you these days?"

Delia smiled strangely. "Things are coming along just fine."

DUFF WOULDN'T SOON forget that day, with its seesaw ups and downs. But being with Delia had buoyed him up. Then he had talked to Carl Wind, the plantation overseer, who had sent him on to the owner, James Lampley. Lampley, having been besieged by all the at-leisure handlers—the liquorheads, the dog-spoilers, the incompetents, the loafers—had begun to be disgusted.

"Well," he said, "why did *you* leave your last place?"

"I couldn't get along with the boss-man is about all there is to it."

"Who?"

"Amos Hawthorne."

"Oh, yes," said Lampley narrowly. "I know of Hawthorne. You couldn't get along with him?"

"Not so hot," Duff said.

"He wasn't too honest for you, I hope," Lampley said.

Duff rose slowly. "I'm afraid you and I wouldn't get along so well either. Good-by."

"Wait a minute," Lampley said. "Excuse it. It's been a sorry procession that's come here for this job, men I don't care for my dogs to associate with. I've got sort of touchy. We won't go into Hawthorne's principles. What I want is a young man with a fair education who can produce winning dogs and not put half the kennel expense money in his pocket. Does it sound like that might be you?"

"I don't know about the winning. The dogs have a lot to do with that."

"My bloodlines are the work of twenty years. I'm just now producing the kind of dog I want. I believe my dogs are about ready. But I'll know whose fault it is, the dogs' or the man's, if they don't win."

"Well, before you go to the trouble of investigating me, I better tell you about a dog I've got. He's a sort of outlaw dog I'm trying to break. I want permission to keep him and work him. He's mean—he's the one killed Ambling Sam. But I'll pen him separately."

"You must be stuck on him, to keep fooling with a dog like that."

"It's just something I've set my mind to do."

Lampley looked at him for a few moments. Finally he said, "The reason I fired my other dog man was because he never set his mind to do anything that seemed halfway hard."

As Duff walked back out to the car where Delia waited, he kept puzzling about what Lampley had said. *I guess I fooled him into thinking I'm a pretty determined sort of a fellow,* he thought without amusement, and without conviction. Lampley would never pass for an easy-to-fool man.

"How did you make out?" Delia asked breathlessly.

"Okay. I've got the job—on trial."

"Congratulations," she said, and kissed him with a warm unexpectedness.

Trial by Marriage

Instantly, as he held her to him, all the dormant emotion flared again.

"I'm so glad for you," she was saying now.

He went around the car and got in beside Delia, and as she started the car back toward Tafton, he looked at her wonderingly. She drove with her eyes concentrated on the road. On her mouth was a little smile.

"Delia," Duff said abruptly, "I'm coming to see you tonight."

For a moment her hand lay in his. "I'll be waiting for you, Duff," she said.

So NOW THERE HE was, with a fine cottage, and a garden, and a kennel of good dogs, and a new girl. From his window at breakfast he could see the trees that hid the Big House, and the pump house with its massive machinery that could supply a small town with water, and the little concrete-guttered road that led to the stables with their first-class horses, and the white-painted kennel pens with hardware-cloth floors so that the dogs lived off the ground, and beyond, the ten thousand acres of rolling quail land.

The only trouble—the cottage, for all its comfort and convenience, seemed empty without Delia there. The days were full—riding endlessly, check-cording, feeding, nursing sore pads, immunizing for distemper. But at night there was this lonesomeness, a desire to tell Delia that Judas had got lost that day and of his own accord returned to the kennel four hours later, and that one of the horses had a heaving cough, and that he had seen several quail already pair off for the nesting season, and things like that. This was an unfamiliar feeling, for heretofore he had always preferred keeping his thoughts to himself.

On nights when he could not get down to Tafton in a borrowed station wagon or pick-up truck, he wrote to Delia. Sometimes on Sunday she drove up to see him, and they spent the day in the cottage, where she would cook the dinner and afterward read the papers with him on the floor. As spring came on, and the woods turned green, Duff made the down payment on a secondhand car. After that he rode to Tafton to see Delia nearly every night.

One day Carl Wind, the overseer, went afield with Duff. Wind was an old dog man himself, and even now supervised the shooting-dog kennel, but Duff presently guessed that his accompanying them today was not accidental or casual. They were discussing Judas, who had run for thirty minutes before bolting, and who was now being pursued somewhere out ahead.

"You ain't never going to break that dog," Wind said.

"That's what they all say," Duff answered.

"No, you won't never break him. But some day or other, he may break himself. You keep hunting him hard, and riding him down, and squalling at him, and maybe some day he'll just take it into his head to behave. You ought to kill a hell of a heap of birds over him, when you get him where he'll hold 'em until you get close enough. You ever see that McTyre dog run? He was as wild as a turkey. One trial the judge told Ches Harris to take that damn dog home and teach him his name. Some crack to make about a five-thousand-dollar dog, ain't it? But Ches says he went home and killed seventeen hundred birds over that dog next season, trying to learn him something; and when it was all over he come back and won the National Championship. But I ain't saying that half-panther of yours will be another McTyre."

"Mr. Lampley won't like the idea of my killing a lot of his birds over a dog that don't belong to him."

"You listen. You show that man you got a field-trial champion in the making, and he'll buy you all the hunting-leases you want. And buy the dog, too. 'Course he'd rather see a dog he's bred himself turn out to be a champion, but it may not work out that way."

"He hasn't said he'd keep me on, yet. This was just to be a tryout for me," Duff reminded.

Carl Wind said, "Well, to tell the truth, that's how come I'm riding with you today. He's going to string along with you. And if you think it's a good idea, he'll let you take about a dozen dogs to Canada this summer. Does that sound okay with you?"

"I'll say it sounds okay!" Duff answered.

FOR A WHILE IT MADE Amos Hawthorne angry when visitors found out that he allowed a dog in the house, but he gradually got over that. Early one afternoon a friend came by to see him, and after a while Amos pointed toward the dog he thought was Ambling Sam, and said, "Having this dog in the house calls to mind a fellow named Barbert, a rich little old man that wore nose glasses, used to come up to Pierson, Manitoba. This Barbert he had a dog named Tarbaby's Rex, and he was so crazy about Rex that he couldn't talk about nothing else. Kept him in the hotel room with him on trials, had a bottle of pills he give him every day for his vitamins er something like that, kept him sheened up like a circus dog. Fer a collar that dog had a silver chain around his neck. Barbert had taught his dog all sort of tricks, like setting up, and going to the grocery fer a package, and stuff like that. Many a time I seen him bring the dog into the hotel dining-room and take him round showing him off to people, making Rex bark howdy to 'em, and playing dead. Got so nobody could put up with Barbert, he was just a bloody damn nuisance, and 'course we all grinned behind his back when he was showing the dog off. Said Barbert had taught his dog every trick in the book except how to point.

"But the truth was that this Rex, spite of all his show dog tricks and manicured toenails, was a ripper of a bird dog; and sure enough, at the Dominion trials he stepped right out and won the Derby stakes. Well, after that there just wasn't no being around Barbert and his dog. I think his wife even come near to quitting him, after being married to him for forty years. The terrible part, young Rex he won again and again; and the handlers they got so they didn't care whether they won the stake or not, just so they whupped 'that damned trick dog.' Then that winter, the end of it came—Rex got hold of some poison a sheepman had put out for sheep-killing dogs. The handlers they said, 'Well, thank God, we're shed of *him*.'

"But when they seen how hard Barbert was taking it, they begin to be sorry for him. Before long they was telling him what a great dog Rex had been, and some of 'em even told him that they hadn't never seen a smarter trick dog. Old softhearted Mel Winder, he give Barbert a fine Air Pilot puppy, and that pepped him up considerable.

Trial by Marriage

Last time I seen Barbert he had that puppy up in his room, trying to learn him to balunst a water glass on his nose. 'Yes, sir, Hawthorne,' he told me, 'he's going to be just as good a dog as Rex. Look how fast he's catching on to this.' "

Amos made a clucking sound with his tongue and the dog in the corner rose and came to the bed. "Now we done made a house dog out of Sam," Amos said disgustedly. "Guess now we have to teach him to roll over, and chase a ball. Sam, you reckon you ain't too old to learn a lot of Goddam foolishness like that?"

"To look at that dog," the visitor said, "you wouldn't think he was eleven years old."

Amos said, "Ner to see him hunt you wouldn't, neither. Hell, this dog ain't hardly started good. Next year, me and him ain't goan miss out on that championship again. I'm goan git that hard-luck monkey off my back, git so I can see and everything." He held the muzzle of the dog he thought was Ambling Sam. "Only way you'd know he's old is by the gray hairs on his face, and by his teeth. Them front teeth ain't nothing but stubs."

The blind old handler leaned over as he spoke, and held the dog's mouth open with one hand. His other thumb found its way between the fangs. "See?" he said. "You can see how them teeth—" Puzzled, he felt the teeth again. They were sharp, not worn.

Amos sat upright in bed. "*Lucie!*" he roared.

Lucie came hurrying in. "What's the matter?" she asked, rushing to the bedside.

"Where's Sam at?"

"Why, right there beside you."

"This ain't Sam. You cain't fool me. *Where's he at?*"

"He's—he's out hunting today."

"Then how come you brought this here dog, and told me it was Sam?"

Lucie struggled for an adequate lie and could not find one. She took a breath and said, "Squire, I'll have to tell you, I guess. Ambling Sam is dead."

Amos lay back down slowly. "I knowed it," he whispered, "soon's I felt that dog's teeth."

"He was killed in a kennel fight. He got one of his cantankerous streaks."

Amos said softly, "I knowed it, soon's I felt them teeth. I knowed he was dead." He lay still, his blank eyes staring at the ceiling.

The visitor stood uncomfortably, with his hat in hand. "I surely regret—"

Lucie gave him a little smile. "It's okay. He had to find it out." She went with him to the door.

When he was gone, Lucie returned to the room. Amos's fingers played with the quilt. She put a lump of coal in the grate fire, and turned her back to it, hoisting her skirt behind to warm her legs. The fire crackled around the new fuel. From out front came the sound of the visitor's car starting, spitting in the cold, then driving off.

The cook came in with Amos's dinner on a tray, covered with a napkin. Lucie could smell the tomato soup. Putting the tray on the bedside table, the colored girl looked at Lucie, then at Amos. "Here's y'dinner," she said, removing the napkin. Now the soup smell mingled with that of turnip greens. In the street outside children on their noon recess were shouting.

"Lucie," Amos said, "if this dog ain't Sam, take him out."

Lucie went by the dresser and got a Kleenex, and caught the tear that had started down her cheek. When she returned from putting the dog in the woodshed, she said "I'll write the *Field* to announce Sam's death."

"No you don't," Amos said. "Just keep your mouth shut about it for a while."

"Why, Squire, for heaven's sake?"

Amos said, "They'll be some bitches sent in here next week to be bred to Sam. You want to lose them stud fees?"

"But Sam's dead."

"All the other dogs ain't dead, though, are they? Breed 'em to some other dog. Won't nobody never know the difference."

"Okay," Lucie said to satisfy him.

She drew a chair near the window so she could raise the shade several inches and admit enough light for reading. Amos heard her sit down and he said, "What you aim to do now?"

"I thought I'd spend the afternoon with you."

"How come?"

"Well, just because. On account of Sam."

"I don't need nobody. You git on out and make sure them damn niggers don't ruin every dog I got."

When Lucie came in that evening, the cook reported that she had taken some orange juice in to Amos and found him asleep, and had not wakened him. Lucie went to the door and softly opened it. Amos lay on his side, face to the wall. She tiptoed across the room, and stood beside the bed, and then spoke to him. There was no movement. She turned the cover back and laid her hand upon his hand, and it was cold, and she knew that he was dead.

DUFF PHONED LUCIE when he heard about the death of Amos Hawthorne.

"I'm coming to see if I can help you," he said. He was at Delia's house but he didn't think he should mention that.

"No, don't come. Everything's working out."

"What will you do?"

"I'm closing the kennel. It's okay, Duff, honest. The Squire had ten thousand dollars in insurance, I discover. He paid it up long ago and hadn't borrowed a cent on it, bad as we needed money lately. I'm a rich gal now, see?" she said. "You can do one thing for me. Find Paul and Wesley jobs."

"Of course. I'll give them work myself, and glad to have them."

HAVING DELIA PHILLIPS for his girl, Duff found, was not particularly peaceful. Their days together—and they were many—were tempestuous, often angry, but never dead. On week-ends they sometimes went to Willow Lake, where Duff liked to fly-fish for bass. Delia had gone in the boat with him once or twice, but she had become tired, and got the twigs of an overhanging limb caught in her hair, and so now she preferred to stay at the swimming-pier.

Two Sundays before Duff was to leave for Canada, he found the bass in a striking mood. As the boat moved slowly along the overhung shoreline, he deftly dropped the

Trial by Marriage

squirrel-tail fly beside the cypress knees, and close to sunken logs; suddenly there was a powerful swirl of water, and a two-pound fish whipped an arc into the slender rod.

"He got you, boss!" the boatman said in glee. "You ain't got him—he got you!"

But Duff finally maneuvered his fish into the open, and there let him fight himself down against the springy pull of the rod, and landed him.

The boatman was putting the fish in the live box when, outside, a speedboat whined by in a white triangle of foam. A man and a girl sat together in the front cockpit, and a yellow kerchief flared from the girl's head.

The waves drifted in, rocking Duff's boat. "Now we got to wait a w'ile," the boatman said, resentfully, "tilst de water gits back ca'm again. Looks like dem speedyboats could do dey whiffing around some other place dan where's we's fishing at, don't it?"

"Who was that?" Duff asked, staring after the boat.

"Don't know who de gennelmun was," the Negro said, "but dat lady, look to me like, was de one you most generally brings down here wid you, wadn't it?"

"That's what I thought," Duff answered.

When he got in, he found Delia lying on her back on the pier, arresting in the clinging yellow Tahitian suit.

"Any luck?" she asked.

"You had some, I noticed," Duff said mildly. "Who was the hotshot in the speedboat?"

Delia said airily, "Oh, I didn't catch his name."

"You mean you didn't even know his name?" Duff asked in surprise.

Delia's eyes darkened threateningly. "Are you going to lecture me, Mr. Webster? You don't expect me to sit around and do nothing all the time you're out fishing, do you?"

"Maybe that's the reason you didn't want to go fishing," Duff answered, now beginning to get mad himself.

And so they had one of their arguments. It lasted for several minutes, until finally they went off in angry silence to their respective dressing-rooms.

It was dark when Duff, now let-down and miserable, finished dressing and went out to his car. It seemed an interminable time until Delia came, and got stiffly in beside him. He fumbled with the switch key, and turned on the lights. The people in the car ahead were waiting for their children to catch the dog, who was darting under the other cars and making a game of it.

Duff pressed the starter button. The car cranked, then choked. Instead of pressing the button again, he reached across the seat and found Delia's hand and drew her toward him. For an instant she resisted; then all of a sudden she was tight-pressed against him, and her mouth was against his, and the argument was over.

"Why do we fight, Delia?" Duff asked finally, holding her close.

"You know what they say about the course of true love," she replied.

"Well, I don't think we can go on like this," he said. "Delia, let's get married. Soon. Before long I'll be going to Canada, and you can go with me."

"Do you mean it, Duff?"

"You know it's what I want."

"If it's what you want, it's what I want," Delia said softly.

IT WAS HOT IN THE church, and Duff felt the sweat dripping down his back as he waited by the side of Carl Wind, his best man. Somewhere behind the ferns and candles the piano played. Out front was a somewhat vague area of faces, and he wondered if the faces had looked that way to Delia when she had sung in the choir and his had been one of them. Uneasily he thought about the ring, then remembered the extra ones Alex had got for Carl from the dime store, so that no matter into which pocket Carl reached, some kind of ring was there; and he thought about the telegram from Raleigh: *Congratulations and best wishes, Lucie.* Now the song of the piano changed to a more dramatic note, and Delia appeared at the archway on the arm of Dr. Phillips in his white linen suit, and even in his tremulous state Duff's breath caught at the calm loveliness of her.

Finally, after a seemingly interminable flow of words from the minister, it was over.

PART IV

NOW ANOTHER MONTH had passed, and Delia stood in the doorway of the Saskatchewan farmhouse they called a training-camp and impatiently looked across the hot prairie for the returning horses, for it was noon, and dinner was ready. The incessant wind, cold in the morning, and hot at noon, whined around the eaves, and she felt the house shudder under its strength. Down on the dry pond, white alkali dustwhirls danced across the bottom, and in the distance she could see the roof top of Benoit's house—Benoit, who Armand said was a beast and should be "troot-fed." For the rest of the vista there was rolling dry land of sage and wolf-willow and Russian thistle like tumbleweed and yellow mustard, and a huge rusting steam-tractor, relic of the days when there were rains enough to grow wheat and money was as plentiful as saskatoon berries in the ravine.

Down at the kennel beyond the barn, the dogs began to howl again, a lamentous, eerie chorus that seemed to portend tragedy and death. Delia angrily shouted, "You hush! Be quiet!"—but her voice did not reach the kennels. Presently they hushed of their own accord, and now the only sounds were the squeaking of the gophers in the yard and the cry of a hawk that beat back and forth over the meadow, and the occasional wind-thumps like a rolled blanket being swung against the house.

Finally they came, Duff and Paul on horseback and the dog wagon, driven by Wesley, far behind on a speargrass flat.

Duff came in and dipped water from the bucket into the washbowl, and bathed the prairie dust from his face and arms.

She said as they ate, "Isn't there some way to keep those dogs from howling?"

"No," he answered, "unless I take them all out hunting at one time. They're not as miserable as they sound."

"They make me miserable. Sometimes I get to thinking your horse has fallen and you're dead, and I'm left in this terrible country all by myself."

"Ah, hell," he said reassuringly.

"It seems like we've been here a year instead of a month."

"This isn't bad. I think it's wonderful country."

"You ought to stay here by yourself all day."

Trial by Marriage

"Maybe you think I wouldn't like to stay here in this cool house all day. What you ought to do is go out on the prairie with me," he said.

"I'm still sore from the last time I rode on that wagon. And you know I wouldn't get near one of those horses."

Duff thought about Lucie—as he often did now—and how she loved Canada. He rose. "Well, I'll tell you what we'll do. You see those hills over there? They're the Moose Mountains. We'll ride over there Sunday, and I'll show you some Indian graves and old camps where they stayed when they followed the buffalo a hundred years ago and more. You can still see the rings of stones they put around their tepees to hold them down. Maybe we can find some ripe chokecherries."

"I don't want to see any Indian graves."

"No," said Duff; "you just want to sit around and gripe. Can't you understand this is my job? It's the only thing I'm fit for."

"Well I wouldn't admit it," she said. "This is no life for decent folk. We're hardly better than heathen gypsies, living out here on this desolate prairie. It bores me silly."

"Hearing you talk like that reminds me of my folks."

"What about your folks?"

"Well, my mother used to nag at Papa like that, fussing at him for being what he was, and he finally tried to change, and it didn't work. It just come to me that it's the same old story." He said evenly, "Listen, I'm doing what I was born to do, and it's hard, honest work and nothing to be ashamed of. I'm as good as any doctor or college president that ever lived. You figured this was a life of excitement or something, just because we travel around. You'll have to get used to your mistake. We have to run bird dogs where there's birds, and there aren't any birds in Times Square or the Loop, not the kind of birds a dog would be praised for pointing, anyway."

"How can you talk like that to me? How can you see me so miserable and lonesome, and not care at all how I feel? You don't give me as much attention as you give one of those dogs out there."

He started to answer; then his shoulders sagged, and he said, "Let's don't fight. It's my fault—I shouldn't have brought you up here. But you had to come. Come, go with us to the bluff and watch us check-cord some puppies, huh? Then we'll run Judas a little."

"That Judas! I'm sick of hearing about him."

"Well, after I run him this afternoon I'll come in, and we'll ride into town and get the mail."

"What fun," she said.

During the hot part of the day, the prairie chickens gathered into the shade of the dwarf poplar groves or "bluffs" and became lazy and even stupid. Duff and the two Negroes led three young dogs on long leashes to the trees. Soon one of the dogs pointed, and Wesley, who was holding him, said, "Whoa, now, boy. Whoa-a-p—" The young dog's tail-tip waved slightly, and he made a leap forward, only to be stopped hard by the tautened check cord. The prairie chicken, an old hen, leaped squawking into the air, banging against the slender poplar branches, and whipped over the bushy trees, only to come down on the other side of the bluff thirty-five yards away. "All right, now, Cap, we goes and gits her again, only dis time recollect what happen to you w'en you fleshed 'er jist den."

For an hour they flushed chickens back and forth and finally the birds had all got enough of it and flown away to another bluff.

"Paul," said Duff, "you reckon your horse is ready for another session with Judas?"

Paul said, "Yes, sir, that race we had the other day didn't seem to bother him hardly at all next day. He's getting toughened up fine."

"Okay, we'll see what that damned-fool dog will have on his mind this afternoon."

They put Judas down. To his collar was tied a forty-foot check cord, and Duff looked forward to the day when Judas would hold a point long enough for him to catch up and grab the end of that line. Lying on top of the wagon dog cage in a semi-comatose state was Blackie, a coyote hound bought from a farmer, whose sole duty was to get on Judas's trail when he got lost, and to find him; Blackie knew his job well and did it capably. Now when he saw that it was Judas who was being released he sat up interestedly, as if hoping his quarry would get lost immediately so he could have some fun.

Saddle girths were adjusted, and bridles straightened. Duff turned Judas loose. Within a few seconds the pointer's swift, effortless stride had taken him over the far rise, and they saw him swinging out to the left. Duff's voice rang out: "Ha-a-ay, Judas!" But Judas didn't turn.

"Get on your bicycle, Paul," Dull said.

Paul's prairie-bred horse raced in pursuit at a sand-muffled dead run, sometimes leaping or swerving to miss a badger hole, but not once slowing or misstepping. Within a few minutes Paul had gained on the dog, and when Judas saw them he knew what they were coming for, and he swung back to the right.

It was hard to believe this was the same dog that had last week chased Wesley out of his pen, for afield his disposition was almost merry, and when he turned back to the course it was with an air of playing a game at which Paul had momentarily triumphed. "Sometime it seemlike to me," Wesley had said the day before, "dat dog ain't ornery 'cept when he ain't hunting. Once you tu'n him loose, seemlike he just happy as a jay-bird in a cherry tree."

Today they noticed the way he swung back to the course, and Duff said, "I do believe he's learned something."

Now Judas was a half mile ahead and to the right, with Paul cruising in the offing in case he needed turning again. Judas turned of his own accord, though, and then they saw him change ends, make several quick nervous casts, then stop cold. Paul's hat went up in signal for the point, and Duff spurred his horse into a fast run over the sage and speargrass.

This was the day for his luck. When Duff slid off the heaving horse, Judas was still there, with his head and his back straight, and his tail stiff as a poker. In his eye was a glint of something like amusement as from the corner of it he watched Duff ease toward him. When the man was almost within reach of him, he plainly intended to leap away again and send the birds a-scattering. But today Judas played the game on too close a margin.

Duff saw the grass stained knot of the check cord lying half suspended over a wolf-willow bush, and he made a headlong dive. Just as his fist closed on the cord, Judas

Trial by Marriage

broke. The few feet of slack evaporated, three prairie chickens burst from the cover, and Judas hit the end of the check cord and went end over end. The shock of the fall stunned the dog, and he sat staring blankly with his tongue hanging sideways out of his mouth and one ear lying on top of his head. At that moment another chicken came out cackling, and Judas made a frenzied leap at it, only to turn another somersault, as Duff shouted, "*Whoa!*" A few seconds passed, and Judas waited, watchfully. Then, with his nose lifted, he turned and, half-squatting, froze into another point.

"Hand me my gun," Duff said sharply. "There's still another bird here. To make a kill over him now will be worth a month's work."

"Mister Duff," Wesley said uneasily, "one dem Mounties liable to be out yonder somewhere and hear you shooting dat chicken out of season."

"You do what I say!"

With the .410, Duff walked steadily toward the motionless dog, saying warningly, "Who-a-ap, now—" and sliding the tight check cord through his left hand. Judas stirred slightly, and Duff put a little more pressure on the line as a reminder.

Then, for the first time, a man stood beside a Judas point. Duff's left hand touched him, and slowly stroked him from his neck to the tip of his tail to quiet his nerves. The dog stiffened in anger under his touch, but held the point. Carefully Duff unbuckled the muzzle and slipped it off. He took one step ahead of the dog, and a prairie chicken jumped from concealment into the air, wings drumming. Judas sprang after it.

The gun went to Duff's shoulder and fired, and the chicken tumbled over into a buckbrush clump. Judas was upon it in one bound. Duff let him mouth the bird for a few moments. Then he drew it away.

"See dere?" Wesley said to Judas. "Ain't it a whole heap' easier to git dem chickens when you behave yo'self and let Mr. Duff shoot 'em, dan to run your feets off up to de elbows trying to ketch 'em? You *sho'ly* ought to see dat, if you got half de sense yo' Daddy did." Wesley turned to Duff. "You see dat look in his eye? Like he saying, 'Well, for de Lawd's sake! Now I begins to see what all dis here running and yelling been about, all dis time.' Yes, sir, Mr. Duff, we is put some numbers in dat dog's head dis day."

Afterward they ran Mr. Lampley's brace of two-year-old pointers. One of them, Tequila, a hot-blooded animal standing twenty-two inches at the shoulders with flaring ribs and a tapered tail and a liver head blazed white between the eyes, was an almost certain winner in the Derby stakes to come, and Duff worked him carefully. When Tequila was taken up they headed back to camp.

After supper, Delia and Duff drove four miles into the village of Leason. The sun had not gone down; an occasional hawk sat upon the crude telephone posts and watched them indifferently. On a rise to the left, Duff thought he saw a jumping deer. At the tiny post office was a letter from James Lampley, saying that he would be at Moose Jaw for the opening trial, and the *Tafton Weekly Times,* which Delia sat in the car and read, while Duff went to the poolroom for a package of Sweet Caporals. Some of the town boys were organizing a game of pea pool; several of them had been stooking and were dust-covered, but liking it—the wheat crop was the first in years worth mentioning. Most of them had grown up hardly knowing how to work, for during the dry years there was nothing to do. But now there was a crop.

Delia had finished the paper when he got back, and by her vacant expression Duff knew she was thinking that there was nothing to look forward to until next week when the *Tafton Weekly Times* came again.

Duff touched her hand. "Listen, in about another month we'll go to Moose Jaw for the trials. I think you'll like Moose Jaw."

She smiled at him. "I'm all right, Duff. Don't pay any attention to me."

AS SOON AS THEY got to Moose Jaw, Duff began trying to make up to her for the lonely time she had spent. The town has a frontier exuberance of its own, and during field trials the dog men are in a convivial state of mind that is not altogether characteristic. There are gatherings in the hotel lobby, and in the rooms, and bottles of whisky and ginger ale are open on almost every dresser. Duff led Delia from one smoke-filled room to another, introducing her to the other dog men and women who sat upon the beds and on the floors and in the windows. Duff couldn't help thinking of Lucie, and how fine this would have seemed to her. For Delia didn't fit, and didn't try to.

"My Lord!" Delia said finally. "Don't they talk about anything but dogs?"

The phone rang. When Duff lifted it off its cradle, James Lampley said, "Webster? How's it been going?"

"All right."

"You and Mrs. Webster are going out with me for dinner. Okay?"

"That's fine."

"Come on down when you get ready. I'm in the lobby."

They walked down Moose Jaw's long street, with its busy sidewalks and neon lights and bright show windows, and turned into a restaurant. The place was crowded, and the juke organ played Tommy Dorsey's new hit record. The juke organ was as magnificent as any in Bill's Tavern in Tafton, with a bright-hued peacock whose tail kept changing colors, and pastel tubes of bubbling green liquid.

"Well, Mrs. Webster, how do you like the prairies?" Lampley said.

"Wonderful," Delia said.

Lampley missed the sarcasm. He turned to Duff. "How's Tequila?"

"He's a mighty good prospect. I post-entered him in the Derby, like you said."

"Is he steady yet?"

"Well, steady enough."

Lampley said, "I hear you've entered that outlaw dog of yours. That right?"

"Well, I may be just throwing away the money, but he's coming around fast, and I thought I might get lucky and keep him on the course. He's getting pretty steady on point, but you have to look him in the eye when you flush because he'll go right on out with the birds if he thinks you're not watching him. What I want to do is stay up until the hunting-season opens so I can kill some birds over both those dogs."

"That sounds all right to me. I'll know more after I see them run."

Delia lit a cigarette disgustedly.

TEQUILA WON SECOND place in the Derby. That was a fine break, placing a young dog your first time under a new boss; and the couple of hundred dollars that went with

Trial by Marriage

the placement wouldn't be hard to use, either. He and Delia might go back up to Orange Lake for a week-end, and do some dancing. She had liked hearing the Canadians sing "There'll Always Be an England"; she said it made her think she was in a foreign country. It was the only thing she had admitted liking.

Before the All-Age, Duff said, "I don't like to try to crowd my luck, but it would really be something if I could win with Judas, too."

"If you still intend to leave his muzzle off, you'll be lucky if he doesn't bite somebody and they sue you," Delia said.

"He's not so bad now; he won't bite you unless you try to pet him and fool with him. He can breathe easier with the muzzle off."

He lifted her into one of the rubber-tired buckboards they call "Bennett buggies"—named after the depression premier—and went back to the dog wagon for Judas. He looped his quirt through Judas's collar and gingerly slipped the muzzle off. The dog lifted his lips and showed his teeth, but that was all. Duff led him up front, through the horses and wagons and pick-up trucks, to where the judges and the other handler with his dog waited.

It was still early morning and chilly, which was good; the chickens would be out feeding. Judas growled at the other dog, and Duff wondered if he had done wrong in leaving the muzzle off. But when the judge said, "Let 'em go," Judas shot away without a further glance at his bracemate. As Duff swung up on his horse, Judas was headed for the outer limits of the course. Paul watchfully reined his horse outward, in case he needed to turn the dog. Now Judas was far away, a spot of white moving distantly on the brown, rolling prairie. They saw him shoot up a rise, then suddenly there he stood on top in motionless silhouette, the sun beyond him to lend an aura. The gallery broke toward him. Duff spurred his horse exultantly, thinking, *Don't you bust 'em, you damn fool!*

Judas held them, leaning forward in his impatience. Duff dismounted and quirted the prairie grass. A fine covey of bleating Hungarian partridges thundered up and streamed down the hillside and lit in a distant bluff. Judas made one jump forward, but Duff had watched for that and was in front of the dog with his quirt plainly visible. Sharply he said, "Whoa!" and Judas stopped, grinning evilly at him.

Now the dogs were out again, and James Lampley rode up beside Duff and said, "You've got a dog there."

Duff said, "He'll cut his throat yet."

Judas hunted as far out as he could and still be in judgment. "Yes, sir," Paul said once during the hour, "he seems to have got the idea, all right."

Then came a drama that was well staged, for everybody saw it. The plodding bracemate of Judas made a point and the flushed prairie chickens flew far ahead and settled on a low ridge. Judas, hurrying across on one of his prodigious casts, passed under the ridge and immediately, as if jerked by a rope, stopped and came back. Obviously he scented the birds, but, as everyone knew, they were above him. He pointed for a moment, then made a violent, frenzied whip through the brush trying to decipher that elusive scent. It came to him strongly again, and he now went uphill in short, tense jumps, straight toward the birds.

A jack rabbit came leisurely out of the sage, measured off a few steps, and sat down. Judas looked around to be sure Duff was not within reach, then sprang at the rabbit, clearing half the distance in one bound. They raced down the slope and across the flat, the rabbit now with his ears laid back, perceiving that nothing less than full speed would be enough.

The amused gallery stopped and watched, waiting for Judas to see that he couldn't catch the jack rabbit and give up. But Judas stayed on, running over the prairie with an effortless freedom. After a mile of it, the jack began leaping sidewise, desperately; Judas leaped sidewise, too. And then they saw the dog close the last inches of the gap, and the race was over. For one moment the dog tarried, shaking the dying jack rabbit, then swung out toward the front.

"Well, boys," a man said, "that outlaw dog put on a show then. But he done a pretty fair job of cutting his throat along with it."

"Even if he didn't cut his throat," another said, "he pumped himself dry outrunning that jack. He won't have enough left to hop into his dog crate with."

Judas now was coming back, cutting directly toward the front of the gallery and moving almost as swiftly as if the jack were still ahead of him. They saw him swing around the bottom of the hill, and then they understood what he was doing, and one man said, "Well I'll be damned!" Judas returned to the precise spot where he had flushed the jack rabbit, and made a short, quick cast downwind, and then froze in a lofty, tail-up point. The newspaper account next day said: *It was as if this bold, brainy dog were saying, "Well, now that I've disposed of that jack, here's those birds I was trying to locate when interrupted."*

Duff flushed the birds and sent him on. The next time they saw Judas, he was a half mile ahead, again on point.

"Pumped dry, eh?" one of the men said.

Another man rode up beside Duff for a moment, and said, "I've been trying to get hold of a dog like that all my life. I'll give you twenty-five hundred dollars for him."

"I guess not," Duff said.

When the heat was over, and Duff and Paul had ridden Judas down and brought him back to the dog wagon, James Lampley joined him, and said, "In that dog and Tequila we've got two of the best prospects anybody ever saw. I'm going to lease a place I used to have in Tennessee, and we'll see what we can do with those dogs. The kennels are gone, but we can use the barn for the dogs; and there are plenty of birds."

"Well, plenty of birds is what will do the trick for these dogs," Duff said.

After loosening the girth of his horse, he tied him to the back of the dog wagon. He wondered what Delia would say when she found out that instead of going back to their cottage in Zurich, they were going to live in a training-camp in Tennessee, nine miles from the nearest village. He walked to where she waited for him.

A COLD RAIN WAS falling when Duff and Delia reached the Tennessee farm that was to be their training-camp. Water stood in the furrows of the bare cotton field, and the ground was mud five inches deep. From the front porch of the old house, the rain dripped steadily. A wet mockingbird sat on the banister. Beyond the house were old chicken houses, and the barn in which they would house the dogs.

"Are you sure this is it?" Delia asked.

Duff said, "Lots of birds in this country."

"What kind of birds—ducks?"

He looked at her quickly, for—he thought with a little pain—it was something Lucie might have said, only in a different way. "I'll drive in the yard so we'll be closer."

"I was wondering if you were going to make me run in through that rain."

He drove the car across the little bridge, and, slithering, turned it toward the front steps. In the soft mud of the yard the wheels spun; the car crawled forward by inches, and eventually would go no further.

"This is pretty good," Duff grinned, "being stuck in our front yard."

"Oh, it's *very* good," she said.

"Listen, if you'll quit that griping for a minute or two, I'll tote you in."

"No. I'll walk."

She opened the door and stepped down into the mud. Holding her skirt with one hand, and a newspaper over her head with the other, she floundered the short distance to the porch. One of her slippers came off in the soft earth but she didn't stop to get it, the stockinged foot sinking ankle-deep in the cold mud. Duff brought the slipper in when he came, and poured the water out of it and handed it to Delia. She looked at him in angry disgust.

"You think it would help your feeling," Duff said, "if I apologized for causing this rain and for muddying up the yard and everything?"

She said, "Have I blamed you?"

"You might as well," he said. "I have to listen to the complaints."

"Am I supposed to like losing my shoe in the mud?"

"It wouldn't be natural for you to like anything concerned with being married to me," Duff said slowly. "Delia, you've got to get used to being the wife of a man who makes his living from field trials. I guess it's like being the wife of a farmer and a traveling salesman combined. But there's no other way."

"You talk like it's all my fault. You don't ever seem to consider my preferences. All you care about is those dogs."

"They're our living, don't forget."

"How could I forget? It's all I hear." She looked around. "My lord, what a place!"

Briefly Duff let himself picture Lucie standing there: *Isn't this something, though, Duff? Look yonder what a big barn for the horses. Look at that open rolling country, with all the plum thickets and lespedeza and bird cover. Gee, and this house—I always did want to camp out. I'll plant some flowers this spring. And put some grass out in the yard—then even a bum driver like you can't get stuck. Okay?* This vision was too painfully precious, and Duff forced himself to shut it off.

He had known, even before the fire that had drawn him to Delia had burned out, that his marriage to her was a mistake. It had been a bitter realization. Looking back, then, it seemed that his life had been a series of mistakes, and he resolved that no matter how bad a mistake this one was, he would abide by it and make the best of it.

He patted Delia's back. "Listen," he pleaded. "Let's make a new start, right here in all this mud and rain. We'll fix the house up, and plant some flowers around it, maybe. What do you say?"

Delia smiled and turned her lips to him. "All right."

Duff kissed her lightly. She complained, "You don't kiss me like you used to."

"Sure I do," he said. "Look. When the big trials get started we'll take them in together. There'll be some good towns along the line, like Albany and Thomasville and Pinehurst and Buffalo. I might make pretty good dough, too, if I'm lucky—five or ten thousand a year, even."

"While you go to your damn trials," she said, "I'm going to visit at home. That one in Moose Jaw was enough for me."

Duff poised on the steps before ducking into the rain to begin unloading their stuff. "Okay," he said shortly.

The horses were stabled near the house Wesley and Paul were using, and the dogs kept loosely chained in the spacious main barn with its half-filled loft of old hay and its mule-chewed troughs. By the time they were ready to start working dogs, the weather improved, and it was soon evident that they had made no mistake in coming here, for the country was ideal—open, slightly rolling, and full of quail. As the weeks passed, the birds that fell daily under Duff's gun gave the dogs a confident steadiness to add to the hunting wisdom they had gained in Canada. Because Delia's continued dissatisfaction made home an unpleasant place, Duff worked harder and longer, leaving in the chill pre-dawn and coming back after dark.

The dogs that seven months ago had been to Duff just a bunch of handsome, healthy pointers had long since become individuals, each with its own personality. Of the Lampley-bred pointers, Tequila was brag dog, already rated as one of the best Derbys, quite steady now unless his bracemate crowded him too close on point, when he would spring in and flush the birds. Then there was May, a little firecracker bitch, and Fred, whom Duff had nursed through distemper—in the kitchen, against Delia's will; and Preacher, who spent his odd time chewing up his food pan, and indefatigable Nate, who never seemed to sleep for eagerly watching for somebody to come into the barn to take him out hunting, and wise old Sunshine Babe, the dam of Tequila and half the others, who lay against her chain post with half-closed eyes following the play of the younger dogs. Judas, chained at the end of the barn, had acquired a certain irritable tolerance; he stood for no fondling or sudden movements, but he submitted to an amount of Duff's routine handling, such as the snapping on of a leash or even the tarring of his feet, with no more than a low, ominous growl like the warning rattle of a diamondback.

In the field Judas was now practically a broken dog; sometimes in the fire of running he forgot himself and left the course, but he eventually came back; and sometimes his lightninglike way of going to scented game landed him in the middle of the covey instead of on the edge of it. But in the main his errors were of overboldness, not meanness. Fundamentally, Judas was the same. His outlook had been changed, that was all; his spirit was not broken, or even bent. What he wanted of any day was to be allowed to hunt as much of it as possible—preferably all—and to be left strictly alone the rest of the time.

After his win at Moose Jaw, Duff decided to pass some of the fall trials up in order to point for the big southern stakes like the Continental, and the Free-for-All, and the Quail Championship, and then, of course, the National Championship.

In January, Duff managed to persuade Delia to go to the Pinehurst trials with him. "Just for luck," he said. The luck that came was of two kinds. Judas, obviously off his nose, ran well but found only one covey of birds. Tequila, on the other hand, was on fire, and he won the two-year olds' stake so positively that even the other handlers admitted it. James Lampley was there to see it, too, and to receive congratulations. But in the last ten minutes of the heat, a broken sliver of cotton stalk rammed through the muscle of Tequila's right hind leg, and he finished on three legs.

"Webster," James Lampley said enthusiastically, "after seeing that dog run this afternoon, I'm convinced that he's what I've been breeding to get. He's worth all the money and all the years of waiting for him. Now listen, take Tequila back to Tennessee and keep him in that barn until he's absolutely well."

"I'm hoping he'll be well for the Derby Championship."

"Don't take a chance on it. There'll be plenty of stakes for that dog to win in his lifetime."

SO WHEN DUFF BEGAN to make preparations for the swing to Georgia, only Judas was to be taken. With the heaviest part of the campaigning ahead, Delia went home for a visit. Duff and Paul drove to Waynesboro, and there they saw that Teague McGinnis's Hotfoot was still the dog to beat—and nobody did it. "That McGinnis is shot in the behind with luck," the men said. "Got the hottest dog on the circuit, and now going to marry that good-looking Lucie Sullivan." Hotfoot took second at the Continental, at Thomasville. At the big invitational Quail Championship at Albany he won first, and this time Judas, handling somewhat better than he had before, won second. Afterward, on the way to Tennessee, Duff thought, *Next time we meet that Hotfoot, we're going to lick the cold hell out of him.*

DUFF'S ROOM AT Grand Junction, facing the main street, was especially cleaned for field-trial week, with the best chenille spread upon the bed and new curtains on the big windows. He had arrived at midafternoon on the Sunday of the drawings, penned Judas satisfactorily in the woodhouse in back, and after talking awhile to the Mrs. Tufts who rented him the room, gone upstairs to unpack. From his duffel bag he took his boots, slicker, spurs, quirt, and sheepskin coat. As he was standing the freshly oiled boots in the corner, a knock sounded on the door, and Lucie came in.

"Hello, Duff," she said. She wore a gray suit, and toeless gray suede shoes with tiny bows, and no hat. Her light hair had blown a bit.

"Hello," he said, swallowing the quick emotion that constricted his throat.

"Is it all right to sit down?"

"Sure, have a seat," he said, when he was able to speak. He still held one of the boots. "I didn't know you were coming to Grand Junction."

"I don't think I'll ever let anything keep me from riding the National," she said.

"You're looking good," he said slowly.

"If you've started passing out compliments, something has changed you," Lucie told him. "Were you tight with them before—zowie! One day you told me I was easy on a horse's mouth, and I had a tough time going to sleep that night."

Duff put the boot down. "How have you been, Lucie?"

Lucie said, "Okay. I come to ask you about Paul and Wesley. Are they satisfied to be away from Tafton?"

"I guess so."

"Well, how's Judas?"

"All right."

"You have a pretty good chance with him?"

"Don't know." Suddenly he said, "Listen. How would it be if I kissed you?"

She looked at him. "You know about Teague and me, don't you?"

"I heard you're going to marry him."

"I am, Duff. No fooling," she said. "You still want to kiss me?" she asked. "Okay. But take it easy. 'Tain't fair, otherwise."

He kissed her gently on her lips. There was an infinite sweetness about the touch of them, and it was almost more than he could stand. Then he went to the bed and sat down, deeply shaken.

"What did that mean, anyway?" she asked.

"It's just something I've missed," he said finally.

"Since when?"

"Since the last time I did it."

"That was a pretty long time ago," Lucie said. "I've changed my way of thinking since then, Duff. I had to, because most of my thinking was about you, and you were gone for good."

"It was the thing to do, all right."

She looked at him accusingly. "Duff, I never thought you'd be doing this."

"Doing what?"

"What you're doing. Throwing a lot of junk at me, just because I'm here in your room. But it just rolls off my back like a duck."

"I haven't said anything."

"You're married, aren't you?"

"Yes."

"I knew I could come and talk to you without getting air bubbles in my blood like I used to," she said, "but I never thought I'd be able to feel like you were somebody I'd never seen before."

"Look, what did I say but that I'd missed kissing you, for gosh sake?"

"That was plenty. I know what that was supposed to make me do. I'm not dumb."

"Well, forget I said it," he said heavily. "Let's don't quarrel; it wouldn't be fair for you to compete with me, because I've had a lot of practice in the past eight months."

"Okay," Lucie answered, fumbling in her pocketbook for her lipstick. "It just made me sore to see the change in you. I was sort of saving you as something to measure people by. For instance the guy my daughter falls for, if I have a daughter." She stood up. "Well, so long. I'll be going."

The door clicked shut, and he stared at it. Now he could hear her little gray shoes tapping down the steps. The sounds faded, leaving him with a sense of profound loss and emptiness. He walked to the chair and touched the back of it. Here she had sat. This was where she had been. Some of the faint, clean perfume of her lingered. But the rest of her, he thought emptily, was gone.

Trial by Marriage

ALL AFTERNOON THE cars arrived—coupés with dog crates, horse trailers, pick-up trucks with especially made dog compartments, expensive sedans. Cars from all the Southern states and many of the others—Indiana, New York, Illinois, Oklahoma. The layers of tobacco smoke began to grow against the ceiling in the hotel and in the drugstore. There were men in boots, and men in English tweed suits, and some of them made three thousand a year and others made a hundred thousand; but this week they all spoke the same language.

One said solemnly, "What I always remember is a piece of salt-pork rind a man found in the crate with his dog the morning before he was to run a second series for the championship. He knew his dog didn't have much of a chance after being given that salt pork, but he ran him anyhow. Not many of us knew anything about it, because this fellow wasn't one to go crying that his dog had been messed with. But I knew it, and when I saw the way that dog ran I got a lump in my throat. He hunted almost at his best and when he found birds he stood them solid as Plymouth Rock, regardless of his guts burning up. But he didn't find birds often, though, because most of the time he was looking for water. I heard one of the judges say, 'I don't think I ever saw that dog do so much aimless running.' And, of course, in the end he lost, because he would've had to be at his best to beat the other dog. But he had beaten the other dog before, every time they met. When the judges made the announcement, the owner rode over to the other handler, who he pretty well figured had given the dog the salt pork, and he shook hands with him and congratulated him, and you'd never guessed that he had been cheated out of something he'd've given an eye for."

"Seems to me," one said, "that if sporting animals could talk, they'd have a damned sorry opinion to pass out on mankind. They go on pure guts, most of 'em, and you'd think it would improve man just to associate with 'em. But, no, somebody's got money to think about. So they feed the other man's dog salt pork, or they give his gamecock aspirin, or they shove a sponge up his race horse's nose."

The talk continued through supper; and afterward, at the hotel, the club secretary had to rap upon the table for quiet. Gradually the room became attentive, and the order of the drawings was given. Judas was called for the third brace, which meant he would run on Tuesday morning against one of the few setters entered, Arnold's Mohawk Pride.

Afterward, Duff went to the drugstore and called Paul, in Leason, who was waiting for word of the draw.

"We go Tuesday," Duff said. "Put the horses on the truck first thing in the morning and come on down, so they'll have a breathing-spell before the running. Take it easy now and don't be in too damn big a hurry, because a crippled horse can ruin us. Be sure to have Wesley come."

"Yes, Sir," Paul said. "He'll be a big help if that dog tries to cover all of Tennessee, like he's liable to."

Duff hung up the receiver. While he talked the crowd had begun drifting back into the drugstore. Sitting on stools at the fountain were Lucie and Teague McGinnis, drinking Cokes. Duff nodded to them and would have walked on out, but Teague said, "How's your dog, since Albany?"

Lucie shook the ice in the bottom of her glass. Her mouth was moist from the Coke; finally she loosened the ice with a straw.

"Just fair," Duff said. "I don't expect him to do a hell of a lot."

"What's wrong with him?"

"Just not going like he should," Duff said. "How's Hotfoot?"

"He's been off some, since Albany," Teague said. "I'm scared he's got a little stale."

Duff knew he couldn't sleep if he went home, so he walked across the railroad tracks toward the house of Mutt Sonderson, where some of the boys were going to start a blackjack game. Down by the depot, an engine sharply sent a geyser of steam through the strata of station lights. Above, the sky was clear, and the stars stood out in cold brilliance.

That lying scoundrel, Duff thought. *Scared he's got a little stale. He'll be stale, all right. But not too stale to run the feet off any dog here. Any dog but Judas.*

The day Judas ran was bad. It was a dismal sort of morning, a morning, it seemed, of impending calamity. No calamity occurred, but the birds must have been affected, for they didn't move. Judas hunted hard and wide, and found just three coveys. His bracemate found only two.

As they went into the third hour, Duff had kept desperately hoping for one more find. *We'll never be called back on three coveys.* Even until the last minute he hoped. But when the judges ordered the dogs up, the bird score was still three coveys.

"Well," Duff told Paul heavily, as they put Judas in the dog crate, "that finishes us."

"Yes, sir," Paul answered in a sorrowful voice, "I reckon so. What we going to do now?"

"Go on back. No use to stay here."

"He ran strong," Paul suggested hopefully. "*Might* be they'll call him back."

Duff shook his head. "Well, if they do want to call him back, they know where we'll be."

AFTER JUDAS'S SHOWING at Grand Junction, where he drew a bad day and found only three coveys, Delia's tongue grew sharper than ever.

"Thought he was such a great dog," she taunted.

"We had tough luck," Duff said gently. "Sometime or other the breaks will begin going our way."

"Oh, sure," she said.

"Delia," Duff said heavily, "losing out was hard enough. I don't see the point in trying to make me feel worse."

"How do you think I feel in this house all day, without a soul to talk to? You go out at daylight, and you come back after dark, and when you're not too tired to talk all you can talk about is Judas, Judas, *Judas!*"

"Maybe if home was a little pleasanter, I'd be tempted to come in earlier," Duff said.

Her cheek whitened in anger. "Now I see! *Now I see!* You've been staying out on purpose!"

"Oh, you're crazy. I said—"

"I heard what you said." She was furious.

"You think I like being nagged at all the time?"

"You think I like living out here in this—this shack?"

"No. You didn't expect anything like this. I tried to tell you, but you thought you were going to be a sportsman's wife, and see the country, and hobnob with the rich folks. You wouldn't believe you were laying your pipes to marry a plain workingman."

"Laying my pipes?"

"Listen, Delia. That trouble with Amos about Lucie—you caused it, and it wasn't any accident. I thought it was an accident until I married you and got to know you better."

Delia's face was colorless, expressionless. "You're crazy!"

"No, not quite."

"My God, how I hate you!" she whispered.

She wheeled and went out on the front porch. She stood at the steps, breathing hard. The night was cold and clear. A frost lay upon the cornfield across the road, turning it white in the winter moonlight. Several minutes later, a cow came down the road, stopping to pull at the vines that grew on the fence. Delia leaned against the porch post, her fingers thrumming nervously against her sleeve.

She lit a cigarette and smoked it angrily, in quick, hot puffs. Down at the barn one of the dogs barked briefly and subsided. Delia stiffened. For a moment she was motionless, poised in sudden thought. Then she threw the cigarette into the yard.

Down at the barn, the chained dogs were bedded deep in their straw, and they raised their heads and blinked sleepily at the match Delia held. One of them, old Sunshine Babe, growled perfunctorily, but quieted when spoken to. Judas raised his head, and his yellow eyes were red in the matchlight. Delia made her way slowly to where the big pointer lay. He rose at her approach, growling warningly.

Now that she was within reach of the dog, Delia hesitated. The match burned her fingers. Determinedly, Delia found the chain and ran her hand down it to the dog's collar. The deep rattle in Judas's throat rose a note, but he let her unsnap the chain.

Delia did not realize she had screamed until Duff came running from the house. She rose from the floor where Judas, in his leap toward the door, had knocked her.

"What is it?" Duff shouted, flashing his light on her.

"He knocked me down!" she said, pulling the hay from her hair.

"Who?"

"Your damned Judas, that's who!"

Duff's light fell upon Judas's empty chain. "Where's that dog?" he demanded.

"He got away."

Duff went quickly to the chain. He straightened and said incredulously, "You turned him loose!"

"What if I did?" she said angrily.

"What if you did?" Duff exploded. "I've worked a long time getting him broke. Now he's running wild again, and in one or two days of that he could forget all I've tried to beat into his head—if somebody doesn't shoot him first."

"I hope to God somebody does shoot him," Delia said.

Duff's hand snatched her around. "You listen to me," he said in cold anger. "The car's out front, and there's a hotel in Leason. You better go right away. Paul will come to town in the truck in the morning with the rest of your stuff."

"Don't worry—I'll go and glad of it!" she said bitterly.

By the time Paul and Wesley and Duff had their horses saddled, the headlights of the car had disappeared down the road. Duff paused before mounting, looking toward the darkness where his wife had gone. He took a deep breath and went into the saddle.

"Okay," he said shortly. "We'll separate and start riding. Maybe he hasn't got off so far we can't call him in."

The three horses galloped out across the frost-covered cornfield.

In the barn, a spark from the match Delia had held worked its way patiently up a straw stem. At the end of the straw was a frayed oat husk. The spark reached this, sputtered, and broke into a tiny flame.

DUFF SAW THE FIRE glow against the sky. He stopped and listened and presently he heard the howling of dogs. He jerked his horse around and kicked him savagely. The horse reared. Duff struck him on the head with his fist, and kicked him again, and the horse flattened out in a wild run homeward.

Emerging from the creek bottom, Duff saw the white-red flames eating across the roof of the barn. Smoke boiled in a flood from the wide door. The howling of the dogs grew frenzied. Riderless, a horse galloped past them, his ears forward in fright, the saddle off-center. Wesley's horse.

Duff hit the ground running. "Wesley!" he shouted.

Then from the boil of smoke in the door staggered a man dragging a dying retching dog by the collar. Wesley's clothes suddenly burst into flame. Releasing the convulsive Sunshine Babe, he turned back toward the barn.

Duff snatched his mackinaw off as he ran. "Wesley, wait!"

The Negro stopped and then saw the fire climbing up his coat. He tried to get the coat off, but it seemed that in his excitement his hands fumbled. Later Duff found out that Wesley's hands were burned.

Duff threw his mackinaw around Wesley, and bore him to the ground.

"Be still, Wesley! You're afire."

"Git de dogs before too late!"

"You be still," Duff commanded. Above the crackle of the flames and the howling of the dogs, he now heard the hollow hoofbeats of Paul's horse.

"Stay here with him," Duff shouted, as Paul sprang to the ground.

"Git de dogs!" Wesley said. Paul knelt beside him. Duff could get no closer than the door. Now the smoke carried tongues of flames, and the heat threw him back. He heard the rattling of the chains as the dogs fought them. He ran around to the back of the barn, but this was no better.

The flames of the burning hay in the loft now spouted geyserlike through the holes in the roof, and the fire crept down the frame walls, like a cat backing down a tree, so that a pocket was left in the center of the barn where the dogs were—a pocket filled with heat and smoke. Duff pried a board from a side of the barn where the fire was thinnest—only to have the opening immediately closed by yellow flame. Farther down he pulled off another board, but the fire licked out and singed the hair off his hands.

Finally Duff went to the house and got his shot gun and a box of shotgun shells. He tore the box open as he hurried back to the barn, spilling part of them.

Trial by Marriage

Standing as close to the big door as he could Duff unbreeched the gun and shoved two shells into the barrels. He fired both barrels through the door. Then he reloaded the gun and fired again. A dog's howl shut off abruptly. Then another. Duff kept shooting.

Finally, except for the dull roar of the fire, there was silence.

Next morning Duff called James Lampley and told him what had happened.

"You mean *every one* of them?" Lampley said incredulously.

"Yes, sir," Duff said painfully. "I'm afraid that's right."

"Tequila, too?"

"Him, too."

Except for the continuous hum of the country phone, the wire was silent. Then: "Webster, I can't quite grasp it. You mean, my bloodlines that I've worked on twenty years are completely wiped out?"

"Yes, sir, that's the way it is."

Another silence. Duff rubbed his finger around the broken edges of the mouthpiece.

"Well," Lampley said at last, "I guess you're out of a job."

"I don't blame you."

"No, you don't understand. It's all right. It wasn't your fault. Perhaps my fault for not letting you build temporary kennels. It's just that I'm washed up," he said heavily. "I haven't got the heart to start over."

Duff paused. "I'd offer you half interest in Judas, only I don't know whether I'll get him back, or whether he'll be ruined."

"No. He's a fine dog, and when I had the others I wanted him. But he's not my creation—like Tequila. I planned Tequila eighteen years before he was born. You see how it is? I made him. Now—he's gone. I haven't got the heart any more."

Duff rang off and walked slowly through the house. Delia's trunk was locked, and her things in it, except for a piece of peach-colored underwear he had overlooked hanging in the closet.

The smell of fire was thick in the house. Duff stood on the back porch and looked out at the smoking ruins. The red-cedar tree, thirty yards away, was burned bare and brown. Stepping over the rubble, he went to what had been the entrance of the barn, and stood by the heat-whitened well bucket Wesley had dropped. Of the barn, little was left. The roof, because of the hay in the loft, had gone first, and the heat of its burning had turned the interior of the barn into an oven. Now there was only the brick foundation, and the iron supporting posts, and heaps of charred, smoking rubbish and ash.

Duff slowly walked into the wreckage. Here was a chain, and at the end of it a pile of bones. This was Nate, who had sat tirelessly watching the door for someone to take him afield. Now he was dead without ever having got enough hunting to suit him. But then Nate never would have got enough hunting to suit him.

The next pile of bones was Preacher, and near by his battered, tooth-marked food pan. Next, Fred, with a buckshot hole in the top of the well-shaped skull. Then Tequila, the hunting heart burned out of him, nothing but leathery-cooked skin and whitened bones left of twenty years of scientific breeding.

Duff stood in silence. There was his kennel—nine chains, nine piles of bones.

Washed up. Yes, that was the word for it. Duff looked at the road that ran in front of the house. Somewhere down that road, perhaps, was forgetfulness; no memory of a ruined marriage and a burned Negro and a gun firing buckshot and a fine, reclaimed dog turning outlaw again, no memory of a girl who had lied to set him free— Down that road, maybe, things were different. He recognized the road—it was the one he used to travel, before he had got the idea that he might make something of himself. Now the idea was dispelled, and the only thing to do was to travel that road again.

He went inside and began packing his old suitcase. When this was done he went outside and set it down on the steps. And there on the front porch lay Judas, asleep. Not running wild, but come home of his own accord, asleep on the porch.

"Judas!" Duff said, in quick exultation.

The dog raised his head. Without thinking, Duff reached out to stroke him. Judas bit him through the hand.

Duff swore; the blood unhurriedly rose in the bluish tooth holes. Judas watched him placidly.

Slinging the blood from his hand, Duff straightened. "If I've put up with you," he said slowly, "I guess I can stand anything."

He took his suitcase back into the house.

AT ELEVEN O'CLOCK, a small blue coupé drove up outside, and Lucie Sullivan, close-wrapped in her tweed coat, got out. She unfastened the gate and strode down the walk.

"I just heard about it, Duff. I had to come to see you."

"Wasn't any need for that," he said.

"I had to come, Duff," she said simply.

"To see me on my back?"

"No," she said. "I wanted to help you."

"I'll make out," he said.

"Duff, don't be so damned stiff and stubborn. I know you're hurt bad; I see it in your face. Please let me help you. Let me do something."

"There's nothing to do that I can't do."

"Oh, you're just crazy."

"Can't you understand anything? I don't need any help. I appreciate your coming, and that's the truth. But I'll make out."

"All right." She sighed. "Will you take me to see Wesley?"

Wesley lay in bed, wrapped to the chin in white bandages. Paul stood by him, attending him, and following the doctor's directions as carefully as any nurse.

"Miss Lucie," Wesley said, "I can hear 'em right on, just howling and crying for me to come git 'em out, and I couldn't do it, Lawd, I just couldn't git 'em out. The closest was old Babe, and I got her chain undid, I can feel it hot in my hand right on, and I drug her out but she was done too far gone." He lay still, his jaw slack. "De first time, I never even got in good, had to crawl out and lay dere, coughing and spewing, and my clothes had cotch, and I beat dem out, and choked-like, couldn't do nothing else."

"Next time," Duff said, "you keep your damn-fool self on the outside."

Trial by Marriage

"Yes, suh, dat's de troof," Wesley said. "Only de good Lawd knows how long dey had been abarking and acrying when I look back and see de fire. Maybe not so tur'ble long, but when I come arunning, de fire was just agoing at it, mostly in dat hay in de loft. Den I run to de well and drawed water, and dey just kept on yipping and barking, and I hollered at 'em, 'Jes' a minute, Preach, old Wes is coming; jes' a minute, Mary, jes' a minute, Teak.' But I knowed dey couldn't hear me; for all dey knowed I was asleep in de bed widout caring where dey was afire er not. I poured de water, and it didn't do nothing but say pshht. Ev'y now and den I let out a holler, so maybe somebody happen to hear me and come he'p—but didn't nobody. Den I went in and drug old Babe out, only she never even had de strenk to stand up."

"You stay on the outside next time," Duff said. "We can raise more dogs, but they've quit making your brand of nigger."

"You reckon I'm got to listen to 'em from now on?" Wesley said. "Barking and barking and barking— Den Mister Duff shooting and shooting and shooting."

"No. You'll forget it after a while," Lucie said gently.

"Just cain't believe my dogs is gone," he mumbled. "Paul?"

"Yes, sir."

"You wid me, son?"

"Right here, Papa."

"Stay wid me, son."

"Right here, Papa."

"Stay wid me."

When they got back to the house, the phone was ringing Duff's number, four longs and one short. He picked up the receiver.

"Mister Webster?" the operator said, above the buzzing wire. "Hold the wire for Grand Junction."

Then came the voice of the field-trial secretary. "Webster? This is Scott. Sorry to hear about your misfortune. All of us here send sympathy," he said. "I called to tell you the judges want your dog Judas here day after tomorrow at eight-thirty."

"What for?" Duff said stupidly.

"To run in the second series, what you think?"

"I can't run. My dog's been out on an all-night hunt. And neither one of my scouts can come."

"Somebody here will scout for you."

"It takes somebody that knows this fool dog of mine," Duff said, sweat standing on his lip. "I just don't see a chance."

"You don't want to scratch the National Championship, do you?"

"No, but—"

"Well, work out something, boy."

Duff stood staring at the broken mouthpiece of the telephone. He gave the crank a turn to ring off; the last note of the bell faded away.

"Duff," Lucie said, "I could scout for you, if you'd let me."

"What?" he said uncomprehendingly.

"I could help you run Judas."

219

"Where did that idea come from?"

"Listen, Duff—and try not to be so all-fired stubborn. I can ride a horse as good as anybody, and I know Judas. Is that true or not?"

"Maybe so, but you're—"

"That's all there is. No maybe to it," she said determinedly.

"You wait. Teague McGinnis is the man you're going to marry. What'll he think?"

"I can tell you exactly what Teague McGinnis will think. He'll think you've had your share of bad breaks, and any help you can get will be okay with him. He'll think it's okay for me to try to win with a dog my grandfather bred. The others may think it's peculiar, but not Teague McGinnis."

"Maybe."

"You let me handle that end of it."

In the first series, four dogs stood out, and it seems to be a unanimous opinion that the judges were entirely right in calling back these four: Daydreamer, Pineview Sue, the spectacular champion, Hotfoot, and the much-discussed Judas. Of these, Judas had the lowest bird score, but the judges wisely took into consideration that he ran on a day when the birds were not out, and no one quarreled with this fourth selection.

Almost as soon as the four second-series dogs were announced, the skies became leaden, and by night on the day before Daydreamer and Pineview Sue were to run snow began falling. Thursday the temperature had dropped to 12 degrees above zero. But by noon the judges deemed it satisfactory for running, and Daydreamer and Pineview Sue were given their chance. These two dogs ran industrious but inadequate heats. It remained for those two super dogs, Judas and Hotfoot, to show what a championship heat should be like.

ABOUT DUSK, DUFF went to the meat market and supervised the grinding of a pound of steak for Judas. He made the butcher put it in an ice-cream carton, because wax paper sometimes disintegrated and got mixed up in the meat. When he fed Judas, he saw to it that there was adequate straw, for it was cold, and the wind was blowing.

There was considerable activity in town, with more cars arriving, muddy cars with steamed windows, people coming to see the champion run; the households of Grand Junction were full; there was not an empty bed left in town.

At the drugstore, the nightly session was on. The young men had got all their heavy-handed kidding and horseplay out of their systems earlier in the week. But the older ones had not tired of recalling the great dogs, and the others had not tired of listening.

"This weather," one of them said, "reminds me of that 1915 championship. Lucie, I guess you heard your grandfather Amos tell about it many times. La Besita was one of his real loves, and I think he would have given anything to have been her handler, though doubtless not even little Bee could have supplanted Ambling Sam in his affection. I remember her clearly, because once you ever saw this fireball little setter bitch, you never forgot her. The night before the second series, she was sick as a goat—some said it was pneumonia. They thought she was dying. Next day she was better, and they let her run, and to the astonishment of all of us she stepped right out and beat that Morris dog for the championship!"

"From the way the weather looks outside," somebody said, "tomorrow might be another pneumonia day. Them pointers will be wishing they was setters."

"I wouldn't worry much about the two that's running tomorrow, if I was you. That Hotfoot, he'll be too busy bird hunting to notice the weather, and that damn outlaw of Duff's is tougher than harness leather."

DURING THE NIGHT Duff heard the wind blowing against the pane, and he put on his sheepskin coat and went downstairs. When he flashed the light into the woodshed, Judas was curled deep in the straw; the dog raised his head and his eyes caught in the light and blinked coldly. Duff went back upstairs. He looked at his watch—3:14. Before getting into bed, he went to the bathroom to get a drink of water, but the faucet was frozen.

He looked out the window to see if he could tell anything about the weather. The sky was black. He got under the thick covers, but no sleep came to him. At six o'clock Duff rose, shivering in the cold room, and dressed. He put on heavy underwear, a sweat shirt beneath his whipcord shirt. The boots were stiff as he pulled them over the woolen socks.

The kitchen was even colder than the bedroom. He was looking for the coffee when Mrs. Tufts came in, squinting her eyes. She wore an old robe and a nightcap.

"You're starting mighty early," she said. "I'll make you some eggs."

"I didn't go to wake anybody up. Just thought I'd fix a little coffee."

"I was about ready to get up," she said.

When he had eaten, Mrs. Tufts said, "I wish you luck, Duff," and he went out to the woodshed to get his dog.

Judas apparently guessed what was up, and he shivered with nervous impatience, and Duff knew enough to be careful about handling him. When he had the leash on him, Judas walked on his hind legs all the way to the car. Duff put him on the back seat.

The starter turned the motor heavily, and finally it caught. Duff switched on the lights, and backed around. The wind blew a paper across the street. At the corner house he saw Lucie's light on. She came out, running for warmth, her breath frosting.

"Hello," she said, climbing in beside him.

"Hello," he answered.

Daylight was showing above the bare treetops when they got to the field-trial grounds. Judas kept yawning nervously on the back seat.

"It's sure going to be a ructious day," Lucie said. "What are you going to do with that check cord, Duff?"

"I'm going to let this dog take some running behind the car."

"Right before he's due to start?" Lucie asked.

"You look at him and see," Duff said. "He's hot as a mail-order pistol."

"Aren't you afraid it'll take too much out of him?"

"He's got to have some of that taken out of him, or we'll spend the first hour hunting for him."

"You're the boss."

After tarring his feet, they put the long leash on Judas, and Duff leaned out the back window and held the other end of the leash. Through winding sand roads Lucie drove at a speed to keep Judas running. Not that Judas seemed to mind. Once or twice Duff said, "Better go a little faster. He's got the line slack again and liable to get tangled in it." Finally Duff decided that Judas's wire edge had been run off, and he stopped the car. Judas breathed rapidly but without laboring. "I'll walk him around and let him blow a minute, and then we'll go on back," Duff said.

As Duff allowed Judas to pull him around, he listened to the gusty winter wind that rattled the stiff bare trees. He looked at his watch—7:44. They were due to turn the dogs loose in forty-six minutes. Day seemed only halfway there; no sign of the sun. Judas was walking on his hind legs.

"Well, I see we didn't run him too much," Lucie admitted.

"He pulled me at a trot all the way up that road and back."

When they got back to the starting-ground the hostlers had come with their bunches of horses, and had fires going. The cars were arriving. "Here you go, boss, best saddler in Lardemore County. Just git on him and take a try, cap'm; he's a Tennessee-walking scoun'l."

Lucie and Duff supervised the unloading of their horses from the truck. They minutely examined their horses' feet and legs and bridles and girths and saddle billets.

"Okay?" Duff said.

"Okay," Lucie said. She smiled wanly at him. "Duff, I wish you luck."

Duff felt a sudden warmth for her that almost overwhelmed him. He said, "I wish *us* luck, Lucie."

Now they were ready, the judges waiting up front. Judas dragged Duff through the gathering gallery, while Lucie followed with the two horses. Teague McGinnis, leading Hotfoot, muttered, "Hope it don't take 'em long to make up their minds. This ground's froze enough to cut a dog's feet plumb off."

The judges looked at their watches. *Time, 8:49. Temperature, 28. Sky overcast, variable winds shifting to the southwest.*

One of the judges blew his nose and said, "All right, let them go."

Duff unsnapped the leash, and Judas jumped away. Both dogs ran hard, each straining to outdistance the other. Then they broke apart and swung out bird hunting, but without slowing. In a few seconds Judas disappeared over a hill, and to the left, Hotfoot disappeared, too.

"Them dogs might as well be running on the pavement as this froze ground," a man said. "And for all the birds they'll find, too."

The horses' hoofs struck with a hollow clopping, and their breath fogged from wet nostrils. Duff and Teague sat loosely in their saddles, occasionally passing a casual remark to show the judges they had complete confidence in their dogs' willingness to stay on the course; but their eyes were sharply searching the terrain ahead. Hotfoot appeared momentarily. "Yon's my dog, judge," McGinnis pointed out, and his confidence became genuine, while Duff's eyes narrowed. Lucie looked at him questioningly, but Duff shook his head.

Trial by Marriage

They surmounted the rise, and Hotfoot could be seen skirting the woods line off to the left. Somebody whistled softly, and told his neighbor to look at that dog go. Duff now rode erect, and made no remarks, casual or otherwise. Then, incredibly far ahead, he made out a spot of white. It might have been a log because it didn't move; or it might have been a dog.

"Yon's my dog, judge," Duff said, "and he's on point."

The judges stood in their stirrups and looked, but they could see nothing. "If you see a dog," one of them said, "you've got better eyes than I have."

"Well, he's there all right."

"I see him," said a man in the gallery suddenly. "Before God, look yonder where he is at!"

Duff spurred his horse, and let out a long squall of assurance to the distant Judas. There was a ride of several minutes to traverse the open stretch and arrive at the patch of sedge and cedars where Judas stood with his tail high and his head back and his mouth cracked in a cocky grin. With his gun in one hand and his quirt in the other, Duff waited until the judges were there, then he strode rapidly out in front, knowing by the elevation of the dog's head exactly where the birds would be. They rose close-bunched, having not yet left their roost place; one of them tilted out and back, flew directly over Judas's head. Judas made a quick about-face but didn't chase, and Duff fired. *There's the dog they said I'd never break,* Duff thought, as he caught hold of Judas's collar. With the dog rumbling threateningly, Duff inspected the pads of his feet; they were already pink.

Now Judas was away again, swinging out in that carefree, tail-whipping run. Ahead was a cornfield that stretched along a branch swamp, and along the edge of it was a continuous strip of weedy cover. Running swiftly, Judas followed this all the way to its end, and at the far end of his cast he suddenly whirled and darted back twenty yards and abruptly stopped, on point again. They all saw it, and looked at each other significantly when Judas stood to wing and shot. Two coveys within ten minutes of each other, on a cold raw morning when the birds weren't supposed to be moving.

Hotfoot's ground work was beautifully capable, and there was a sparkle about his manner of running that gave the illusion of tremendous speed. He disappeared behind a roll of land, then swung back in beyond it. Ten minutes later Hotfoot made his first find, and Judas, crossing the field, saw him a hundred yards away and backed. Lucie looked at Duff and smiled. Duff thought, *There's the boy I wasn't going to break.*

The sun came up, and before long the ground had thawed. Instead of ice there was a coating of cold, half-frozen mud upon the earth, and in the low places the horses sank over their pasterns. The wind rose, burning the reddened faces of the men. A half hour later, as if the day weren't already bad enough, a thin, stinging spray of half-sleet, half-rain came with the wind, and it grew colder again. The men pulled their heads into their collars. The judges began looking at each other questioningly. But gradually the sleet subsided, and that seemed to settle the matter.

Not that the dogs minded. Both of them ran with the air of being out on a bright fall afternoon, and except for the difficulty of finding birds they might well have been. But after Judas found his third covey, Duff saw that his pads were now cut and slightly bleeding, and half-frozen mud matted between his toes. *I guess now's the time to call up some of the guts you're supposed to be so full of.*

Instead of slowing his pace, Judas seemed to quicken it, darting down through a cold branch-head, whipping back around and then leveling off for the fields ahead; and whenever he pointed, he did it with such smash and intensity that even the most frostbitten novice was jolted upright in the saddle.

"You reckon the judges aren't going to put a stop to it?" one red-nosed man asked, after a while.

"Mister, if them judges are seeing the same dog race I am, you couldn't stop 'em with a blizzard."

The American Field said: *Cast off on that great open flat, Judas soon demonstrated that he was at his best, for he smashed across those vast lespedeza fields, his great white form silhouetted on the gray background of trees and sky, always appearing somewhere ahead just when the judges would begin to wonder. In less than twenty minutes he had the entire gallery with him. Not that Hotfoot was outclassed, for this dog is hard to beat anytime. His work was done in his usual scintillating fashion, and the mistakes he made were negligible. But the weather seemed to hamper Hotfoot somewhat; not much, but a little. On the other hand, Duff Webster's fiery pointer seemed contemptuous of the killing weather, contemptuous of the gallery, and even contemptuous of his handler.*

As this heat wore on while the judges were trying to find enough difference in the dogs to reach a decision, it became apparent that in this mighty pointer we were seeing one of the great dogs of the year, possibly of all time. Just when we were deciding this about Judas, he cast over some hills, and in a little hollow Hotfoot was seen to flash into point. As McGinnis came up, the dog seemed to realize that he was pointing downwind, and then he did a piece of work very much like an expert chicken dog will sometimes do. He made a swift dash downwind and came back with the wind in his face, not in a crawling, creeping manner, but with snap and decision; in another moment he froze. The birds were there, and he was as steady to wing and shot on this, his fifth covey.

Judas retaliated a few moments later, with his superb, inspirational handling of the covey in the gully...

Occasionally both dogs were out of sight for several minutes and the scouts rode out wide, searching. At first Duff had been doubtful about Lucie's ability to keep up with Judas; but she soon proved that she knew what she was to do, and, more important, that she knew what Judas would do.

She rode back in and joined the gallery and whispered to Duff, "How are we doing?"

"All right."

"Just all right, huh? You're crazy." She said it with the old lilt, and Duff liked it.

The course became almost serpentine, and every time they made a turn Duff was in a nervous sweat until Judas, guided by the rolling Ha-a-ay, Jude! bent around and appeared ahead again. Once, after a five-minute absence, he showed again at exactly the right place, and a man rode up to Duff and said, "If he wins, I'll give you five thousand dollars for him, and you to campaign him for me and take the winnings."

Duff said, "I'll think about it after he wins."

The man turned his horse, then came back and said, "I'll pay it whether he wins or not."

"I'll think about it."

"Boys," an old man said, "you watch this race and remember it, and tell your children, because you've never seen one like it before."

"I saw Doughboy run in 1924," another answered.

A lawyer from Cincinnati said thoughtfully, "Gentlemen, you take a careful look at that dog. Judas? Take a look at him. That's no Judas, that's old Ambling Sam come to life again!"

They looked, even the judges; and they saw it. For it did seem to be a reborn, rekindled Ambling Sam.

"You see it, Miss Lucie?" he asked. "Isn't it so?"

"Yes," Lucie said, "it's true!"

"Look at him hit those birdy places. You remember his crossing over to find that last covey in the brier patch in the middle of that field? When he did it, I said, 'Now what dog was it used to pick out places like that?' and it came to me. Then I could see it in that short-coupled gait, and the way he cracks his tail. Don't believe Sam was quite as big-going, but then he wasn't as all-fired independent, either. Otherwise, that's old Sam, all right!"

Lucie's throat suddenly grew hot; the resemblance between Judas and Ambling Sam was uncanny. She could almost imagine old Amos up front, unsmiling, attuned to every move the dog made.

Now she saw that Duff was watching Judas too, and that he was nervous, often standing in his stirrups when the dog was overdue to show back on the course. Lucie's breath quickened, for all at once she knew Duff's thoughts as plainly as if he had told them to her. And she knew why he was so deeply intent on winning. Duff was thinking that this, in a way, might at last be Ambling Sam's championship.

Now they watched Hotfoot across an opening grass area where a covey had flushed wild, and saw him cast nervously about several minutes before going on; then Judas swung over and passed the same place and gave the lingering scent only one fling of his head, knowing the birds were gone. Five minutes later Lucie found Judas pointing on the edge of a series of gullies. On the other side, where the dog was looking, was a weed patch which conceivably held the covey.

Well, you've picked a damned good place to cut your throat, Duff thought uneasily as he drew his gun from the saddle scabbard. Judas stood as if on tiptoe, his nose high, his breath hasseling audibly, the cold, wet hide of him stretched tight over his flared ribs. Duff skidded down the red-mud side of the gully.

As he started up the other side, a shadow flicked across his vision, and he looked up to see Judas pass overhead in a great leap. "Hey!" Duff yelled, and swore in bitter anger. But there was no whir of wings. Duff climbed the wall of the gully, and there stood Judas. He had landed on point in the patch of grass.

There was hardly room for a covey of birds, but Duff kicked around in the cover. Nothing happened. Puzzled, Duff gave a sharp blast on the whistle. Immediately Judas leaped as if touched with a hot wire, across a second gully. He landed in a half-crouch, tail up, frozen. And this time Duff knew the birds were there. He crossed the gully and flushed then, and they boiled up from all sides of the motionless dog.

Out of the corner of his eye, Duff saw the judges conferring, their horses drawn in close. As he got back to his mount Lucie was grinning and winking at him, knowing, as he did, that the judges were on the verge of telling him to take his dog up, and that he had won. Then a long halloo reached them. On the far hill was Teague McGinnis, and McGinnis's hat was raised high—signaling a point for Hotfoot.

After that there was nothing to do but run them longer. Now the sun was out, and there was no wind. Both dogs reached out to the horizon in their casts, and the day had suddenly, now that the race was in its last stage, become almost pleasant. Quail were moving—the gallery rode up several coveys.

The course made another right-angle bend, and the handlers squalled at regular intervals. Five minutes passed and neither dog showed. Far out to the side, Lucie could be seen riding hard, searching and calling. Duff signaled her further out to the left.

"Durned if I ever seen two dogs have the pure hair run off of 'em, and still be tough enough to get lost!" somebody said.

The judges and the gallery stopped and waited. Another five minutes passed, and still no sign of either dog. Duff and Teague now rode the surrounding woods desperately, kicking their horses without mercy; all of them knew that, in all likelihood, the first dog found would be given the stake.

Then, in a heavy cover beyond a chill branch, Duff saw something white. As he approached he knew it was a dog. The horse splashed through the branch and galloped up the hillside; and there, half-hidden in the brush, stood Hotfoot, pointing birds.

Duff rode back out into the cornfield and help up his hat. The gallery broke and came toward him. To the right of them, Teague McGinnis appeared, and Duff motioned to him.

"Yonder's your dog, pointing," Duff said to Teague.

"*My* dog?" Teague said, staring at him.

"Right yonder," Duff said, and rode on out to continue the search for Judas; but there was no hurry, for he knew it was over and Hotfoot was still the champion.

A few minutes later Lucie found Judas nearly a mile away, directly on the course, on point. Now there was no gallery. Duff walked up to Judas. For a moment he stood there beside the dog, watching him. A big drove of doves passed overhead, swerving around the bare treetops. Somewhere in the distance a crow cawed. Duff walked out in front. The covey whirred up, and he leveled his gun and pulled the trigger, and a cock quail fell out of the streaming flight. Judas retrieved the bird, and Duff pulled off the head and let him eat it.

"Duff, you told me to go out to the left," Lucie said.

"It wasn't your fault. I guessed wrong, I reckon. All we needed to do was follow the course; he was right where he was supposed to be."

When they got back, most of the cars had gone. The hostlers were leading the horses away. Two men were trying to get a rearing horse into a trailer. Fires smoldered here and there, where the hostlers had waited.

Trial by Marriage

Duff took Judas's muzzle out of the trunk of the car and put it on him so they could dry him off thoroughly without being bitten. Lucie held him while Duff rubbed him with a croker sack. She stroked the dog's head gently. Judas didn't like it.

"Duff," Lucie said thoughtfully, "you just had to report Teague's lost dog, didn't you?"

"Sometimes I think I don't have a hell of a lot of sense."

"But you had to do it. You couldn't simply ride on past and keep looking for your own dog. No, not you. Not Duff Webster," she mused. "That's you, all right. But I knew you were like that long ago. I guess that's why I used to love you."

He stopped rubbing. "I'm sorry it has to be 'used to,' Lucie."

She answered, "It doesn't have to be. It isn't."

"Honest, Lucie?"

"Oh, Duff, you know it as well as I do!"

He kissed her hard on the mouth, all the months of missing her suddenly consummated. "I thought I'd quit loving you once, Lucie, but I found out different. Things have been in a tangle, but they're straight now."

Lucie suddenly took his hand and kissed the back of it, in the way he remembered. She said, "Duff, do you think things might be the way we used to say they would? About summers in Canada on the prairies, and campaigning the dogs round the circuit, and all that you used to tell me about the ivory table and the amber studs?"

"Yes, that's the way it will be," Duff said. Then he added, "And next year we'll win this championship."

Lucie looked at him. "What did you say, Duff?"

"Next year," he said determinedly, "we're going to win this championship."

She smiled softly and somewhat sadly, remembering that her grandfather, Amos Hawthorne, had said that every year. "Yes, Duff," she answered finally, "next year we will win."

Duff said, "Hold him still so I can dry him under here."

Judas stood still while Duff rubbed his belly and legs with the croker sack. The dog was growling, but in an absent-minded sort of way, for his eyes were looking out toward the cornfield and the sedge that bordered it, where there should be a covey of quail.

Prairie Dogs

You would think that any place with a name like Moose Jaw, Saskatchewan, would be a frontier outpost on the last geographical fringes of civilization, but, as a matter of fact, it's an alert and modern town in the center of the Canadian prairie country. Here, in late summer, the bird-dog men gather for the first major field trial of the season. Because Moose Jaw is the opener, and breaks a summer of hard work on the lone prairee, the occasion is mildly festive, and the hotel lobby is crowded with wealthy dog owners and their wives, local sportsmen, the trainers and the judges, all talking about bird dogs.

But every now and then you see the odd bit, as the Canadians say, of gloom; and this comes when one dog trainer asks another dog trainer about his prospects. The kennels of Ed Mack Farrior and V.E. Humphreys and Earl Crangle were in a pitiable state, to hear them tell one another about it; they had no chance of winning, and had come up just to be with the crowd—Farrior, who had Crooked Creek Jake, a young fireball pointer just getting hot; Crangle, who had Hillbright Susanna, a tiny, hustling dog anxious to prove herself the best setter on the major circuit; and Humphreys, who had Young's Billie, the dog that, the Friday following, won the Saskatchewan championship.

Dogs like these, and like Lester's Enjoy's Wahoo—son of Enjoy, owned by Doctor Lester, in case you're wondering about that jawbreaker name—and Farmwood Traveler and Surracho are the highest development of the bird dog. Their owners pay the trainers twenty-five dollars a month per dog, pay the trial entry fees—fifty dollars or so—and give the trainers whatever purses the dogs win. The owner's share is pride of possession. But he isn't getting the short end of the stick. He's willing to spend an unlimited amount to be able to point out a field-trial champion and say, "That's my dog." And the published list of higher-bracket-income men doesn't include any dog trainers.

The owner could perhaps get additional value for his money in watching his field-trial dog in the formative period. Of no other sporting animal is so much required. Greyhounds and horses simply run, retrievers retrieve, hounds follow their noses, gamecocks fight. A field-trial dog's training begins at six weeks of age; by the time he is three years old he should have begun to reach a finished state of development. Then, when he enters a trial, here's what he's supposed to do: run big—meaning at a good distance—a half mile or so—ahead of the handler—without getting lost; he must also run fast and jauntily throughout the one to three hours of the heat. He must use initiative and judgment in hunting birdy places, and yet handle easily. He must locate game decisively, and point with intensity and style, and honor another dog's point upon sight. And finally, he must be steady to wing and shot, standing until the birds have been flushed and the gun fired—into the air; the birds aren't killed—and the handler commands him to get going again. You can see that a dog wouldn't learn all that in one day.

Neither does he learn it in one place. Most field-trial trainers are located in the South. But when summer comes, the Southern woods and fields are hot and rattlesnake-infested; and the trainer, with several assistants, forty-odd dogs, saddles, clothing and miscellaneous equipment, travels 2000 miles to work his dogs on the rolling prairies of Southern Saskatchewan or Manitoba.

Here the game is plentiful, there are no venomous snakes, at least the early part of every day is cool, and the country is wide open enough to invite a pointer or setter to go his doggonedest.

At the camp of Ed Mack Farrior, outside the village of Forget—pronounced "forjay"—breakfast is by lamplight. The camp personnel consists of Houston Nichols, Farrior's assistant from Alabama, and Gordon Dunk, the Canadian, and four Alabama Negroes: Johnny Hooks, who has helped the Farriors train for fifteen years; John D., his son; Oscar, the wagon driver; and Man, the cook. By the time breakfast is over, the Negroes have the dog wagons ready and the horses saddled, and forty-three noisy dogs leap ecstatically about the pens, each trying to state that he would like to hunt this morning and, if chosen, would show some really extraordinary bird-dog work. Finally the two outfits are loaded and drive out, one turning north, one east, followed by a prolonged chorus of brokenhearted howling from the dogs who are left behind.

The first dog to go down is Jake. In the dew-wet early morning, his feet are smeared with a protective coating of tar—his "travelin' shoes," Johnny Hooks says—and then he is turned loose. A few weeks ago, Jake was just a fair-going dog, but lately something has happened to him—something that happens often to dogs on the prairies; he's simply taken it into his head to go. Now he is a half mile away, a spot of swift-moving white against the yellow mustard. His ground-eating speed electrifies the men, and each responds in his own idiom.

"Lookit the bloody thing move!" says the Canadian.

"Yes, suh," agrees Johnny, "ole Jake is sho vappin'! He's cut him a long walkin' stick dis day!"

Jake's run even stirs the unexcitable Farrior, who in his twenty-eight years has seen many first-class dogs, one of which, Air Pilot's Sam—national champion in 1937 and one of the best dogs that ever lived—he raised and trained. Farrior went to college to become an engineer. But after finishing, the call of the fields got him, and like his father—who has now quit field-trial campaigning for the comparative quiet of game-preserve management—he became a bird-dog man.

"Look a-yonder! He's got 'em, Mr. Eddie Mack!" calls Johnny, pointing to the distant patch of buffalo willow that almost hides the immobile Jake.

Instantly the little training caravan is galvanized into action, with the horsemen spurring their mounts into a dead run across the badger-and-gopher-hole-infested

Prairie Dogs

plain. ("De old badger, he don't have to dig dem gophers out," Johnny Hooks says. "He just blow is bref down de gopher hole, and de gopher got to come out.") The wagon follows, rocketing and bouncing, with the shaken dogs howling and fighting in the excitement.

Farrior's horse plows to a stop, and the trainer is off and runs to where Crooked Creek Jake stands on a lofty and stylish point. Incidentally, as to bird-dog style, the important thing about a point is intensity; the ideal point is erect, with head up and the tail above the level of the dog's back—the higher the better. Some people think a cautiously lifted front paw is the *sine qua non* of bird-dog style, but a good dog is supposed to be bold and positive, not cautious; you see the raised forepaw on calendars, not often at field trials.

Farrior runs in front of the dog, quirting the sage and buffalo willow, and eight scattered prairie chickens burst into the air with indignant squawks. The impatient Jake makes a leap forward, but Farrior "squalls" at him, and the dog stops and watches the trainer guiltily. Ed Mack makes him stand for a moment, then gives him an encouraging slap on the ribs and Jake is gone again, with flying feet and merry tail.

Thirty minutes later, the next dog called from the wagon is Surracho. His name, properly spelled "Sirocco," means a hot wind, and is somewhat apt, for this rangy goose-necked pointer is a fast and fiery bird dog. Last year he was a winner as a derby two-year-old; he is as deadly on game as any backwoodsman's meat dog, and no dog makes more stylish, breath-taking points. But for the chicken trials this year Surracho is out with a sore foot.

Farrior leaves the lemon pointer down only a few minutes. But even in that time Surracho has reached a bluff—willow and white poplar patch—and pointed.

"Look at de ole fool puttin' it on," Johnny grins.

Farrior flushes the birds and fires into the air and Surracho stands there like Plymouth Rock. Johnny lifts the dog and carries him to the wagon, where the healing pad of his foot is treated with flexible collodion.

Surracho's owner, W. F. Miller, has never seen his dog work, and only through Ed Mack Farrior's thorough-going sense of honor does he happen to own him. His father having been a bird-dog man, Miller wanted to acquire a field-trial dog simply for sentimental reasons, and asked Farrior to sell him the likeliest-looking puppy he had. On the day the check for $300 arrived, Miller's brand-new dog died. Farrior offered to return the check. "Or," he wrote, "I have another puppy that may make a good dog. I'll give you this one for yours that died, if you prefer." Miller agreed to the second suggestion, and the dog he got is Surracho, now in his first all-age year, one of the class dogs of the major campaigners.

Another pistol ball of a dog who changed owners is the diminutive setter, Hillbright Susanna, or, as she is known in the kennel, Dot. About three years ago I saw this dog run in the amateur puppy—under one year old—stake, as a brace mate for her litter sister, who had drawn a bye. Puppies are not required to run well; but Jeanette found birds and pointed them steadily, and Dot, coming upon the scene, instantly honored the point. Last year the brace was broken when Jeanette died under a truck.

Dot's pedigree name, then, was Sealey's Momoney Dot, and she belonged to Bob Sealey, of Donaldsonville, Georgia, who used her principally as a hunting dog. As far as Sealey was concerned, Dot was God's best job in the bird-dog line. That also went for M.G. Dudley, of Greenville, South Carolina, who had bred the puppies. On every occasion he badgered Bog Sealey to sell him Dot. Sealey laughed.

"Tell you what I'll do," Dudley said in desperation. His own vocal cords having been removed by an operation for cancer of the throat, he talks quite plainly with an artificial larynx. "I'll give you a thousand dollars for Dot."

"No, I don't want to sell her," Sealey replied. "And I've been offered fifteen hundred for her anyway."

Dudley mulled this over a day or two. Finally he concluded that Sealey would not be persuaded by any normal approach to sell Dot, and he decided to use strategy.

Susanna Changes Owners

He visited Sealey's hotel room, innocently accompanied by a witness, and he said, "Bob, I'll make you a final proposition. I want Dot, and I'll strain a point to get her. I'll give you fifteen hundred dollars for her. You ought to give me the option, since she's from my Hillbright kennels."

"No soap."

Dudley sighed. "Just out of curiosity, what would you take for that dog?"

And Sealey, thinking to discourage Dudley for all time, said airily, "Oh, I'll sell her for twenty-five hundred dollars."

"Sold!" said Dudley instantly, and whipped out his checkbook, while Sealey blanched with horror at what he had done.

So now Dot's name on the books is Hillbright Susanna, and she has been steadied by Earl Crangle into a first-class field-trial dog, all thirty pounds of her.

THE NEXT DOGS THAT ARE taken from the Farrior dog wagon are eleven-months-old puppies. They hit the prairie with joyful yelps, streaking through the prairie grass and mustard, eager for something to chase. One of them bursts into a covey of Hungarian partridges and sends them hell ascattering. Presently the other one jumps a big jackrabbit. The jack gallops away with the puppy in frantic pursuit.

"Shucks," Johnny says, "that ole rabbit ain't halfway runnin'. Ain't even got his years laid back yit."

Bird-dog puppies have a terrific time. When they're six weeks old and eating solid food, a pistol is shot over them at mealtime, so that they associate the firing with something enjoyable; that way, they won't by gun-shy later. Their training is in the yard, where they are taught to come at command, to retrieve, and to stop at command. But afield they can do as they please. They can chase deer, jackrabbits, coyotes or birds. During this wild and gay period, the love of hunting becomes deeply rooted. Furthermore, an intelligent dog will begin to learn such things as the proper use of a downwind, and that prairie chickens are often to be found in wolf-willow patches, in bluffs, around old buffalo wallows; that only gophers inhabit bald prairie ground.

Prairie Dogs

Then one day the puppy finds a collar around his neck with a check cord attached. He attaches no importance to this slight encumbrance, and joyfully beings bird hunting. When the hot scent of the first covey burns his nostrils, he pauses in an instinctive flash point, then prepares to bust cheerfully in and send chickens squawking everywhere. This time, though, he hears a sharp "Whoa!" The young dog knows what that means, but perhaps thinks, "To heck with him! I took orders in the yard, but out here it's different! There're birds right ahead!" And he leaps forward—only to be suddenly jolted to a stop by the check cord. "By gum," the dog thinks ruefully, "I believe he meant it." He's a puppy no longer; play days are over.

When the puppies are put back into the dog wagon, the outfit heads for dinner. By now, the sun is hot and dust devils dance in the wind. For the country around Forget is dry, with almost no rain, and no wheat crop for ten years. They say a young boy walked out of a Forget store one day just as it began to rain. When the first drop of water struck him, he promptly fainted. However, some man with presence of mind poured a bucket of sand on the boy and revived him. Another weather hazard is wind, which sometimes blows for days without stopping. They say it once blew a dog against a grain elevator and held him there until he starved, but I doubt if this is literally true.

Points on Pointing

In the hot early afternoon, the prairie chickens become lazy and congregate in the shade of the bluffs. This makes an excellent training item for the dog men, for they can put the young dogs on check cords and give them endless bird work around the bluffs. The chickens are reluctant to fly, and when they do flush, they go only fifty yards or so. The trainers follow, and the dogs are allowed to locate the birds and point them again and again.

The apparently mysterious tendency of a dog to point game is really not mysterious. Many carnivorous creatures freeze momentarily before springing upon their game. It's somewhat a matter of getting set. Watch a spider sometime, or a cat. Man saw that dogs paused stiffly before seizing rabbits and fowl, and he trained the dog to exaggerate the pause. There is a quite reliable case on record of a pointing pig, which was used for a shooting animal in England. The pig, according to the record, would point quail, woodcock and pheasant; it would also retrieve, and even honor the point of a bird dog. Mr. Ripley, perhaps, wouldn't believe this, but a dog man would.

Many puppies make their first points on prairie chickens. It's a heart-warming sight to see a young dog suddenly slow up, then freeze, his muscles taut and his nose twitching. The trainer walks carefully to the side of the dog, and strokes him, running his hand from the dog's neck to the tip of his tail, which soothes the animal's nerves.

Some dogs are precocious, and begin pointing game at four or five months. Others go for two or three years before they can be "stopped," or broken. Like Terry, a handsome setter, son of the great Equity. Terry is now three years old and still thinks that the fun of hunting is trying to catch birds on the wing—he occasionally does it, what's more—instead of pointing them. He's a fine, big-running dog, though, for all his hardheadedness, and when Farrior can bring him to his senses he will make a field-trial dog.

Another dog that needs special treatment is Jack, a derby pointer. Somebody was careless with Jack when he was a puppy, and now he is gun-shy. Ordinarily, a gun-shy dog might as well be given up as a bad job, but Jack, like Terry, is worth the trouble. He runs wide and merrily, points with cold accuracy. When the gun comes out of the saddle scabbard, though, Jack is through for the day. The standard treatment for gun-shyness is the starvation method. The dog is offered his food pan to the accompaniment of blank-pistol fire. He of course forgets his hunger and dives back into his kennel. Next day, the same thing again. Finally the dog's hunger overcomes his fear of the gun, and he eats with the shooting ringing in his ears. Jack went eight days without eating, and you could count his ribs. On the ninth he ate. Now the gun is shot over him at every meal, and though he still doesn't exactly reach heights of ecstasy when he sees Farrior coming with the gun, he manifests his disapproval only by a couple of barks of protest. Before you condemn the treatment as cruel, remember that it lasts for only a few days, and a gun-shy dog is worthless as a hunter and will either end up with a humane bullet in his head or as a fat and lifeless pet in some spinster's apartment. But if you cure him, he again gaily ranges the countryside for bird scent, doing what God made him to do—hunt.

Jack is the dog that pointed the prairie chicken in the tree. After a short cast, we found Jack on point behind a dead poplar, and on a bare willow limb ten feet in front of him a prairie chicken sat, plainly silhouetted—a remarkable sight. The chicken seemed more curious than alarmed, and allowed me to work fairly close with my camera before she flew.

Much of the special treatment that the dogs get is medicinal. On the lone prairee, there's no veterinarian to be phoned; the trainer is his own doctor. Sore feet—prevalent during the early part of the season before the dog's pads are hardened—are treated by antiseptic, by flexible collodion which forms an artificial skin over the wound, and by confinement of the dog. Occasionally there are fight wounds. At the beginning of a training season the dogs are carefully watched, and any two dogs that seem always to have conflicting opinions are separated. However, the number of pens is limited, and separation can go on just so far. One noon we came in to find two pointers silently locked in what would have been death combat. When they were, with difficulty, pulled apart, they looked as if they'd got caught in a threshing machine. Curiously enough, these pointers belonged to the same owner, and had been raised together. After the fight they behaved better, but for the rest of the summer they muttered harsh things at each other.

Forty Supper Thieves

Another hazard of the prairies is spear grass; the seed pod of this weed is a tiny barb which often gets in a dog's mouth and works into the flesh, making a bad wound. Every time a dog is taken up, his mouth is carefully wiped out with a cloth.

But for the most part the treatment of the dogs is preventive—among other things, thorough drying of a dog that has run in dew-wet cover, periodic worming of the entire kennel, and an occasional sprinkling of cod-liver oil on the daily meal of cracklings and shredded wheat.

Prairie Dogs

Because of the tendency of a dog to prefer his kennel mate's supper to his own, the feeding of the forty dogs at one time without general warfare would seem a problem. The solution, though, is a number of short chains with snap hooks, spaced around the pens; before feeding every evening, each dog is fastened so that he can reach neither the food pan nor the throat of his friend near by.

A dog that gets fat easily has to be worked over time, but most of them burn excess weight off without any trouble. Sometimes, to keep a dog in condition without risking staleness by too much bird work, the harness is brought out, and for an hour the dog is "roaded"—allowed to pull against a check leash. That way he goes to the trials eager to hunt, as well as lean and tough.

Field-Trial Veterans

And he has to be tough to keep whipping out the miles campaigning from August to March. The major field-trial circuit begins at Moose Jaw, Canada, on prairie chicken; it ends in late February with the national championship on quail, at Grand Junction, Tennessee. Of the scores of trials in between, a big-time dog will make from five to twenty-five starts.

At Moose Jaw and Grand Junction, and occasionally in between, the dog will be under the surveillance of Dr. Benton King, the best-known field-trial judge in the sport, and perhaps, by his eternal insistence on fast and stylish bird-dog performance, more than any other living man responsible for the top quality of the modern bird dog. "When you're running a dog under him," the handlers say, "you better have a dog that will hump." Doctor King is a small and amiably crusty Tennessean, who quirts his horse in wild, thundering flights across the buffalo wallows and badger holes of the prairies, or the ditches and stumps of the Southern piney woods, but in an automobile regards as blinding speed anything above forty miles an hour.

Riding up front with the judges at the important trials will be a man who looks like a movie sportsman, George Rogers, reporter for *The American Field*. *The Field* calls itself an all-around sporting magazine, but in reality it is a field-trial newspaper, and the dog men read it the way a priest reads his prayer book. Rogers is there to see every point at every big trial.

Probably present also will be the veteran Jake Bishop, with his spectacles halfway down his nose, a first-class dog man who this year trained in Canada for the thirty-eighth summer; and big Ches Harris, who has won more national championships than any other living handler, and the Crangles, father and son, and a loquacious, hard-riding little Texan, V.E. Humphreys; and the fashion-plate handlers, Clyde Morton and Dewey English. Some of the owners will be there, too; possibly Gerald Livingston, and Carl Duffield, the wealthy setter man who trains his own dogs and wins with them, and M.G. Dudley, and Udo Fleischmann, and W.C. Teagle, and E.J. Shaffer, and Miss Claudia Phelps.

Practically everybody attending the trial will have a different idea about which dog won. Who really won is not a matter of fact but a matter of opinion. Unless some dog got hot and kept everybody standing excitedly in his stirrups throughout the dog's heat, the judges' announcement is usually greeted with several looks of puzzlement and disappointment, and that night in the hotel there'll be many confidential exchanges, such as, "I'll tell you frankly, I don't see how they could help giving it to old Jap, after that big race he ran, and making five finds without a damn bobble."

But to the owner and the handler, the winner was a foregone conclusion. "Yes, sir," the owner will tell you proudly, "when Dan swung in from that long cast, just before they ordered him up, and pinned those Huns right out on the open prairie, I knew there wasn't any doubt about which was the best dog."

One Man's Dogs

There's a pointer lying on top of the doghouse watching as if he's king of the kennel. He's not the best dog of the lot, but he is good. And he *is* the boss. Perhaps his story will illustrate something of what it's like to be a bird-dog man.

On a cold day, a couple of years ago, we stopped at a little country store and sounded the horn. A tall countryman in boots came out and he was the man who was to show us the hunting land.

"You got any dogs?" he asked. "I got two we can take."

We had brought our own dogs but I told him to bring his along, too.

As we rode to the hunting place we began to get acquainted. Our new friend had a certain hardness about him that is not typical of our Southern country people.

He asked my name again and then said, "You any kin to Judge Bell, the state judge used to be solicitor of this circuit?"

"He's my father."

He was silent for a while and finally he said, "He prosecuted me one time."

I asked, "What were you charged with?"

"Murder."

As you will guess, this caused the conversation to drag. In fact, it almost rolled over and died. Although I am a writer, whose job it is to unearth as much of a man's story as possible, I must say that this was one time when I was willing to change the subject. Later in the day he indicated that he regarded my father highly—but that was later.

It was the bird dogs who remedied things. First let me say that every bird-dog man thinks his dog is the best in the world. So I thought his dogs would be ill-bred potterers, and he probably thought mine were half-wild idiots that didn't know a quail from a joree. We were both wrong.

After we had been hunting a while, he was moved to tell me that I had a couple of pretty nice dogs there, and true praise from another bird-dog man is a rare thing. But top dog for the day was his two-year-old pointer Fred, which he put down after my dogs had hunted a couple of hours. This was a fleet-footed rambler, and he covered those flatwoods. He found several coveys, handled them properly and pointed them stylishly.

"There's a dog," I admitted finally, "that I wish was mine."

After that, things went along fine. We ate sandwiches by the bank of the river and talked about the war. He had been in the Rainbow Division in the other war. But mostly we talked about bird dogs, and when he started home that night, he mentioned that he was willing to sell his pointer. So Fred became my dog.

Like many dogs raised and hunted exclusively by one man, Fred did not quickly get used to changing owners. Fred's training was of an old-fashioned severity—judging by the birdshot to be found even now here and there under his hide—but for many months, his heart still belonged to the other man. His hunting for me was only fair; just when he was about to get his mind on his business, he would suddenly stop and look back at me and then wander on half-heartedly.

Before long, his health began to fail. He lost weight and became anemic. I won't say all this was caused by grief. I only say that Fred got sick, and three very good veterinarians in turn failed to find any specific disease. For months, we worked on him, feeding him liver and meat and eggs and milk, and injecting vitamins, and finally we got him well, in spite of himself.

With health came belligerence. Fred is boss of the kennel. He eats his food leisurely—"He likes to just mench along on it," says colored Henry—returning several times during the hour to take a few bites. When he is not eating, he doesn't need to stand guard over the remaining food. Although there are two or three larger dogs in the kennel, not one of them will touch Fred's food.

Furthermore, he now hunts the way he did that day I first saw him. Apparently he is satisfied with me as a master, or at least he has become too polite to show his feelings.

Snow was a similar case. Snow was a "drop," half pointer, half setter. Setters and pointers should never be crossed, for the result is usually a defective and mongrelish animal, and even the occasional excellent drop does not justify the cross. However, Snow did not look as bad as most; in fact, I didn't know he was a drop until later; I simply took him to be a setter of not simon-pure ancestry; and he was a good hunting animal.

Snow was raised and trained—and, like Fred, trained by harsh methods, judging by his tendency to overcaution in pinning his game—by a snuff-dipping backwoodsman friend of mine. I first saw Snow at work in the blackjack-oak woods of his owner, who had told me he had a dog to sell. Snow made a prodigiously long cast and pointed, and when we fired, two birds fell. I fired at another but apparently missed. Snow retrieved the two birds and we went on. Presently Snow returned from somewhere with another bird in his mouth. The bird I though I had missed had fallen at a distance, and Snow had found it and brought it in. That is retrieving of the highest quality.

Snow was a peculiar dog. Whereas most bird dogs—especially setters—show a marked affection for human beings, Snow quite obviously cared for nobody. I had noticed his indifference to the farmer before I acquired him. Snow would stand still and allow you to stroke him, and would even wag his tail politely, but he really preferred to be left alone. What he wanted was to lie sleepily in the shade all summer and hunt all winter, with as little human contact as possible.

One Man's Dogs

Although a one-man dog heretofore, from the first, Snow hunted quite industriously in my company. Only in one way did he ever show that he knew he had changed men. He never retrieved again. I hunted him for two years but not once in that time would he ever bring a dead bird to me.

The Affectionate Butch

Butch is as different from Snow as a dog could be. Butch is a small pointer, not yet two years old, and her idea of heaven is to be in my lap licking my face. She is intolerably affectionate. In fact, she's a nuisance in a car, because she absolutely will not stay anywhere but in my lap, wriggling and nuzzling and licking at my face. Push her away and she comes back immediately. Slap her—if you can force yourself to do it—and she cringes for five or six seconds and then she's at it again. The only way she can be transported inside a car without making you a menace to traffic is short-leashed on the back seat.

Unlike Snow, Butch's happiest moment is when she is bringing me a bird. In her play about the yard, having no bird to retrieve, she brings me sticks, old bones, or anything she happens to run across. Afield, she occasionally runs across a box turtle, and no matter if she is a quarter of a mile away, she stops hunting and brings the turtle proudly to me. This trait might become annoying if it weren't for the fact that the turtles aren't often encountered in the wintertime.

I might add that these turtles seem to have an odor similar to quail, because many perfectly good bird dogs point them. Jake Bishop, the veteran trainer, once had a dog that would pick up any stray box turtle and continue hunting with the turtle in its mouth; and if it happened upon another turtle, it would put the first one down, pick up the second and go ahead with its hunting.

Last spring, I sent Butch to John Gates, one of the better professional dog men, for training. About a week later I got a letter from him saying that he thought Butch could be a winner in the major field-trial circuit. Now a good steady shooting dog is one thing, and an open-field trial winner is quite something else.

"I want you to come up and see Butch go," John Gates wrote. "Her range is widening each day and she hunts every minutes she's down."

Appearances Are Deceiving

Arriving at the village where John Gates lives, I suffered the ecstatic osculations of Butch, and we started to our hunting land.

"I'm going to hunt some territory I haven't used before," John said. "I'm taking along a farmer who'll show us the land lines."

The farmer was a six-footer, about sixty years old, with big hands and feet.

"Mr. Gates," he said, "I'd like to take them two puppies of mine and see what you think of them."

Since he was being good enough to give up his day to go with us, we could hardly refuse, although we had misgivings. He went back to his corncrib and let out two ten-months-old lemon-and-white pointers. One of them, the male, was a surprisingly fine-looking dog; however, the bitch was undersized, too sharp of face, and pretty scrawny all the way around.

"I'm gonna have to git shed of these durn dogs. They've took to killing chickens, and my wife ain't gonna put up with it any longer," the farmer said.

However, we weren't interested in the puppies—we were interested in Butch. We put her down and she started hunting while the puppies chased each other and barked at the horses and made nuisances of themselves generally. But it was at once apparent that something was wrong with Butch. She didn't have her customary sparkle; she seemed stiff and sore. We stopped and examined her, but could find nothing wrong with her pads.

Later, the veterinary diagnosed the trouble as a temporary ovary condition. ("Oval trouble," Henry called it.) We thought it might be helpful for her to stay down and work out some of the soreness.

Gates and I were disappointed, and it looked like a day wasted, except that our farmer turned out to be as entertaining a talker as you'll find anywhere. His job was to point out land lines, and he not only did this, but told us bits of country history to go with it.

"Used to be birds aplenty in this country," he said. "I used to git me a quart of whisky and hitch up my buggy, and me and my bird dogs would ramble these woods. Done got too old now, though, and had to cut out whisky and woods rambling. An old man ain't fit for much, boys," he said matter-of-factly. "See them woods yonder? Four of my daddy's brothers got a bait of fighting the Yankees and they deserted and holed up in them woods for four years. Kept their horses tied and ready saddled on the edge of the camp for lookouts, and whenever the horses sensed something coming, the boys they mounted and rode off the other way. See that lime sink yonder? One of the boys had a fast mare, and one night the soldiers jumped him and they had a race for the woods, with them shooting at him with buckshot. The mare come to that lime sink unbeknowing, and there wasn't nothing to do but jump it or fall in, so she jumped it. They come back next day after the soldiers had give up and gone, and measured it, and it was thirty-two feet across."

It would be a poor writer who couldn't make a story out of material like that. I remembered everything that had been said, and after a time the finished story developed in my mind, and I wrote it, and then Collier's bought it. A day wasted?

John Gates had been listening, too, but he hadn't forgotten that he'd made big talk about Butch and she had—through no fault of her own, of course—let him down.

Now he said, "Butch is feeling better. She's really going now! Look 'way over yonder on that rise."

We looked, saw a swiftly moving spot of white flicking through the woods. But then, just ahead of us, Butch appeared, still jumping along stiffly. Happily trailing behind her, stopping to peer into bushes and sniff at grasshoppers, was the well-built male puppy.

"That's not Butch," I said in amazement. "That's the other puppy!"

The dog making the beautiful swing ahead was the undersized bitch named Sister that I had dismissed without another glance. She had quickly tired of her brother's puppy-dog play and had gone hunting. And she kept it up. It was obvious that she was no ordinary dog. Furthermore, although her general conformation was all a mistake, her stride and style afield was that of a class dog.

I watched her for a while longer, saw her find and stylishly point a covey of birds, and I said to the farmer, "What do you want for your puppies?"

A Matter of Finance

It took him about forty minutes to get around to giving me an answer. We rode on, and he talked about other things, and finally he complained, "Well, I hate to just come right out and say what I'll take for them. Might be you'd give more than I'd think to ask, and then I'd cheat myself."

But he finally named a price for the two of them, and it was not high, and so I said, "I'll pay that, and only take the little bitch. The dog is a nice-looking animal, but I don't want him."

"He is a damn'-fool sort of dog, ain't he?" agreed the farmer, and the deal was closed. Sister is now fourteen months old, and a good one.

But for every good dog you get—by raising or buying—there are dozens that you reject. Mostly they're simply inferior animals, without the deep will for hunting, or they may be good hunters and bird finders, and yet not have the style and dash that really tingles your blood.

It's the outlaws that break your heart. There was a setter bitch named Rose, for instance. Never have I seen a dog better at going to game—by which is meant locating the birds after the first vagrant scent has been struck. Upon finding scent, Rose would go into a frenzy of action. Most dogs slow up and pussyfoot around. But not Rose. She would whip back and forth—then stop for an electric second—then move up and stop—and she had them. Somehow she could get smack into the middle of a covey without accidentally flushing a bird. All her flushing was on purpose. She would hold her point a few seconds, then jump forward and flush them and follow the streaming covey out of sight.

I never broke Rose. During her puppyhood, she and a litter sister used to get out and self-hunt. When they got to killing goats, her owner gave her to me. This was two weeks before the end of hunting season. I hunted her by herself every day, and in a few days she was holding her birds long enough for me to get there and shoot. I believe if I could have kept hunting her, she'd have been saved. But by the time next season came around she had slipped back into her old ways.

Her worst trait—and I never came even close to curbing it—was her jealousy. When another dog pointed, she inevitably dashed in and sent his birds scattering—a habit she had acquired, I'm sure, in her puppy days when she had roamed through the woods with her sister.

Rose had a way of whipping her tail against her sides and she kept the tip raw, so that when she hunted, her side usually became blood-streaked.

Once a Negro woman stuck her head out of her cabin to see who was passing, and she exclaimed, "Lawsy, Boss, you done shot your dog, ain't you?"

After I'd given Rose up as a hunting dog, she used to slip off to the woods self-hunting, and I'd know what she had been up to by the splotches of pink on her sides.

Tall Tale

Rose was very different from a dog a friend of mine claims to have had. Old Spot his name was, and his stanchness on point was absolute. Once Spot became lost while hunting, and my friend, almost sure that the dog was pointing birds, searched for him for hours. Finally he gave up, hoping that Spot had found his way home. But Spot never came home. Next year, my friend happened to be hunting in the same territory and came upon a skeleton of a dog, and it was standing there with head and tail up in a stylish point, and he knew it was old Spot. Spot was still holding his birds, for huddled there in the grass in front of him were twelve tiny quail skeletons.

Or so my friend says.

About the Artist

Marguerite Kirmse was without doubt one of the best canine illustrators of the 20th century. Her popularity as an artist reached its peak in the early 1930s, and for many years her etchings ranked among the nation's top sellers.

She was born in Bournemouth, England, in 1885 and trained both as a musician and artist during her youth before moving to the United States. She was eventually offered a job as a harpist in the Seattle Orchestra, and it was only the lack of the initial union dues of $100 that prevented her full-time career in music. Later, she would recall in an interview, "In 1910 I came to the United States on a visit and was fortunate in securing orders to paint dogs and horses. For a number of years my time was divided between music and art until finally the press of artwork forced me virtually to abandon my music. Recognition as an animal painter brought added commissions to paint portraits of dogs and horses as well as to make sketches for various publications. This put an end to music as a career. In 1922, I began making etchings of dogs in drypoint and also began illustrating animal stories." She soon became one of the most popular animal artists in the country, able to work from a studio in New York and on her 150-acre retreat, Arcady Farm and Tobermoy Kennels, near Bridgewater, Connecticut. She was always surrounded by dogs of all shapes and sizes and maintained an impressive kennel.

In addition to the dozens of titles she illustrated, classics like *Lassie Come Home, Greyfriar's Bobby,* and works by Rudyard Kipling, she published two books of her illustrations with Eugene Connett at Derrydale Press, *Marguerite Kirmse's Dogs,* in 1930, and *Dogs in the Field,* in 1935. Today, these titles are exceedingly rare and expensive, the former selling for around $500 and the latter often over $1000.

Despite her enduring fame for both drawing and breeding Scottish terriers, she had a special affinity for bird dogs and always kept several at Tobermoy. She was particularly adept at capturing the expressive language of the dog's body, the majesty of a beautiful pointer or setter on point, while avoiding the cartoonish appearance so often seen in dog illustrations during this era. She worked in many different mediums, including oil, pastel, pencil, etching, and even bronze, but her work is most often seen today in her wonderful etchings and drypoints (a method similar to etching, but without the use of acid). She received little formal training in etching, reporting once that she had simply picked up a phonograph needle one day and started doodling on a piece of metal. From that humble beginning, she produced some of the best drypoints and etchings seen anywhere in animal art.

She died at the age of 68 of a heart ailment, having survived her husband, George Cole, an importer by profession, who died in 1945. The etchings, drypoints, and pencil drawings seen in this volume represent but a fraction of her excellent work, and her etchings remain highly sought after by collectors and dog lovers around the world.